THE FIELD OF CROWS

ROBERT GARROD

For further information:

www.robertgarrod.co.uk

www.facebook.com/fieldofcrows/

Cover illustration by Joolz Denby

www.joolzdenby.co.uk

My name is Wulfred, son of Saxmund.

I belong to a place that is lost, to a people who were scattered, to a time that many have already forgotten.

The first thing I can recall is war. I only pray it will not be the last thing I recall.

I remember Harold Godwinsson's great hall above Llyn Rhydderch.

I remember the smells of brewing ale and roasting meat, the sound of song and music in the smoky twilight, and the fire-shadows that haunted the high beams of the roof.

I remember the great gateposts hewn from oak trunks too thick for me to reach my young arms around, and the damp days of golden leaves and misty sunshine when the earl and his men were chasing Welsh raiders through the hills and the women sang bright songs and chattered over the looms, the spindles and the cooking pots.

I remember standing at the door, watching the red sun sinking to its rest among the dark Welsh hills.

A lifetime has passed, but I can still hear the braying of war horns and the warning cries as I rushed into the hall at my mother's side, running and stumbling through a swarm of feet. It was only my fourth or fifth summer in this world. My brother Oswold was little more than a baby, bundled up our mother's arms. As the men of the village struggled to close the heavy doors, I saw the warband howling through the valley, dark and fierce in their shirts of mail, leather and ragged furs. I remember the shields, painted with eyes and serpents; swords and axes bright against the shadows of the hills, and the long spears promising death. Their eerie battlecries shivered through the dusk.

They threw blazing torches into the mean huts of the village, but none stopped to look for spoils there - they came on, running as if pursued by all the terror of the gathering night, towards our hall. The great doors were heaved shut, and as the cries of fear and panic faded I heard the grim rhythm of axes beating against the heavy planks.

The women scrambled for places to hide, dragging their children with them. The village men - shepherds, stonecutters, ploughmen, basket weavers - stood fearfully awaiting the enemy, their knives and cudgels as clumsy in their hands as hoes and willow rods were comfortable.

I had lost my mother in a moment of sudden darkness as the doors closed, so I scrambled under a drinking bench and curled up to make myself as small as possible. Trembling in the shadows, I watched as the beams across the door split apart, and saw the raiders crash through, their spears held aloft, with cries of triumph. Howling desperately, two of the villagers ran at them carrying a long bench like a battering ram.

"Godwinsson!" they yelled, in imitation of the Earl of Weesex's warriors on the field of battle. There were vicious curses and crashing sounds as the first of the enemy stumbled. But in the torchlight I saw more spearmen pushing through the broken doors and those two brave and unwarlike men were cut down and trampled underfoot. The rest of our defenders died on spears and swords with hardly time to scream. Scrabbling along the splintered floor, shivering with the panic of the weak and helpless, I huddled further under the bench, further into the shadows. I wanted to call out for my mother, but terror took hold of my throat and I could not utter a sound. All my young life, I had heard warriors tell tales and sing songs of battle, but never before had I seen the wild fury of men whose joy is to kill and plunder. I saw them breaking open chests and boxes, searching for the gold and silver taken by Earl Harold's army, and tearing rich cloths and tapestries from the walls.

One mail-clad man leapt across the bench I was hiding under. The thud of his iron-shod heel was loud on its rough planks and I clamped both hands over my mouth to silence a scream. The mailed man reached into a pile of furs and dragged my mother out by the wrist. She was screaming and beating her fists against his neck and chest. He was roaring something in Welsh, grinning drunkenly through the sweat and grease of his beard. Two more men ran past, carrying loot from the back of the hall. The torch flames spread into the straw and rushes of the floor and I cowered away from the flickering light, trying to push myself down into the planks. My mother screamed again, spitting and clawing at her attacker's face. He struck her around the head and knocked aside her linen scarf so that her hair, golden in the shadows of the hall, spilled across her shoulders. The grinning Welshman grabbed a handful of it, pulled her towards him and I ran out, desperate to save her, screaming in rage and terror, beating my puny fists against his leg.

"Wulfred, no!" I heard my mother cry, and the raider laughed as his fist slapped numbly into the side of my face and I fell, rolling across the floor and tasting blood.

Then the hall bellowed with new warcries and I saw more men rushing in through the broken doors. At their head was a long-limbed, iron-grey figure with mailed boots, mailed gloves, a bright sword cutting through the smoky light and a mask of mail hanging from his helmet, leaving just two dark spaces for his eyes.

It was a demon from a world of death, but it was a demon I knew. This was my father, dressed in the fearsome war gear of his youth. He brought death against death and his presence only stilled my fear enough so that I could howl out into the twisting light and shadows of the hall.

He saw my mother and ran towards us, his footsteps thundering, and with a cry of vengeance that sang around the walls he brought down his sword and cut the bearded Welshman from shoulder to belly, kicked the body down, pushed my mother to safety, then plunged on into the burning hall, howling for more blood. The doomed raider fell only a footstep from where I lay. A pool of thick blood spread around him and his breath came in desperate, gurgling sobs, each one a little weaker than the last. His fingernails clawed at the floor planks. And, with his death-gaze, he saw me. My mother had always told me that the eyes of men and women shone with the light of God's love, but this man's eyes were just grey as they took their last fading view of this world. As cold as the first day of winter and as dark as the blood that bubbled from his mouth. His skin was like ash in the morning. There was a pleading expression on his face, as if all the sins of his life had come back to destroy him and he would give anything to escape them. Those songs of battle I had heard said nothing of the final choking, twitching, weeping moments of the slain. The chill of his death shivered through my body. So many times since have I seen that face dying in my dreams, slipping in pain and terror from this world into whatever lies beyond.

The sounds of fighting began to fade. Still trembling, I pushed myself away from the corpse and looked out into the hall again. Shadows grappled at the door where firelight and smoke mingled. Dropping their heavy shields, some of the raiders broke out and fled into the black valley beneath a waning moon. My father threw himself on his horse, swung his sword in the air to call for men to follow, and led the pursuit away into the darkening night. The valley enfolded their hoofbeats with silence, leaving only the whimpers of the dying and the stunned whispers of survivors.

The years since our world was made are as many as the raindrops in a spring sky, and this shall be the story of just one of them. But it was a year which England's elders will recall for many lifetimes to come. A year of battles, betrayals, and dark smoke carried on the autumn wind. A year for the grey wolf and the carrion bird, gathering to fill their bellies after the last summer of a broken land.

8

It was the nineteenth year of my life, the year our priests numbered ten hundred and sixty-six. It began with the death of a king and it ended with the death of a kingdom.

This winter is a cruel one, and many will not see its end. I am growing old now. I feel the shadows of my life gather around me in the dim corners of the house and between the bright stars of this cold sky. But there are many worse things in the world than the ghosts of a man's life. There are stories told in victory and in defeat which bend the truth like a rod of soft iron at the forge. Stories that make heroes of men who made only slaves and corpses. Some tell of a conqueror who saved England from a usurper who would have damned us all in the eyes of God. Others tell of a great king who would bow before no other to defend his people from tyranny. They do not tell the truth. When I was a young man, I saw the truth. I saw men and women slaughtered to uphold the pride of kings and of men who would make themselves kings.

Tonight is quiet and still. Frost holds the fields in slumber, the hills are hushed by snow and the stars are like splinters of ice on still water. Tonight folk will gather at the hearthside and hear the tales I tell. They will ask me what it was like, that day in the grey murk of the past when I stood in the shield wall of Wessex beneath the banner of Harold Godwinsson, as if it is a thing to be proud of. Few of them had even slithered into this world when these things happened. Even fewer have stood alongside kings and shaped the future with the sword's edge. I do not doubt that they are luckier than I, but they narrow their eyes and grumble to each other when I say that were I to live my life over again I would put my sword in the ground and stay far away from that place of blood, steel and crows.

They may not like the things I say, but still they ask for my tales. And I will tell them, because I am growing old and perhaps I have more tales to tell than I have years to live. And because I must tell the truth of the land and of my people, before it is drowned forever in a tide of lies and forgetfulness.

My eyes are not as strong as once they were, but from the doorway of my house, in the day's last light, I can see a ring of black rocks standing on a hilltop. The people who placed them there have passed even from memory. They leave only their ancient stones and a few dark grave mounds that folk stay well clear of on even the stillest winter night. Their names are gone, their gods have faded into shadows, their memories have passed into the hills and their proud lineages are only so much dust on the summer fields. Their stories are lost upon the west wind and, one day, mine will join them.

1. THE FALLEN CROSS

"We have sinned o Lord! We have strayed from the righteous path and your anger is just! We beg you, Lord, for your forgiveness and your guidance." Father Cuthred raised his thin hands towards the freezing sky as if the mercy of Heaven was something he could touch. The sparse crowd groaned in agreement. Wrapped in cloaks against the biting cold of dawn, many of them turned their faces to Heaven. Others gazed balefully down at the thick wooden cross that lay in the snow, torn from the roof of the village church by icy winds in the night.

"The worst storm since that tree fell on Eohric," I heard one man call it.

"The Devil's work," his wife replied, making the sign of the cross.

But most of the villagers were still asleep, slumbering off the ale and mead of the great feast of Christmas, and I wished I was among them. My father had found me lying on the floor of his hall, among the bones, the crusts and the spilled ale and had knocked the sleep out of me with a blow from his staff. Now I stood beside him in the blinding white, wind-whipped morning, my head throbbing and the cold cutting through me like a spear. And I was listening to the shrill lamentations of the clergy.

"Why doesn't he just nail it back on?" I whispered.

"Show some respect Wulfred!" my father snapped. "Our people have seen a terrible omen. It is our duty is to console them and help in any way we can." He stamped his feet and brushed a few snowflakes from his beard. "However ridiculous it may seem," he added under his breath.

11

"All is lost!" wailed Grimstan, a younger and even shriller priest. Groaning, he touched his face to the snow and marked it with spots of blood from where he had recently shaved the top of his head. Although he was probably about twenty years old, Grimstan's skinny frame, a wasted face haunted by the demons of scripture and the tonsure shaved into his limp shock of red hair made him look like an old man. Cuthred kicked a patch of snow aside and knelt.

"Oh, Lord of Earth and Heaven, we beg you hear our prayer…" he began, reaching out to touch the fallen cross.

The huddled villagers knelt obediently. I stood there and shivered. My father tapped his staff impatiently on the frozen ground while the priest offered God abject apologies for the heathenism and debauchery of all mankind.

"Cuthred. Grimstan," my father interrupted. "You cannot set right the house of God alone. My son and I will help you in this holy task." That was an unwelcome suggestion. I was hoping to be asleep again before the sun rose much higher.

"No man can undo this Devilish work!" wailed Grimstan. He turned his face skywards again and sobbed like a child.

"Do you truly believe God listens to these two fools?" I muttered.

My father jabbed me with the end of his staff. "If you cannot say anything useful then be silent," he growled. Cuthred's ancient knees cracked as he rose to his feet. His eyes were bright with fear and sadness. Father Cuthred was a gentle old man and I immediately regretted calling him a fool.

"All things must be set right through prayer. Only by repentance shall we find redemption," he mumbled. I noticed frost dusting the sleeves of his priestly cassock. How long had he been out here praying beside his church? I wondered if I would ever reach Father Cuthred's age and if I would spend those distant years peering, like him, into the mysteries of the next world. My father shuffled his feet again, drew his bearskin cloak tighter and sighed a long white plume into the chill air. He was probably thinking about a warm fire and a good breakfast. I was sure his idea of putting things right involved more nails than prayers.

"It shall be fixed," he said, nodding at the broken cross.

"The holy cross is smashed beyond repair," Cuthred sniffed. Grimstan, his eyes rolling back in his head, raised his arms to Heaven and howled like the wolves of the great forest that edged our village.

"It is a foul, foul omen!" he shrieked. "Satan's host roams the land, spitting smoke and lightning! Out of the heathen realms of the north they ride - raising columns of fire that split the very sky apart! A great star shall fall and God will send a terrible host to vanquish all men, both the sinful and the just. By the sword ye shall perish and by fire shall thy bones be consumed. Be ready to look upon the face of God!" The little crowd gasped and shuffled back. I put my hand on my father's staff and inclined my head towards Grimstan, suggesting that the situation might be improved if one of us dealt the priest a sound blow to the head. My father shot me a warning look and wrenched the staff back.

"We must make another cross," he said, deciding that Cuthred remained the priest most worthy of his attention. "Show the Devil whose side we're on!" The two of them stared up at him like frightened toddlers. "Ragnald will cut the timber for it." Grimstan covered his face with his hands, curled up into a ball and shrieked. Cuthred fingered the clumsy wooden cross that he wore on a piece of rope around his neck.

"Ragnald the Dane?" he whispered.

My father nodded. He turned to look across the snowbound village and gave me a shove to let me know that I should accompany him and the priest to Ragnald's cottage in the shadow of the forest. I shot him an angry look over my shoulder and he scowled back at me.

13

An owl shrieked somewhere to the west where the black branches of elms were bent under heavy snow. To hear an owl during the day was an omen of death and darkness. I scanned the forest's edge, looking for the bird that had called out, but the wind gathered snow from the high branches and drove it into my eyes. My father tramped along without even turning his head. Across the village, the little huts and houses lay half buried in the night's blizzard and the tangled riverside willows away to the east had become a wall of snow. What god worth worshipping, I thought to myself as I stumbled through knee-high snow, would demand that a man deal with the clergy so early on a winter's morning after a feast? My father, for once, echoed my thoughts.

"At least when I fought the battles of lords and kings we had a decent breakfast before we started," he muttered under his breath.

"Ragnald!" Cuthred demanded as he stepped through the cottage doorway. "The storm of this past night has torn the Lord's cross from our church. We need wood to replace it." My father and I followed him into the little house. It was dark and held a stubborn chill that a new-kindled fire was not yet starting to tame. The walls were hung with axes, knives, saws and other tools of a woodworker's trade. A low table and a few rough stools stood among clay pots and sacks and in the middle of the floor a cauldron hung from a tripod beside the stone hearth. I knew the house well. Cuthred was less at ease, frowning darkly at the bundles of herbs, twigs and berries that hung from the roofbeams.

And before the hearthfire, staring at the little flames, knelt Ragnald himself, bare-chested despite the cold, a young man with the burdens of a longer life somehow etched across his face. I nodded to him in greeting, but he did nothing to acknowledge us. His long straw-coloured hair and beard hung loosely, tangled with broken twigs and a few dry leaves. His cloak lay sodden across the table. He glanced up at Cuthred, and his eyes were ice-blue, bright and unreadable.

"We need timber Ragnald," Cuthred repeated, but he spoke more quietly now and was fiddling with his cross again. "Perhaps you may atone for your ill attendance in the house of the Lord." Ragnald's eyes strayed to the fire, then he moved his head slowly up to look at Cuthred again. As white as the snow outside, his face was eerie in the gloom.

"Priest!" Ragnald finally whispered. He turned to my father and spoke with the heavy accent of the Danes who dwelt in England's northlands. "Why, my lord, does this priest disturb me in my home?" My father bit his lip. He liked Ragnald - particularly the fierce way he swung his axe against the great trees of the weald - and had little time for the fussing of priests. But a lord must support the Church or face its wrath.

"The wind has blown the cross from the church. We need wood for a new one," he said.

"And I am sure the holy Church will pay you well," I added, grinning at Ragnald. The shadow of a smile flickered in his pale eyes. My father growled and jabbed me with the top of his staff again. Cuthred shook his head in disapproval.

"Ragnald, you are called upon to serve God. The Lord shows great mercy in Heaven to those who do his work on Earth." The priest's voice lingered in the white plume of his breath for a few moments. Ragnald turned those piercing eyes away from us and looked back into the fire, collecting his thoughts, struggling to see something. A floorboard creaked as my father shifted from one foot to the other. Somewhere out in the weald, a great snow-burdened branch snapped and fell, its sound rolling like the hoofbeats of a thousand horses across the frozen land. The flames in the hearth rose and crackled a little, but something cold still waited in the shadowed house. The howling voice of a wolf rose out of the forest and faded away on the wind.

"A new fire for a new year," said Ragnald, still staring at the rising flames. And as he spoke, a little colour stole like a blessing across his face, the ghostly light passed from his eyes and some kind of spell seemed suddenly to break. Wordlessly, he plucked a black branch covered with dry leaves and shrivelled berries from a rafter and held it just low enough over the flames to make it smoulder. One at a time, the blackened leaves flared. The dry berries hissed and burst. The ends of the twigs caught fire, their flames crawling slowly along the wood. The fire was still small but I felt its warmth and I was glad of it. Again we heard a wolf crying out from deep among the trees, then another and another until their voices gathered into an otherworldly chorus, before fading to echoes and finally silence. Cuthred drew his thin priest's robe closer around himself. Ragnald watched unblinking as fire gathered on the branch. I followed the tiny movements of his eyes and the light and shadow passing across his face, but his expression told us nothing. Cuthred clutched his cross and my father shuffled his feet. At last, Ragnald flung the charred branch on the fire and turned to us.

"Your church will meet its end before the year does," he said, looking into the eyes of the frightened priest. "I will make a cross, if that is what you wish. It may bring comfort for a time to those who have faith in such things." He picked up an axe and strode out. I followed him into the dazzling white world about which I had almost forgotten.

Cuthred shivered as he left the house, whether from the cold or from what he had just seen and heard I could not tell. He looked even older and frailer in the harsh light. Feeling guilty for calling him a fool earlier and for mocking the rewards of Heaven, I took off my thick cloak and placed it around the priest's shoulders.

"Thank you and God bless you," said Cuthred, "but I fear there are men far greater than I who will be undone by the storms of this winter."

Eohric, the old brewer, was sat just inside the door of the hall with two other men of the village. Grinning with his toothless gums, he was cackling his way through a story about a girl he once knew way back in the days of his long lost youth. In one hand he clutched a drinking horn with golden mead sloshing at its rim and with the other he made a gesture to demonstrate the size of this girl's breasts. He had been drinking all day and all night and he would continue to drink, to tell tales and to sing songs in his raggedly perfect voice until sleep stole over him.

My father grunted something about breakfast and strode off into the shadows, towards where the smoke from the hearth drifted up and misted around the roof beams.

The whole hall creaked and shuffled with the sounds of the sleeping and the reluctantly waking. The low thatched roof and the plank walls held a welcome warmth after the bone-biting chill of the morning, but somewhere beneath the woodsmoke there lingered the smells of sour ale and vomit. The floor was scattered with wooden cups, bread crusts and greasy bones, the remains of the great feast of the night before.

I found Godric and Idwal sat at a bench close to the ale-splattered patch of floor where I had sprawled in sleep for an hour or two at the end of the night. Idwal was eating, poking a crust of bread into a bowl of barley stew. His frayed cloak hung about his shoulders and mingled with his black hair, giving him the look of a lean mountain crow as he hunched over his bowl. Godric held a horn mug full of ale, but seemed dazed and reluctant to drink from it. His sister, Hildelyth, lay asleep in a heavy brown cloak on the floor near their feet. I remembered how her head had been pillowed uncomfortably on my stomach as my father's staff jabbed at my shoulder. She had replaced me with a clump of straw and slept serenely on.

I sat down with Idwal and Godric, leaned my elbows on the bench and shut my eyes for a moment, enjoying the relief of being off my feet again. When I opened them, both men were looking at the snow melting into my cloak and hair.

17

"There was a storm in the night," I explained. "It blew the cross off the church roof. The priests think the Devil's at large and my father decided I should help him deal with it." Godric smirked. He suspected that what my father really wanted was to make me suffer for the ale I had drunk during the feast. Godric was a peasant, a year or two older than me, his dark hair forever tangled by the wind and his body made thin and wiry by working the land. But his mind was quick, his eyes were questioning, as blue as a summer river and lively with ideas, though more often than not his ideas concerned getting a free meal or avoiding a day's work. If fate had played more justly with our lives, perhaps it would have been Godric's task to tell this tale.

"The cross has fallen?" Idwal smiled. "Your priests will be in a panic. That's worse than finding a frog in the holy water." His voice danced through the words as if they were poetry. Idwal came from a place called Caer Myrddin, far beyond the great river that divides the English from the Welsh. He was a poet and a minstrel, wandering the roads with his flute and his songs, bringing music to the halls of lords and warriors, earning his food and drink and a few coins wherever he could.

Godric put down his ale, blinked a few times and looked curiously at Idwal.

"It is an omen, my friend," explained the Welshman. "The closer a Saxon is to Christ, the more he fears the Devil. Those priests see the Devil's work in all things and the glory of God in almost nothing."

"An omen of what?" Godric wondered.

"Another bad harvest?" I suggested. We both smiled at that. Godric's family were among the poorest of the poor, living at the village's edge in a cluster of huts and hovels thrown up in the shadow of the forest. They farmed a few weed-choked scraps of land wedged between the trees and the great barley fields of my father's estate, growing just enough grain and beans to feed themselves. Three summers had passed since they had paid my father any rent.

"What about the king?" Idwal glanced across the hall as he spoke, wary that my father should hear him speak of such things. Godric and I fell silent. "He is sick, is he not?"

"So they say." I said quietly. The failing health of a king was not a matter to be spoken of lightly. I took a swig from Godric's ale and swilled it round my mouth to get rid of the dry taste of the smoky air.

"I heard news from a priest in Cantaburh just a week ago." Idwal looked around cautiously as he spoke. "He said your king has been struck by blindness, sleeps for most of the day and has barely the strength to stand."

"And the falling of the cross foretells his death?" I wondered. It was a dark thought. The death of a king and an empty throne were always invitations to the grim gods of war. Godric bit his lip and Idwal nodded.

"Last night you toasted the health of your king, but I'll wager all the silver a Saxon lord keeps hidden beneath his privy that you'll be drinking to a new king before the winter is out."

Godric gave a whispered laugh and raised his ale cup. "Then we'd better drink a toast to King Edward's cock. He's spent too long building churches while the queen lies alone and leaves him heirless."

Idwal leaned in and spoke in a hushed voice. "It's too late for that my friend. The wretched fool of a Saxon! How can a man call himself a king, but let age shrivel his balls before he's filled his wife's belly?"

"I'll shrivel your balls for you if you don't shut up," Hildelyth grumbled. "It's like trying to sleep in a coop full of hens." She rose up on her knees, let her cloak fall to her shoulders and blinked at us. Hildelyth was tall, with the healthy figure of peasant girl in the months of the harvest and the livestock slaughter. Her face was gently rounded and her eyes glimmered with the light of fields and woods.

She sat on the bench and leaned against me, pushing her hair out of her face. It was the same golden colour of barley fields at the height of summer and it flowed half way down to her waist, tangled with bits of rush and straw from the floor of the hall. It was the will of God, Father Cuthred perpetually told us, that all women should modestly plait their hair and cover their heads in order to spare men the lustful thoughts that might stain their souls. But as soon as they were away from the church, the village girls tended to ignore Cuthred and men's souls were generally stained.

"What are you talking about anyway? The sun's hardly up," she mumbled.

"We were talking about the king," I explained, wondering just why I had talked about the king when I could have been asleep.

"Bollocks to the king!" Hildelyth snorted. She spat out the words, but at the same time she smiled like the coming of spring. And for a moment I was lost in the music and the dancing of the night before, the swirling sound of Idwal's flute, Hildelyth smiling and laughing, the whole village dancing, their hands and eyes mingling in the firelight, Godric staggering around in a devilish green mask and with a tail hanging from the seat of his breeches.

"Bollocks to your king indeed," laughed Idwal, a little too loudly. "Perhaps they will help him beget an heir!"

"Mind your tongue when you speak of England's king." My father had come over from the hearth, chewing on a piece of the yellow cheese that grew tougher and smellier as the winter progressed and giving us all a hard look. In the weak, smoky light the grey streaks in his hair were hidden and his jagged teeth, broken by the blades and the fists of uncounted battles, gleamed yellow in the darkness of his beard.

"King Edward is old and has no heir," I said, wary of how he might react. "Who could rule when he's gone?"

My father growled. "I am loyal to King Edward of England. My sword is his. My tongue does not speculate idly upon his death." There was a brief silence while his eyes held us darkly. Then he finished the cheese, wiped his fingers on the edge of his cloak and sat at another bench facing us. "But tell me, who does England have who would make a worthy king?" A mocking smile stole across his face, a smile that told me any answer any of us gave would be wrong.

"Edgar?" Godric suggested. "He is of the royal line of Wessex, a cousin to King Edward, and is the true aetheling."

"A feeble choice," my father snapped. "The atheling is a child." An atheling was a son or close kinsman of a king and the person expected to succeed to the throne.

"The Witan could act as his counsellors until he comes of age," I said. Godric took another gulp of ale and looked pleased that someone else had spoken.

"The Witan?" my father gave a savage laugh. It had seemed like a ridiculous idea even as I had said it. The Witan - the great council of England's highest lords and churchmen. It would be hard to find a less united or trustworthy body of men.

"Oh to see England ruled by it's most noble men!" scoffed Idwal. "So they can fight each other for the best whore in Lunden while the bastard-born Duke of Normandy makes off with the ale and meat!"

My father gave the Welshman another hard look, but there was truth in Idwal's words and he let the comment pass.

"The Norman duke does look to England for a crown," I nodded. "And King Edward hasn't spoken against him."

"But the great lords of this land have!" My father banged his fist down on the bench and his eyes gleamed with a memory of battles past. "Edward brought his friends from Normandy to this land and our earls drove them out. When Edward is gone nobody will support a Norman king."

"So who else is there?" I wondered aloud. "The Danish king might wish to claim England's crown, but he cannot hold onto his own. There is only Earl Harold."

"King Edward hated the earl's father. He would not want the son of his enemy on his throne," said Godric, but my father had smiled as soon as Harold's name was mentioned.

"England is an empire, ruled by Wessex," he said, leaning forward and eyeing us keenly. "But it is an empire surrounded by foes and it needs a warrior king whose strength can bind the earls to his will and whose courage can put our enemies to flight wherever they come to meet us. The lords of Mercia and Northumbria have never accepted the rule of Wessex, and the Viking Sea is an open road for Norse and Danish fleets. The Scots, the Irish and the Welsh are hungry for English corn and cattle. And, of course, the Norman Duke seeks to make himself a king. Only a great lord of warriors can lead England in victory through the years ahead."

"And Earl Harold is that lord?" I asked. He brushed some grease from his beard, looking intently at me all the time.

In those days Harold Godwinsson was the Earl of Wessex, the most powerful warrior lord in the land, the eldest surviving son of old Earl Godwin who had quarrelled endlessly with King Edward. There were many who believed that all it took to rule a land was a thousand mailed men with bright spears and strong shields, and if they were right, then Harold could already call himself England's king.

"He is," my father murmured, his voice now as dark as the grave. "I have fought at his side and I will proudly do so again. And why should Harold not become a king? Wessex has rejected

Norman lords, and the Viking kingdoms make war with one another. If King Edward's days are few, then he must declare that neither Norman nor Viking will wear his crown. The Witan must choose a king of Saxon blood. Earl Harold is the only lord with the strength to hold England."

I felt a coldness even deeper than the wind which gusted in the hall's thatch suddenly creep through the dawning year. A king's life was ebbing into the chill of winter, war was edging closer and the faces of those dead men of Llyn Rhydderch stared, blood-slick and hollow-eyed, through my memory. I had grown from a child to a man since that day, but still they haunted me.

Idwal, however, shared none of my fears. He was grinning like a man who knows he is about to say that wrong thing, but must say it anyway. "And when the men of Normandy have driven shield-splinters into your king's arm," he cried. "And when Vikings have hewn the head from his spear, then my people shall fly from their mountain eyries to tear off the rags of his cloak, sweep him into the sea that brought forth his forefathers, and claim once more the land that was taken from us."

I shook my head and gritted my teeth at Idwal, warning him to say no more. But it was too late. My father's eyes were already flashing with the joy of a man watching his enemy fall.

"And you and Godric can go and hide in the forest like you always do when there's work or fighting to be done." Hildelyth whispered. She leaned close and said it quietly enough for my father not to hear. But she need not have worried. His ire was already roused and it was aimed like an axe blow at Idwal.

"Be silent!" he shouted, lurching to his feet and pointing a finger that killed Idwal's laughter in his throat. "You are a man of ale and music. You know nothing of war. Use your voice for song alone or I'll see you hang from a tree at the village gate."

Idwal lowered his eyes, but my father's rage-red gaze stayed on him. Across the hall, we heard the shuffling of people roused by his voice. My father picked up his staff and stamped off towards the door at the end of the hall.

"Wulfred, come with me," he snapped. Reluctantly, and grimacing at my friends, I followed. His anger was fierce and could simmer for days and weeks. A Welshman had already angered him and he was in no mood to have his son disobey him.

"The men of the northlands believed that the world began like this, in ice and snow and emptiness." He pointed his staff out of the door that creaked on its worn leather hinges, and my eyes followed it across the snow-covered country. "Before the truth of Christ was brought to them, of course," he added, as an afterthought.

Ellasham, our village was called. A huddle of little houses, a hall and a church all embraced in the curving arm of the River Leman as it split the ancient kingdoms of Kent and Sussex and coursed its way seawards to the harbour town of Riaburh about half a day's walk to the south. The great port of Lunden lay far to the north, a full day's journey for a rider with a swift horse; nearly a week away for a man travelling on foot. My father's land and his right to be called a lord of men were things he had won with the sword's edge and although years of peace had swollen his belly and etched lines across his face, it was on the field of battle that his soul still dwelt.

"Ever since that time our people have been warriors. Neither the god of Christ nor any gods who went before have freely granted anything to our people. The sword and the spear have been the tools with which we've shaped this kingdom. At Aella's side we drove the Welsh into the hills of the west. With Aelfred we held the Viking hordes at bay and with Athelstan we covered the earth in the bodies of Scots and Northmen." Slowly his gaze moved across the quiet, snow-covered country. "The chain forged by our ancestors cannot be broken. I became a warrior like my father and his father and a thousand fathers before. Last night, at the great table at the

24

head of the hall I sat with men at whose side I fought in my youth and with your brother, Oswold, who wears his sword proudly and longs to do battle at our side. We told the tales of mighty kings and lords of war and we sang the songs of battles long past. And where were you?" His eyes were fixed upon me and I tried to hold his gaze.

"I was with..."

"I know who you were with, Wulfred. With idlers, drunks and vagabond poets, with the men of the fields and their filthy women. They are our people, but they are not our sword-brothers, they are not the ones who will stand with us in the wall of shields when the ground runs with blood and the air is thick with the din of battle."

"A lord must be loved by his people as well as his sword-brothers," I ventured, knowing even as I spoke that it would be wrong.

"He must not. Our duty to the men of the fields is to rule and protect them. We don't need their friendship. I had fought battles by the time I was your age, Wulfred. I'd held the shield wall against charging foes and watched them flee before my spear, I had twisted my sword in men's bellies and stood alone between my lords and greater warriors than I. I was wounded when I was not much older than you." He tapped his staff against his left leg. "Speared above the knee while I fought at Earl Harold's side. And all you choose to do is drink and vomit with that louse-ridden pack."

"I've guarded the borders of England," I pointed out, but he just grunted dismissively. Over the previous two summers I had played the obedient son and ridden to the edges of the Welsh kingdoms with Leofwin, the Earl of Middlesex. I had gone with weapons, shield and armour and with the horror of war and death like a lump of ice in my belly. But I had also been lucky. The rebellious King Gruffyd of Gwynedd had fallen the year before I came of age as a warrior, and those were peaceful summers. My father was deeply disappointed that I had reached my nineteenth year and still not killed anyone.

Now he gave his words time to sink in as he looked away across the white and distant flatland of Walland Fen, the great sea-marsh that lay east of the River Leman.

"It may not be right to speak of these things, but King Edward's life is coming to an end and these soft times are ending with it," he eventually said. "The Witan must give the crown to Harold Godwinsson, but it is we who must hold it for him. This kingdom has so many foes. Even our fellow Englishmen cannot be trusted. Barely two months have passed since the men of Northumbria drove out Earl Tostig and the law of Wessex and chose instead a man who will look across the Viking Sea to seek a king. Armies will gather like the winter crows, Wulfred, once King Edward is gone."

"Why?" I snapped, angry at his blind devotion to duty and war. "Why must men butcher each other on the whims of a king?"

"Because it is the way of things as ever it was," he shouted, banging his staff on the thick boards of the hall's threshold. "Why must you ask such a foolish question? How have I raised a son who would rather spin wool like a woman than wield a sword? Men fight. The brave and the battle-wise win victories, their people prosper, and those who shirk battle die as carrion or live as slaves." There was an uneasy silence. This was the hateful destiny I had been born to. An endless saga of blood and battle, to be played out from the misty dawnings of our people until the last day of the world.

"When a new king rules, he will need every warrior in this land, Wulfred," he went on. "You and me and your brother Oswold and all of the sword-men and spearmen bound by oaths." He held up his right hand to show the gold ring on his middle finger, given to him many years ago by an earl to seal a blood-oath. "When towns burn, when rivers run red with blood, when fields roar with the death-songs of swords and wherever our enemies dare to defile our land. There will be no hiding place for cowards in the days that are coming." He beat his staff on the boards again as he spoke, its sound reaching across the winter land like an echo of the beating of weapons on shields before the clashing of armies.

"You mock poets and bards," I said. "But you speak like them."

"There may be fire and iron in their words, but how many makers of songs have braved the battle line? Many times have I stood beside the earls of England in battle, Many times have we put our foes to flight and we needed no men of flutes and dancing to help us." Warmed by memories of blood and battle, his breath plumed white against dark clouds that gathered, cauldron-black with a promise of more snow. He leaned on his staff and flexed his knee.

"Oswold will find battle fame as a lord of men," I said. "But perhaps my fate lies elsewhere."

"It does not. You do not have a choice, Wulfred! What you have is the skill, the quickness and the clear mind of a warrior. I know - I have trained you from childhood. You are afraid to face the enemy, afraid to face your own death. Your life has been too easy - you have never had to triumph over fear. But soon you will be tested on the battlefield and you will find that rage, that warrior's fire in your heart. For a man's life has no true worth until he has bargained with it in battle."

"And a man's death?"

He paused for a moment. A strange kind of peace was stealing over him, as if a part of himself already dwelt among the warrior-ghosts that roamed that winter landscape.

"A man's death awaits him always. He must find a place and a time to die. If a man falls beside his lord in the midst of battle, then he has come to a good death and it is the price we pay to hold our land for our people. Your heart is filled with fear, Wulfred, but you will find your courage and you will leave your fear among the dead, upon the field of crows which follows battle."

2. THE MESSENGER

Something was moving among the snow-bent saplings just ten paces in front of us. Oswold and I crouched behind the roots of a fallen tree and stared hard into the cold sunlight that fell in shafts through the winter forest. We waited, watching, until a mass of snow, melting in the sun's thin warmth, fell from a treetop beyond the saplings. Then two black dots appeared in the tangled branches – the ear tips of a white hare, sitting up and scanning the woods for whatever had broken the silence. My brother and I were on our feet instantly, but the hare caught either the rustle of our boots in the snow or the faint creaking of our bows as we drew the stiff cords.

It was gone in an instant, the tips of its ears and the soles of its feet blurring into a dark streak as it raced up the woodland path and vanished in a flurry over the crest of a ridge. Our arrows chased it in vain, mine sinking into the snow and Oswold's flying just a hand's breadth over its back before thudding into a tree.

Oswold smiled and shook his head.

"The hare is quicker than men. Even a pack of hounds couldn't touch that one."

Quicker than men. It was strange to hear my brother speak of himself as a man. He was sixteen years old – only two years younger than me but those two years had always made a difference. For as long as we had been able to stand, our father had made us fight and spar with one another, first with wooden swords, then with spear-long poles and finally with heavy shields, axes and blunt-edged training swords. Those two years of extra height and strength and cunning had always allowed me to break his guard and knock him to the ground. Do not let Oswold win, my father had always told me. A young warrior needs to be beaten in order to learn from the skills of his opponent. Then he would take up his own sword and show Oswold what he should have done, usually leaving me bruised.

But now Oswold was a man. The summer before we had fought each other to a standstill while the people of Ellasham toiled in the harvest fields. He was as tall as me now and I could tell that the muscles of his arms and shoulders were as strong as mine by the way he drew the powerful hunting bow. He even had the beginnings of a beard, wispy and blond and looking as if a gust of wind might blow it off his chin. My beard was thicker and my hair darker, but we must have looked very alike as we trudged through the snow with our bows.

We were both men now. Old enough and strong enough to stand at our father's side in battle. Old enough to kill and be killed. To Oswold, battle was a bright destiny, a thing of savage joy. To me it was a horror from a place far away in time and distance but as close in memory as a hand on my shoulder.

"You and Hildelyth are still closer than our father would like," said Oswold as he used a knife to carefully work his arrow out of the tree it had struck.

"Yes," I smiled. "Last year he said that as a man of high birth I had every right to take a girl like Hildelyth to my bed, but he wanted no children of his line born of her. If she fell pregnant, he said I should make her drink thyme and rue to kill the child. I think I'd marry her just to see the look on his face."

"Why don't you?" said Oswold. "You've never worried about what he thinks before."

He was right, of course. It was usual for the sons of warriors to wed the daughters of other warriors and to forge alliances and blood-bonds among the lordly families. But although I saw no reason to care for what was usual, I was stopped in my tracks by my brother's bold suggestion.

30

"Oh God, no," I stammered. Then I wondered why not. "Marriage makes men and women old. She'd start talking about cooking pots and cloth and spoons and children, and I'd have to think about cattle and corn and collecting rents." Also, marriage is for men who are steering a bold course along the path of their life. Men who can keep a wife and pass something on to their children. Peasants with rich fields to farm, traders with ships and good reputations in ports and markets. I was a warrior and to forge my path and earn my fortune I would have to fight and kill in the shield wall. Oswold grinned cheerily at my discomfort.

"You'll have to think about those things one day, Wulfred, when you inherit this land. Even if you don't seek war-fame, you'll still have to deal with crops and payments and arguments about fences." The waiting burden of mundane things weighed suddenly on my shoulders.

"There are better things to live for," I mumbled after a while, looking up through the treetops where a daytime moon, a pale shadow of its midnight self, hung tangled in the high branches.

I had grown up with Hildelyth. The young children of lords, priests and peasants ran wild in the villages of Wessex, unaware of the mysterious order that separated their parents. During the long days of childhood, we had hidden together in the forest and in the reedbeds across the river. Our parents had always had tasks and duties for us, but in the wilderness there had been better games to play. As we grew up, we learned to steal ale from the barrels at Eohric's house at the bend of the river and spent our nights stumbling through Andredsweald in search of sprites and the ghosts from fireside tales, forging memories and secrets that would stay with us forever. She was as beautiful as a summer sky and when I remember Ellasham, I remember Hildelyth in those last sweet years before the dark times came.

"Let's head towards the river." Oswold's voice broke through the fog of my thoughts. He had teased his arrowhead out of the tree trunk and was gently straightening its barbs. "One of the village

31

lads saw a stag drinking there yesterday. A pot of venison would make us plenty of friends tonight."

We both laughed as we trudged on into the snow, but Oswold was right. Everyone in Ellasham had eaten fresh meat a week ago on the night of the Christmas feast, but that was the last of the winter slaughter. What cattle remained were shivering on a patch of land close to the hall that we called the Winter Field, being fed on hay and taken into the hall for shelter during the worst of the weather. There were sheep huddled in rough shelters on the fields to the north and south of the village where wheat and barley grew in the summer, and a few families shared their houses with a sow, but these were the beasts kept alive for breeding. All the meat that remained after midwinter was hung from roofbeams to dry like old leather in the smoke of hearthfires, or preserved in barrels of salt, half rotten and tasting as foul as seawater.

The great trees loomed over the pathway as we trudged through the quiet woods and I listened to the breeze whispering in the high branches, tasted the cold air and tried to push aside all those thoughts of the future Oswold had awakened. This was Andredsweald – the great forest of Sussex that stretched westwards from Ellasham, reaching out towards the setting sun over forty or fifty miles of wild and sparsely settled country. Loud with the cries of birds in summer and haunted by wolf-cries in winter, it was so close to the village that its shadows darkened our hearths in the evening.

The path we followed curled around the foot of a high clearing called Blood Hill - a strange and quiet place where a bright stream of water bubbled up from the earth and where old fireside tales told of a battle fought in the times when our ancestors first came to this land. Ragnald the woodsman had a hut up on the clearing for when he was working deep in the forest, but it was not a place where many folk would willingly go.

As we rounded the foot of the clearing, Oswold froze and grabbed my arm. We both peered through the winter tangle of dead brambles and weeds and out onto the open land across the river. Four or five deer – brown and stark against the snow – were making their way across a great empty meadow. Oswold said nothing, but his eyes asked a question, I nodded and we moved forward.

We walked like ghosts then. The snow hushed our footsteps and we slid between the clumps of brambles and the frost-crisp nettle beds, even crawling on our hands and knees under branches to avoid causing any sound or movement. And eventually we reached the cover of a big willow tree beside the winter-swollen river.

Icy water dripped from the tumbling branches and ran down my neck. I hunched my shoulders and tried to lean forward a little, but still the drips soaked through the hood of my cloak. I dared not move any further. Now that we could see them clearly, there were more than a few deer. It was a big herd of about twenty. Each animal took a step or two then stopped, pricked up its ears and listened, eyes bright and coat shining in the stone-cold sun, scanning the landscape for wolves and men.

"We must get closer," Oswold whispered.

"I think I can hit one," I said. The deer were a little over two hundred paces away.

"If you miss they'll be gone." He pointed across the river and away to the north where the rising ground ran into thick woodland. The herd shuffled across the meadow, nuzzling in the snow to reach the brown grass and the new shoots beneath it and watching, always watching and listening. Despite the hard weather, many of them still carried the fat of autumn and just one would make a good meal for the whole village.

Oswold laid his bow across his knees and shook his head. A blackbird gave its alarm call from somewhere in the trees to our left and the whole herd looked up as one. My brother and I froze. For a moment we did not even breathe. Just the faint plumes of our breath might be enough to give away our position among the riverside bushes. Slowly the herd relaxed.

33

"They might come to the river to drink," said Oswold, but I shook my head.

"They're moving away." On the sides of the hills that faced the sun, there would be slushy pools of water from melting snow. There was little need for this herd to drink at the riverside where wolves might lie in wait. I grinned at my brother and nocked an arrow to my bowstring. Oswold shook his head again, but I half drew the bow and raised my knees off the ground ready to stand. The longer the bow, the further the arrow flies and my bow, when unstrung, was almost my own height. I had to stand to draw it fully and I had to draw it fully to have any hope of hitting the plump doe I had singled out at the rear of the herd.

I tried not to rise too suddenly. The herd would see me, but perhaps I would not alarm them straight away and gain a fraction of a heartbeat in which to take aim. But once I was on my feet I stopped thinking. As I stood, I pulled back the cord until the arrow's fletching touched my cheek, and looked down the shaft to see the doe raise a front foot and turn its head towards me. I raised the bow a little higher to give the arrow the extra yards of flight it would need, then felt the bowstring whip into the hard leather strap that protected my wrist. The doe took a step forward as the arrow streaked across the river. Then the rest of the herd bounded away towards the woods and the doe suddenly leapt up and kicked out, with the feathered shaft skewering it through the neck.

With a great whooping sound, Oswold also leapt up into the air.

"You hit it!" he shouted, pointing and jumping up and down. The stricken beast flailed its hooves and twisted, red blood spraying out against the white landscape. Then it fell, just a few steps from where I had shot it, its legs still kicking the empty air. I lowered the bow and felt a chill breeze wash the dank smell of winter across my face. And I grinned while Oswold jabbered in amazement.

We crossed the river where a half fallen willow stretched just far enough across for us to leap from its thicker branches into the

34

shallows of the opposite bank. Oswold pulled down some ivy to use as rope and I used my seax – a heavy, single-edged hunting knife – to cut a pole from a young ash tree. Then we tied the deer to the pole and carried it back to the ford just north of Ellasham. The trail of blood it dripped into the snow would bring foxes and maybe wolves close to the edge of the village that night, but we had keen-eyed shepherds with the flocks in the fields and most of our livestock could be brought into houses or the hall for safety. Fresh meat in winter was always worth a night of extra vigilance.

"Your bow-skill should bring us more than meat," Oswold told me as we tramped over a bridge of thick oak beams that spanned an old defensive ditch. "Arrows like that, shot over shields, could break a host of enemies." He was like our father in his keenness for the field of battle. I stopped and sighed and looked across the village. Folk had trodden pathways into the snow between the houses and the thin grey smoke of hearthfires seeped from beneath the eaves of turf-roofed huts and cottages of planks and mud.

"I've often thought of it," I said. "It must be better to drive off our enemies with flights of arrows before warriors have to meet and cut each other to pieces."

Oswold thought for a moment. "Perhaps," he pondered. "But it would make for a strange sort of battle. What would men sing of at feasts in the halls of their lords?"

Life and love and rich harvests and the sun and rain sweeping across the land. The world had so many things to sing of. But I did not answer my brother. We tramped on in silence towards the village.

As we neared the little huts and cottages, we heard the first voices, faces appeared at doorways and people came wandering out in the snow to greet us. Old Eohric shuffled from one of the houses, clutching a wooden cup and roaring joyously

"Light your fires and fill your cauldrons!" he called out to the village in general, "For we are gifted by the gods of winter and sons

35

of Lord Saxmund!" He took a great swig of ale and hissed his cackling laugh into the cold air as a small crowd began to gather.

Oswold told everyone about how far I had shot the arrow and they all congratulated me heartily. They were obviously hungry, but I smiled and enjoyed their praise.

Idwal, trapped in Ellasham by the snow for more than a week now, grinned broadly.

"You should have taken me hunting with you," he said. "I would have shot you three more."

Eohric's shouting even brought out the priests, scuttling up from their church and holding their cassocks out of the snow like a couple of nuns. Cuthred frowned at Eohric as if to suggest that if he mentioned the gods of winter again, the Christian god might well turn him into a toad. Grimstan looked darkly at the deer I had shot. He disapproved of folk feasting when they should welcome hunger as a punishment for their sins. And Eohric got more than a look from him.

"Hold your tongue old man," he squawked. "Your blasphemy is fuel for the fire of Hell."

"Hold your cock young priest," Eohric rasped back. "Lest you displease the Lord God by fuelling the fire of some young girl's belly." He sank to his knees in the snow, breathless from laughter and Cuthred had to take Grimstan aside and speak to him calmly.

Still wearing the long greyish tunic that he slept in, my father came out of his house, a sturdy log and plank built dwelling on a patch of higher ground above the river, and Oswold splashed up to him through the slushy mud.

"It must have been four hundred paces away," he said, as proud as if he had shot the deer himself.

"It wasn't that far," I protested.

"Nevertheless, a fine shot," my father smiled. He smiled a little reluctantly. He enjoyed the hunt himself, but to him it was a grand affair with horses and dogs and a pack of noblemen drinking mead and bellowing about battles past and battles yet to come. Sneaking around the woods with a bow was the work of poachers and thieves.

"If Wessex had fifty men who could shoot like that in battle," Oswold went on, "our enemies would piss themselves in terror of us." My father's smile hardened.

"The bow is not a weapon of war," he muttered. "A true warrior stands face to face with his foeman."

"Doesn't a true warrior seek victory by any means for his king and his people?" I said, planting the end of my bow in the. My father just scowled at me.

"There are Welshmen who use the bow in battle," said Oswold and our father scowled at him too.

"Indeed there are," he growled as if that in itself was a good enough reason not to use it.

"I shall warn my countrymen," Idwal said, "that Wulfred of Ellasham is almost as skilful with the bow as an old woman of the Dyfed Hills. They may send you a gift of strong wine before battle in the hope that it causes your eyes to cross and your hands to fumble."

As we stood there in the cold, my brother telling everyone I had shot an arrow half the length of Wessex and the villagers making hopeful mutterings about venison stew, the sound of hoofbeats arose from the north.

A rider, dressed in vivid scarlet against the winter landscape, forded the river and rode towards the village. The breeze caught his cloak as he approached along the muddy pathway, and I saw the emblem sewn in golden thread.

"The Dragon of Wessex," I pointed out to a couple of puzzled-looking villagers who stood close to me. "He is Earl Harold's man."

"I have news for Lord Saxmund of Ellasham," the rider, a plump-faced youth with a patchy beard, called out, looking doubtfully at our small gathering. Oswold and I were mud-splattered and wearing old cloaks of faded green. Our father was still dressed in his nightshirt. He stepped forward and addressed the messenger.

"I am Saxmund." The horseman did not look convinced, but he dismounted and bowed before my father.

"I ride from the royal hall at Westminster," he said, "where there is great sorrow, for the blessed King Edward has departed this life to dwell among the saints, but rejoicing also, for Harold the Earl of Wessex is already crowned the king of all England."

There were a few gasps then a moment of silence.

So what we had spoken of had come to pass. My father's hopes and my fears. The wind gusted in from the west and clouds piled upon the murk of the horizon, dark and inevitable, like the warrior's destiny I had always looked away from. A chill much colder than the winter's day shivered through me.

"Go back to your homes. Have you no work to be doing this day?" It was my father's voice that broke the silence. "We will speak of this later," he added as the villagers wandered away to return to their winter tasks of field and hearthside. He beckoned Oswold and I and the messenger into the house.

"What news of the Norman duke?" I asked the news bearer as he sat at the hearth and set about a plate of bread and sausage and a cup of hot spiced ale. My father and brother were busy changing into more lordly clothes for the occasion. I suspected that this young man had set out especially early in order visit as many halls and villages as he could, knowing that each one was likely to provide him with a free meal.

"What of him?" he shrugged. His vacant look suggested he might never have heard of the Norman duke.

"He has claimed that the kingdom of England was promised to him."

The messenger shrugged again as if it was no concern of his. "I know only that upon his deathbed, the blessed King Edward entrusted the kingdom to Earl Harold and that the Witan approved his choice," he recited.

"And if the Witan has chosen Harold," my father thundered, "then, according to the laws of Wessex, Harold is our king!" He stamped around now, dressed in his finest red cloak and tunic, irritated by my questions.

"The Witan," I pointed out "is mostly Harold's brothers and the archbishop's supporters - the Church would put the Devil himself on the throne before it chose a Norman. And King Edward fought for years with Harold's father. Why would he want his son as a successor?"

"Show some respect Wulfred!" he boomed. "The Witan holds the wisdom of our most noble lords and clergy. Our duty is to uphold its decisions - with our lives if necessary."

"Maybe so," I conceded. "But it seems odd."

"Show some respect!" I heard one of the planks of the floor crack as he beat his staff on it with each word. "It is not our place to judge the words and deeds of a dead and blessed king, nor to question the right of a living one."

The hall at Llyn Rhydderch, where I spent my early childhood, was a fortress of jutting wood, carved with the scowling faces of beasts and planted on a craggy border hillside. A place of kings and spearmen, where a thousand broken-toothed warriors would drink hugely, sing horribly and pledge their swords to the mightiest lord.

Its walls were brightly hung with painted shields and on its floor beat the footsteps of those whose iron strength could chain a restless land.

By comparison, the hall at Ellasham was poor and rustic. A gathering place of farmers, the rough benches along its bare plank walls seated a hundred or so folk. Our winter grain was stored in sacks on a platform at the far end and the roof was not high enough to spare us from the smoke when a fire was lit in the central hearth.

It was a place where we celebrated life, not death and battle, though my father would happily have had it another way.

"People of Ellasham. Men of Wessex," my father began. The long benches were full and a brazier of dry logs flickered before his raised table at the head of the hall. He stood to address his people in the evening of that winter day and I sat dutifully at his side, looking far into the smoky shadows at the faces of the villagers. They looked back at us, curious about the day's news, but probably more interested in the big iron cooking pots suspended over the smouldering firepit with the promise of hot stew as soon as he finished talking. "People of this kingdom of England. News was brought this morning that the sun has set upon the reign of the blessed Edward. King Edward who brought strength and plenty to our land is now among the saints of Heaven, and with the dawning of this new year, the sun has risen on a new age..."

Thus Lord Saxmund spoke to his people. And maybe in towns and villages all across the kingdom under the dark skies of deep winter, other lords and earls and bishops also addressed their people, while in the halls of power in Lunden and Wintancester there was singing and celebration for the new king.

My father spoke of a warrior king who would lead his people to victory. Harold would lay waste the Norman host, should the Bastard Duke ever dare to set foot on English soil. He would drive the Vikings back into the sea as had the great King Alfred of old. He would put the Welsh and the Irish to flight as had our rulers of

40

elder times. And the north - the troubled earldoms of Mercia and Northumbria – would again bow and tremble before the strength of a Wessex king.

But there under the roof beams of Ellasham, I saw children shivering in the half-light, and faces that were downcast, a few eyes even bright with tears. For the common folk of England, especially in those more prosperous parts of the land, Edward had been a popular ruler and a father to his people. The earls had quarrelled with him, but not in a way that touched the lives of the folk who worked the fields. In their eyes, his love of the Church had brought the whole kingdom closer to Heaven. The peace of his long reign had allowed people to reap good harvests and to save a little silver. To them, and to me, a new king meant change, and change from what was good could never be welcome. I saw the worried glances of the women, exchanging silent fears of what they may now lose to the hungry gods of war. Old men - they were few, but Edward's reign had spared more from the scant mercies of the battle-line than had the bloody reigns of earlier kings - just bowed their silver heads.

It was not a long speech that my father made. And when it ended there was fresh bread and the meaty stew, bulked up with blood sausage, beans and barley, was welcomed with much more enthusiasm than the new king. Lord Saxmund bade his people plough deep furrows and sow a generous crop to feed the army that would defend England, and to keep their knives sharp for the day when every man was called to his king's side. A barrel of ale was opened and the murmur of voices crept through the hall's silent space again.

I was dressed like a lord of men that night, in a tunic of bright blue hemmed with red silk and a fur-trimmed cloak embroidered with images of stags and eagles. Also, at my father's insistence, I had a sword sheathed in leather at my belt, a blade from the long wars of the Welsh border. He had given it to me four years earlier, as soon as I was strong enough to handle its weight. The lead and copper in the pommel balanced the blade perfectly and it slid through the air with only the slightest guidance. Oswold had a similar blade and he needed no encouragement to wear it, even just to wander around the village. But I was never comfortable with mine, especially on that night of change and uncertainty.

"I suppose if your father's war does come, it might not be too bad," muttered Godric. "If England is attacked, it will be the men of the fields who are called to the king's side as well as the men of swords. We kill our enemies, steal their silver and one day I'll be a lord like you. Better than working these fields all my life." He gave a snort of laughter and we raised our cups of ale. I suppose it was possible for a man who worked the land to rise up and become a lord of men, but I do not think such a thing had ever happened.

Ragnald stood before the smouldering brazier, his eyes sometimes watching flames coiling around the beech logs and sometimes wandering among the faces in the hall. I remembered his strange words of prophecy about the church and I wondered if he was searching for glimmers of the future among the embers that night.

But before I could speak to Ragnald, my father sidled up next to him. "Your axe will serve us well in this coming year," he said, clasping the woodsman's shoulder.

Ragnald only frowned. "If you demand it, lord," he replied. Brichteva, the daughter of one of our herdsmen, handed Ragnald a cup of ale. Her eyes followed his and they whispered to each other as if the hall was filled with their enemies. Brichteva was tall and slim with an unruly mass of dark reddish hair, but she was not a very pretty girl. She had a look that might entice some men, but would chill the hearts of most. She would catch you in a glance and her eyes could make your soul shrivel as if they knew every secret you had ever tried to conceal. For that unsettling look and for her quick and stubborn temper, the young lads of the village were apt to say that Ragnald was welcome to her. There was a dark air about the pair of them that night.

42

By the cooking fire, my mother was supervising the village girls who tended the pots of stew and carried bread and ale around the hall. Estra was my mother's name. Estra, after an old goddess of the dawn. She still had the slight, girlish figure and that pale golden hair of her youth, though it was dusted now with strands of silver.

"He is happy tonight." With a sad smile she nodded across towards my father, who had given up on trying to coax any enthusiasm out of Ragnald and was using his staff to show a group of men how to distract an enemy and get a spear past his shield.

"He's waitied a long time for a day like this." I said

"So has Oswold." There was a tremor in her voice. She watched Oswold join my father, holding up a shield against his staff and against one of the village men who came at him with what looked like the shaft of a hoe. Then she closed her eyes, sighed and turned back to the cooking pots and the platters of bread. My mother was younger than my father, but I saw the faint lines the years had drawn around her eyes and at the corners of her mouth deepen as she watched her husband and her youngest son rehearsing their battles.

"So your father would have you put your sword to good use would he?" Hildelyth laughed as she put some empty platters down on a table. She grinned at me and her eyes flashed mischief in the dimness. Before I could think of a witty response, old Eohric shuffled between us, seeking the warmth of the fire.

"I was a warrior," he croaked, leaning on a staff and pulling his cloak about his shoulders. The usual liveliness was gone from his face and his voice was weak, yet still it rose above the hall's chatter. "When Aethelred Unraed raised the great fyrd of England against Swegn Forkbeard. But then Swegn became our king, so we stopped fighting him." Eohric paused, trembled and took a steadying draught from his cup. "After that we were led by Edmund... Edmund Ironbelly or something, they called him. We fought Cnut – he was Swegn's son - at some cold place in Essex. The ground was

43

burned black there. Whole villages destroyed. The men were killed and the women were driven away, whoring themselves and their children for scraps and shelter. Then Edmund was killed and Cnut was our king, so I came home. It is not good, the life of a warrior." He turned to stare into the flames again. "There are many better ways to live."

Another barrel of ale was broken open and the children fell asleep, huddled under blankets on beds of straw. We heard the cries of shepherds out in the freezing night as they drove wolves away from their flocks. Somewhere out there the stars of midwinter shimmered on a frosty land, and the battle-slain of a thousand years looked down at a kingdom on the cusp of great darkness. And we drank and we talked and we even sang songs, but all I could feel was those old ghosts watching across the bloody years.

3. THE MERCHANT'S SON

"If our faith be strong, our limbs shall also be strong!" Grimstan shouted, waving his arms about as if to attract God's attention. Father Cuthred looked doubtful. The new cross was made from two stout beams of elm and was the height of two men. Ragnald and I were strong, but still we had struggled to carry it up the muddy pathway to the church.

"We can help you," I suggested to Cuthred. It was Grimstan who replied.

"The holy cross shall shall be raised by those who are virtuous in the sight of God," he cried. "The Lord will give us strength." The two priests bent their backs and lifted the heavy timber. Cuthred wheezed and staggered. Grimstan hefted the top of the cross onto his shoulder and stumbled around, struggling to straighten his scrawny legs, his limp hair flapping in the breeze. I sensed Ragnald stifling laughter as we waited to see which priest would drop his burden first.

Unfortunately it was Cuthred. The butt end of the cross fell a few feet from the hole in the thawed earth where it was to be planted. The elm beam landed with a heavy thud. Grimstan staggered for a moment then let go of his own end before he fell beneath it. Cuthred stood there groaning and rubbing his back, the younger priest looking at him as if to suggest it was his unworthiness in God's sight that had caused them to fail.

"Rest, Father," I said to Cuthred, stepping in to take his end of the cross. Ragnald moved in and grasped the middle of the shaft, smiling at Grimstan in a way that was more threatening than helpful.

"And you should stand aside too," he grinned. "We don't want to see a priest killed by his own cross."

"The holy water!" Grimstan shrieked. "Wash their hands before they do God's work!" Cuthred picked up a leather flask and splashed water on my hands, muttering prayers as he did so. Then he moved on to Ragnald. The woodsman held out his hands and looked suitably solemn. Grimstan watched with beady eyes and seemed disappointed that neither of us burst into flames.

Blessed and cleansed, we hoisted the cross and dropped its end into the newly-dug hole in the soft earth. Then we packed gravel and stones around it while Cuthred looked on with relief and Grimstan with resentment. In the afternoon of that damp winter day, the new cross stood tall, a brave silhouette against grey sky and half-ploughed fields, as if the work of winter's storms had been undone. As if work done by the hands of men could hold back the destiny of kingdoms.

Ragnald came from Northumbria, a place more Viking than Saxon, a place where men were not so closely tied by rule and custom to their lords and where the law of the land was something vague and unwritten, something still half-hidden among stories and legends. There were some who said the men of the north were more free than a man of Wessex could ever be. But many more said they would steal the very beard from your face should you dare to travel their roads unarmed. All we heard of Northumberland were rumours of vicious outlaws and rebellion against the king's justice. It did not seem strange that a man should leave so harsh a land and wander away into the peaceful valleys of Wessex.

"Grimstan's an ungrateful bastard," I said to Ragnald as we sat at his hearth after the cross was raised.

"I made the cross for Cuthred and for the folk who fear dark omens," Ragnald grunted. "Cuthred is a good man and I suppose he is a good Christian too." He sighed and looked across the hearth to

46

where Brichteva was scraping the last slivers of flesh from the skin of a hare.

"But Grimstan is a worm not fit to eat turds in a midden," she snarled. "There are too many like him."

"He is. He stole a chicken from my coop once. Said God had taken the bird as a punishment," Ragnald shook his head. "I'd mixed milk and herbs for a sick child, but Grimstan said it was blasphemy – it must be left for God to decide who lives and dies."

"They still think of you as a Dane from the north," I shrugged. "No priest of Wessex will trust you easily."

Ragnald smiled at that thought. "The Church is slow to forget. Ten generations ago it was my people who slaughtered monks and stole the wealth of monasteries."

"And brought the old gods back to Christian England," said Brichteva with a wicked smile.

"A crime far worse than theft and murder," Ragnald grinned. A cold draught gusted around the hearth and pricked at my memory. I turned to Ragnald again.

"When the old cross fell, you watched a burning branch and spoke of Father Cuthred's church in flames. It was like the heathen magic that priests fear."

Ragnald gathered his thoughts before he spoke. His voice was quiet and strangely flat. And he did not look at me. It was as if he addressed something unseen in the half open doorway of the little house.

"My uncle was the last in our village to renounce the old ways. My father never did. The bishops of York and Dunholm say they hold the land for Christ, but even today there are those who honour the older gods. The priests called us devils, witches and filthy heathens, and one night my uncle led priests and monks and madmen to our house. My father called out the names of his gods.

He drew his sword and cleaved his own brother's skull before the rest of them speared him to death in the doorway. They caught my brother, my mother and my sisters and tied their hands and feet, but the man who held me down was old and feeble. I opened his fat belly with my hunting knife and ran into the darkness. In the morning, the house was burned to ashes and my family were gone – killed or banished I do not know which, but I never went back to that village. Cuthred's god might forgive what those men did, but I never will."

A stillness seeped through the cottage. For a few heartbeats the only sound was of Brichteva's knife scraping away at that hare's skin. Then Ragnald stirred himself. A shadow passed from his face as he leaned forward and poked a stick around in the hearth embers. When he spoke again his voice was stronger.

"On the day Cuthred came to my house I saw his church in flames with the leaves of autumn scattered on the graves, many more graves than lie there already. It may mean nothing. Every summer ends among dead leaves - perhaps the church will not burn for another hundred years. And there were grey shadows of people running, like ghosts fleeing from the fire. Did you hear the wolves?"

"Yes. Hundreds of them."

"Maybe from this world, maybe from another. But the grey beasts are waiting, my friend. They gather for a feast of some kind. The darkest days of winter have passed, but still the wolves are waiting."

Oswold's sword swooped like a falcon against the blue sky and I raised my own to parry it. The clang of iron rang out across the field and I struck low at my brother's leg. But before the blow could land, he skipped aside and with lightning speed he struck me on the hip. It was an old blunted blade that we used for training and I was wearing a thick padded coat, but I still felt the force of the blow and I staggered to keep my balance.

"Another Norman bastard dead!" he grinned. I smiled back at my brother, but his words made me uneasy. I liked to spar with him, as we had done since childhood. To me it was sport, a game of strength and skill. But to Oswold it was a foretaste of the battles he and I were born to fight. When our swords crossed, a look as as sharp as pain flashed through those wide grey eyes that had once gazed out at the world in wonder. And since the death of the old king, his enthusiasm for battle had consumed him.

A few girls from the village had set up a big iron cooking pot over a fire at the field's edge. Now they chatted and giggled, occasionally poking the smouldering fire or stirring the pot with an iron ladle. And as the smell of herbs and onions stewing with the barley was carried across the field, the men began to leave their work and drift towards it. Some were working in the long baulks and furrows, carefully hoeing out the first weeds that come before the barley has even sprouted. Others climbed cold and muddy out of the ditches that edged the field, clutching shovels. The land to the south of Ellasham ran alongside the River Leman and unless the ditches were dug deep and wide in the spring, the south field would remain a swamp until after midsummer.

"You should stick to the bow," crowed Oswold, still flushed with his victory. I did not answer my brother. Instead I shot a sly grin at the girls by the cooking-pot and whirled around, aiming my sword with a two-handed blow at Oswold's midriff that would knock him to the ground. But he was quick. So much quicker than he had ever been in the summers of his boyhood. A grimace of battle kicked the smile from his face and his sword was a swift streak of grey as he lowered it to block me. The clang of blades rang out once again. Oswold's teeth showed white, but he was unprepared and his feet were off balance. Before he could gather himself and hit back, I brought my right hand up from the hilt of my sword and pushed him hard. To the scattered cheering of the girls, Oswold stumbled and fell on his back into a puddle.

"Treacherous fucking bastard!" he shouted, but the mask of battle was gone and he smiled at me as he sat up in the mud. The men from the ditch were laughing and as I turned to acknowledge them, I felt Oswold's hand grab my ankle, pull and twist and before I could do anything I was sprawled in the mud beside my brother. There was another cheer from the men. I pushed myself up and looked at Oswold and he looked at me and we both fell back, laughing as if our lives were still the summer games of children.

"It's good to see the king's warriors are ready to face their foes," Godric smirked as he filled his wooden bowl with barley stew from the big iron pot.

"Good indeed," said another man. "I saw two eagles this morning. One flew from the east and one from the south. One for the Danes and one for the Normans. We won't know peace for much longer."

A man with a grey beard nodded solemnly. "Aye, the birds of the air dwell close to God, they know the future better than we."

"If the Bastard Duke of Normandy was coming, he'd be here by now," a younger man sneered. "It's been three months since they crowned Harold."

"He'll come when the roads are dry and the barns are full of grain," muttered the grey-bearded man.

"So will you show us how to break a shield wall?" asked Godric with the look of a man who was in no hurry to go back into a ditch and shovel mud.

"You won't be breaking any shield walls," I said, and I noticed that a silence quickly fell and thirty or so pairs of eyes were all turned eagerly towards me. "If you are called on to fight, it'll be in the fyrd. You'll have whatever weapons you can lay your hands on – axes, knives, clubs. The king's trained warriors will stand at the front of the battle line. It'll be their task to break shield walls. The fyrd's job will be to chase them down when they try to flee. Without shields and mail you'll be swifter than the trained men." That band of mud-spattered peasants looked at me like children keen to hear more. Their lives were hard and monotonous and the thought of fighting and killing and plundering the corpses of rich warriors must have been a grand prospect for to them. But I felt a sickness in my soul as I looked back into their eager faces and thought of them being cut down by a merciless and well-trained enemy.

"We could still teach them what to do," Oswold suggested. He picked up an iron-edged spade which one of the men had dropped on the ground. "Sharpen this up and it could take a man's head off." The men looked at their tools and began to jabber excitedly.

So when they had eaten, I organised half the men into a small shield wall and Oswold led the rest in a charging wedge that might break it. We used old willow hurdles from a rotting fence as shields, but they soon broke apart when Oswold's men smashed at them with their shovels. Godric had picked up a hoe with a long pole and he thrust it over our shield wall, knocking down one of Oswold's shovel-men. Two more of Oswold's men tripped over the fallen one and the men at my side rushed forward into the gap with a great cheer and a wild flailing of shovels and poles. One man threw a bucket, and the whole scene was suddenly so chaotic that he stood as much chance of hitting one of his own side as an enemy. The man who had earlier spoken of eagles flying from the south and east thrust his spade at me and got it caught in the splintered willow rods of my makeshift shield. As he struggled to free it, I saw his face twisted by the same snarling mask of war that I had seen on Oswold and a cold fist tightened around my heart. If I had any kind of duty to fulfil, surely it was to protect and defend my people. And there I was on the south field, beside the river swollen by the rains of spring, preparing them for the field of death.

We were all flailing, shouting and trying not to be hit in the face by muddy shovels when two riders came up the riverside pathway

51

from the south. The fighting mass immediately broke apart to see who it was. It never took much to distract fyrdmen.

"Perhaps we can get them to charge us," said Oswold, rubbing the side of his head and nodding his admiration at the man who had hit him with a mattock. "See how you'll stand up against Norman horsemen."

"I think they're the merchant's sons." I said as the riders drew closer. "We won't get much sport out of them."

But Oswold hailed them cheerfully and they cantered towards us. I knew these two young men by sight and by name, but had rarely spoken with them. Their father was a rich merchant who traded wine and cloth across the Narrow Sea and had a small estate of land further down the river.

"What brings you to Ellasham?" I called out.

"We come to see the thick crop of barley sprouting in the south field." Richard – lean and fair-haired with what he hoped was a commanding look in his eye - reined in his horse and gave a little grunt of laughter as he cast an eye across the muddy furrows.

"The crop will grow," said Oswold. "These men are clearing the ditches to drain the field."

"These men are merely your labourers?" Richard feigned surprise as he looked down at our bruised and mud-spattered band of peasant-warriors. "We thought it was King Harold's great army preparing to face the host of Normandy." A couple of men muttered and a shadow passed across Oswold's face.

"You're not journeying with your father in such fine weather as this?" I asked before Richard could annoy my brother further. "There must be good trading to do now the seas are calm again."

"The Lord Sigered is entertaining guests," said Odda. Odda – shorter than his brother with a shock of dark hair that he constantly had to shake out of his eyes - seemed nervous, but the friendlier of the two. Richard kicked him in the leg and shot him a look that suggested their father's business was none of ours.

"Your father is no lord of men," Oswold muttered.

"He holds five hides of land, so he is a lord," Richard snapped, still looking down at us from his horse.

"A lord has land granted to him in return for his service in battle." I shot a warning glance at my brother, but his voice had an unfamiliar shaft of cold iron running through it and he ignored me. "How did your father get his land? He rents it from the Bishop of Hrofceaster I believe, for a bag of silver and the promise that he'll build a church." There was a ripple of laughter from the village men, who watched keenly, excited by the glimmering prospect of a real fight.

"Will you join us?" I suggested, trying to keep my voice friendly. "Try to break our shield wall with horses." It was a fairly stupid idea and I suggested it more in the hope of breaking the tension than of them taking it seriously. Norman warhorses are trained in battle as rigorously as men. Richard and Odda's ponies would have probably just cantered up to our shields and stopped. Richard waved a dismissive hand.

"We would not flail about amongst men of the fields," he sneered.

"These men are as good as any you will meet in a hall of warriors." I said. "Or in the marketplace."

The girls from the village had gone down to the riverbank to scrub out the cooking pot, but now they returned, two of them carrying the big pot between them. Sitting bolt upright, Richard turned his horse in a tight circle and twirled his hand limply in greeting. A few of the girls giggled. I grimaced at Oswold and Oswold grimaced back. I hoped the merchant's son might have made his point and be ready to ride off, but it seemed he still had more to say.

"So, how will your warband fare against the might of Normandy?" he asked, curling his lip and smirking again at the muddy villagers. I smiled back at him. I did not want to smile. I wanted to pull him from his horse and stamp on his face. But a warrior's greatest skill is to control his anger and only unleash when it is needed, so I smiled.

"We'll be a match for the Duke of Normandy," I said. "With the army of Wessex we'll soon drive him back into the sea."

"And what about you?" Oswold growled. "Are you and your brothers ready to fight for your king?" Richard bit his lip and furrowed his brow.

"We are oath bound to no lord. We are not led into battles like sheep." He glanced briefly at the watching villagers then he turned back to me.

"You've ridden to the west twice, haven't you Wulfred? How many of the Welsh have you killed?"

"The border's been peaceful these past two years. We've not needed to fight. The Welsh piss in their britches at even a rumour of the spears of Wessex."

"And how many battles have you fought in Richard?" My brother's voice cut across mine and rang out across the field like the meeting of blades.

"Our family has enough silver to buy the swords of a hundred hireling warriors in Flanders. We've no need to squabble with frightened Welshmen or play games with peasants." He glanced over again at the girls watching beside the riverbank.

"I asked how many battles you have fought in." Oswold's voice drew all eyes towards him. "As many battles as you have bollocks is my guess."

"We are busy Richard," I said. "If you have no business here please leave us." Odda looked like he wanted to go but his brother gave a grunt and sprang down from his horse. I think I was pleased to see him ignore me. This son of Sigered had angered me and I wanted to see him put down in front of the men and women of Ellasham.

"I think I have business here," he hissed, approaching Oswold with his hand on his sword hilt. The sons of Sigered were not known as warriors, but they still wore swords - out of vanity, I had always supposed. "I was taught swordcraft by the finest warriors in the Frankish realms. Our father gave more silver to our tutors than yours has ever seen."

Oswold laughed in his face. "Is that really a sword? I thought you'd just bolted the hilt to a scabbard to make yourself look pretty." It was exactly what our father would have said. Richard spat on the ground and drew out the blade.

"There'll be no killing here today." I stepped between them and held up the blunted blades Oswold and I had used earlier. "I don't want to have to wash your blood off our good land," I said to Richard. He looked down his nose at the dull old swords with their edges ground away, but when he saw Oswold take one he reluctantly snatched the other from my hand.

"Or perhaps you could not afford to pay the weregild," he spat and in truth, that was something that worried me more than Richard's life. The weregild was the life-price which had to be paid in recompense for killing or wounding a man and Sigered would no doubt demand a huge sum for the death of his son. Some villagers were already placing wagers on the outcome. Within moments there were at least four chickens at stake.

At first, they eyed each other and weighed the swords in their hands. With the blunt training swords they fought only to humiliate, not to kill, but the hateful glare of battle was bright on both their faces.

Richard leapt forward first. Graceful and deadly, he slipped past Oswold's guard and lunged with his blade. Oswold leaned back and twisted awkwardly, only just turning the sword aside before it could hit him hard in the belly. Such a blow from a sharp sword could have killed him, even through mail and leather. With a blunted blade it would have at least winded him and left him unable to resist while his opponent beat him to the ground. Instantly, Richard stepped to the left and pulled the sword into an arc over his head, aiming to bring it down on Oswold's shoulder. It was a predictable move and Oswold could have stepped away, but instead he brought his blade up with both hands and knocked his opponent's aside with a ferocious clang of steel. The blow jarred Richard's arm, but he recovered fast and stepped back. It was clear that he could handle a sword, but that Oswold had trained harder and his strength was much greater.

Oswold stepped forward and attacked but Richard parried skilfully and moved fast, leaping aside from one blow then stepping back to beat off the next. After blocking a cut aimed at his neck, he flicked the sword back, showing surprising strength with his thin wrists, and tapped Oswold on the shoulder. With a smug expression, he pranced elegantly and nodded to the girls watching from around the rough grass at the riverbank. Oswold looked at him as if he was mad. A man who taps an enemy on the shoulder and prances is a man who dies quickly on the field of battle.

"Save your dancing for the mead hall," my brother growled, but before the words had left his mouth, Richard feinted towards Oswold's chest then swung his sword up into a chop aimed at his head. It was a clumsy manoeuvre, learned but not practised, and Oswold had time to parry hard, then he stepped forward into a counterstroke, the strength of which half spun his opponent round. Seeing his opportunity, Oswold aimed a ferocious blow at Richard's midriff which would probably have knocked him down whether his blade had stopped it or not. But instead he twisted aside, leaving Oswold flailing from the force of his own stroke. Lightning fast, Richard swung his own sword at Oswold's face and all my brother could do was drop to his knees to avoid it. Richard kept control of his weapon, pulled it back over his head and came in with the same stroke again, only cutting down lower this time and now Oswold leapt from where he crouched in the grass and sprang inside the arc of Richard's sword, lunging up so hard that his blade would have taken half of Richard's face off had his arm not got in the way. Richard's swing and Oswold's lunge met at the inside of Richard's elbow, in a gout of blood and tearing flesh as the tip of the sword, blunted though it was, drove through bone and muscle and ripped out through the skin of his upper arm.

Richard screamed and Oswold gave a roar of victory as he pulled his sword back in a flying arc of blood droplets. Richard collapsed onto the ground and kept on screaming.

Suddenly there were people everywhere, swarming around the fallen man.

"I hope he's got a lively young girl for his bed," grunted one of the villagers. "Because he'll not be pulling himself off with that arm for a while." A couple of others laughed, but most of them just stared unhelpfully. Odda knelt in stunned silence at his brother's side, his face pale as he stared at the blood was spurting from Richard's arm, the splintered shaft of bone sticking out through the mangled flesh, and at Richard's other arm and his legs which thrashed in the mud and the grass. I swallowed hard at what I saw - a wounded man, screaming against the great darkness of more pain than he had ever known, a boy condemned in a moment of rage to live life as a cripple, or to face the creeping death of fever and rotting flesh.

"Give me your knife, Wulfred." I turned to see Cuthred standing beside me. Taking the knife from its sheath on my belt, he cut a strip of cloth from his own cassock and bound Richard's arm tightly above the wound to lessen the flow of blood. The priest muttered prayers and the wounded man's screams subsided into ragged breaths. Someone held a leather bottle to Richard's lips and he drank, gasping with pain between gulps. Then Cuthred used some of the water to clean the wound. I had to kneel on Richard's left arm to keep him still, and Godric held his legs while the priest poked about in the bloody mess trying to straighten out the bits of broken bone before he finally bandaged the arm.

Late in the afternoon, we placed Richard, weak but conscious, on a cart and sent him back to his father. Odda rode alongside, talking to his groaning brother to keep his spirits up and Grimstan knelt in the cart, ordered by Cuthred to stay at the wounded man's side and pray for his recovery.

"Why can't he ride back?" Oswold muttered. "I only cut his arm."

"He can't ride or walk because he's bled out half the blood in his body!" my father snapped. "Do you realise he'll never use that arm again? And we'll have to pay the weregild. God knows how much silver that bastard Sigered will demand for an arm."

"He deserved it," Oswold muttered.

"I'm sure he did. Sigered is a worm who thinks his silver can buy land and power and his sons think they are as great as any true lord who has earned his status with sword and blood. I'm sure his whole damned family deserves as much, but I'm going to have to pay for it."

Twenty pounds of silver was the price Sigered demanded for his son's arm. Odda was sent back to Ellasham, backed up by four other riders. Two of them were mailed men with swords; the other two had the restless look of thieves, dressed up in padded leather coats and having trouble keeping their horses still. It was an absurd price that the merchant could not have expected anyone to agree to. He wanted payment in three days otherwise Oswold would be called before the hundred court at Riaburh. And if such a court was convened, my father would be one of the men to sit in judgement on his own son. So on the morning of the third day he went down into the dark oak-lined chamber beneath the house where he kept a cask of silver, along with chests of shield bosses, axe blades and spearheads, all wrapped in greased cloth and ready to arm a war host. He gave Oswold two leather bags, each containing three pounds of silver coin.

"Give one to the merchant willingly," he instructed. "Three pounds of silver is more than enough to pay for that miserable boy's arm. "Give him the other if you have to."

"It feels like I'm apologising," Oswold muttered as he mounted his horse. "Why should I apologise? He wanted a fight and he got one." The knot of anger that had strained and burst beside the river still throbbed in my brother's voice.

"It's only the law," I said to him. "Just give him the silver. You don't have to apologise. You don't even have to speak to him."

We rode southwards, following the path along the river. The trees were still bare, but rooks fought and bickered around nests in the high branches. Oswold was silent for most of the way and it was the best part of an hour before we reached the land that Sigered called his estate.

If the merchant's sons had indeed come to see the barley sprouting in Ellasham's south field, I could understand why. There were no crops growing here. To our right was an expanse of brown, scrappy land littered with the stumps of trees. Gangs of sullen-looking men were digging at their roots and hauling on ropes to pull them out of the ground. They stopped work as we passed and watched us in silence, with the lowered eyes of men scheming to attack and rob us.

"These are the men Sigered has working for him?" Oswold whispered.

"This land was waste when the Church held it," I explained. "Forest and marsh. There was nobody living here to work it. The merchant must have hired whatever men were in need of a master."

"Nothing-men. Lordless men at the end of their luck."

59

"And those running from debts and from the gallows," I added. Some of them wore a patch over an empty eye socket as a sign that the law had already had its dealings with them. Others were branded on their forehead and thus marked as outlaws, men whom the law did not protect, men who could be killed without consequence. Such men were forced to live as fugitives or seek protection from any lord or rich man who might find a use for them.

To our left, a wide expanse of land between the pathway and the river was green with sedge and moss. There were gangs of men working here too, knee-deep in mud and water, digging ditches to drain the soil. It would take years of digging, I thought, to turn that marsh into land dry enough to graze cattle or grow corn. The stone-scattered pathway snaked southwards and on either side was waste and ruin, peopled by the broken and the damned.

But Sigered's house told a different story. It stood in what would once have been a natural clearing in the woods and it looked more like a hall than an ordinary house, long and low with a grand doorway at one end, window-spaces with shutters and leather curtains, and its thick posts and planks washed with lime to shine out like a beacon from the wretched landscape. It was roofed with shingles – round-edged tiles cut from white ash and pink-tinged cherry wood. They were expensive, they let the heat of a fire escape and they needed replacing more often than thick reed thatch. But they shone out boldly from the marsh and the ruined woods, declaring that here the hand of man was taking hold of this wasteland, and the hand of a rich man at that.

As we neared the house, one of the diggers in the marsh threw down his spade and sprinted ahead to warn his master that riders were approaching. The doors opened as we drew near.

"Sons of Saxmund," Sigered greeted us, stepping out of the hall's shadows. His expression was grim. Dressed in fine silk-trimmed blue cloth, he must have been about forty years old – the same age as my father. And like my father he was tall, though his gait was more stooped and when he spoke we could see that he had a full set of teeth – the mark of a man who eats fine food and has not known battles or tavern brawls.

"Greetings Sigered," I said. I knew immediately from his look that he would have liked me to call him lord, but I did not wish him to think the sons of Saxmund were grovelling for pardon. "We bring weregild for the wound your son received." I glanced at Oswold but he said nothing. He looked, or tried to look, like our father, with his jawline set firm and a hard glimmer in his eyes.

"Come inside," the merchant said. There was a warning in his voice and his eyes were dark and sad beneath a furrowed brow. It was not a hospitable invitation. We dismounted and followed him through the doors.

Inside, the big house was dimly lit and it stank of sickness. I looked again at Oswold and now his steely expression only flickered. He knew as well as me that something was wrong. There were chairs and benches covered with fine cloth and cushions, a big table with plates and goblets of silver. Candles of expensive beeswax illuminated wall hangings sewn with golden images of holy saints, trees laden with fruit and the beasts of distant lands. But what caught my eye and twisted my stomach was the wooden bed beside the glowing hearth, made up with blankets and a straw mattress, where Richard lay, his face moon-white, slick with sweat and turning from side to side as he groaned and sighed and retched with every breath, like a man lost in an ocean of pain.

Slowly we followed Sigered, shuffling towards the hearth and horror of the wounded man. A woman sat at Richard's bedside, a plump woman, well-dressed and with a thick braid of mouse-brown and silver hair hanging down her back, whom I assumed must be Sigered's wife. Tearful beside her groaning son, she wiped the fever-sweat from his face and whispered to him in a voice which was at once soothing and urgent. As we drew close, I caught the hellish stench of decay, the smell that lingers over a field when a sheep has died in the heat of summer and lain undiscovered for a

61

week, the smell of maggots bursting out through the black slime of ruined skin.

The wound had festered and Richard was dying. I gagged on the stench and took a step back. Sigered turned to look at us, his eyes accusing, his silence worse than any curse. Oswold stepped forward. The control he had fought for was gone and now his face writhed with horror.

"Six pounds of silver coin," he said, his voice and his hand trembling as he held out the leather bags. Sigered took them. He looked defiantly at Oswold.

"I asked for twenty." I think he was going to say more, but his wife interrupted.

"Sigered! Do not argue over a price when our son is dying!" Her voice, though cracked by grief, was breathy and musical, the accent coming from somewhere across the seas.

"You must pray," said another voice, and the skinny figure of Grimstan rose from across the bed. "It is for God alone to choose who lives and who dies. Only entreaties to the Lord of Heaven can help this son of an earthly lord."

Sigered's wife sobbed quietly and in the dim light I could see something that was too dark to be the clean blood of a healing wound soaking through Richard's bandage. Grimstan came around the bed and advanced towards Oswold, his eyes alight with menace.

"You," he said. "Oswold, son of Saxmund, sinful man that you are. You struck the blow that cut down our most pious brother. You must do penance. Stripped naked, you must walk a path of shattered stones, whipped by willow rods, your hands tied together in prayer by a twisted bough of thorn. And you must pray beneath the sky for three days and three nights so that God might see your anguish and perhaps heal our worthy brother by increasing your suffering." Oswold stared back at Grimstan. The anger that had struck down

Richard flashed across his face again but this time he did not know what to do. I touched the sleeve of his tunic.

"Come outside," I whispered, stepping slowly away from the sobs of the dying man's mother, the clinging stench of sickness and the accusing eyes of Sigered and Grimstan.

"Penitence and prayer!" Grimstan repeated as we moved towards the door.

"He will die," I said to my brother when we got outside, but he just looked away into the welcome brightness of the day, grinding his teeth as if a sullen scowl was enough to stave off a man's death.

"I only wounded his arm. We've paid the weregild," he grumbled.

"The wound you gave him has festered. Such wounds do not heal. They rot until they poison the whole body. When he dies, Sigered will have the right to demand much more than we've given him."

"Indeed I will." We both looked around to see Sigered coming out of the house behind us. He stared at us both, the unyielding look that had cut through his sorrow seemed even harder in the sunlight. "Tell your father that my son is dying and that if the Lord God does not intervene to heal him, I will demand the south field of the estate of Ellasham as weregild."

I tried to look Sigered in the eye, but it is hard to know how to face a man whose son is dying.

"That land is not my father's to give," I said.

"It was entrusted to him by a king," Oswold added. "Land is not a thing that can be bought and sold in the marketplace." I glanced a warning at my brother. Starting an argument could only make things worse.

"But your family must pay the price for murder," Sigered hissed. "And we shall see how this matter is viewed when the Shire court meets at Easter."

Murder. Neither Oswold or I had seen it that way, but that was what it was. An argument, a fight, a death. Murder. Sigered muttered a bitter farewell and stepped back into the house.

"So what do we do?" I asked my brother.

"He picked a fight and I fought him. I murdered nobody." Oswold clenched his jaw again and narrowed his eyes.

"It's only murder if he does die," I said.

"It's not murder!" blustered my brother. "He wanted to fight me!"

"Go back to Ellasham," I told him, because I had had an idea and because Oswold's refusal to face what he had done was not useful. I had remembered Ragnald talking about the time he had angered Grimstan by mixing medicine for a child's fever. "Go and tell our father what is happening. I'm going into the weald to look for Ragnald."

"Ragnald?" Oswold's stubbornness gave way to confusion.

"Ragnald knows about healing," I explained. "The priest in there will not like it, but he may how to save Richard's life."

Darkness had fallen by the time we arrived back at Sigered's house. I had ridden half way back to Ellasham with my brother, then sent him home with both our horses and headed off along the narrow pathways of the weald which were only accessible for a man on foot. Late in the afternoon I came to the windswept clearing of Blood Hill, where two fresh mounds of turf covered heaps of chopped wood ready to be burned for charcoal. And shortly after I found Ragnald checking fishtraps beneath the half-fallen willow where the River Leman curls   around the foot of the hill.

"The flesh of his arm has died. The arm must be cut off above the wound, the stump cleaned and bound and cleaned again and again if it is to heal," he said when I told him of Richard's sickness. He frowned and picked up a saw which hung from the wall of his log hut in the clearing. "The teeth of this blade were made to cut wood, but they may be strong enough for bone."

"Grimstan will be there," I warned him as we set off down the hill. "He's praying for Richard's life. He won't want you to intervene."

Ragnald shrugged his shoulders dismissively. "I think Sigered is wise enough to see that prayers are of no use."

Under the cold light of the moon, we came out of the briar-tangled forest and hurried across the rough field of weeds and tree stumps towards the merchant's house. A roosting grouse screamed out its warning cry and rattled up from under my feet, disappearing into the darkness beyond the river and alerting two men with spears to come scrambling across the broken ground to intercept us.

"This is the estate of Lord Sigered. Who are you?" demanded the foremost of them. He had a mark in the shape of a half moon branded onto his forehead. His companion was not scarred, but he prodded his spear towards us and looked keen to stab more than just empty air. Although the men were dressed in poor cloth and shabby leather, their spears were bright in the moonlight.

"I am Wulfred, son of Saxmund of Ellasham. I was here earlier today. And this man is Ragnald, also of the village of Ellasham. He may be able to heal the wound of your master's son." They both looked at as with narrowed eyes, disappointed not to have apprehended thieves or poachers.

"You are the man who attacked the Lord Richard?" hissed the man with the lively spear.

"That was my brother," I said. "They fought. My brother won."

65

"Come with us," the branded one grunted. He led the way across the rough ground while his friend walked behind, his spear never far from our backs.

"Wulfred? Why have you returned?" Sigered scowled as we were pushed into the house by a spear butt.

"This is Ragnald. He knows about the healing of wounds." I placed a hand on Ragnald's shoulder in a gesture of confidence. "If we act quickly we might save your son's life." Sigered looked Ragnald over, a wild-bearded, pale-faced man with wood chippings and dead weeds from the forest clinging to his patched cloak. But Sigered himself did not look at his finest, his hair hanging over his eyes and his face lined through lack of sleep. The stink of rotting flesh in the house was keener now than it had been in the day. Richard still lay groaning on his bed and his mother stood and turned to face us. But as she did so, Grimstan leapt out of the shadows.

"Spawn of Hell! Be gone from this good place!" He clutched at Sigered's sleeve and pointed at Ragnald. "Lord," he babbled, "One son of Saxmund has tried to kill your son and now the other brings a servant of Satan to curse your godly house. God commands you, Lord, to cast out this demon." Grimstan's bony hands and elbows twitched and flailed as if he had no control over them and his hair flapped like broken wings on either side of his head.

"I will not speak with the priest." Ragnald's voice was steady in the shivering candlelight. "But I may be able to help your son."

"Lies Lord, lies and witchcraft! Only prayer can heal. Spare us your heathen spells"

"Prayer Grimstan?" I said. "And how have your prayers helped Richard?"

"Only prayer can heal!" the priest shrieked, and I took a step back as he pranced and flailed. "Only almighty God can choose who lives and who dies! These men are sent by the Devil, Lord,

66

sent to try your faith. You must dismiss them." Grimstan's eyes were like two white embers in the gloom, but the merchant just stared back blankly at him.

"Sigered, obey the priest if you wish. I came only to offer my help." Ragnald held out his hands and the openness of the gesture seemed to shake Sigered out of his daze.

"My son is dying," he murmured. "What can you do for him?"

"No, Lord! They are not men but demons. Look to your Christian soul!" Grimstan picked up a wooden cross with a carved image Christ and held it just a finger's breadth from Ragnald's face.

"Odda," Sigered called to his younger son. "Take Father Grimstan outside. I must speak with these men." Odda, shy and overawed, shuffled out of the shadows and took hold of the priest's arm.

"It is the Devil's craft, my lord!" protested Grimstan. "If they practice their witchery, then God will curse you and all your line."

"Take him out, Odda." Odda was afraid, but Grimstan was weak and scrawny and although he struggled, Odda soon bundled him out into the dark night.

"What can you do?" Sigered asked. His wife now took a few cautious steps towards us.

"Can you save my child?" she whispered. Child seemed like the wrong word to describe Richard. Ragnald crossed the room to look at the dying man and I followed him. I tasted the poison of his rotting flesh in my mouth. Richard lay sweating with fever, moaning with pain and unaware of our even being there. His arm was bandaged, but the skin of his hand was turning a bluish grey and that terrible black ooze still soaked through the cloth binding his wound.

"The flesh has died below the wound," Ragnald said. "If he is to live, we must cut it off." Sigered's wife gasped and raised her hand to her mouth.

"It must be done," said her husband, putting an arm about her shoulders. "Our prayers have come to nothing. It must be done."

Ragnald worked quickly. First he took my knife and placed it in the embers of the hearth. He asked for a plank of wood to place under the rotting limb and tied a strip of leather tightly below Richard's shoulder. Then he took out his own knife and cut quickly into the flesh below the leather strap. Richard sprang out of his fever and howled.

"Hold him!" barked Ragnald. Sigered took hold of the boy's other arm and I grasped his legs. His mother knelt down so her face was close to his. She stroked his hair and spoke to him gently in a language I did not know. It only took a moment for Ragnald to cut through the flesh of his arm. While Richard screamed and writhed and tried to kick me away, he picked up the saw.

"Odda!" he called out. "Where is Odda?" Odda's footsteps came rushing back across the floor and his face, pale with horror, emerged from the shadows. "Hold his legs," Ragnald commanded. "Wulfred, hold his arm here. Keep the severed flesh apart – I need to see the bone." I moved around the bed, leaned over the stricken man, and grasped the butchered flesh on either side of where Ragnald had cut. Although the leather strip had held back the bleeding, the skin was still sticky and slippery with blood. Raganld took a few deep breaths, placed the saw to the white bone and began to cut. Richard and his mother both screamed, Odda looked ready to vomit, Sigered muttered prayers and I felt my heart beating in my throat as we listened to the rasping of blade on bone. Richard screamed again as the teeth of the saw jarred his whole body. He shook and sweated and spluttered snot and dribble. Odda closed his eyes and tried to join his father in prayer until the saw cut through and the rotting arm fell to one side. I snatched my hand back, disgusted by the dead thing I had been holding. Ragnald swiftly retrieved my knife from the embers and started to touch it carefully onto the parts of the wound from which blood was oozing. The scorched flesh hissed and little plumes of steam, stinking of burnt meat, rose and Richard's mother began to weep again. Her son had slipped out of consciousness, but his chest rose and fell steadily. When Ragnald called for wine, Sigered picked up a jar from the floor.

"Father Grimstan would call this witchcraft," he whispered as Ragnald bathed Richard's stump then laid some leaves that he had collected on our way through the forest against the grisly lump of flesh.

"It is healing." Ragnald did not look up from his work. "For many generations while Wessex followed the word of Christ and laws of holy books, my people – the Danes of the north – kept the knowledge they had known since the birth of the world. Perhaps prayer can help to heal wounds, but we have seen that wounds washed with wine do not fester as easily as those washed with river water. Certain herbs and leaves will keep a wound clean. The priest would call it witchcraft, but you must choose what to believe. Change the bindings at dawn and at nightfall. Wash it only with wine. And pray for him. It will do no harm."

Richard lived. Or at least we assumed he lived. The days lengthened, the elder trees came into leaf, the village children walked the baulks between the seeded rows of the great fields to drive off hungry crows and starlings and we had no word from Sigered. No demand came for payment for his son's life and it became clear that Ragnald's skills had worked and that my father would keep the south field.

Eventually Cuthred received a message from Grimstan to say that by constant prayer and by the mortification of his own flesh he had fought night and day with the Devil until Richard's wound began to heal. But Sigered and his family had strayed from the path of true godliness by allowing a witch to work foul magic in their house. God's will, Grimstan believed, was that he should stay with them and use Sigered's money to build a church beside the river and to pray for the saving of their souls.

"We must thank God," Cuthred concluded as he handed the messenger a coin and sent him on his way, "for the sweet mercy He has shown."

4. THE SLEEPING GROUND

Easter is the greatest celebration of the Church's year. With the coming of spring we are reminded of the joy of Christ's return from the cold grave and of the miracle of life's triumph over the long dark death of winter.

Yet it comes at the cruellest of times. While winter is bitter and the fields lie barren, at least there is grain from the harvest and a little meat from the slaughter of the beasts. In the spring, as the land comes to life once again, folk have little but coarse, gritty bread from the dwindling supply of corn and whatever roots and herbs can be gathered from the hedgerows. I remember the villagers of Ellasham, their eyes sunken from the cold and hungry months, the flesh and sinew of autumn replaced by cloaks and scarves, passing bowls of thin curds made from goats' and sheep's milk around their hearths. They soothed each other with talk of the calves that would soon be born and the rich, fatty milk of the cattle, and the looks that stole across their faces were like those of warriors whispering tales of hoarded gold.

The old and the very young die in spring. Hreth's month was what the older folk called the time leading up to Easter. Hreth was an old goddess of death and she gathered her harvest in the spring when those weakened by hunger and frost would finally succumb.

On the day we remembered the crucifixion of Christ, Cuthred carried a cross of twisted iron at the head of a procession through the village to the unlit church. His eyes shone with the wild light of something more glorious than this world could offer, as he spoke of the sinfulness of all mankind and of the suffering we must endure because of it. The most devout wept for their saviour's pain, their tears mingling with blood drawn by crowns fashioned of thorn boughs. And on the day of the Resurrection, every candle in the church was lit and the people crammed themselves inside to hear words of Latin they did not understand, and to gaze in wonder at the

71

bright paintings blazing from the walls. The creation of the world covered the back of the church, with Adam and Eve shamelessly naked before the serpent's eye. On either side were displayed the feast of Heaven and the hunger of Hell, but it was at the front wall, behind the altar where Cuthred stood, that most of the candles were placed to illuminate the figure of Christ himself, rising in blue and gold majesty into a world of green hills, clouds and angels.

Then the congregation walked barefoot, still following the stark, forge-blackened cross, to my father's hall where we honoured the occasion with a meagre feast - usually a stew made with tough roots and salted offal. Grimstan once struck a cup of ale out of Godric's hand at Easter, shouting that our lord had taken no comfort but a sponge soaked in vinegar as he suffered on the cross. Godric told the priest what he could do with his sponge soaked in vinegar and had to be dragged out of the hall before he earned himself some terrible divine punishment.

In the spring of 1066, Cuthred's hands shook and his voice throbbed around the candlelit church as he intoned those Latin verses and spoke of his crucified lord. Already there were rumours and whispers spread by the trading folk who crossed the seas and walked the roads that the Pope in faraway Rome had spoken against Harold Godwinsson and favoured Willelm of Normandy as the true heir of King Edward. But such things meant little to Father Cuthred. He prayed for the souls of the people of Ellasham and the world of kings was nothing but a dim shadow in the furthest corner of his long life.

And I wished that world could be only a dim shadow in my life also.

Some of my father's old warrior friends had come to celebrate Easter at Ellasham. There were four or five of them and I shall not name them because their names are not worth remembering. Pompous old greybeards who had stood alongside my father in the battles of his youth, men whose swords had stilled the hearts of many foes and who believed the world should bow down to them because of it. And their sons, who curled their lips and sneered bitter curses against the Normans, Danes and Welsh they had been taught to despise. They came to hunt boar in the forest, to try their swords against one another, to roar and bluster about battles past and battles to come, to shuffle their feet impatiently through Cuthred's mass, and to eat the bread that should have fed our people until the next harvest.

After the Easter service, the guests and villagers knelt one by one before Father Cuthred and received his blessing. My father, the last to be blessed, thanked the priest for his prayers and handed him a small purse of silver.

As we filed out into the bright spring sunshine, one of my father's friends – an old warrior with plaited moustaches and a deep scar across his forehead - greeted us with a broad smile and a voice like a bull with its prick caught among brambles.

"With the blessings of God and the swords of the sons of Godwin, how can England ever fail?" he roared.

"Wessex will stand when even the mountains beyond the Severn are levelled!" my father bellowed in response. I looked at my mother and she silently rolled her eyes and shook her head. Oswold looked like he wanted to join the shouting, but did not want to risk saying something the others might think foolish. One of the old warrior's sons, a pointed-faced youth twitching with excitement, pulled out his sword and got its hilt tangled in his cloak. I quietly hoped never to get stuck beside him in a shield wall.

"I have named her Bastard-biter!" he gibbered, when he had freed his blade and held it out before us. "In honour of the Bastard Duke himself." The old warrior laughed and clapped a proud hand on his son's shoulder.

"I hope you're ready for battle, boys," he said to Oswold and I. "I know a trader just back from Normandy. He says half the forests of that land are felled and at every port men are building ships to carry an army to England. We'll give the wolves a feast of Norman flesh before this year is out." He leaned back and laughed like a madman.

"Oswold here will be the scourge of our enemies," my father declared, slapping Oswold on the back. "A month ago a lad from down the river – a fool of a merchant's son, but a swordsman nonetheless – picked a fight with him. Oswold ripped the flesh from his arm with only a blunt old training sword." Oswold grinned as the scarred man and his sons gathered around to congratulate him.

"We should have the lads learn to fight with sharp swords," bellowed another old fool. "Sharp swords and no armour. They'd learn some skills quick enough then! Those who are wounded or killed would be no use in battle anyway." I saw my mother shoot the man a look of disgust, but there was a quiet sadness in her face when she saw Oswold's and my father's hands slipping instinctively to their sword hilts.

"Yes, it was just an old sparring blade," my father went on. "As blunt as a pair of buttocks, but he thrust it right through the lad's arm. Wulfred," he called to me, "go fetch the sword your brother fought with. Let's show these warriors the kind of men Ellasham will send to the shield wall of Wessex."

I looked at my father and he looked back at me with an expression that warned me to stay silent. Had we been alone I would have reminded him that Oswold's swordsmanship had almost cost him a crippling weregild and it was only my quick thinking and Ragnald's skill that had spared him from it. But I did not want to hear a dozen voices all telling me that to kill a man is a much better thing than to save a life, so I walked away.

At first I stamped off towards the house, clenching my teeth in anger, but dutifully going to fetch the sword. When I looked back though, I saw the little crowd ambling towards the hall and I heard their laughter and their boasting carried on the breeze and I wanted nothing more than to be alone, or in any company other than theirs. So I turned towards the river, towards the quiet bubbling water and the willows that swayed over its banks, their branches bright with the hope of a new-born spring.

At the river's bend, close to the weed-filled ditch that surrounded the village, stood Eohric's house. There were old barrels heaped around the dilapidated cottage and a fine smell of brewing ale lingered in the air.

"Good morning Wulfred," Ragnald called, rising from a tree stump where he sat beside the old brewer. His hair and beard hung loosely, tangled with wood chippings, straw and last year's dead leaves. "You come at a good time, as always. We've just finished working on the roof." About a third of the thatch on one side of Eohric's house had been replaced and the old man grinned toothlessly up at me.

"I'd rather mend every roof in the village than listen to my father's friends a moment longer," I said, sitting down on a barrel among the sprouting weeds.

"Ha! A sturdy roof can only keep the rain at bay. A well-swung sword can lay hosts of men to waste," Eohric laughed, mocking my father's voice.

"Have you seen my good friend Grimstan?" asked Ragnald with a dark smile.

"Not since we were at Sigered's house."

"Grimstan passed through Ellasham not a week ago. It is good to know that our lords are watching over the land with the keen eyes of moles." Ragnald shook his head and Eohric hissed his dry remnant of a laugh.

"Grimstan's a bitter little turd." I said. "Why do you care what he does?"

Ragnald looked suddenly serious. "Aye, a bitter little turd he is. But Grimstan's a man of ambition. He'd make a reputation for himself. He'd have his voice heard in the great councils of the church. I'd wager that all the bishops of England were turds like Grimstan once."

"So where do you think he was going?" I asked. "Up to Lunden to look for a whore?"

"The Devil's arse will fart forth wine and honey before Grimstan finds a pretty girl who'll spread her legs for him," rasped Eohric. Ragnald ignored the old man and leaned forward.

"He came to my house on the eve of his Sabbath to offer me baptism or eternal damnation. Eternal damnation! How could anyone but a fool believe that Grimstan has such powers? Eternal damnation and the wrath of all Christian folk. He stamped into my house and bleated like a sheep at the slaughtertime, until Brichteva came over from the hearth and bared her tits at him. That got rid of him, but he stopped for an eyeful first. She gave him something better than his crucified god to think about when he got home." Eohric doubled up with such laughter that he struggled to breathe.

"It will not have been the hand of God," he cackled, "that came to the Turd Priest's aid that night." Ragnald passed him an ale jug to slake his ancient throat.

"As if standing in a river while some fool of a priest mutters makes any difference to a man's life or death." He paused to pull a thorny twig out of his beard. "Long ago, I learned to hate the priests of Christ. Nowadays I can live with them, but Grimstan would take me back to a place I walked many years ago. If he can, he will rouse the faithful against me."

"Not in Ellasham," I said

Ragnald smiled again. "I used to watch Grimstan sneaking around dropping eggs in the henhouses while Cuthred said his Mass. A fair way of rewarding their prayers, I suppose, but he went out before everyone woke to steal those same eggs. I think the folk here only go to church because they believe Christ makes their hens lay."

A fish jumped in the shallow ford, just a few yards from the cottage and a gangly-legged heron swept over the riverside trees. Ragnald fell into silent thought and Eohric started fishing about in his jug of ale, trying to catch something. Eventually he lifted out a white butterfly, its wings soaked and stained. It fell from his hand and strutted on the ground in a confused circle.

"A sign of hope at the end of a dark winter?" Ragnald grinned. "But hope somehow sullied by the ale-pot?"

"It carries a thousand omens," Eohric cackled. "Everything does." The butterfly spread out its wings to dry them in the breeze. "I say the white wings stand for Grimstan's purity and Christian chastity and the ale shows how it was forever tarnished when he looked upon Brichteva's tits." At the sound of our unholy laughter, the butterfly took wing. Then Ragnald sat forward again.

"We've spoken enough of priests," he decided. "For six days I've laboured in the weald and now I seek rest. Eohric, open the mead jar." The old man picked up a clay jar and his gnarled fingers fumbled with the wax-sealed lid.

"Mead brewed with forest honey and the juice of apples," he explained to me. "In which elfcaps have been steeped all winter."

"Elfcaps?"

"You don't know of the elfcap?" Eohric stared at me mockingly. "The little mushrooms that cover the fields' edges each autumn before the oaks turn. They have power," he grinned with his gums. The wax crumbled away and he shook the jar a little and peered into it. "There are sounds and beings which are hidden from us. The priests say they come from a world of demons. But priests know little." He poured the mead out into three wooden cups. We picked them up and raised them to each other.

"Here's to Grimstan's world of demons," Ragnald chuckled, lifting his drink to the blue and cloud-blown sky.

"To a world in which my father's friends shut their mouths and leave their swords to rust," I added, watching the golden light and the golden liquid blending in the cup.

"And here's to Brichteva's tits," laughed Eohric. "The only pair Grimstan will ever see." He swilled his the mead down in one long swallow. Ragnald did the same - only I paused to taste it. It tasted a little of honey and apples, but mostly of stale mushrooms. Eohric looked disappointed.

"Every year," he lamented. "Every year I use the ripest apples and the finest honey. And every year the elfcap makes it taste like I've pissed in it."

In the herb garden and the reed thatch of Eohric's house, weeds were waking to the spring sunshine and the hills stretching away to the north were warm and round. I laughed at the weeds and the hills and at Eohric's wispy white beard that danced in the light as he spoke. The old brewer's concoction took hold of me and dimmed all the sorrow and anger of the world as a more golden light fell like warm rain.

I remember walking away from where we sat, wading through the knee-deep ford, where the water moved like twisting fingers that could have pulled me down and drowned me had they not been so fantastically gentle in the sunlight.

From the opposite bank, I could still see Eohric and Ragnald, but the river's rolling voice drowned any words they might have called to me, so I turned away from the village to face the land into which I had crossed.

We called it Oxeneye - the Isle of Oxen, where we pastured ploughbeasts and sheep during the summer, and on whose western flank I had shot a deer in the dead of winter on a day when news of a new king was brought to us. Its grassy hump was plainer than the dark weald or Walland Fen, but as I walked I remembered the old sleeping ground where the dead of ancient times were buried. It was high on Oxeneye and it was a place feared by many, where some folk said only a ghost could walk unmolested.

Higher on the hill, the gathering wind tugged at my hair and my cloak, and I watched the grass at my feet spiralling, a thousand shades of green rolling into one another.

Three hares bounded out of the grass in front of me, their big eyes shining and their long bodies stretching and flying towards the distant woods. My eyes wandered from the treeline to the bare flank of the hill where the growing grass shivered, and for a moment something flashed along the horizon, like an army with banners flying and shields bright beneath the sun.

And from the hilltop, in a great upturned bowl of blue sky and boiling, rolling clouds, I looked back into the valley of the River Leman.

The river snaked along far below, kingfisher blue and twisting among trees and fields, glistening greenly in a world coloured by the changing season.

Beyond it, Ellasham was minute but perfect in every detail. The little huts and houses scattered by a careless hand, the thin white smoke from their roofs tracing brief journeys through the air. Distant people moving along the pathways, their dreams of rich harvests, strong children, sweet ale and lost loves drifting away into the infinite sky.

And I turned to the east. My feet walked and I followed them down the slope, where the hill rolled towards a wooded gully and where the old field of the dead faced the rising sun each dawn.

Although our priests had long insisted that the dead should moulder away in the cold earth beside the village church, a few still left their bodies on this hilltop, this place used by our ancestors

79

since a time when even the immortal oaks of the weald were young. The remains of a staked fence surrounded it, breached by the wind and by villagers whose fear of the dead was not as great as their need for winter fuel.

The rotting wood of an old post gave way beneath my feet and I crossed into a crumpled field of mounds and ditches - the corpse-beds of England's ancestors. Our ancient dead were honoured - or dishonoured - in the memory of our people, not in crude words of Latin chiselled into cold stone. Their silent sleeping places took many shapes. Great barrow mounds reached up towards the sky. Lower mounds were ringed by shallow ditches that overflowed with grass and wheeling buttercups. Here and there I saw a cairn of stones and from dark places between the rocks the eyes of the dead seemed to glimmer back at me.

Two swallows, the first of the spring and bright as beads of glass, swept up from the wooded gully and circled around a straggle of blossoming thorn trees. For a reason I did not know, my eyes followed them and there among the bursting leafbuds and the mist of blossom, like a swift reflection in a shimmering pool and for just a fragment of a moment, I glimpsed a woman's face. I stopped and I stared into the clustered bushes. There was nobody there. The face had gone, but in a heartbeat I had remembered every detail - the curling hair that fell darkly across her forehead; her eyes wide and watchful, tawny brown and shimmering with a question I could only feel; her cheeks full and flushed by the sun; her mouth opening anxiously to speak, to call to me to follow. To walk into her world as if something terrible waited in my own.

I scanned the white-blossomed branches for a long time, as the wind twisted them into shapes that melted through the clouds and sang a high and fading note like a flute reaching the end of its song. And at last I caught a glimmer of her again, further away and flitting along the line of bushes, vanishing into a thicket of elders. And this time, I followed.

I stumbled along a soft path of moss and fern, watching the bushes and the saplings. Again and again she flickered briefly like a distant fire in a moonless night, twisting through nettles and stones, treading bright flowers, but never so much as rustling the leaves. And all the time she seemed to glance over her shoulder with an expression that called me onwards.

At last I saw her slip out of the shadows, a brief blaze of white and the brown murmur of her hair and she was gone behind a turf-covered mound. I ran after her, springing up from the soft ground with every step. A flock of tiny birds arose from a briar thicket beside the mound, strewing their songs across the quiet graves. I followed their undulating flight, shifting between the land and the sky.

And I saw her, and she was still.

She stood on a green slope of cropped grass in the middle of the sleeping ground, looking down, half-smiling, silently welcoming me. She wore a white robe so light that even the softest whisper of a breeze caught it and bore delicate shapes into the air. Faint shadows seemed to linger after the linen had shed its twisting forms, and they faded slowly away through the graves. The wind blew her hair up across her face and back onto her shoulders. And she smiled with all the brightness of summer. There was much more than beauty in her face. Time was resting there. She looked as young as any pretty girl in the blossom of womanhood, yet as old as the world and all its lost dreams. At her back was a tall standing stone - something planted on the hillside thousands of years ago, its purpose long lost to the rain and the ghosts that wander the land.

She held out a plain wooden cup and without speaking, she commanded me to drink.

I drank. Something cool slid down my throat and when I looked up again, the girl was gone. Not to lead me through the mounds of Oxeneye, but gone entirely from the world. My hand was still curled around the wooden cup, but my hand was empty.

I did not fall, but suddenly I was on the ground, pushing myself up.

There was no sound among the rolling clouds, no more chorusing of birdsong, only the breeze whispering its rumours through the graves. The sky was warm and blue with a few clouds following their unceasing journeys. There were still a thousand shades of green at my feet, but it was only the grass.

Suddenly feeling tired, I leant against the ancient stone and touched its rough surface, its frost-shattered scars, the marks of ancient hammer blows. I strained to hear the falling of hammers, the chanting of songs and the crackling flames of long forgotten feasts. But there was nothing. The hills were silent and the wind was still.

"Wake up you oaf. Your father's had people looking for you all day." I looked up, and the shadows of the trees and the standing stone had stretched and turned to the east. Hildelyth was prodding me with her foot.

"On a Holy day when we have fine company," she went on, putting her hands on her hips and imitating my father's sternest voice, "he sends you on a simple errand and you disappear without trace."

I put a hand on the mossy stone and hauled myself up. Light-headed from sleep, or from Eohric's mushrooms, I stumbled towards Hildelyth and caught her in a hug. She made a quiet sound and put her arms around me. She was thin from the hunger of spring, but I felt the warmth of her body and it was good to hold her.

"I was dreaming of the weald, of walking through the weald with a thousand crows flying above the treetops," I said, because I was not sure whether I was still dreaming. Hildelyth lifted her head and gave me a quizzical look. Her cheeks were red and her lips roughened by the winter frosts, not like the girl I had seen standing

82

by the stone, whose face was as perfect as if it had been smoothed from changeless marble. I felt my senses settling and I knew what was real and what was not.

I kissed Hildelyth, because she was beautiful as the light of the fading day passed across her face. And we looked down at Ellasham, where the long shadows of my father's friends, prancing about and sparring with their swords, crossed those of men and women returning weary from the fields.

As I should have expected, my father was angry.

"Why do I have a son who would wander the hills like some crazed hermit rather than try his sword against great men and hear tales of battle?" he blustered, and tugged on his beard in irritation.

"I know how to use a sword. I don't need to prove it to men who'd gladly watch their sons kill each other." One or two of my father's friends glanced at me with disapproval, and I saw a wild flash of rage blaze across his face. He took a step towards me, his fists clenched and for a moment I thought he was going to hit me. But I planted my feet in the grass of the sloping field beside the hall and I looked him in the eye and he held my gaze. We both knew that a warrior's greatest skill is to know when to unleash his rage and when to hold it back, and my father was not going to let a disobedient son get the better of his self-control. Instead he raised his hand and in it was my sword. He drew it from its sheath and handed it to me.

"Your sword and your war-skills are your life, Wulfred. What would become of this land if all our best men wandered off to get drunk as soon as an enemy came to our shores? What would become of our people?"

"Warriors do not fight to protect their people, only for their own glory." I slammed the sword back into its sheath in what I hoped was a defiant gesture.

83

My father gave me a hard look. He ground his battle-broken teeth together and stayed silent for few moments.

"You will learn soon enough why warriors fight," he eventually growled. Then he turned away and looked up into the evening sky. For the dusk of that Easter Day had brought a new strangeness.

In the east, where the constellation of the swan winged low between quiet Oxeneye and the mists of Walland Fen, a new star had bloomed in the fading of the day. It glimmered brightly in the deepening blue of the sky, and unlike the other stars it trailed wild slivers of light, like fine hair blown by the wind, as if it was falling away towards the silhouetted trees of the southern horizon.

We were gathered on the open ground beside the hall. A few of my father's friends still wore the mail and leather they had donned for sparring and they sweated in the scant warmth of the spring evening. A few villagers were there too, and in the dim light I could see that all over Ellasham people had come out of their houses and gathered in small knots to gaze up at this mysterious thing.

"It is a sign from God!" one of the warriors hollered, causing Father Cuthred to throw him a cautionary look. "A warning at last that the land won by the swords of our forefathers is in danger. We must saddle our horses and rally to King Harold's side!"

"You'd look a fool galloping to Wintancestre to tell the king you've seen a star," said another grey-headed man, raising a little laughter from those around him.

I turned away from them and made my way to the edge of the little crowd. We all feared omens and portents and signs from places beyond our world. People told tales in hushed voices of a time when the sun had darkened, when the moon had turned the colour of blood, or when a comet like this one had blazed across the empty sky. And in nearly every tale they were the harbingers of war, famine, plague or of whatever curse God saw fit to throw across the earth. Looking up at that weird light in the eastern sky I could well imagine the eye of God peering down into the world,

84

seeing the just and the sinful and deciding who was to live and who to die.

"The Hairy Star," said Eohric. Fearful muttering passed among the villagers, but Eohric's lined face was filled with child-like wonder and there was a quiet joy in his hoarse voice. "I have forgotten much, but I remember this as I remember yesterday, as I remember my childhood, as I remember my first love." He paused for a long time and I looked at him curiously, wondering just how well he could remember yesterday.

"You've seen it before?" I finally asked.

"When I was a child," he replied, staring upwards as if his memories were written on the sky. "In the reign of Aethelred - before the Danish kings and long before the days of Earl Godwin and King Edward. I remember nothing before and little for a long time after, but I remember this. My father told me that if I sought wisdom and shunned glory, then I might live to see the Hairy Star again. My father fell to the spears of the Danish shipmen later that year." Eohric leaned heavily on his staff and searched among the faces clustered about him. Hildelyth took his arm to steady him and the old man's eyes wandered briefly across the curve of her breasts beneath her thin cloak. "It takes not much less than a hundred years to return. I must be so old now."

At the riverbank below us, a small group shuffled into the cold water and knelt to pray.

"My grandfather said something strange would happen," said Godric. "His sow's been restless all day."

"She probably saw the way you were looking at her," Hildelyth grinned.

"So, is it an omen of our doom?" asked an anxious woman who stood behind me. Eohric turned to face us and when he spoke, his voice was barely more than a whisper.

"For some, perhaps."

Eohric was dead three days later. One of our shepherds came to find me in the early morning and led me across the ford to the foot of Oxeneye. The morning sun cast a long shadow pointing down from the standing stone to where the old brewer lay on a death bed of thick grass and spring flowers, young lambs suckling just a few yards away. An eternal smile wreathed his face and his eyes seemed bluer and brighter than I ever remembered them in life as they stared blindly up into the dawning sky.

I knelt beside Eohric's body for a long time. And I wept for him, because he was a good man and when a good man dies all the world dies a little with him. Eohric had lived without bringing harm to anyone. He had gathered stories from his life and told them in his old age and he gave us joy and laughter in hard times and easy times. He must have been young once, but I have no memory of that. Even when I was a child, Eohric was a mischievous, spirited old man, joking with the women, dancing with a confused shuffle at feasts and telling unlikely tales to the children. He had lived a long, long life, but now his life had ended, and I was no longer the child who had laughed at his tales, and strange stars filled the sky with dark omens, hard-faced men talked of war and all the good things in the world were passing.

Old Eohric was gone and the ale would never taste so good again.

It was the hour before dawn when we laid Eohric in his grave. Cuthred may have quietly wished the old man to be buried in the cold earth beside the church, but he knew that he had lived a life somewhere beyond the Church's power and that Eohric's spirit must now dwell among the mounds of Oxeneye, where the tall stone throws its shadow and the spring days would warm the soil around his old bones.

There was little ceremony at the graveside. My mother said a prayer and we knelt and murmured with her. My father knelt alongside the rest of us. Perhaps it would have been more fitting that he, as a lord of men, should have spoken, but he had only words of war and this was not the time or place for such words. My mother's voice was gentle in the silver light of dawn.

"We must remember that God sees and hears all. He will hear the words of Christians even in this old and heathen place, so we must not fear for the soul of our brother Eohric. He was a good man and a friend to all and is surely worthy of Paradise."

Grimstan would have condemned us all to the torments of Hell just for setting foot on the old sleeping ground, let alone waking its ancient gods by planting a new corpse there. But Grimstan was far away and we laid our friend in a shallow pit at the foot of the standing stone, and the women sang songs - not the dirges of monks, but bright songs of love and summer and happy times. Hildelyth sang about a wife who tricked her drunken husband into a life of sobriety by combing her hair over her face to look like a beard and make him think he had mistakenly gone to bed with a man.

My father stepped forward and placed a jar of strong mead in the grave and it seemed enough to send the brewer on his new journey with. Then he stepped away from the grave and faced Oswold and I.

"I am glad we still have men who will rest in the soil of Oxeneye," he murmured, looking around at the weed-strewn resting places of the dead we had never known. "The men who fought on Blood Hill lie here. Our ancestors - the kin-folk of Aella, the sons of Woden - lie in this ground and that is what makes the land ours. When the time comes, we must defend the bones of our forefathers." Oswold nodded and closed his eyes as if he was taking in words of great wisdom. My father looked at me silently and with eyes that sought to hammer something into my soul.

Dawn broke slowly in shades of blue and pink - a few clouds that hung on the horizon blazed from below with the promise of the bright day returning. We fell silent, watching the eastern sky. Out in Andredsweald and in the gully below us, the sun painted silhouettes of trees with colour. Thousands of birds sang to welcome the light. Brichteva stepped away from Ragnald's side and stretched out her arms to the kindling sky. And as she did so, the sun erupted over the far hills in red and yellow fire, and a crown of light tore through cloud, stretched high across the heavens and flooded the whole world.

We filled Eohric's grave as the sun rose. I took up a wooden shovel and joined in with the village men, allowing the day's first light to mingle with the earth as we piled the mound high to honour his memory. I saw his shrouded body vanish beneath the earth and I was not the only one who stifled a sob at the thought of never seeing him again.

Hildelyth and her young cousin Frithe gathered flowers from the green spaces between the graves, to scatter across the dark earth and as I paused to watch their silhouette figures gliding across the sunlit hillside, I heard the sound of a flute carried on a warm breeze that sprung up suddenly from the west.

"I have brought the summer to you!" called a voice as the music stopped and a figure appeared from behind a cairn of stones.

"Idwal!" I called back, and hurried over to greet my friend as a burst of chatter broke out behind me.

"So, the old brewer is gone," said the Welshman with a solemn expression that seemed wrong on his face. He looked tired and ragged, his cloak trailing on the grass as he stuffed his flute into a leather bag.

"He knew the comet would take him," said Ragnald, who strode up behind me and greeted Idwal in turn. "It is the harvester of contented souls. Those whose hearts are drained and broken do not live to see it twice."

"A sad day," Idwal murmured. For a moment he managed to keep his solemn look, but only for a moment. "Who will keep you drunken Saxons in ale now, eh?"

Idwal was a wanderer of the roads, so it was not unusual for him to appear unannounced and unexpected in this way. The villagers crowded around to greet him, asking for a tune or two in memory of Eohric and asking about his travels since he left us in the depths of winter.

"I walked to Lunden after the new king was crowned," he announced. "I sang in the taverns, drank with shipmen and danced with whores." He gave a lewd laugh. "They were good times, my friends. I went up the river on a trader's boat to a place called Oxenford. More song, more ale, more women. Then I took the roads back to Caer Myrddin and when spring came I crossed the Severn Sea and travelled south. I was in Hantone at Easter, on the shore of the Narrow Sea, playing fine music for the lords of Wessex and their men."

When he had greeted everyone, Idwal took up his flute again and handed a goatskin drum to one of the villagers. They played graceful tunes in the warming air of the hilltop and we danced around Eohric's new-filled grave, and the old man would have been happy that we did.

Before the sun was far risen, the villagers bade their last farewells to Eohric and headed back to the great fields which would need hoeing as weeds sprang up to meet this new warmth. Some of the women were still singing as they walked away and their voices carried far into the sky.

"Lord Saxmund," Idwal turned to address my father who had walked in silent thought around the grave field while we danced. "You have heard the news from Wyt?" My father showed his teeth and frowned.

"News from Wyt?"

"Yes, lord, the isle just off the coast at Hantone."

"I know where Wyt is, Welshman. What news?"

"Wyt is burning, my lord."

"Burning? From whom do you have this news?"

"I left Hantone four days ago and many messengers riding from the town have passed me on the road. They say Wyt has been raided by a fleet, its halls robbed and its villages burned."

"A fleet?" I interrupted while my father continued to frown at Idwal as if he was lying. "The Norman Duke cannot have built a fleet already. Is it the Danes?"

Idwal gave a bark of laughter. "You Saxons – as slow witted as ever. The only things you do with any haste are eating and drinking. And probably fucking, though I am pleased to say that when I was a boy the Saxon herd was kept far distant from me. Your land is being raided by Tostig of course."

"Mind your tongue Welshman. You're not among the pigsties of Caer Myrddin now," my father growled, but his expression had softened with interest. "Tostig Godwinsson?"

"Of course. Your king's brother with thirty ships from Flanders and vengeance in his heart. Harold sat by and watched as he was driven from Northumbria and now he returns. The warriors of Wessex are being summoned to defend ports and towns along the coast."

"So we are at war." It was Oswold who spoke now, a thrill in his voice and his fingers curling around the hilt of his sword. His words were like an icy fist in my belly and I swallowed the fear that rose up my throat. First a comet flashed like a beacon fire in the night, then Eohric was taken, and now news of war came like another wave of a dark tide.

"If the Welshman speaks truly, then war has indeed come," my father said. He cast a grave look at Oswold and I, then he turned and

90

hurried back towards the village, eager to be at his hall when the expected messenger arrived. Oswold clapped a hand on my shoulder, grinned and hurried after him. I looked curiously at Idwal. It was unlikely that he would risk my father's anger by joking about something like this.

"So, my friend," he said. "Shall we fight together on the shores of Wessex?"

"What?"

Idwal drew himself up to his full height, breathed deeply and stared out across the wide, open landscape. "War comes," he said, nodding to the far horizon, "and I shall stand in the line of battle. Not for the land you Saxons took from my people, but to learn the skills of war, so that I might be ready when my people's time comes." He swept his cloak open to show me a sword hanging from his belt.

"You've stolen a sword?"

"This blade was given to me in Hantone by Earl Gyrth Godwinsson. One of your king's brothers raids his land while another gives swords to the men of Caer Myrddin. Harold needs to watch his brothers as keenly as he watches his enemies." The Welshman laughed, but I was still staring at him as if he had gone mad.

"Why did an earl of England give you a sword?"

"In Lunden I had suffered to hear some tuneless oaf of a Saxon deep in his cups and singing a dirge in praise of Harold Godwinsson and all his little triumphs. So in Hantone, I sang the same song, but changed Harold's name to Gyrth. The fat drunken fool gave me a sword. He said that if he was loyal to the house of Godwin, even a Welshman deserved the right to bear arms in defence of the English kingdom."

Idwal drew it out and turned it slowly in the sun. It was a plain old sword, but he had cleaned it up and honed the edge and it was

91

light enough for an untrained man to wield with ease. Its hilt was bound with leather and its square pommel decorated with copper rivets. A gust of wind rushed across Oxeneye and hummed a song of battle about its edges.

"You could sell it." I suggested. The idea that man who lived by good things like music and song should take up the sword made no sense to me.

"Oh no." Idwal smiled and something bright and distant slipped into his expression. "In halls I have sung of battle. And at quiet hearths I have told great tales first wrought by the tongues of warrior-bards. But the time must come to live what I have only sung, to feel my life cradled in the hands of God." He thrust the sword back into its sheath with what looked like a move he had been practising. "She is yet a virgin, but soon the blood of warriors will warm her." Idwal's sword did not look virginal. It looked like an old Danish blade and I would have guessed that it had bludgeoned many men to death in its time.

"It is said that Magnus, the son of your king is gathering warriors to defend Riaburh," he went on, with the calm expression of a man abandoning his life to the throes of fate. "So we shall fight side by side my friend, and we shall see our foes flee before us."

We walked down the hill together and at my back I left Eohric's body to the worms and his spirit to the gathering summer. And before me, the fate I had long feared came rushing in like a winter tide.

5. THE FIRST BATTLE

People die so easily. Women die bringing children into the world. Children die from summer fevers and winter chills and perhaps because they see the cruelty of the world and no longer want to live in it. It seems like a work of madness that we should seek ways to kill men too, but that is what we do. I was born to be a warrior and however much I may have wished it otherwise, a warrior is what I became.

I fought my first battle in the spring of 1066. It was not an awesome clash of great armies. I have heard no songs or stories that tell of it, and very few of the few who fought there can be alive today. Lords and kings and the poets who strive to make them immortal have much to say about shining armour and bright shields and armies of thousands hollering their warcries to the braying of horns and drums. Of clashes that would shake the gates of Heaven and the destiny of kingdoms. Of blood covering the great wide fields that lay between hosts too brave to be forgotten.

It is mostly nonsense, of course. I did fight in one great battle upon which hung the future of our land, but more often war is battered out between small bands of men beside quiet rivers and at the gates of little towns. The stories of these fights are told at winter hearths by grey old warriors with shaking hands and failing eyes and when their voices fade, their memories are lost forever. Such was my first battle. And perhaps I am the last who still speaks of it.

We rode out of Ellasham well before dawn. In the evening of the day when we buried Eohric, a message bearer arrived at our hall with a dozen warriors. The news was just as Idwal had told it. Tostig Godwinsson had brought thirty ships from Flanders, crewed by gangs of hired spearmen and his own supporters from when he was the Earl of Northumbria. They had laid waste the island of Wyt

93

and now they turned their ships to the east. The king and his hearthtroop, an army of a thousand of his greatest warriors who called themselves the Dragons of Wessex, were riding hard for the far coast of Kent, where Harold expected his brother to set up a base among the islands and inlets within striking distance of Lunden. All other warriors who served King Harold were to head for the ports of Sussex and South Kent. My father, Oswold and I were ordered to Riaburh where Earl Leofwin of Middlesex, another of the king's brothers, and Magnus, Harold's eldest son, were gathering warriors to defend the town.

"Today you will become men at last," my father said to us as we rode south along the riverside pathway and the first light of dawn crept through the damp woods.

"You think Tostig will attack Riaburh?" I asked and he sighed in irritation. The prospect of a battle was still uncertain and he did not want to be reminded of it.

"We'll have a quiet time in Riaburh," said one of the warriors who had come with the messenger. "Tostig surprised us at Wyt, but he knows that next time he'll have to fight, so he won't risk his fleet here. He'll attack somewhere richer. Why stick your cock in a scabby little whore like Riaburh when there's Dover and Sandwic waiting round the coast like fat tavern girls laid on their backs." He bellowed with laughter and my father laughed along through gritted teeth.

"If they don't attack Riaburh," he growled, "we'll ride east and join the king in Kent. War has come and we will fight."

In the years of peace, Riaburh's defences had decayed. There was an untidy ditch ringing the town and a bank of crumbling earth scattered with the rotten planks of an old fence. A grey-haired spearmen stood guard by the pathway where it crossed the ditch.

"Who approaches the gate of Riaburh?" he called to us.

"Saxmund of Ellasham and men who are loyal to King Harold" my father called proudly back. "We come to join our lords Leofwin and Magnus."

"Then you'd better hurry," said the old warrior as we drew level with them. "Ships have been sighted approaching the headland. If we're going to wet our spears on Tostig's crews, it will be today." He smiled at Oswold and I. He saw two young warriors eager for their first taste of battle. I felt a shiver pass from my stomach to my fingertips. I glanced at Idwal who rode unsteadily beside me on a borrowed horse. He smiled back and a wild light flickered in his eyes.

There was chaos in the market square as some warriors arrived and others emerged from the halls and houses where they had spent the night. They had to fight their way through bands of townsfolk and merchants pushing handcarts of wares and belongings, trying to get out of the town before raiders arrived. A group of men and dogs were herding sheep along a pathway between rows of houses and taverns.

"My Lord Leofwin!" my father shouted when he spotted the earl among a group of spearmen in the middle of the muddy square.

"Saxmund, my old friend!" Earl Leofwin swayed towards us raising a horn of ale in salute before clasping my father a in a rough embrace. He was tall and slim in his polished mail, with straw-coloured hair and plaited moustaches. His quick smile made him look younger than my father though there was probably little difference in their ages.

Above the shouting and the noise of horses, dogs and sheep, came the sound of timber splitting and falling. Idwal and I looked up to see a tall ash tree crash down beyond the buildings that edged the square.

"Felling trees into the river," Leofwin explained to my father. "Stop Tostig's ships from reaching the docks."

"So where do we fight them?" my father asked him.

"On the bank of the river south of the town." Leofwin took a deep swig of ale and wiped his mouth on his sleeve. "There's a bank of shingle at the riverside there. It's the only place below the docks where a ship can land." Waving his drinking horn in a southerly direction, the earl turned to face us.

"We'll lie in wait in the old ditch – let them think the town's undefended. Then we'll take them by surprise – attack before they can form a shield wall. And Magnus will have his men hidden in the woods to the west. He'll attack them on the flank while they're fighting us." The men around me muttered in approval.

"This will be the first battle of my brother's kingship, and it will be a victory to sing great songs of," Leofwin concluded, raising his drinking horn to the sky. The group of warriors who stood around him cheered and raised their own cups. Most of them were middle-aged. Some were grey-bearded, some looked as if the thick muscle of their youth was dissolving into fat. All of them were drinking ale.

"If your men are sober enough to climb out of the ditch," said another voice. I looked to my right, where the crowd parted to let a younger man through. He was also clad in mail with a battered shield across his back. His hair had been cropped down to stubble and there was a vicious, sneering look about his face.

"They'll leap at our foes like wildcats, Magnus," Leofwin replied. "And don't look so sour. It is good to drink before battle. A man must meet his foemen fearless and strong."

"Indeed he must. Not stumbling and half asleep." Magnus cast a disdainful eye over his uncle's men. Half a dozen of his own warriors stood behind him. The eldest of them must have been in his mid-twenties and they all looked like their lord – shaven-headed, scowling and ready to fight, to kill and to enjoy it. They stood firm in a grey block of blades and armour and I was glad not to be the enemy who would have to fight his way through them.

96

"Have we enough men?" my father asked Leofwin. "If Tostig has thirty ships he could have close to a thousand warriors." Leofwin waved his horn around in a dismissive gesture.

"Tostig has already lost control of his fleet. Small bands are breaking away to raid villages. If a hundred or so men land here, we'll crush them in moments."

"We've got a hundred and eighty-three men," added Magnus, his voice like a creeping shadow. "If Tostig lands his whole force here then we burn their ships while they plunder the town and wait for my father to arrive with his heathtroop." A few of Leofwin's men raised their voices in protest, but Magnus wasn't listening. To my horror, he fixed his small, cold eyes on me.

"You," he said, pointing with a gloved and mailed hand. "What's your name?"

"Wulfred, lord, Wulfred of Ellasham."

"You are a bowman?" He waved his hand at the bowstave I had brought with me. My father had said I would bring ridicule on myself by coming to do battle among honourable warriors with a coward's weapon. But now I was standing before the king's son clutching a bow, so there was no use in denying it.

"I am, lord," I said. And I straightened my back and I looked him in the eye as I spoke, because I could tell he was the kind of man who would sense fear and weakness and strike at it like a snake.

But a look of interest crossed his face. "And you would use the bow in battle?" he asked.

"I hunt in the forest, lord," I said. "If an arrow can kill a deer, it can kill a man." I was afraid of Magnus, but I thought this was the kind of thing he would want to hear. He answered with a smile, and I judged that to be a rare thing.

"Can your arrows pierce mail?"

"Yes," I showed him an arrow from the bag that hung at my waist – one with a needle-thin point of hard steel made to drive between the rings of a mailshirt.

"And can you hit an enemy from a hundred paces away?"

"I can hit a deer at that distance. A man is no different."

"Suppose he fights sword on sword with your brother? Could you hit the right man?"

"Eight times out of ten perhaps." I grinned at Oswold.

"Eight times out of ten! Ha!" Magnus was actually laughing. He turned to a group of Leofwin's men. "Eight times out of ten, how do you like those odds?" From the looks on their faces they did not.

"There's a slope of gorse and elder that rises from the riverbank," he said. "I've got ten bowmen who could hide there and harry the enemy while they fight my uncle's warriors. Weaken them, confuse them before my men charge from the woods." He paused briefly and grimaced. "They may not be reliable. I want you to lead them, Wulfred of Ellasham. Make sure they don't shoot too early or run away. You'll join my men when we attack. Then you'll fight alongside the Bloodhelms – the Spears of Glowcestre." A few of his men cheered on hearing the name they gave themselves.

"This isn't the way we fight battles Magnus," Leofwin cut in. "There's no honour in putting an arrow in a man's back."

"This is the way to win battles," Magnus muttered. His voice was low, but his eyes were like a winter dawn as he faced the earl. "There's no honour on any field of war - only steel and blood."

"Put the bow away lad," said a black-bearded man who stood beside the earl. "It's a woman's weapon. A true man of Wessex meets the enemy face to face, sword on sword."

My father said nothing. But the look he gave me told me I was a man now and I must make my choice. He may have disapproved of the bow, but the king's son was offering me an important role in the battle plan, and he knew well that war-fame gathers around those favoured by kings and princes.

But for me it was the chance to stay out of the blood and terror of the battle line for a little longer that beckoned. Perhaps I should have refused Magnus' offer. It would have been a perfectly honourable thing for me to say I would rather stand beside my father and my brother. But I was young and fear was a greater thing than honour and the market square of Riaburh was filled with men far braver than I that morning.

"Ships are coming! Five ships are making for Riaburh!" The rider crashed through the crowded square in a whirl of mud and hoofbeats, yelling his message. Suddenly shouts and orders were coming from every direction.

"Men of Wessex!" Leofwin shouted. He drew his sword and held aloft as a rallying point for his warriors.

"Leofwin!" roared a few of the warriors around him, and the command spread quickly across the square.

"Wulfred, this way." Magnus grabbed me by the shoulder and hauled me away. There was just time for my father to raise his fist in a warrior's salute before the tide of imminent battle swept me away.

"These are the men you'll command," said Magnus, pointing at a surly group dressed in faded cloth, crouched by a mud wall and guarded by spearmen. "They are poachers and robbers – thieving bastards to a man, but they might be able shoot a straight arrow. This is Wulfred of Ellasham," he said to the bowmen. "Do as he says. And it's death for any man of you who steps out of line or tries to turn his bow on the army of Wessex. Now move, all of you." The spearmen jabbed at them with their spear butts and they shuffled forward with the rest of the warriors.

And I marched to battle alongside the men who called themselves the Bloodhelms after their habit of daubing their

Helmets red to represent the blood of their enemies. And I was commanding men as reluctant to do battle as I was. It was a time when all the madness of life and death might have weighed on my mind, if there had been time to think.

"So, my friend, we shall shed the blood of many foes this day, eh?" Idwal clapped a hand on my shoulder and spoke quietly amid the clattering of shields and the rattling mail. It was the first time he had opened his mouth since we arrived in the town. We both knew that, unless he was singing and strumming a lyre, the voice of a Welshman among these warriors of Wessex would be poorly received. He had swept his cloak aside so all could see the sword hanging at his belt, and a shield that my father had frowningly given him hung across his back, but he wore no mail or helmet and had drawn a few dubious looks from the warriors in the square.

"March with them," I whispered, thrusting him towards the bowmen. "You might not stand out so much."

As Idwal fell in alongside the thieves and poachers of Wessex, the foremost three of them ducked between the spears of Magnus' men and sprinted down a muddy alley. Half a dozen mail clad warriors turned and lumbered after them. Two fell as they got wedged in the narrow passageway, but one of them leapt and bounded forward and caught the flapping cloak of the slowest bowman. He fell, and the warrior held him down.

"Leave them." Magnus called out as the two fleeing men vanished around the side of a long hall. "We're too close to battle to hunt them down. Bring the other one here." He drew his sword as the captured man was brought to him. It was a weapon of strangely dark steel, as if the smoke of the smith's forge had mingled with the blade, and he called it Ironclaw.

"Running away in the face of battle," Magnus roared, pointing the sword at the panic-stricken man. The Bloodhelms had stopped to watch, while Leofwin's followers glanced across as they marched on. He raised a leather-booted foot and kicked the bowman, a

100

weary-looking, grey-haired man, down. He fell gasping for breath on the dung-strewn ground at the foot of a building. "Your life is mine, thief. You could have saved yourself by proving worthy in battle. But now your life is finished."

The man half sat up and opened his mouth to plead but before any sound came out, Magnus drove Ironclaw hard into his stomach and up under his ribcage. He screamed and choked, his body shook and blood gushed from his belly and from his mouth. Magnus stepped back and wiped his sword on the edge of his cloak. The stricken bowman shrivelled into a ball and pressed his hands into his open belly as his screams faded to a croak and a groan and finally a whimper.

"A sacrifice before battle. Like the old times." Magnus spat on the corpse then snarled at me. "Don't lose any more of them." For a moment, he ground his teeth and glanced at his men, wondering whether put one of them in charge of the bowmen and send me back to his uncle. But there was little time to spare and he turned and marched on, waving Ironclaw in the air for his men to follow. Idwal picked up the dead man's bow and took the string from his leather pouch.

"I suppose I'll take his place," he smiled.

I wrenched my eyes away from the spreading blood pool and the twisted face of the dead man and looked at Idwal.

"Can you use a bow?"

"I come from the valleys of Dyfed, you fool. My people shoot Saxons for sport. There's no man west of the Severn who cannot shoot an arrow to kill his foeman across the full breadth of that great river."

We marched on at the rear of Magnus' column, passing over the wooden footbridge that marked the southern gate of the town and out in the scrubby, salt-scented landscape where the River Leman met the sea.

101

"Line them up among the gorse there," said Magnus, frowning as he indicated the undergrowth on a slope facing down towards the tidal expanse of the river and the neglected ditch around the town where Earl Leofwin's men, my father and Oswold among them, were taking cover. "Let them fight for a while. Don't shoot until they start pushing my uncle's men back. When men taste victory they become careless. Remember," he went on, turning to face the ragged troupe of bowmen, "freedom for any man who shoots four enemies." He turned back towards his warriors, pointed Ironclaw towards a clump of birch and ash trees further up the slope and they rushed away to take cover. And I was left on the empty hillside with the threat of battle drawing close and men under my command.

The bowmen had spread out a little and found themselves vantage points, crouched behind the cover of the gorse bushes. The riverside and the town ditch where we expected to fight were only a hundred or so paces below us. I went along their line, a warrior in mail and leather with a shield across my back, among men unprotected from the spears of their foes. I wished them all a steady aim and a portion of luck and I tried to shake each of them by the hand, although most only grunted and looked away. But the last man grasped my hand firmly and told me his name.

"I am Ulric," he said "of Aethelingey." He was a little older than most of them, probably in his thirties and had the warm accent of a man from the far west of Wessex. His face was scarred by pox, but his eyes shone out brightly from beneath his leather cap. "The king has an estate there where I used to hunt," he added with the shadow of a smile.

"What's the deal Magnus made with you?" I asked him.

"Our arrows are all marked with different colours," he held up a bag of a dozen arrows each painted with a red and a blue ring below the fletching. "A man who puts four arrows into the bodies of the enemy will serve the Lord Magnus. Any man whose arrow strikes one of Earl Leofwin's warriors will to be put to death. Those who do neither will face justice at   the next shire court."

102

"I'd rather be whipped half to death at the fucking pillory than spend another day serving that bastard Magnus," spat the man next to him. I was inclined to agree with him and I almost said so, but Idwal grabbed me by the shoulder and pointed out towards the mouth of the river. I rose to peer over the gorse bushes.

Below us the thatched and shingled roofs of the town lay to the left, silent in the morning sun, and the brown river gurgled through a mesh of newly-felled tree trunks and branches. To the right, beyond the long flat riverbank and the wind-troubled branches of a few rowan trees, the river Leman met the sea, wide and empty, apart from a few gulls and curlews squabbling on the mudflats.

"There's nothing there," I whispered to Idwal.

"As keen eyed as a mole," he muttered. "Look to the headland." I strained my eyes, staring into the distance. At first I saw only the morning sun glinting on the water, and the dark mudflats. But then I caught a glimpse of long, low shapes, the same black shade as the coastal mud, shivering between flashes of reflected sunlight.

"Five ships," said Idwal. "Long ships. If they have four dozen oars to a boat, then the enemy is greater than us."

"But they don't know we're here," I said, to myself as much as to Idwal. He just shrugged

"Only your strange Saxon gods can aid us and I expect they're still sleeping off last night's ale." He nocked an arrow to his bowstring. "See how the ships stay close together? They have the look of hunted deer."

A flight of plovers rose squawking from the mudflats as the ships rounded the distant headland, sailing away from the sun-splashed sea and into plain view.

"They should have come at dawn," said Ulric the bowmen. "Raiding is like hunting. You must walk unseen through the shadows. Magnus is a bastard, but he knows how to fight. If the earl's men can hold them for a while then we'll have a victory." I

103

smiled and nodded at Ulric, then at the other bowmen, though I did not feel his confidence.

And then we waited as the ships drew near, driven by a southerly wind up the quiet river. Their white sails billowed and turned and there were battle-scarred shields raised above the gunwhales, some plain discs of black or red, others painted with horses, eagles and a few other beasts. I watched the men at my side stringing their bows and flexing the cords and going through their bags of arrows to select the straightest and the best-fletched. I glanced behind me at the woods where Magnus' men were hidden, knowing that if I turned and fled from the enemy I would meet the same fate as the man who died in the town. Then I looked down towards the ditch where Oswold and my father lay in wait and I told myself that I had to shoot my arrows fast and true for their sake, as the force that forged its way up the river would certainly outnumber Earl Leofwin's little warband. There was fear somewhere – a tightness in my stomach and my legs felt unsteady, but I was in control. I knew how to shoot an arrow. If I had to, I could kill an enemy at this distance and perhaps that was all that would be necessary. My helmet, plain iron with an angled nasal guard, hung from my belt and I put it on, fumbling to untie the strap then tie it again under my chin as I watched the ships on the river.

They came closer, gulls and curlews taking wing from the riverside as they passed. The carved beast-heads of their prows showed starkly against the bright water, warning that the men on board brought only murder and destruction.

The five ships hit the beach as one. The crunch of their hulls on the pebbled shore and the wind-snatched shouts of men were carried towards us. The first of the raiders were swiftly ashore. They were heavy, muscled men, wearing coats of iron mail as easily as another man might wear a cloak. They had swords and axes at their waists and wide shields across their backs. They thrust the shafts of their spears into the riverbed for support as they leapt from the boat.

"Hired men?" whispered Ulric and I was glad that he spoke because his voice broke the silence that my fear was filling with the shadows of death.

"The ones with blank shields are hired," I told him. "Those with horses and eagles painted on their shields are Northumbrian – the men who fled with Tostig last year."

"There are a lot of them," he remarked. He said it calmly, as if commenting on a big flock of sheep.

"The more glory to us when we cut them down," said Idwal. He held the dead man's bow in one hand and he had the other on his sword hilt, as if he wanted to draw it already.

"Glory? You sound like my father. Was it glorious when Magnus killed that man on the edge of town?"

"The gods of war must reap their harvest." Idwal shrugged, and turned his eyes back towards the warriors assembling on the shore.

Their spears had nine or ten foot shafts and long iron points. Such weapons were meant to be wielded two-handed, to charge a shield line with enough force to break the wall of wood and leather. Many of them had barbs just behind the blade, used for hooking over a shield and pulling it open for another spearman to make a kill. Their ships were only half beached, moored with ropes, ready to be boarded and rowed quickly back to sea should Riaburh prove to be well-defended. And these shipmen were forming into a watchful shield wall, a far cry from the charging rabble Magnus and Leofwin had expected to face.

Behind their line stood six more warriors with prancing horses painted on their shields, and a seventh, a grey-bearded beast of a man with a livid purple scar where his left eye might once have been, stood at their centre.

"Is he a big enough target for you?" whispered Idwal.

"Shut up!" I snarled at him. "And keep your head down.

The big man stepped forward in front of the shield wall, walking stiffly in leather breeches and a long mailcoat.

"Harold! Gyrth! Leofwin! Lesser sons of Godwin!" he called out in the rough accent of the half-Danish north. "I am Anlaf, oath-man of Tostig, who is the true earl of Northumbria. Show your whimpering faces so that I might give your souls to the shadow-world and your skins to my lord!" He thumped his spear butt on the ground, but was answered only by the birds that flitted about the gorse and by the wind that twisted his hair.

"Where are the women?" one of Anlaf's men shouted. "Bring us gold and women and perhaps we'll spare your town."

"We'll have their wives and daughters," Anlaf laughed "If they hide them away, we'll take the rumps of their men and boys." He drew an axe from his belt and thrust its shaft violently up into the air in front of him. There was a burst of savage laughter from the warriors.

"Oh, true Saxons, they are!" Idwal sniggered, but I did not dare speak or move to silence him.

Then Anlaf began to beat the axe against his shield in a slow rhythm that was quickly taken up by the rest of them. Still there was no response from Leofwin's men in the ditch.

"You fear me!" he shouted. "Pigs and shit-hounds of Wessex! Sheep-fuckers of Sussex! You fear me! You hide like virgins from the swords of men. You piss in your breeches! Today the ravens will strip your bones and men of the north will fill your wives' bellies!" The beating of weapons on shields quickened while Anlaf's men roared and bleated like sheep. But still they were answered only by the birds and the wind. He shrugged his shoulders and turned to face his followers with the jagged grin of an old warrior.

"Wessex has fallen to the rule of lesser men. Men too frightened to defend their towns. Gold and women for all!"

106

Maybe if a song had ever been made of the battle at Riaburh, those shipmen would have charged like wolves against the walls of the town, howling their battlecries, their swords scything through the brightness of the dawn. In reality they just walked as quickly as they could while keeping their shield wall intact. But that was a deadly enough threat for Leofwin. He had hoped to face a blundering mob intent on pillage and destruction. But our foes were not fools, and even with the town apparently undefended, they did not break their battle formation. I watched from the slope above, knowing that the only choice for my father and brother was to charge into a hedge of spears.

When the enemy were just twenty paces from the ditch, Leofwin's banner, a blue cloth sewn with the golden image of a hawk, was suddenly raised in front of them. Cries of "Godwinsson!" and "Wessex!" rolled across the peaceful riverside and the earl and his men leapt forward in a rush of shields and steel blades. Or at least, most of them did. Leofwin himself, hurling a spear into the advancing enemy, sprang up like a hare as did the men around him. Oswold and our father quickly made a shield wall with the warriors on the right flank. But on the left, as Magnus had feared, some of the older, fatter and drunker men stumbled and slipped. The line was incomplete and with a cry from their leader, the shipmen also charged. Over such a short distance their own shield wall held at a run, and the warbands met, shield on shield and sword on sword.

The poets sing of such clashes as thunder in deep valleys and the breaking of storms against a rocky coast. But I heard only the cracking of blades against shields and the occasional cry of a warrior rising from the flat ground below me. Those sounds were small in the spring morning. The sun was a little higher now and in the cool shadows, finches and warblers flitted through the gorse, building nests and seeking food.

Then the first man died. The warrior beside my father choked and fell with a spear in his neck. My father lashed out and struck the killer a vicious sword-blow on his shoulder, but the man did not fall and Leofwin's line crept back towards the ditch. Closer to the river, two more fell in a desperate fight where the line was ragged and broken. With a roar of triumph, four or five of the shipmen drove into the gap, but one of them stumbled, his ankle broken by a low spear-thrust, and somehow Leofwin's outnumbered warband held on at the edge of the ditch.

I saw Oswold raise his black and red shield against the sweeping arc of a long-shafted axe. It was swung by a bare-chested, bald-headed warrior who stood tall above the rest of the line. The top of my brother's shield splintered and the axe hooked over it. The axeman pulled his weapon back, opening Oswold's shield and a spear stabbed in from the side to strike him low in the chest. The horror of my brother's death cut through me, and my legs trembled as I stood and lifted my bow above the gorse bushes. That spear-thrust was weakened by a sword swung from Oswold's right and it merely ripped into his mailshirt and the stuffed leather coat beneath it. But his shield was still open and there was already another spear snaking towards him as I drew back the bowcord and, without even pausing to aim, released the arrow.

The axeman fell forward as the feathered shaft thumped into his hip. Oswold dragged his shield back and beat the second spear aside with its rim. Then Idwal's first shot glanced off a helmet and span away over the ditch. He cursed his aim and drew the bow again as the arrows of the other bowmen scattered along the line of warriors' backs and into the long grass at their feet. I saw Oswold raise his spear and stab it down into the wounded axeman as Idwal loosed his second shot. It thumped into the back of a Northumbrian, knocking him forward onto a spear. Idwal screamed in victory and leapt up, punching the air with his fist.

"Caer Myrddin!" he hollered.

Some of my bowmen began to scramble forward through the undergrowth to get a better aim, but I just stood among the yellow-flowered gorse, feeling as light as the air that rushed through my lungs, drawing back the bowcord again and knowing that I had saved my brother from the edge of death, that I was the bringer of victory, that I had control over that field of battle. The arrow flew and skewered one of the Northumbrians through the shoulder.

Then Magnus charged. And that was a sight that poets could sing of without stretching the truth. But it was not something bright and glorious. It was a scene from Hell.

"Glowcestre!" was their battlecry, the name of the town near the Welsh border where Magnus had his hall, and it promised death to all who heard it. In a tight wedge, sixty of them crashed out of the trees where no men had seemed to be. A solid pack of warriors, edged with shields and bristling spears aimed at the heart of that northern warband. Their blades, their armour, their shields and faces were smeared with a mixture of soot and grease that had let them lurk unseen among the shadows of the trees. The shipmen looked up and saw an army of black demons howling towards them.

Idwal threw down his bow and drew his sword.

"And now we break them!" he yelled, grinning like a madman. Driven on by a power I had never felt before, I ran after him. I was mail-clad and helmeted, with a shield in one hand and a long spear in the other, but I felt lighter than the empty air. The rest of the bowmen ran beside us, without armour but carrying axes and knives and faces dark with murder.

Magnus hit the enemy moments before us. A few of the shipmen struggled to make a second shield wall facing backwards, but they wavered as the black warriors ploughed into them. Some dug their spear butts into the ground to hold the line, but Magnus' men knocked the shafts aside and plunged headlong into the faltering enemy, their own spears driving in at eye level.

109

It takes some skill and rare courage to break a shield wall, but the Bloodhelms of Glowcestre smashed through as if they did it every day. I was slowed when a slaughtered warrior fell in my path, his skull cracked open by a spear rammed hard under his helmet. He gibbered and shook as his brains oozed out onto the grass.

Idwal screamed something in Welsh, leapt over the dying man and threw himself at one of Anlaf's bodyguards. Untrained in swordsmanship, he lashed out wildly to knock the man's spear aside, but his blade cut into the wooden shaft and stuck there. With a practised twist, the Northumbrian warrior tore the sword from Idwal's hand and pulled the spear back, ready to skewer the Welshman. But I was still possessed by the gods of battle and I hammered my spear hard at the edge of the man's shield, buying Idwal a moment to roll aside. The Northumbrian turned towards me. I pulled back my spear, planted my feet solidly in the grassy ground and for a moment I saw everything as clearly as if it had already happened and I was telling the story of my victory. He would feint high, hoping to make me raise my shield over my face so I would not see where the real thrust was coming, but I would step aside and in the same movement go forward, draw my sword, get inside the reach of his spear and drive my blade down into his neck.

But he did not feint. He came towards me, his spear tipped with iron sharp enough to shave a man's beard, and his eyes locked onto mine. He lunged low and fast, trying to stab under the rim of my shield and into my groin. I pushed my shield down and heard the spear scrape along the skirt of my mail. But now the sharp focus of the world had suddenly blurred and I had no idea what this warrior, this man who had probably killed a hundred men, would do next. I stumbled back, struggling to keep a grip on my shield, the spear hanging useless in my hand as he came towards me again, seeing my weakness, seeing my death as clearly as I had seen his.

Then Ulric the bowman hurtled in between us and used his axe to pull the Northumbrian's shield open. In a flash of resurging clarity, I saw the chance he had given me and without thinking I

110

dropped my own shield and threw all my weight into a two-handed spear thrust. I heard the blade split his mailshirt and felt the thick leather beneath give way, then I saw the look of horror on his face as the iron point tore into his stomach. And the joy of victory rushed out of me like vomit.

He was lying on his side, one hand clawing at the grass and the other fumbling at the blood-slick spear sticking out of his belly. He opened his mouth as if to speak but instead a wretched blood-stifled groan fell from his lips. And his eyes were fixed on me. And for a moment the crashing of weapons and the cries of warriors, the charging of Magnus' Bloodhelms, the desperate struggle of Anlaf's raiders – it was all gone. And once again I was a child of five summers huddled in the dark in the hall at Llyn Ryhdderch watching a man's life ebbing away. He gasped with pain and clenched his teeth as he tried to pull the spearhead out of his body. I had dropped the shaft of the spear and just knelt on the grass. The man was my enemy and wounded beyond help, but for some reason I shuffled a little towards him. Fear flickered across his dying eyes and he dragged a knife from his belt, then threw his head back and gasped again as the movement sent new pain surging through him. A torrent of blood suddenly gushed from the rip in his mailshirt and he slumped back on the grass.

"Well done, boy. A good kill." It was the voice of one of Leofwin's warriors hoisting me to my feet. "Now let's finish them." He lumbered off towards the river where Anlaf's routed followers were fleeing for their ships. Stunned, I stumbled after him.

But the fight was already won. Magnus' men had hacked through the shield wall and Leofwin had rallied the men on the right of his line. Some of the raiders had turned to run before they could be surrounded. The men of Wessex fought hard, crazed by blood and the taste of victory. They hammered swords and spears into the dwindling band of shipmen caught between the ditch and the river and they chased the others along the shoreline, dragging them into the grass and mud and cutting them to pieces. And I stood in the midst of it all, watching Death reap its harvest. I saw one of the bowmen trip a fleeing warrior with a spearshaft, then saw another leap on the stumbling man's back and smash his skull with an axe. I saw the warriors of Wessex picking up fallen spears and hurling them at the backs of the fleeing men.

It was quickly over. Anlaf was killed by the water's edge, his one-eyed corpse falling into the river so that his blood flowed back out towards the sea that had brought him. Some of his men tried to surrender. They fell to their knees on the mud and shingle and begged for mercy, but it made no difference. Kneeling men made easy kills. Others fought on. I watched the ending of the battle and I wondered what they thought as they battled without hope - did they still believe they could reach their ships and escape? Did they pray for the intervention of a warrior god? Or did they look to the sky, taste blood on the air and sense the hall of their forefathers' ghosts waiting for them?

Along the riverside, blood mingled with mud, splintered bone and the offal that oozes from broken heads and bellies. The dead lay still, smashed and impaled. The wounded twitched, writhed, tried to crawl away. I stepped over the corpse of a man whose eyes stared with blind horror into the sky and whose dead hands still clutched the purple innards hanging out of his body. Some dying men wept. Some prayed and some gasped for every last moment of life. A warrior no older than me lay screaming out for death, a spear through his groin pinning him to the ground.

One of Anlaf's ships did escape with a dozen men fighting to control the big vessel as spears and axes rained from the riverbank. Just a handful of men who lived to rejoin their fleet and fight again. The rest lay butchered under the spring sky. Gulls wheeled high above the shore and hungry crows were already gathering before the swords had fallen silent.

One of my bowmen was killed in the fighting and another had been cut down trying to flee as the Bloodhelms had charged.

"You men shot well," said Magnus, addressing two of the survivors on the corpse-scattered riverbank. "Four arrows each in the bodies of our enemies. You'll shoot for us from now on. We'll teach you how to use a spear as well. You three," he turned to the others "will face the pillory or the gallows."

"This man fought bravely," My throat was dry and my mind still numb, but Ulric had saved my life and I had to speak up for him. "He attacked an enemy, used his axe to open his shield so I could kill him." Magnus frowned. Good bowmen he could use. He had no need for bad ones. But as a lord he had to be seen to reward bravery.

"Very well," he said, pulling a sour face. "Ulric will dig latrine ditches at our camps until he learns to shoot straight." A few of his men laughed and the other two bowmen looked at me hopefully, but I said no more. I had seen neither of them fight, only killing the wounded and plundering the dead.

My father bellowed proudly as he put his foot on the corpse I had made and pulled my spear from its belly.

"So, we have made a warrior of you after all," he cried, and slapped me hard on the back. "Did you see his face as you drove the spear in?" he asked. The blood of other men was drying in his beard and his face shone with a savage joy.

"I did," I mumbled, looking at my father because I could not bear to look at the dead man on the ground.

"Good. That is the moment when a man becomes a true warrior, when he sees Death working at his command."

Oswold, his shield smashed and his mailshirt splattered with blood, had killed three more men as the enemy were fleeing for their ships. He was grinning like a drunkard, but he saw my face and he knew what I was thinking.

"We saved the town, Wulfred," he said. "We saved the men from the sword, the women from rape and slavery. They could not have bargained with Tostig's men."

My brother was right, of course. Riaburh stood, its traders and craftsmen, its women and children lived and the shipmen lay slaughtered. Briefly, I had felt what fighting men call the joy of battle. It had come like fire across a dry field, but it had faded more quickly than any joy I had ever known. And now the whole world stank of blood and I had taken a great step along a path from which I could not turn away.

Early the next morning, Idwal and I stood on the hillside overlooking the river again. There were black ribbons of cloud across the eastern sky, but the pale light of the dawn was still bright enough to sting my eyes. The army of Wessex had drunk and roared and bellowed all night to celebrate the first victory of Harold Godwinsson's reign. And I had joined them, hoping the ale and wine might drown the memory of battle.

"I'm going back to Hantone," Idwal said, blinking in the harsh light of morning and looking down at the riverside where a few shuffling figures moved among the dead, stripping off any clothing that could be used or sold and throwing the bodies into the outgoing tide. "Perhaps I'll find a ship that will take me west along the coast, back to my homeland."

"May we meet again in better times," I said, though something told me that better times were a long way off. Idwal shook his head at me and immediately groaned and put a hand to his temple.

"These are the good times, you fool. Ours were deeds that will live forever." He glanced down at his leather bag, heavier now with rings of silver and beads of amber taken from the dead. "My eyes have seen and my heart has felt the truth of battle," he went on, and the sunlight burned my eyes and I hoped it was not going to be a long speech. "But there are battles still to fight, my friend. The foes

114

of Wessex are gathering, the men of the west are stirring, and when next we meet, the shield wall may stand between us."

"My blade knows friend from foe. And you, Idwal of Caer Myrddin, need not fear it." I somehow lost my footing on the level ground of the pathway and staggered to one side.

"Of course not," Idwal replied, suddenly grinning as fiercely as he had in battle. "When the kings of the west arise, your blade will rest in its sheath and you will hide up a tree as far from the field of battle as you can get!"

We laughed and we said our farewells. I turned and wandered back to the town. The lonely cries of gulls soared high above the shoreline and a bell rang in a monastery across the river.

And on the silent riverside below, the souls of those slaughtered warriors arose to begin their own journey.

6. GRIMSTAN'S DAY

The first fyrdmen arrived in Ellasham a week or two after the fight at Riaburh. On the far coast of Kent, Tostig's fleet had slipped away into the mist of the Viking Sea and rumours of a great Norman fleet being built in harbours across the Narrow Sea to the south were spreading like summer fire across the kingdom. So the fyrd had been raised and a state of war had come to all of England.

In Ellasham, as in many villages across the south of Wessex, bands of these peasant warriors were given battle training by local lords, before continuing their march to the coast, where they would await the war host of Normandy. A dozen sailcloth tents had been sent from Lunden to house the fyrdmen, and I helped a group of Ellasham's men to pitch them beside the river.

"I hope the king's going to be feeding these bastards," grumbled Godric. "We can't spare anything."

"They'll want ale as well. And women," grumbled another man. "Any fyrd bastard comes near my wife, I'll beat his balls back up into his belly."

"They'll carry food with them," I assured the men. "And if you give your wife what she wants, she'll fight the fyrd off herself."

But the men of Ellasham were right to be worried. The wheat and the barley were still green in the fields and the lambs and piglets born earlier in the spring were only half grown. There was no meat in the village and bread was too scarce to be spared. And in the end the men were doubly right, because our first group of the fyrd, a sullen band of thirty or so from a village far across the Thames in Essex, came carrying nothing but the cocksure manner of men far from home and convinced the whole world plots to rob and beat them.

On the evening of their arrival, they banded together and marched on the hall, demanding to be fed with the little grain that was still stored there. The villagers barred their way and as the sun began to set there were fifty or so men kicking and flailing and swinging cudgels about on the edge of the village.

My father, Oswold and I had to break it up with shields and axe shafts.

"Where's the food you brought with you?" my father asked the Essex men.

"What food? We didn't bring any," spat a tall man with a shock of red hair. He was the lord's reeve of the estate they came from, and the man who had led the fyrd on their journey so far. "We're here to fight for the king, so the king can feed us." He stood tall, planted his feet solidly on the ground and looked my father in the eye. Behind him, his companions muttered their agreement. My father dropped the axe shaft he carried and punched the man hard in the face, sending him sprawling across the ground with blood gushing from his nose.

"While you're on my land, I am your lord and you'll call me lord!" he bellowed, kicking the prostrate man in the belly.

"The law of Wessex states that fyrdmen must carry enough food for their journey." I said. I scanned the row of angry faces lined up on the field in the fading light and in truth I felt sorry for the them, sent many miles from their homes to face death for a king they cared little for.

"And if Essex has any laws," my father added, "you can wipe your arses on them. Now where is your food?"

"We weren't given any, lord," replied another man.

"Weren't given any? Would you be spoon-fed like babies at your mothers' knees? You should have brought bread from your homes."

117

"My lord, would you have us carry food away from our wives and children?" The red-haired man was on his feet again, wiping blood from his face, and the men gathered behind him muttered in agreement.

I stepped back to my father's side. "There's wheat and barley for sale in the markets at Riaburh," I said quietly. Irritated, he shot me a warning look, then turned back to the gathered fyrdmen.

"We have no food to spare here," he said. One man spat on the ground and turned his back, saying that he was going back to Essex. Another had overheard me and shouted something about moving on to Riaburh where there were warehouses stuffed with meat and ale.

"Let them go back to Essex," yelled Godric. "We don't need these starving shitsacks here." He stood shoulder to shoulder with his friend Ecgbert, who had blood all over his face and a chunk missing from his left ear, and at least twenty other grim-faced village men. One of the Essex men raised a cudgel and advanced on Godric, hoping others would follow, but I cut him off with a thrust of my shield. The others held back, their eyes bright with nervous defiance. They were hungry, and it takes more than pushing and shoving to make hungry men back down.

Night fell, and after a long stand off, we agreed to feed the men of Essex. To lose thirty fyrdmen who were later found looting the warehouses of Riaburh would not have done my father's reputation any good. He agreed to give them grain, ale and onions and allowed them to set eel traps in the river. He promised the villagers that he would send someone to the market in Riaburh to replace what they lost. He also muttered darkly about sending a bill to whatever estate these men came from.

"I expect Essex is rolling with fat women and bloated great children while their menfolk feast on our grain," he muttered as he sent Godric and I to fetch a couple of sacks of corn from the hall. "And give them the rotten stuff," he added. The warmth of spring sometimes caused a kind of mould to grow on grain that had been stored all winter and when eaten, it could have a similar, but more frightening, effect to the elfcap. People sometimes went mad in the spring, thinking they were being burned alive, chased by demons or torn apart by birds.

That first group of the fyrd, with their broken-nosed leader and their mouldy corn, remained sulky for all of the week they were with us, but those that followed were not so bad. Some were resentful at being dragged across the country while they had fields to tend at home, while others looked forward to battle and were eager to learn how to fight. They came from all over Wessex and East Anglia. Those from the east scattered words of Danish amongst their speech and were full of tales about the wondrous things they had seen as they passed through Lunden on their journey. One group of men from the far west of Wessex regarded our ale as a rare delicacy, as the land they came from was too damp to grow barley.

In the afternoons, my father had the fyrdmen work on clearing out the old ditches and rebuilding the wall of stakes and planks that had once defended Ellasham. And in the mornings Oswold and I trained them for battle. Each day the sun rose a little earlier and each day we set out for a corner of the south field where smoke from their riverside campfires trailed through the misty light and where the hard rain of early spring had washed out the seedcorn and left the ground barren. There we made shield walls with flimsy wooden boards and we taught them how to use axes and hooked poles to open enemy shields.

The sun was warm, the spring rain was fresh and we joked and laughed as we thrashed about for little victories in the dust and mud. Sometimes I forgot that I was training peaceful men of the fields and herds how to kill and how to cripple.

It was late in May, and the whole world was green. Those who worked the land were known to call it the month of three milkings,

119

because the new grass grew so fast that they could sometimes milk their cattle three times in a day. New calves were trying their spindly legs on the hillsides and the cuckoo sounded in the woods. It was the time of year when the green of the hills and fields seems like it could stay forever – long before the ripening corn drains colour from the land and reminds us that the wheel still turns and the grey ghost of winter is only ever biding her time.

"Frithe was talking about finding a husband among the fyrdmen." Hildelyth looked away as she spoke, staring into the bright-leaved branches of an ash tree. Across the river, the last of the villagers were wandering away from the field of green, knee-high wheat, their hoes about their shoulders and the evening sun throwing their shadows far across the ground. Hildelyth's cousin Frithe was slim and pretty with blue eyes and hair as bright as spring blossom. She must have seen fourteen summers by then - ripe for marriage before the year was out.

Hildelyth was a couple of years older. Many girls of her age already had husbands and children, but marriage was something she had never really spoken about.

"Good luck to her," I mumbled, knowing that, like Hildelyth, I was saying none of the things I was thinking.

Everything was changing. Since the winter-dark nights when storm winds tore the cross from Cuthred's church, all the pieces of our lives had been falling like leaves from an autumn tree. And on the river's edge at Riaburh, I had killed a man in battle. That spear pushed through mail, leather and flesh was the final step onto a pathway I had always tried to look away from.

"You could be a merchant," said Hildelyth, as if the thought had fallen down to her from the evening sky. She sat up and clasped her arms around her knees "You could live like Sigered. Buy a ship. Take grain and fleeces across the sea, buy wine and fruit and spices to sell in Lunden." Hildelyth looked at me, eager for a response, her brown eyes glinting in the evening light. It sounded so simple, but I

120

had never even been on a ship, let alone sailed one, and money was something the poor struggled for scraps of and the rich hoarded in oak chests and which I rarely thought about.

"How would I buy a ship?" I wondered aloud.

"You know where your father's silver is hidden." Her grin was bright with the mischief I had long loved in her. "We could be across the sea before he knew it was gone."

"But I know nothing about trading. Or the languages of the people I would trade with. Or how to sail a ship." Sigered was a trader and a traveller because his father had raised him to be one. He had learned the value of goods, the ways of the sea, the many different tongues of the marketplace from the day he could first walk. In all the years of my life I had only learned to use a sword and spear to kill men.

"So you would be a warrior. As your father always wanted." There was a cold edge of contempt in Hildelyth's voice and she looked away into the fading light.

Hildelyth was of the land, and the land taught its people that clever or desperate ideas could sometimes hold back the relentless advance of cold and hunger. I had always lived within a dream – a flimsy dream that war might never come to England, that the skills my father taught me would never be needed. I had dreamed that nothing would ever change and that is the most foolish dream any man can have. To dream of such a thing is like dreaming that the mists of October will never leach the hot green summer from the woods.

In the days and weeks that followed the fight at Riaburh, I felt the weight of change dragging me down and spreading like a shadow across the green fields of gathering summer. But I could not face that shadow. I could not shed my old skin, cut myself new robes from the darkness of the coming storm and emerge into the calm sunlight beyond with my destiny clutched in my hands.

Instead I clung to a world that had faded to little more than an ember. And Hildelyth knew that warriors did not return victorious from battle to marry the poorest girl in the village. She knew that my future was now a thing to be hewn by swords and shaped in the halls of earls and kings, and that hers lay among hearthfires, turning seasons and strong children raised to steer the plough and swing the sickle. But we had lived on my foolish dreaming for so long that neither of us could find the words to speak of it.

So we lay on the grass in silence while the river gurgled along and the new-leaved forest trembled in the breeze. A pair of nightjars whirled through the empty sky above the weald's edge, clapping their wings an uttering their strange throbbing call. I followed their flight out across the quiet village, and on the far side of Ellasham, between the river and the south field I saw lights moving in the darkness of the landscape.

"What's that?" I said. Hildelyth turned towards me. There was still a sullen look in her eyes, but she peered into the distance and her face softened.

"Torches?" she said. "Is it the fyrdmen?"

"The fyrdmen have had a hard day digging out the ditches. They'll be drinking in their camp by now."

"Unless they've run away," she said, with a barb twisting her voice.

"Go home," I said to her. "Warn your family there are strangers out tonight." We both slipped separately into the gathering dusk, and I hurried down from the weald's edge towards my father's house.

"Father Grimstan has returned," My father muttered. We could hear the familiar tone of the priest's voice, rattling on the edge of madness, but from where we stood in the doorway of the house, his words were as blurred as the distant faces he addressed. There was a

122

small crowd gathered around the priest on the edge of the south field. By the light of their torches we could see that many of them carried cudgels and hoes, but shadows hid their numbers.

"God is with us! Slay the heathen!" chanted their voices, carried on the breeze in a sudden moment of chilling clarity.

"He's come for Ragnald," I said and looked at my father, expecting to see his anger rise. But instead, he turned away and said nothing. "Grimstan has no business here. Your word is enough to stop them." Ellasham did not have a gate we could close and bar, but it would be easy enough to block their path with a few spears and a group of village men. Some men from the fyrd camp by the river had wandered over to see what was going on and Grimstan started shouting at them too.

"Grimstan is a priest of the Holy Church," my father sighed. "He can come and go as he wills."

"But you are lord of this place. What will you do?"

He turned to face me again. "What will happen if I stop them?" he snapped. "If I stop them, they will come for me next, only it won't be a rabble. If I defy the Church, it will be a bishop's spearmen who come to haul me away to a trial in Cantaburh for obstructing the work of God."

"So you'd knock down a fyrdman asking for food, but let a mad priest lead a mob to murder your people?"

At the sound of raised voices, Oswold and our mother looked over from the hearth where they sat in awkward silence, obedient to the command that none of us should get involved. My father glanced across the dusky village again, then turned back to me and beat his fist against the frame of the doorway as he spoke.

"We live in a kingdom just a hair's breadth from war, Wulfred. Already we hear news that the Holy Father in Rome has taken the side of our foes. Would you have the lords of England defying the Church?" As quickly as the fire of anger had sprung into his eyes, it

123

faded and he looked down at the floor, muttering as if he despised his own words. "The merchants say there are five hundred ships at harbour in Normandy, waiting to carry the duke's army, and more being built. There will be strife in England soon enough. Until that time we must keep what peace we can. If I do not intervene, the kingdom will be stronger for it."

"And Ragnald? Will he still fight with the fyrd and stand beside you in battle?"

"Ragnald will take care of himself."

"Grimstan wants blood. You don't raise a mob like that to give warnings."

My father closed his eyes and drew a deep breath. I had never seen him look so weak. "If Ragnald has eyes and ears and sense enough to use them, he will be gone deep into the weald before Grimstan gets anywhere near him. Our people have no quarrel with Ragnald. He will return safely and soon enough."

I glanced at Oswold but he too spoke without conviction. "Ragnald knows we cannot defy the Church, Wulfred."

The crowd – it looked to be about fifty strong - began to move. Their tallow torches flickered into the village, between the houses and towards Ragnald's cottage at the forest's edge.

And, leaving my father standing uselessly in the doorway, I set off at a run into the darkening night.

Ahead of the mob, I slipped between the thatched sheds used for drying wood and through the doorway of Ragnald's house. He was stood by his dwindling fire with a heavy basket strapped to his back, but swifter than a hawk, he pulled a langseax - a single edged hunting knife with a blade as long as any sword - from a sheath at his belt and whipped around. Seeing me, he lowered his weapon.

"Have you come to bid me farewell?" he said with a grim smile. All the tools, the cooking pots, the blankets – all the things that Ragnald valued – were gone from the house. Although the light from the hearth was dim, I could sense an emptiness in the way his voice rang against the walls.

"You know they're coming?"

Ragnald grunted angrily. "I've been watching Grimstan. Outlawed men have come from across Kent and Sussex to work on his church. Sigered feeds their bellies and Grimstan poisons their minds. They believe that if they build the church and work his will, they'll be assured of a place in Heaven." He hitched his basket into a more comfortable position and took a final look around the darkened walls. The yelling and the chanting outside grew closer.

"Where will you go?" I asked, following him out of the house and down into the shadowy ditch that surrounded the village.

"Hurry up," he hissed. "I don't want them to see me leave." The mob was close enough now for us to count their bright torches and to hear their footsteps. "I'm going to the hut on Blood Hill," he grinned, clambering up the other side of the ditch towards the weald's edge. "Now the evenings are long, the nights are hot and men are restless. This will all pass over by harvest time." He let out a small laugh, but it died in his throat as we saw Grimstan's face, sharp with purpose, slither out of the gloom.

"Creature of Hell! You will answer to the holy law of God!" the priest screamed, storming into the house. "Vile demon! Come out of the shadows!" The mob fell into a disappointed silence and I heard Ragnald chuckling quietly to himself as Grimstan raged out of the house, angrier than ever. "This devil has transformed himself into a low beast of the night! He crawls among us! Seek him out and stamp the life from him!" Some among the crowd looked puzzled, while others shuffled about stamping their feet and bashing their sticks on the ground.

"Goodbye Wulfred. I'll see you again before long," whispered Ragnald's voice as he scuttled into the black undergrowth, his footfalls quickly silenced among the new leaves of the forest. A few dim silhouette figures were poking around the woodpiles and the back of the house.

"The Son of God will return to us, and the rule of Heaven will return to this world with him. But only when we have scoured His kingdom of heathen filth!" Grimstan raised an improvised cross made from a broken axe shaft tied across an old spear. The crowd stabbed their blazing torches at the sky and cried out for Ragnald's death. To avoid their searching eyes, I backed a little way into the forest, crept along a rough pathway and emerged from the trees and the ditch at their backs.

"Wulfred?" a voice called out and I saw Father Cuthred shuffling towards me. "Is Ragnald safely gone?"

"Long gone," I lied, wary of listening ears. "Is this what God demands men do?"

"No," Cuthred sighed. "This is the work of Grimstan's ambition and it saddens me that he has the support of the Holy Church."

I peered around again at the crowd's faces. Among them were many men scarred by brands and some with ears and noses mutilated from past encounters with justice. As Ragnald had said, these were Sigered's men.

"I wanted my father to stop this," I muttered.

"I hoped that I might stop them," said Cuthred. "I told Grimstan to let Ragnald be – that it is for God alone to judge such men as he. But Grimstan hears only the voices in his head and he believes them to speak the word of God." He sighed again and looked up to where the stars were obscured by the light of burning torches.

"This beast offended the Lord of Heaven with the pagan spells he used against the son of our earthly lord Sigered," screeched Grimstan's voice. "I witnessed this dreadful thing and only my

126

ceaseless prayers saved Lord Richard's life. Now the heathen must answer to God!"

"Your father was wise to stand aside," said Cuthred. "A man accused of using heathen magic - sadly such things are common. But a lord of men cannot risk standing against the will of the Church."

With Ragnald safely gone, I started to think my father might have acted wisely after all, but then Grimstan clambered up onto a log pile. His face loomed red, thin and scowling in the firelight. He held the shaft of his cross before him in both hands.

"The Devil has fled and the spirit of our saviour Jesus Christ is with us!" he howled. "But his whore still brings shame upon our Christian souls! She must taste the fire of holy justice! The land will be made clean! The glory of Heaven will descend to Earth!"

The crowd bellowed and pushed one another in every direction until Grimstan leapt down and led the way.

"No!" wailed Cuthred, hurrying into the mob in search of anyone who might listen to reason. "Brichteva is little more than a child - she knows nothing of..." He was cut short by a blow from a sword-pommel on the side of his head. It was dealt by a hard-faced, wiry man with a livid half-circle branded onto his forehead. The crowd rushed on after Grimstan and I bent down to help Cuthred to his feet. The swordsman had lashed out wildly, cutting a shallow gash in the old man's temple. Had he troubled to aim the blow, it could have killed. The priest stammered and mumbled as I hauled him staggering back up the hill towards my father's house.

Lord Saxmund sat hunched over his table. My mother was sweeping ash from the hearth. Oswold chopped logs into smaller kindling to drown the uneasy silence of the house and the sounds of Grimstan's followers shouting and tramping along the planked

127

pathway through the heart of the village. My father took one look at Cuthred's bloody head and assumed that I was to blame.

"What in the name of almighty God have you done?" he cried, rising from his seat as we tumbled in through the doorway.

"They've gone after Brichteva," I gasped, breathless from half-carrying Cuthred. "They'll kill her if they find her."

"What has happened to Father Cuthred?" he demanded. My mother brought a cloth to wipe the blood out of Cuthred's eyes and helped him up from the floor where I had dropped him.

"One of Grimstan's men hit him with a sword hilt," I explained. "They've gone after Brichteva. They'll kill her."

"Where is Ragnald?"

"Ragnald is in the weald. Ragnald is safe as you said he'd be. They've turned on Brichteva."

"Father Cuthred, what has happened? Has my son's interference made things worse?"

With an unsteady hand, Cuthred pushed away the cup my mother held to his lips. "Your son did nothing but help me," he murmured. My father looked at me doubtfully.

"Brichteva has harmed nobody," said my mother.

"To those men, she might as well be the Devil himself," muttered the priest, making the sign of the cross.

"The fire of holy justice. That's what that bastard Grimstan said." It was not the proper way to speak of a priest, but nobody objected.

"We have to stop them." It was Oswold who spoke. My father and I looked at him and he seemed to regret opening his mouth. A long silence followed. Slowly, my father walked back to the bench and slumped down on his seat. As if he was cast in lead, he

128

struggled to lift his head and look at me. His eyes were like ash in the morning.

"I cannot intervene," he mumbled. "Ragnald knew what he did at Sigered's house might lead to this."

"What Ragnald did at Sigered's house saved you from losing half this estate in weregild," I protested. "Brichteva is accused of nothing. You must protect your people!"

"I cannot act," he groaned. "Only the laws of men are forged from reason and justice. The laws of God come from holy books and the whims of priests, but they are mightier. No man can defy the Church."

I struggled to believe the things I heard. For the first time in my life I was ready to fight in anger and I wanted my father at my side as we faced our foes. But he only gazed down at the table to avoid my eyes. Cuthred and my mother stared at me as if pleading with me to understand.

I looked at Oswold. Oswold knew right from wrong. Surely he would stand up against those who brought murder among us. But Oswold just shook his head. His father had spoken and the dutiful son would not defy him. I gave him a hateful look then, because he was closer to me than any man and he should have stood beside me. He lowered his eyes to the axe and the log that hung uselessly in his hands. Outside in the night, the crowd's chanting rose again and there was the sound of a commotion somewhere nearby. Despite the warmth of the spring evening and the glow of the hearth, a chill ran through me as I realised I was alone.

I stamped across the floor, kicked open a wooden trunk and lifted out my swordbelt. The blade was there as always, hanging from the belt in its leather sheath, its copper and silver-laced pommel gleaming in the soft light. So many times my father had ordered me to wear the sword at feasts and occasions when he wanted me to look like the son of a lord, not some vagabond of the wild hills. Even at Riaburh, on the very edge of battle, I had been reluctant to strap the belt on and its weight had hung on me like a curse. For the first time my father saw me take up the sword willingly. I looked at him, and at Oswold, but still they did not move. Buckling on the belt as I went, I left the house again.

The leather scabbard beat against my leg as I ran out into the darkened village. Grimstan's mob was heading back towards the cottage at the weald's edge, but a few familiar faces were emerging from darkened houses.

"Lord Wulfred!" It was Brichteva's father. His name was Edwy and he was known for the tender care he gave our cattle, from the birth of the calves to the slaughter time. But his face was bruised and there was blood at his mouth and matting his greying hair that night. He clutched a heavy sickle and wore a wild and murderous expression. "Grimstan has taken my daughter. I must speak with your father."

"My father..." I began, but I chose to make no excuses for him. "Come with me," I said instead. "We'll deal with this." I glanced briefly at the other men who had gathered around me – Godric was there, and Brichteva's brothers and uncles, and three or four more villagers. They carried clubs and axes and the darkness in their faces filled me with determination. Blind courage is a fool's virtue, but with these men at my side I felt ready to face Grimstan and his host.

We hurried between the little vegetable gardens that edged the field beside the hall, stopped behind a hedge that overlooked Ragnald's house and I glanced over my shoulder. My little warband were there at my heels. Godric knelt beside me as I peered into the gloom. Grimstan's followers had dragged their captive to the woodpiles. Tallow flares threw sparks into the black sky and light across their faces. I searched for Brichteva among the crowd and Edwy looked at me expectantly, as if I should know exactly what to do. A ring of torches formed outside Ragnald's house and the priest's voice screeched from its centre.

"Kneel, witch! Kneel before the judgement of almighty God! Where is the demon called Ragnald?"

"Touch me and I'll tear your cock off!" Brichteva screamed back. "You're a worm and Ragnald will crush you!"

"Where is he? Where is the devil you lie with?"

"He watches you, priest. You'll hang yourself from a noose of your own guts rather than face his vengeance."

There was a sudden sound of scuffling, of slaps and punches. Then, in a flash of red hair and rage, I saw Brichteva dragged by four men to the far side of the circle. Although she was lightly built, she had a spirit far greater than her stature and she fought like a vixen at its den. Grimstan strutted over and pulled her up by the hair. I saw the torchlight glance off Edwy's sickle as he pointed its blade at the priest. I drew my sword and felt its calm movement in my hand. The unsuspecting wall of backs that we faced would break, I knew that immediately. These were people who had fled from debts or justice and sought refuge in working for the church. There was nothing among them that possessed the grace or the otherworldly power of my sword. Its blade would flash and fly in the flamelight and Grimstan's mob would break, with Godric and the others to chase them out of our village.

Brichteva screamed. It was a scream of anger rather than pain and I heard the answering howls of at least two men.

"Fire!" Grimstan raged. "Pile the wood and light a fire. We'll burn the heathen's whore in his own filthy hole." The crowd roared and cursed. Grimstan dragged Brichteva across the circle of torches and hateful faces, holding the spearhead of his cross at her back, and threw her into Ragnald's cottage. A tall man with a thick staff moved to guard the door while others threw logs on to a pile.

131

A few stars had begun to shine in the blackening sky. Briefly, I thought of the eyes of my ancestors watching from across the great void of forgotten years. A breeze stirred the leaves of the weald's edge, touching my face like a cool hand. And with a quick gesture to tell the others to follow, I leapt over the hedge and ran as fast as I could at that line of unsuspecting backs.

It was like Riaburh, when I had panicked my foes with arrows and then charged at them alongside the Bloodhelms of Glowcestre, feeling like a god in control of the whole world. I remembered that day as I glided swift and silent over the cold grassy ground. There were only a dozen men at my back, against a mob of fifty, but the battle-rage told me that such odds would only make my victory greater. The enemy expected no fight, and when blades and cudgels stormed out of the black night, they would run as if the demons of Hell were biting at their britches.

I heard howls of anger from the men behind me and a few heads among the crowd began to turn. Faces moved, fast and frightened, but they moved too late to stop me. Choosing the back of a head that still stared dully at the growing pyre, I sprang forward and hammered my sword pommel into it. The man fell like a cornstalk at harvest time and, as I had expected, the mob stumbled apart before me. I wheeled around, scything the air with my sword to check anyone who might have regained their balance. And, leaving them to my followers, I raced for the doorway of the house.

"Out of the way!" I yelled at the man with the staff, swinging my blade at his head. He lurched aside and I kicked open the door.

Inside the cottage the fire still flickered. And in its weak light I saw Grimstan, his pointed face scratched and bloody, pinning Brichteva down on the floor. He pushed her face into the dusty planks and ripped her skirts up over her buttocks. His own priest's cassock was already hitched above his belt. Brichteva spat and growled and as the priest tried to force himself between her legs, she twisted her head around to bite his hand. Grimstan snatched the

132

hand away and brought it down as a fist high on her back, knocking the breath out of her.

"Leave her alone, priest!" I shouted, and he flung himself across the floor. His spear was rammed upright between two of the floorboards, but just a little too far away from him. I kicked his head as he dived for it then lashed out at the weapon, sending it clattering away to the wall. Brichteva leapt up and ran for the door. As Grimstan fell, I dived on him and dragged him to his feet, pushing my swordpoint into the small of his back. He was scrawny and feeble and although he tried to writhe away, I could easily grip him by the neck with one hand. My throat was too dry to insult him so I just I hauled him roughly out of the house to face Brichteva and her father and whatever remained of his mob.

But there was no sign of the men who had charged at my back – just the sound of scuffling and shouting from the darkness beyond the circle. My followers - probably undone by the warning their voices had given - had failed to follow me. The ranks of torchlit faces remained - confused now, but still simmering with hatred. Brichteva was pinned down again by the weight of three men. There was blood on her clothes – probably enough priest's blood for any Church court to hang her.

"Let her go!" The fear I had felt none of before suddenly came surging back and I heard my voice croak rather than shout. "Let her go or the priest will die!" Every face looked coldly at me. Grimstan breathed hard in my grip and struggled to regain a little dignity by unhitching his cassock from his belt to cover his wilting cock. Threatening to slay a priest was a rash move, but in that moment it was all I could think of.

"You kill the priest and we will kill you." A heavily built man with long moustaches and a big axe stepped forward to face me. I recognised the axe. It was one of Ragnald's - a tree-felling blade. Although it was a woodsman's tool, it was similar in size to the feared Dane axes of the Vikings – a shaft the height of a tall man and a blade that could behead a horse. The axeman stepped forward into the circle as if to challenge me and I wondered who he was. Over his plain brown tunic he wore a jerkin of padded leather - the kind of thing a farmer might wear for protection when called on to fight in the fyrd. There was no brand or mutilation to mark him as an outlawed man, but he was clearly no nobleman either. But he was tall, standing a good head above most of Grimstan's followers, and his anger was ice-cold.

"God will strike you down - you and the witch," piped another voice from the crowd. "You're going to Hell!"

"The priest tried to rape her!" I shouted back. "Would you work the will of such a man?"

"We do what God wills." The voice came from somewhere to my left, but the whole circle grunted in agreement. I spat out the strands of Grimstan's hair, which had caught in my mouth as we fought.

"The witch will die," said the man with the axe, his voice like a frost among thorn trees. "Will you die with her?" If he was a fyrdman, he was not one who had passed through Ellasham.

"Ragnald has stood no trial!" I pushed the sword harder against Grimstan's back, hoping he looked suitably terrified as he arched away from it. "And you have nothing to accuse Brichteva of!"

"She's a witch, a pagan's whore. She drew the blood of a priest." The axeman said dismissively. "Let Father Grimstan go and maybe you will die by iron and not by fire." He lifted the axe with the confidence of a man who had killed before, but I gathered my courage and threw him a questioning look.

"I am Skerne the Heathens' Bane," he smiled coldly. "I have slain pagans in the lands of the north and in Ireland. And now almighty God commands that I cleanse the filth from this pig shed of a village." The crowd cheered him on and called for my blood. Skerne was a Norse name, from the land where the pagans had been converted at swordpoint and with much slaughter less than a lifetime ago. The Heathens' Bane was clearly something he had made up and I baulked at being cowed by a man vain enough to invent his own name.

But the crowd were closing in on me, and death stalked a little nearer with every heartbeat. I shook Grimstan by the neck.

"The priest will die!" I stammered. I felt my sword point cut into his skin. He whined and his bowels emptied in a rush of terror. The axeman grinned again. With Grimstan under the sword, he had become their leader. If I slew the priest, the sin would be mine to account for and theirs to avenge. I remembered how my father had talked of a good death as the year dawned in snow and omens, but the only good thing I could think about death was the faint chance that it might not happen now.

I ought to kill Grimstan, I thought. He deserved to die. If I killed him before the axeman came close, then maybe I could recover my blade in time to fight. Then fifty crazed maniacs would fall upon the priest-killer. Perhaps avenging a priest's death was an even surer route to Heaven than obeying one. I watched the axe blade swing lazily through the air a few times. There were beads of sweat running down my neck. That axe was a clumsy weapon, but if Skerne had a warrior's skills he could be deadly with it.

"He'll cut your liver out and feed it to the pigs," Brichteva howled. Someone struck her across the face with a log and she screamed. My sweat was cold on the sword's hilt. The crowd began to chant for my blood. Grimstan, probably feeling certain of his doom, whimpered a prayer. I tensed my sword arm, ready to drive the weapon through his back then twist it free to defend myself. Perhaps I could slip around the side of the cottage and escape into the trees. It would not save Brichteva, of course, but maybe she would get away in the confusion. If I thrust Grimstan's bleeding body at my attacker, it might buy me a little more time to get away.

"Ready to meet God?" I whispered in the priest's ear. To slay a priest in cold blood was a death sentence in itself, but my mind was

135

reeling in a world already ruled by death. The axeman stepped closer. His eyes were pale and without feeling. The faces of the crowd burned with anger. They were banging out a rhythm with their feet and the shafts of their makeshift weapons. The world beyond their dreadful circle seemed like a lost dream. The future was short, black, filled with panic and pain and it would begin in the moment that Grimstan's body fell from my sword. My arm felt suddenly weak and the blade heavy. The priest's life was the only thing that stood in death's way.

But as the heathen-slayer raised the axe to his shoulder, a clash of weapons broke out among the crowd to my left.

"Stand aside," someone shouted. A couple of men were knocked to the ground and a black and red-painted shield appeared where they had stood. Then suddenly it was my father's face, scowling in the torchlight, to which the crowd turned. He growled as he swung his sword around to clear a way through the mob. Oswold followed him, with Godric and the others close behind.

"Let my daughter go," shouted Edwy. The men who were holding her glanced nervously at Grimstan and Skerne.

"Let her go!" my father roared at them.

"Who are you to bend the will of God?" Skerne sneered.

"I'm Saxmund, King Harold's thane and Lord of this place. What you do in Ellasham you do with my blessing or with my sword at your throat." He raised his sword up in the dancing torchlight for all to see where his authority came from. A small man with flapping arms and an indignant expression stepped forward to speak.

"You allowed the heathen to work his spells. You bade him use witchcraft to take the life of Richard, the merchant's son. When you do such things, you forfeit lordship." A murmur of agreement started, but the indignant man had spoken unwisely. My father

136

grabbed his groin in a mailed fist and twisted viciously. The man shrieked, fell to the ground and lay there gasping.

"Speak again and I'll tear them off!" my father shouted. Then he turned back to the men holding Brichteva. "Now let her go!" He pointed his sword at them and all the rage he had earlier hidden throbbed in his voice. The men he addressed looked desperate to obey, but the axeman was not yielding.

"Servant to England's king you might be," he mocked "but you're nothing in the eyes of..."

"Oswold! Kill him!" my father roared. "Rip the bastard's belly out!" Oswold advanced hesitantly, but Skerne stepped towards him swinging the big blade with a wild cackle. For a heartbeat or two they sized each other up, then the big man raised his axe and howled out as he rushed forward. His howl became a scream of agony as Godric smashed his knee with a low cudgel stroke. Oswold stamped hard on Skerne's belly until he vomited, then held his sword at the man's throat. As one, the crowd began to edge back. My father hissed a vicious laugh, spat in their direction and turned to me.

"And Wulfred, you fool, drop that piece of dung."

"When they free Brichteva," I growled. I pulled Grimstan onto the point of my sword again, just to let him know that death was still close. Edwy picked up the fallen axe and joined my father, advancing on the three men who had held his daughter down. But already they were trying to melt into the crowd. For a moment I tightened my grip on Grimstan's neck, but I knew now that the priest would survive the night and I was as relieved as he.

"Release him!" my father ordered again. "We do not slay priests. God shall be his judge." With the hilt of my sword, I punched Grimstan hard between the shoulders, the way he had hit Brichteva earlier. He collapsed onto the trodden soil and struggled to his knees under the disappointed looks of his followers, but he could rise no further and just knelt there whimpering for breath.

Edwy draped a cloak around his daughter's shoulders and led her back into the dark village. She clutched him tightly, her defiance suddenly gone and her eyes shining with the fear she had fought so well. And around its fringes, the crowd prepared to fade into the night as Lord Saxmund's voice roared out again.

"You who serve the rat Sigered and the turd Grimstan when you should be serving your king with the fyrd, crawl back to your hovels and never dare to soil my land with your footfalls again." His face that had seemed so grey in the house that evening now burned with the joy of victory. "And step forward the worm who struck Father Cuthred."

"Him," I added. I had seen the wiry man branded with a half circle and I pointed my sword at him before he could edge away into the shadows. The frightened crowd pushed him forward and he stood limply before my father, all the hatred that had burned in his face replaced by whimpering fear. Cuthred also stepped forward, a bandage tied around his head.

"I have forgiven this man," he pleaded. "And if he repents and lives in virtue, God will forgive him too. Already too much blood has been shed tonight."

"If God has any wisdom at all, he will forgive none of them!" Cuthred winced as my father's blasphemy echoed against the black walls of the sky. "Draw your sword, outlaw. Let's see who God truly favours." Grimstan, still hunched and abject on the ground in front of me, raised his head and breathed in sharply to speak. But whether he would have spoken up for his follower I did not wait to find out. I kicked the priest down with the heel of my boot and he kept quiet.

The branded man was terrified. He looked fit and his sword looked like a well-forged blade. But he did not look like a man with a lifetime of fighting behind him and my father sensed his fear.

"Did you kill a warrior in battle, or did you steal that sword from a better man than yourself? Is that how you got your outlaw's brand?"

"I fought the Welsh," he said, the desperation hint quivering in his voice.

"When you carry a sword, outlaw, you proclaim yourself a warrior. It is more than feeble old priests you must fight." He threw down his shield to make the fight fairer and stamped impatiently on the ground. "My blade is called Skullbreaker," he hissed. "And she has earned that name many times over." He gave a dreadful grin full of promised death and tapped himself lightly on the side of the head with the flat of the sword. The branded man glanced at his own sword and I could see the sweat of fear shining on his face

"This is not the way of law," he said. "I did the priest wrong. Let him name my penance."

Renewed anger flared across my father's face. "You are marked as an outlaw. The law does not protect you!" he shouted, and he lunged forward with the sword Skullbreaker. With a speed that surprised me, the outlawed man parried the blow. The ring of faces – Grimstan's few remaining followers and people from the village who had come out to watch once danger had passed - looked on expectantly.

My father made a short stab at the outlaw's belly. The leaner man stepped aside, again more speedily than I would have expected, but he missed the chance to attack my father's briefly exposed left side. They faced each other and shuffled sideways in the silent ring.

My father stabbed again and again. Every time, his wiry opponent dodged aside, but failed to get in the quick counter-stroke that could have saved him. When their swords clashed, Lord Saxmund raised his knee hard into his foe's belly. The outlaw stumbled back and fell. He rolled away as my father came after him. When he stood, he was backed against the wall of Ragnald's cottage. He did not have time to parry the stab my father aimed hard

139

into his neck to take his soul. There was a moment when death seemed to choose its victim. Whether my father cried in triumph or whether the sword itself screamed for blood was impossible to tell. But the blade did not feast. The outlaw slipped sideways to the ground and rolled again. The sword stabbed with a brittle sound into the dry mud and wattles of the wall and the other man scrambled out from under my father's legs. He took a firm grip on his sword as he sprang to his feet, ready to strike before his opponent could free his blade. Splintered wood flew, then sparks tore into the darkness as my father dragged Skullbreaker from the wall and into a vicious parry. The outlaw winced as the blades collided, but he had proved that he was not as weak in battle as we expected. His eyes glanced around, looking for open space. He knew that to keep moving was his best chance of staying alive and that staying alive might lead his opponent into a clumsy mistake. My father lunged his blade at the man's shoulder. He dodged again, and this time he got in with a swift counterstroke that my father had to twist awkwardly to avoid. He stumbled, twisted his knee and kept his balance only with difficulty.

Oswold whispered to me. "He's tiring - he's limping already."

"Surely not," I whispered back. "He never limps when there's fighting to be done."

But my brother was right. That stumble must have jarred his leg and now he dragged it behind him while the branded man danced around seeking a weakness. My father grunted and lashed out at his midriff. It was an easy blow to dodge, but instead the outlaw chose to bring his own sword up to meet my father's. The crashing of steel was answered by the screech of an owl in the forest.

I glanced at Oswold again and it was obvious from his face that he felt the same fear and doubt as me. Because our father had stumbled back again and now the outlaw looked him in the eyes. His fear had fled and suddenly he was master of the field. Torchlight caught his face, his hard eyes shone wolflike. For such a man to kill a king's thane in combat was a great feat indeed and the law could not touch him as my father had already placed the fight in the hands of God. Now he bared his teeth and growled. And now he advanced. He stabbed and cut. My father hobbled back across the woodyard, his breathing hard and the sweeping arcs of his sword growing clumsier. Oswold nudged me with his elbow. He wanted to intervene, but I shook my head. No proud warrior such as he would wish to be saved dishonourably on the field of combat. And yet there was no mercy in the outlaw's eyes, and I knew that in the end neither of us could stand back and let our father be slaughtered.

Again he retreated from his opponent's blade, limping back to the cottage wall. I saw the glimmer of steel at my side and Oswold's sword was in his hand. The outlaw swung his sword in a great swipe that could have taken our father's head from his shoulders, had not Skullbreaker caught it low, close to the hilt, with a sudden twist that sent it flailing from the man's grip. The crowd, villagers and Grimstan's men alike, gasped as one, then held their breath as the outlaw dived across the ground and recovered his blade. My father should have chased him and cut him down before he reached the weapon, but he just leant weakly against the wall, his hair tangled in the splintered wood from his earlier blow.

Enraged, his foe snatched up his sword and charged back at him. He let out a howl of victory and brought down his blade again. Oswold began to run across the woodyard and I followed him. But this time, my father stepped forward. Springing away from the wall, he met the outlaw head on. He beat his sword aside with a two handed blow. Then, balancing on the leg that a moment ago he had seemed barely able to touch to the ground, he kicked the man down and at the same time smashed Skullbreaker deep into his left shoulder with a terrible crunching of bone. Oswold and I were still five or six paces from them. The outlaw hit the ground and screamed. Then, grunting with pain, he tried to push himself up using his sword arm.

A heavy silence fell over the watching crowd, broken only by the wounded man's tortured breaths. Oswold and I stood as if

141

frozen, waiting for Skullbreaker to make its kill. Clouds drifted apart and a sickle moon silvered the bright-leaved forest. Finally my father spoke.

"God has made his judgement!" he said in a loud, clear voice. "Ragnald is a friend to myself and to my people. If the priest Grimstan has a case to bring against him, then let him bring him - if he can find him now - before the chosen men of our shire for judgement. Let him stand trial according to our laws. The priest Cuthred is my friend also. A man who strikes Cuthred strikes me." He pressed his sword against the skin of the outlaw's throat and the injured man withered under Lord Saxmund's glare. His left arm trailed like something dead and blood soaked his mangled shoulder and his chest. We all waited for him to speak.

"I am sorry for what I did," he eventually gasped. "Father Grimstan said..." He glanced at the dishevelled figure of Grimstan, huddled on the ground then he thought better of it. He alone had wounded Cuthred and to lay the blame on another would have been cowardly. "Please have mercy," he whimpered instead.

"Mercy is for the weak to give and receive!" muttered my father. He smiled cruelly as he lifted and flexed the leg he had pretended was lame. For a few more heartbeats, another great silence fell. Again we waited for the killing blow.

"All that you own, outlaw, now belongs to Father Cuthred. That is my judgement. And your life..." He let those words hang in the air. Would my father kill a man already broken and beaten?

"Please, Lord," the man sobbed.

My father watched the thick pulses of blood running down the fallen man's chest and grinned through his broken teeth. "You placed your life in the hands of God and there it will remain. Grimstan's prayers did nothing to save Richard when my son's sword took his arm. Let's see what they can do for you."

He wiped the blood from his blade and slipped it back into the sheath. The last of Grimstan's followers slipped away, one man helping the limping Skerne. The wounded outlaw screamed as two more men tried to pick him up. His arm was hanging by shreds of flesh and the wound was a horror of shattered bone.

Wordlessly, my father turned to walk away and beckoned Oswold and I to follow. Grimstan struggled to his feet. He looked at me with curses in his eyes, but I still had my sword in hand and he stank of his own shit. I spoke first.

"Will you go bragging to your bishop about what you tried to do tonight? Does he reward murder and rape?"

"You are doomed. Hell will be your reward for this," he mumbled, but his voice was broken and he hurried quickly away.

"Wulfred!" my father called. "Leave that priest alone. You've made enough trouble already."

"Would you rather they'd killed Brichteva?" I protested, running to catch up with him. The night was suddenly cold as if the chill of winter had returned.

"I would rather have not made an enemy of that bastard. Maybe he'll think twice before running to his bishops, but he'll forget nothing."

We walked home in silence. I tried to thank my father for intervening – for saving my life - but he shrugged me aside and walked more quickly. The wounded man cried out again as he was carried from the village.

I had an uneasy feeling in my stomach. A heavy, empty feeling, like hunger - like a hunger that might never go away. And although the house was warm, I found it hard not to shiver. My father pulled off his boots in silence and before he climbed the ladder to the sleeping loft he turned to me with an unreadable expression.

"You showed your courage tonight," he said. But he growled the words through gritted teeth and made them sound like a reprimand.

"You did what was right, Wulfred," Oswold said, but the shadow of his father's anger lay across him and he retired to his curtained bed at the back of the house without another word.

Instead of trying to sleep, I sat by the hearth with my mother and told her what had happened at Ragnald's cottage. She listened in silence, sometimes watching my eyes as I spoke, sometimes staring into the embers of the hearth.

"Oswold was right," she eventually said. "You did what you should have done."

"He doesn't seem to think so," I muttered, gesturing towards where my father lay. I kept my voice down, not knowing whether he was asleep. "And Grimstan still lives while another man will probably die because of his meddling."

"But Brichteva would have been murdered. The man your father fought knew what a man risks when he carries a sword. He knew as well as you did." I realized that I had thought very little of what I risked when I drew my sword earlier that evening. She untied the linen scarf she wore on her head and the gold and silver of her hair fell down her back. For a shattered fragment of a moment I remembered her hair flying in the twisting firelight at Llyn Rhydderch as she fought for her life so many years ago. She reached forward and poured out a cup of mead from a jar warmed at the fireside.

"Mead?" I asked. My father had always insisted that good mead was a reward for hard fighting and was only fit for feasts and celebrations.

"You'll need it to sleep tonight." my mother smiled. "Your father said that if you returned alive, then you should drink a warrior's drink." She smiled again, fondly mocking his words.

144

"But he was angry with me."

"He was angry that he could not defy the priest. All his life, your father has fought for his king and his lords, never for what he believed in." I must have looked puzzled. "Tonight he had to defy the Church in order to save his brave and foolish son. If he is angry, it is only because you made him do what he should have chosen to do."

We sat in silence for a long time, staring into the glowing hearth and listening to the sounds of night beyond the walls. The cries of owls echoed softly across the dark fields and the river gurgled away, snaking south under the trailing willows. Death had come close to Ellasham that night and death was still out there in the darkness. I struggled with the grey dawning knowledge that another great change had slipped into my life. Finally, I found some rough words for it.

"Before we fought at Riaburh, Father always thought me a coward, and that never troubled me. But now I don't know what I am." My mother laid a hand on my shoulder. The embers crackled and I swallowed some more of the sweet mead.

"You're a man, Wulfred," she sighed. "Men are restless. They see enemies everywhere. Some men fight for their lords, some for themselves and some fight for those too weak to defend themselves."

"But there are enemies," I said. "Should we be blind to them? Should we let people suffer and die?" She stirred the embers with a spoon handle.

"No," she sighed. "Men are not always wrong to fight. But it makes me sad that only being blind to the world can make them happy."

7. SUMMER

"Stand your ground! Hold the line!" The fyrdman facing me
looked up, distracted by my orders to the men at my side and I hit
him on the head, knocking off his leather cap as he obediently fell
to the ground in feigned death. But the men on either side of me
were in trouble. Half of them slipped over as the charge hit them
and Oswold's men drove through our right flank. Warriors wear
nailed boots, which can grip even on wet grass. Fyrdmen and
villagers do not. Fyrdmen and villagers fall over if they are ordered
to hold a shield wall. I shouted at my remaining men to turn and
face a threat now storming in from two sides. I also trod on
Godric's foot and he cursed loudly. Pushing Godric aside with his
shield, one of Oswald's men, weasel-faced with concentration,
poked me on the shoulder with his pole, I dropped and they seemed
to regard that as enough of a victory, grounding their weapons with
a burst of cheering and whooping.

It was midsummer. The sun's wheel was as wide as it would
ever be and the shadows of evening stretched further and further
into the night as if to touch the light of dawn. And Earl Leofwin had
sent word that he would be passing through Ellasham on a journey
to the west, joining us for the feast of St. John the Baptist. My
father had decided that the fyrdmen should entertain the earl and his
retinue with a display of their military skill. So Oswold and I were
practising with them – Oswold leading our visiting fyrdmen and I
leading the men of the village as one side formed a shield wall and
the other charged it, wielding long poles for spears and shorter
sticks for swords and axes.

"I don't see why we have to pretend to fight for the earl. It's his
men who are the warriors – they should do this while we drink,"
said Godric, nursing his bruised foot. Godric's enthusiasm for

battle, I had learned, began and ended with the idea of looting silver from the bodies of fallen warriors.

But only Godric was complaining. The rest of the men helped each other up and laughed and talked and fought among themselves with their poles and their flimsy shields. Many had never seen an earl before and they were keen to do their best for him.

"And what about the wheat and the barley?" Godric moaned. "We'll go hungry this winter because we ran around with sticks while the fields were choked with weeds."

"The Earl's bringing two of his daughters," I said, and Godric's face glowed briefly with gap-toothed lechery. Then he scowled again as he used his pole to push himself to his feet.

"Not even a lord like you stands a chance of getting inside an earl's daughter!" he grumbled. "If he'd bring a few of Lunden's whores with him, then it might be worth all this. Why's he bringing them here anyway?"

"To find them husbands among the idle and ill-favoured of Wessex?" Oswold grinned. He had dropped his shield and stick to help roll a barrel of ale up to the hall.

"Wear your best breeches, Godric – that pair with only one leg chewed by rats," called out another man struggling with the heavy barrel. Godric pulled a sour face. I slapped him on the back and told him to cheer up.

"It's not every day we have princesses of Wessex come to feast with us. If either of them drinks like their father you might have a chance."

"Princesses of Wessex!" he muttered. "The way the spawn of old Godwin breed, Wessex must have more princesses than it has dungheaps."

Earl Leofwin came early in the afternoon. Two horsemen crossed the ford near Eohric's old cottage and announced the imminent arrival of their lord. My father greeted them as men who had fought at his side at Riaburh, though they did not much resemble the scruffy warband of a few weeks before. They wore bright blue cloaks embroidered with hawks and eagles; their hair and beards were trimmed, their shields newly painted and their sword-hilts, buckles and cloakpins flashed in the bright sunlight.

My father had ordered Oswold and I to don our war gear to impress the earl, so we stood sweating in heavy mail, padded leather and helmets, clutching spears and with shields slung across our backs while Leofwin and his retinue thundered through the shallow river and into Ellasham. He had twenty or so warriors with him and they too had been scrubbed up since their stumbling battle at Riaburh. Some even looked slimmer and stronger. Perhaps they had been training with the fyrd like Oswold and I. Leofwin, I supposed, had no intention of letting his nephew's men outshine him in battle again.

"Not too many of them," My father muttered approvingly. He had been grumbling darkly all morning about the calf and the two half-grown pigs that had been slaughtered to feed the earl and his followers.

Leofwin himself rode at the head of the column, with his usual careless smile, the hawk banner carried at his side and his gorse-bright hair streaming behind him. And at the rear was the carriage in which his daughters rode. I call it a carriage, because it was a small improvement on the old ox-drawn farm carts in which local lords dragged their womenfolk around. It was larger and sturdier, draped with cloth of blue and yellow, drawn by heavy horses and furnished with benches.

"Welcome to Ellasham Lord," my father called out as Leofwin reined his horse to a halt.

"My friends!" cried the earl, leaping down and staggering on the rough ground. "It's a fine thing to see you again. Ready for another battle, eh?" He rapped on my helmet with his knuckles and, unsteady on his feet and reeking of ale, embraced us all in turn. Then he stepped back, threw his arms wide and looked around in mock surprise at the groups of villagers gathered to greet his arrival. "All these men are in fine shape to serve in the fyrd," he said. "With Saxmund for a lord and his son Oswold, we expected to find a whole village of one-armed men." There was laughter among the earl's warriors. Tales of my father and brother's exploits off the field of battle must been spreading around Wessex. "And there is news from the north," he went on as one of the women brought him a cup of our best ale. "The rebel fleet is destroyed. The earls Edwin and Morcar trapped Tostig's men on the banks of the Humber and cut them to pieces."

"Ha!" my father cheered. "And what of Tostig himself?"

"My once-brother fled to Scotland with just a remnant of his force. What we began on the Leman's banks, my friends, the lords of the north have finished beside the Humber."

"This is great news," cried my father, smacking Leofwin and I hard on the back with his mailed gloves.

"Could he persuade the Scots king to attack us?" I asked.

"He can try. But he'll have no luck there."

"The Scots fear us," explained Leofwin. "Their kingdom still cowers in the shadow of Brunnanburh, and well it might. The Wessex of Athelstan lives on." He raised a clenched fist and his men cheered again.

The battle of Brunnanburh had taken place over a hundred years before – when Wessex had stood alone and triumphed against an alliance of Scots, Welsh, Irish and Vikings. The Scots had paid homage to King Athelstan afterwards and although they no longer

149

bowed before a Saxon king, the ire of Wessex was still something they feared.

"So the north is safe and we turn our spears towards the ships of Normandy," my father grinned.

"Aye, into the bellies of our foes," roared the earl, grabbing my spearshaft and shaking it at the sky. "They say the Bastard Duke has a thousand ships ready to carry his war host to our shores, and more still being built. My brother the king has commanded that the warriors and fyrd of Wessex must march to the coast before this month is out to keep a watch on the sea roads and make ready to defend the kingdom." My father and Oswold smiled at each other as their hands shifted to their sword hilts.

"My daughters!" the earl suddenly shouted as if he had just remembered they were there. "You must meet my daughters." The two girls dutifully stepped down from the cart and were introduced to us. My father immediately looked embarrassed. Apart from my mother, I hardly ever saw him talk to a woman. Oswold flashed me a sly grin.

"Herlesa and Aelfwyn," Leofwin slurred, waving his arms around and not making it clear which was which, "I present to you Saxmund, my shield-brother of many battles, and his sons Wulfred, who fought like a wild fucking bastard at Riaburh, and Oswold whose spear ran with the blood of our foemen." My father grinned awkwardly while Oswold and I kissed the girls' hands and mumbled a few shy greetings. The earl was embarrassing, but I supposed young women admired the mighty warriors who would defend them from their enemies. One of the girls was tall, angular and severe. She looked like a particularly humourless nun. The other was shorter and very beautiful. Something about her was inseparable from the bright summer day. She smiled at me and I grinned foolishly until Oswold trod on my foot.

The girls were ordered back into their carriage by their father and Leofwin's warriors escorted them across the village and up to the hall. Through the dust kicked up by the horses, the pretty one waved at us, and the severe one looked at her disapprovingly.

The earl had brought a piper with him and a couple of the village men had drums made from pig and goat's skin stretched over wooden hoops. So once Cuthred had preached a solemn sermon about the baptism of Christ and about faith being the only sure route to Heaven, the ale barrels were tapped, the cooking fires lit and the doors of the hall were thrown open to let the warm air, scented by ripening barley, chase out the hungry old ghosts of winter.

The village girls had weary feet that day, as their menfolk, the fyrdmen and Leofwin's warriors all pushed and elbowed and tripped each other up in order to dance with them. Hildelyth and I whirled around the hall to the sound of the pipe and drums, spinning through the dust raised from the floor and the beams of sunlight flashing through gaps in the hall's high timbers. We laughed and stumbled our way through the doors and onto the sunlit field outside. Among the tussocks of grass there were groups of men singing bawdy songs, there was a wrestling match going on to the sounds of wild shouts of encouragement and there were men competing to throw bags of sand across the river and to run from one side of the village to the other carrying heavy logs. I looked around and wiped a few beads of sweat from my forehead. My mind was quickened by ale, the shadows of my destiny had been melted by the summer sun and I felt only the warmth and closeness of Hildelyth and the joy of being alive with her on that bright day. But when she looked at me there was no joy in her eyes, only a quiet anxiety that had made me want to hold her and to get away from her at the same time.

"Do you like the earl's daughters?" she asked in a small voice. She looked at me as if she was trying to shut out the rest of the world. It made everything else – the sun on the hillside, the singers and the drinkers, the wrestlers and the runners – all the more distracting.

151

"No," I lied too quickly – why did I lie to her? She had been my friend for as long as I could remember. There had never been a time when we could not speak the truth to each other. "They look like nuns." Hildelyth said nothing and I found myself awkwardly trying to fill in a strange silence that suddenly lay heavy amidst a day of celebration. "And anyway, their father is an earl. He'll want to find them princes for husbands." At first it had seemed like a good thing to say, but it made Hildelyth look away from me, which was somehow worse. And before I could say anything else, she wandered away saying she needed to speak to one of her cousins. At another time I would have gone with her, but now something unspoken rose between us to and as she turned her back I wanted again both to hold her and to get away.

The fyrd fought as the sun was sinking towards the weald, throwing the last of its light across a swallow-filled sky. We used a patch of flat ground behind the hall, having discovered earlier that if we fought on a slope, the side facing downhill always won. The women and children of the village gathered close to my shield wall, shouting encouragement to husbands and fathers. Leofwin and his warriors stood on the other side of our battlefield, making bets every time Oswold's fyrd charged at us on whether the shield wall would break this time.

Three times their wedge of thin shields and poles battered against us and three times the village men stood firm at my side and we beat off our attackers, to the cheering of the women and of those who had wagered silver against Oswold. Most of us were bruised and some men were bloodied as they picked themselves up to regroup. But they laughed and they smiled and they raised their shields in salute to us and prepared to do battle again.

As we faced them for the fourth time, Godric wiped the sweat from his face and muttered.

"If we just let them beat us we could get back to the ale. This time I'll get killed early, at least then I can lie down." The lowering sun had not yet brought the coolness of evening and the men were all wearing the thick caps and padded coats that would protect them in a real battle.

And the thoughts of Leofwin's men had also turned to those barrels waiting in the hall. On Oswold's fourth charge, a dozen warriors joined him, pounding along at the rear to push the fyrdmen hard into our line. They came straight at me, hoping that if I fell, my shield wall would sink into confusion.

"Men of Ellasham, let them hear you!" I called out as Oswold's men stumbled over the rough ground. My men all hollered out the name of our village, some called out my name and others just screamed in defiance. Oswold's charging men closed in fast and as they did so, Godric roared a shrill battlecry and leapt out of the line. Swinging his spearshaft like a man knocking apples out of a high tree, he bludgeoned a sour-faced faced man leading the charge, but as he did so three or four other spearshafts beat him about the chest and shoulders. The man who had stood behind Godric was not quick enough in taking his place and Oswold stormed to the front of the charge and crashed through the tiny gap in the shields. My headless spearshaft crunched into a shield and the weapons that had taken down Godric suddenly snaked in behind my own shield and under my exposed arm. As I fell to the ground I saw the line of men who had stood to my right collapse under the weight of the charge and for a while I lay among rushing, trampling feet listening to cries of victory and mock-death as the men enacted the thing which seasoned warriors long for and fear the most – the crazed slaughter of a broken army.

When Oswold's victory was complete, Earl Leofwin walked among the victors and the fallen, laughing and helping men to their feet, congratulating and commiserating. He hauled Godric up by the elbow and turned to face the rest of us.

"This man is the hero of this field of war," he bellowed. "He threw himself on the spears of the enemy to stop a charge and save the life of his lord." He gestured towards me and I gave him a quizzical look. I was certain that had not been Godric's intention. Godric shrugged his shoulders and smiled.

"Swegn," Leofwin called to one of his men. "Bring me that knife – the one you took from that Dane at Riaburh. This man must be rewarded for his bravery." One of Leofwin's warriors stepped forward. With a frown he unbuckled a sheathed knife from his belt and reluctantly handed it to his earl, who gave it to Godric.

"There my friend. A prize for your courage. Bury its blade deep in the foemen of Wessex."

"Thank you lord," said Godric, happily accepting the earl's praise. As Leofwin marched his men off to the hall for a night of meat and ale, Godric drew out the knife. The blade itself was strong and sharp, hilted plainly with rings of wood and iron. But the sheath was of thick, pale leather, edged with polished copper and engraved with a beautifully worked image of a hare in full flight over a furrowed field with a swirling sun floating above it. Wax and charcoal had been rubbed into the engraving to make it show more boldly. The men clustered around to look at it and to heap upon Godric more congratulation than he deserved.

A few of us lingered outside long into the evening. The hall was filled with the shouting of warriors, with fyrdmen basking in their drunken glory and with the heat of cooking fires. It was easy enough to wander in to get a plate of bread and meat and a jug of ale to share with a few friends, outside in the cooling air of a summer evening. As darkness was getting close I made my unsteady way, carrying a big empty jug, into the hall.

The ale barrels were balanced on strong frames behind the benches where Leofwin's warriors sat drinking and eating, their trimmed beards now running with ale and fat. I filled the jug,

154

jammed the wooden spike back into the barrel and turned to leave. But I had chosen my moment badly.

"I will sing for you," slurred the earl, rising to his feet and pressing his palms heavily into his bench for support. My father was sitting beside him and a stormy look passed across his face. "I shall sing the song of Aelfred." His warriors gave a cheer that was more dutiful than enthusiastic. The piper tried to strike up a tune, but he squeezed his bag too hard and let out a shrill farting sound. I glanced around, hoping I could slip out unnoticed in the moment of laughter that followed, but my father had seen me.

"Stay, Wulfred," he called out. "Stay a moment and hear the earl sing!" He did not quite grit his teeth, but there was a threatening look in his eye - the look of a man who was about to suffer and the more people that suffered with him, the better. Oswold sat, as dutiful as ever, with Leofwin and my father. My mother was at another bench with the earl's nun-like daughter and her servant girls. The daughter's face was very ghostly pale in the dim-lit hall. She looked as if she would be having a miserable time even if her father had not threatened to sing. The other daughter was nowhere to be seen – probably hidden behind the screen that had been put up at the far end of the hall to give the ladies some privacy. The piper got his bag under control and it began to parp something resembling a tune. And Earl Leofwin sang. He had a good voice – as deep and powerful as you would expect of such a man. But he struggled to remember the words. There are many songs of Aelfred, the king who drove the Vikings from Wessex, and most of them have thirty or forty verses. I thought about pretending I needed to go outside to vomit.

Leofwin's song seemed to go on for a very long time, with the earl's voice trailing off in confusion several times while his men stamped along, pounded their benches and joined in from time to time. In end, with the piper red in the face and the warriors weary of beating their feet on the floor, Leofwin bellowed a final verse and gave up before he had a chance to get muddled again. There was

155

wild applause and cheering as he slumped back onto his seat. Even the morose daughter clapped politely.

As I left the hall, I tripped on a broken plank and clutched flailingly at a doorpost for support. There was a quiet laugh somewhere nearby and I looked up to see the earl's other daughter smiling at my drunken stumbling.

For a moment I was held fast where I stood. Her eyes were dark, but they gleamed in the fading of the light and she looked back at me with a questioning and perfect smile.

"Aren't you one of Lord Saxmund's sons?" she smiled.

"I'm Wulfred," I said. I was staring at her, afraid that she might vanish if I glanced away. "And you're... Aelfwyn?" I guessed. I chose Aelfwyn because I thought it a prettier name than Herlesa. She laughed again. "Is it Aelfwyn? Your father didn't really say – he was..."

"Drunk?"

I grinned, and nodded, and must have looked like a witless oaf.

"I'm Aelfwyn. My father always drinks when he's with his men. My sister finds him very embarrassing. I just think he's funny." She laughed and shook her head and dark hair flickered across her forehead and curled loosely over her shoulders.

"Funny? Where were you when he was singing?"

"It is better if he doesn't sing". She raised a hand to tuck some stray hair behind one of her ears. "That's why I didn't join my sister with the other ladies?"

"Not because she'd be frowning at you again?" I attempted to imitate Herlesa's stony frown and probably looked like a man with a mouthful of sour ale, but Aelfwyn smiled and her eyes flashed back the firelight of the hall.

"You saw that? I only waved to you boys – you looked so uncomfortable with your shields and armour in the hot sun. But Herlesa says it was an undignified way to behave – we should think only of God, not of men."

"You wouldn't want to be as dignified as her. She looks like a nun."

Aelfwyn laughed again and gently touched my arm. "Come outside," she said "My sister won't miss me for a while if she's got our father to frown at, and all the men are too drunk to notice. Show me your village before it gets dark."

Some fat dripped from a roasting pig's carcass, crackled in the fire embers and sent a flare of light streaking through the hall at our backs as we stepped into the red twilight. The air was cool now and it rang with the songs of crickets.

"Do you really think Herlesa looks like a nun?" Aelfwyn giggled.

"Beside you, my lady, she is as plain as an old broomstick." I cringed with embarrassment as soon as I had said it, but Aelfwyn took it well.

"Your lady?" she grinned, pretending to be shocked, but her fingers brushed my arm again, as if she was touched by the clumsy compliment.

The sun's trail lingered above Andredsweald. Owls called from deep among the trees like the souls of ancient Saxons and druid-warriors still squabbling over Blood Hill. A few huddles of villagers sat drinking around the twilit hillside and the thick summer grass hushed our footsteps. Godric's drunken voice cackled across the dusk and I guessed that after my disappearance he had found his own ale. A crescent moon shone golden in the great blackening sky over the willows of Walland Fen. Aelfwyn watched it as we crossed the grassy field around the hall, then she sank into the long grass and pulled me down beside her.

157

We sat there in silence for what seemed like a long time. Aelfwyn gazed at the moon, half smiling and half wandering in a dream and I watched its light brush silver beams and shadows across her sun-darkened skin.

"The moon travels south towards the sea," she finally said. "If you watch carefully you can see it move against the trees. I thought I could hear the sea just now, but it must have been the breeze in the grass." She touched her hair again and that breeze ghosted along the fine silk edging of her white robe. The curiosity with which she had regarded me in the hall was there in her voice too, somehow welcoming everything and judging nothing.

"The sea's a few hours' journey south of here," I said. "Where are you travelling anyway?"

"We're going to Glowcestre." She paused, her smile suddenly passing into something uncertain. "Our father wishes us to take a ship to Ireland. He wants to find husbands for us among the rulers of Dublin." A coldness rippled through me when I heard those words, but Aelfwyn was a daughter of the royal house of Wessex and I had no business wanting her for myself.

"You've come from Cantaburh?" I asked.

"Yes, Cantaburh," she sighed. "That's where we live now. A horrible place - just the bones of a city. The old stones of the Roman people sink into the ground and we live among monks and rubbish heaps. My father's hall is there, near the archbishop's palace. He thinks being close to God protects him from the Devil." We both laughed. With Leofwin for a neighbour, I was surprised the archbishop had not moved out.

"When I was a child, we lived in the Cilterne Hills," she went on. "There's an old hall in a valley above the Thames, where my father sends his children and his womenfolk when they annoy him."

"Isn't that a dry and barren place?" I felt that I was asking too many questions, but I suddenly wanted to know everything about her and I would gladly have listened until the world ended its days.

"Sometimes," she shrugged, shaking her hair back over her shoulders and letting the moonlight wash across her face again. "In the summer, when the rain doesn't come. We lived in a valley where the hills sheltered us from the wind and cattle grazed on the summer pastures. The hall was old and draughty and the other women moaned all the time, but I loved it." She paused to wind a buttercup stem around one of her fingers. "There was a garden. It ran along the valley, full of flowers and apple trees. I used to sit outside in the evening and watch the hilltops turn red in the sunset. Then my father's spearmen would order me back into the hall where my sisters talked about their fine clothes and their jewellery and the silly young men who came to flatter them. The sons of lords used to boast about their land, and their horses and how many spears they commanded and my sisters would smile and gasp like dying fish. I'm glad they didn't talk to me." She gave a little snort of laughter.

"Why didn't they talk to you?"

"Once I met a young nobleman from Mercia – a nephew of the northern earls – he bragged that, as he held five hundred hides of land, that made him a hundred thanes in one man. I told him I hoped the other ninety-nine would be staying in Mercia. After that the boys left me alone."

"I would have come to see you," I offered awkwardly. "I'd have ridden up into the Cilterne Hills and we could have watched the sun setting on the hilltops and laughed at your sisters and their noblemen." I cringed inwardly once again, but Aelfwyn looked at me a bit her lip in a kindly smile and I thought it would be best to change the subject again.

"I met your cousin Magnus a few weeks ago. That was a joy indeed." I grimaced and I expected her to laugh. She nearly did, but it quickly turned to a sigh as she stared down towards the silhouetted willows of the riverbank.

"Why," she began, her brow knitting slightly "when peace brings us so much that is good, do men still worship war?"

"We don't all worship war! I don't worship war." A bittern's song boomed somewhere deep in the marshes, its echoes moving across the shadowed land to be drowned out by a burst of drunken singing from the hall.

"But you take men from the fields and put spears in their hands. And you fought with my cousin at Riaburh."

"I didn't want to be in that fight. I went with my father and brother and a foolish poet who wanted to live the battle songs he had sung. My father's not a man to shirk the sword or let anyone else do so." Aelfwyn gazed intently at me for a moment, weighing up my excuse. Then she turned to face the moon again.

"So you all go off to battle. For your fathers or your god or your king. With swords and songs and polished armour. And you limp back stinking of blood and sweat, for your dutiful women to bandage your wounds. And weep for the dead. Why weep for the dead? If they did not wish to die, why did they become warriors?"

"We don't choose to be warriors. My father is a warrior. I was born to be a warrior." The words sounded terrible and hopeless on my tongue and Aelfwyn looked at me doubtfully. "What choice do we have? Should we have abandoned Riaburh to our foes? Should we lay down our swords and give our land to the Norman duke?"

"Why not?" There was a new intensity on her face as she spoke. "Does it matter whether my uncle or some Norman wears the crown? This land is rich. Our cattle are growing fat in the valleys, the corn will soon be ripe, the rivers are full of fish. The sun will rise, the birds will sing, the rain will fall and we'll still gather at our hearths in the dark of winter." She looked up at the blackening sky again. "Those stars will always shine above our land. Because it *is* our land, whichever fool wants to call himself its king."

She spoke with the certainty of one who has never blistered in the summer heat to bring in a barley crop before the rain comes, never watched helplessly as sickness lays waste a herd, never struggled in torrential rain to save a house from a flood and never stood at a child's graveside when spring has finally made the ground soft enough to dig. Her words were a dream, a beautiful dream.

"But you're not going to be a great warrior like your father, are you Wulfred?" Whether it was a question or not, I could not tell.

"No," I sighed, but I smiled as well. "I don't think I am."

"I thought not as soon as I saw you. You looked different. You were looking at the sky when my father's men rode past. And you were slouching against your spear. If you'd have looked like your father I don't think I'd have waved at you." I laughed quietly while fireflies speckled the air, rising from the long grass and tumbling down towards the river where bats swooped between the trees.

"My father's trained me for battle all my life and I've grown into a man who slouches on his spear."

"Stay that way. The old warriors sing songs about dead heroes and spit on the memories of cowards who fled from battle. But those who fled are the men who went home and rebuilt their villages and ploughed the land and fed their people. A hero can only feed the ravens." Her eyes glinted in the silver light and I knew she spoke a long forgotten truth.

The moon climbed a little higher towards the south. Over the horizon of trees and onwards, to pass among the bright constellations of the summer night. The songs of grasshoppers wandered like lost ghosts across the valley and a white owl drifted out of the weald, gliding low over Ellasham. Time moved as slowly as the growing oaks behind the hall. Every breath seemed to take a

161

lifetime, every sound and every shimmer of the night moved in perfect detail.

"Some folk are afraid of owls," she said, when the white bird settled in a tree close to the river. "But my mother used to tell me that they guard us in the night, from the evil spirits that come to harm us."

"Then they'd do better to guard us in the day. If there is evil in the world, it walks among us in daylight, among priests and kings and their bloody plans. When the sun sets, sleep and ale lull them all and the shadows of night will bring us no harm." A small breeze crept through the grass, as if the darkened world agreed with me.

"It's a time of life, not death," she said. She turned her perfect face towards me again, as if searching for some kind of response, though whether it was words or something else she sought I could not tell. I remember looking back at her, framed by stars and meadow-grass, but I cannot recall whether I said anything.

8. THE SHORE

All day I stood on that hill, with the army of Wessex at my back and the yellowing woods beyond. My shield was all that stood between me and a horror of blood and steel, of thousands of men, their faces twisted by rage and terror, screaming out for the deaths of all who stood in their way, their blades hacking and whirling in the still autumn day. And arrows rained from the blue sky upon warriors who fought because their love for a king was greater than their love of life, and among fyrdmen who left their fields and families and walked into battle like blind fools, thinking they could profit from the bloody work of their masters, and on men like me, who had not found the courage to walk away.

The memory of battle has always followed me. In the summer months I work in the fields and the woods alongside men and women for whom that day of blood is little more than a thing of legend, and the memories of happier times are strong enough to keep the ghosts at bay. But when the winter comes, the wind howls through the dark valley and around the walls of our houses with all the pitiful moans of the dying and the roars of those who would kill a thousand men just to live another moment. And when the silence of a night frost grips the land, the faces of the dead flicker in the light of the hearth. The faces of men biting through their own tongues in the pain of mortal wounds, the glimmer of white bone amid butchered flesh, the sight of brains and guts spilling from bodies twitching in the last desperate moments of life. Those are the nights when sleep comes sparingly and only with dreams of terror; the nights when I must either tell my tales or suffer to live through them again.

Perhaps I should have died that day, among the sword-feast and the wreckage of flesh that folk now call the Great Battle. If I had fallen on the hilltop when the shield wall of Wessex finally broke,

163

maybe my people would not have been slain and scattered as they were. Or perhaps it would have made no difference.

Unlike so many others, I left that terrible field with my life. But I have seen so much death that sometimes I can think of little else. Men die. Women die. That summer passed and whole villages died in the dark times that followed. I have seen two generations grow up since the battle, and still they live in a land chained by its new lords, a land broken by the swords of both Normans and Englishmen, a land whose fields give up their wealth to line the purses of cold-hearted men in halls of oak and stone who bring only death into this world.

I think often of my own death. It may still be distant, but it will come and I wonder what will follow it. It may be that the priests and the monks are right and that there is a kingdom called Heaven where the good and the holy will dwell in peace forever. Will I be permitted to enter? It is true that I have sinned. I have killed men – I have broken that great commandment and no doubt many others too. But there are priests of the church who do not hesitate to kill and to do much worse, so it cannot be so important. Father Cuthred used to tell us that simply to believe in the truth and the love of the Christian god and his son Jesus Christ is enough to allow a man to enter Heaven in spite of all the sins of his life. But it is a long time since my heart has truly believed in these things. And would I really want to dwell forever in the kingdom of Grimstan's spiteful God?

And what of Hell? What punishment could Hell devise that men and women have not already suffered?

Perhaps there is a great hall of warriors beyond this world, the feast of the battle-mighty that the Danes of old longed for. And, I believe, the otherworld that my father and many others secretly sought. Although I never felt like one, I did live as a warrior, so perhaps I will pass through the great gates of the war god's mead hall. Will I meet again the men I slew? How will I greet them? Will we be doomed to fight out our battles for all eternity? I could happily feast and drink through all of eternity, but the boasting and brawling of warriors seems as bad as the Hell that priests speak. And I think of such a world as a place of men, where a woman's purpose is to serve and be silent, and in that case it is only half a world. Maybe less than that.

Perhaps I will one day meet with the shadow of that Welsh warrior lord who fell to my father's sword at Llyn Rhydderch so many years ago. And I will tell him that the child I once was witnessed his death and never wanted to see another man slain. And he will tell me in Welsh that he does not understand me and I will not know what he is saying, but maybe we will raise our ale cups to each other and drink because the chaos and the suffering is finally gone. And then Earl Leofwin will start to sing.

In spite of all I have lost, I truly hope my life in this world is yet a long one. If my soul is to live beyond my body, then I hope it will return to Ellasham and that all the souls of that last summer will be there too. And we will tell our stories over Eohric's ale in the firelit hall and we will dance and sing the songs of happy times and we will walk as fading ghosts in the sunlight along the edge of the weald and the world will never change again.

I left Ellasham in high summer, just days after Leofwin's visit. The king had given his orders to the men of Wessex and, still wearing my destiny like a yoke I could not shed, I obeyed the orders of my king.

My task was to patrol the shore with a little band of Ellasham's fyrdmen between Riaburh and a little cove to the west called Farenley. Oswold and my father were also out on the coast somewhere, with their own little bands of fyrdmen.

I led my men back and forth along the coastal pathways and we watched the sea from windswept sand dunes and shingle beaches that only the gulls called home, where the voices of the drowned were carried on the waves and an invading fleet could easily land. At first the villagers were nervous to be away from home, but quickened by the thought of imminent war, straining their eyes to the far horizon, expecting that any one of those long salt-tinged days could bring ships laden with spears and armoured men. But the days became weeks and the green fields became speckled with gold and the sea remained as empty as the sky above it.

There were times when I felt strangely happy as that summer ripened. There was a sword at my belt and I was following the will of England's king, and yet I was still among friends and we talked of times gone by and times yet to come and we laughed as we would have done back in Ellasham, and it was as if all my fears of a warrior's fate had come to nothing but this.

One night, we camped in a hollow beneath two high sand dunes. Between the tapering ends of the dunes we could just see the sea glimmering green and gold like a witch's brew in the last light of the sunset. And above us to the north loomed the dark bulk of a beacon fire built on a patch of high ground. The beacons were spread out on ridges and hilltops all along the coast, covered with greased cloth to keep the wood dry, and each one just in view of the next. If a fleet of ships was spotted out on the sea, the nearest beacon was to be lit, then a chain of fires would quickly flare up along the shore, their light and smoke alerting every armed man who served the king to rally to the source of the flames. Down in the shadows of the dunes, we lit our own little campfire, but I was careful to stop the men throwing too much wood on, lest it should be seen from a afar.

"If the Norman Duke comes," asked Godric, taking off his shoes and emptying the sand out of them, "and if he defeats our king in battle and becomes the ruler of England... what difference will it make?"

"He will be the king of all England," I replied. "And in the lands across the sea the king is a much more powerful man than here. A foreign king would rule without the counsel of his nobles. There would be one king who would rule alone and everyone from an earl to a beggar would be subject to his will."

"That doesn't sound much different," Godric grumbled. "We work like oxen now for our lords, but if we are defeated we will do the same work for a king,"

"Judgements of law in England are passed by lords and chosen men of the shires. In Normandy only the Duke has that power. If he were king he'd wield the same power here." I did not know if that was quite true, but I had once overheard an old Wessex warrior who had once served the Duke in Normandy trying to explain something similar. In fact, I did not think things would change much under a foreign king. I supposed that, if Wessex were defeated, many warriors and lords would die at their king's side and the rest would simply pledge their loyalty to a new lord, and life for most people would continue much as it always had. I remembered the things Aelfwyn had said about kings and warriors and when I thought of Aelfwyn it was hard to think of anything else.

"Is that what happened under the Danish kings?" In the dark shadows of the dunes, I could not see who had spoken, but I noticed that six pairs of eyes were looking at me, all a little doubtful, but eager nonetheless to hear what I could tell them. The Danish kings had ceased to rule England six years before I was born, but I wanted to answer knowledgeably. I wanted the men who followed me to think I was wise enough to be a worthy leader.

"Denmark is ruled in a similar way to England. The earldoms were established by King Cnut and he gave us many of our laws," I said.

"So would it be better to be ruled by Denmark than by Normandy?" asked a man with a big nose and a bushy beard who had been sharpening his knife. I glanced at Ragnald, recently returned from the weald now that the threat of war overshadowed the bickering of priests, and I hoped his Danish blood carried with it a little knowledge of Danish customs. He nodded and grimaced at the same time, as if the law in Denmark was something made up from day to day.

167

"Maybe," I finally said. "I think the church is stronger in Normandy. A Norman archbishop would be as powerful as a king."

"The archbishop can jump in a dungheap," spat Godric. "If the Church thinks we'll hand over even more of our harvest to keep their priests fat then the Church can think again." He threw a piece of driftwood into the fire. The flames crackled against the whispers of the sea and the sun faded beyond the far horizon.

Later that night, long after the sound of waves had lulled us to sleep, Ragnald shook my shoulder. We took it in turns to stay awake and watch the sea and I assumed he was waking me to take over from him.

"To the west," he said, pointing across one of the dunes. "A fire."

"A beacon?" I sat up and threw aside the cloak I had wrapped around myself in the chill that followed sunset. Ragnald beckoned me to follow him and we scrambled up the side of the dune. Away on the western horizon, a ball of orange light shimmered against the great black sky. I felt fear like a cold fist suddenly closing around my heart, and for a few moments I just stood there staring across the dark land. It was Ragnald who spoke first.

"Look at the sea," he said. I looked to my left, at the black expanse of rolling water, silvered here and there by moonlight catching the edge of a wave. I turned back to Ragnald and shrugged my shoulders.

"Would a fleet at night have lanterns?" he said.

"It would." I suddenly understood what he was saying. "So the ships at the rear of the fleet have something to follow."

"So there is fire on the horizon, but nothing on the sea." Hearing our voices, the others began to stir beneath their cloaks and I tumbled back down the dune towards them.

168

"A beacon has been lit to the west," I said.

"Is the Bastard Duke here?" asked a voice from the shadows. I saw a glint of steel where the man who had spoken was already clutching a knife.

"There's no sign of a fleet. I'll ride west. The king's orders are that when we see a beacon lit, we should light the next." I hesitated then. I should also have told them to follow on foot to wherever the king's army was mustering, but I could not bring myself to order my people into war. "Stay here," I told them instead. "Light the beacon and wait for news."

I ran across the sand and the dune grass and mounted the horse that we had used to pull a light cart with our food, weapons and armour. And I kicked it into a gallop away into the quiet, moon-silvered west.

The air was chill as it rushed past me, and the moon lit up the pale, dry earth of the coastal path as I flew through the darkness, like a moth towards the flames on the far hilltop. After two or three miles, I halted my horse on a headland of low cliffs where the wilderness of Andredsweald crept down close to the sea. The beacon loomed closer on the skyline now. I could even see flurries of sparks rushing up into the black sky, and behind me the beacon lit by the men of Ellasham blazed on the eastern horizon. But across the dark water there was still no sign of any fleet. I sat there looking out to sea, and listening to the gentle sound of the waves on the shore as my horse shook its mane and cropped the short grass. Why, I wondered, did I ride so swiftly and so willingly to war? The beacons stretched all the way along the coast to Wyt and Hantone and beyond. I could see no enemy ships on this strip of coast, but that did not mean that they were not somewhere away to the west. War and death might well be gathering to the naked blades of warriors far along the coast and I was galloping to join them. A gust of wind rushed through the trees to the north and in my head I heard my father's voice shouting about the glory of battle and of our duty to our lords and the honour we earned through serving them. Those despised words had taken root in my soul and I had ridden towards the beacons without a thought. And I saw Oswold holding his sword and shield before him, his eyes wide and every tensed muscle of his body eager to join that great line of warriors from which he sprung. And I thought of what fools they were. My father and my brother and every man in Wessex who carried a sword that night and rode hard to give up his life so that one man might be called king rather than another.

I began to wonder what else I could do. If the men of Wessex fought a great battle and drove the host of Normandy back into the sea and I had not been among them, then what would happen to me? Could I let my father and brother face death in the shield wall and not be at their side?

But I had no time to make a choice. From the black woods at my back came the sound of hoofbeats and six riders, all in helmets and mail, came thundering out of the trees.

"Who the hell are you?" shouted the foremost of them. He had drawn his sword as soon as he saw me and now he held it at the ready. He had a thick beard matted with grease and dark hair jutted out from beneath his helmet. His face was just two angry eyes in a mass of hair. "And why the hell are you skulking here when there's a battle to fight?" The other five surrounded me and levelled their spears.

"I'm Wulfred of Ellasham," I said. "I ride west towards the beacon fires." The hairy man lowered his sword, but still regarded me with suspicion.

"You're riding nowhere. You're sat there like a carving of the Holy Virgin." He paused to allow his warriors to laugh then he turned to me again. "And where's your armour?" In my rush to do what I thought best, I had left my shield, spear, helmet and mail, and even my bow, in the cart back at the sand dunes.

"My fyrdmen are bringing it," I said. "I ride quicker if I ride light."

"Idiot!" the hairy man snapped. "What use is a shieldless man to his king. If we fight today, you'll be the first to die."

Another warrior trotted his horse forward, poked his spear into the folds of my cloak, and spoke in a shrill voice. "I'll do the fucking Normans' job for them right now, Bera. I'll wager a pound of silver this cowardly lump of shit was running away." Bera. The Bear. The hairy man had an apt nickname, but it was an apt one.

"Enough!" shouted Bera, nudging his horse sideways and knocking the man's spear down with the flat of his sword. "We'll escort this bastard to the king's side and make sure he dies in battle."

Bera sheathed his sword and kicked his horse into a gallop. And I followed, with men who wanted to see me dead riding on either side.

We were the first to arrive at the beacon fire, but only just. As we reached the flat summit of the hill where the fire blazed, I could hear the hoofbeats and see the silhouettes of fifty more horsemen galloping up the other side. And three figures darting away from the fire towards the trees.

"Bring them here!" Bera shouted to his men and they immediately kicked their horses on towards the treeline. Two of the running figures made it into the tangle of branches and brambles where a horse could not follow. But the third, slower than the others, was brought down by a blow from a spearshaft and dragged back.

"Why is the beacon lit? Where is the enemy fleet?" yelled Bera, leaping down from his horse. He was a stocky man and he hit the ground hard in his coat of mail. The captured man shrank away from him.

"Answer!" Bera roared again, grabbing the man by the front of his tunic and shaking him. "I see no fleet. Who lit the beacon?" The man cowered away and stuttered. He was an old grandfather, thin and grey-haired. He must have been sixty. A line of horsemen thundered across the hilltop and reigned in their mounts. Some looked on as Bera demanded answers from the old man and others turned to each other and muttered.

"Wulfred!" My father cantered his horse towards me. Oswold was at his side. "What's happening? Has the fleet been sighted?" They both wore their mail and had shields across their backs. My father glanced despairingly at my own unreadiness.

"I don't know," I said, and he looked at me as if I should have known. "Bera caught this old man running away when we arrived."

"Where is your lord?" Bera shouted. "Answer me you oaf or I'll cut your throat out!" The bright steel of a knife glinted in the warrior's hand now. Oaf or not, this was no way to treat a frail old man and I felt a powerful urge to grab Bera by the throat and wave my own knife in his face. Then the old man finally found his tongue.

"Our lord went to the village across valley, lord. There is a tavern there." A few of the assembled warriors laughed, but Bera was not among them.

"And why has the beacon been lit? Bera shook the old man and he sobbed with fear. "Answer me, may God damn your soul, or I'll throw you into the fire." The old man curled in on himself and whimpered his reply.

"We were cold, lord. Our lord left us no fuel for a fire of our own."

There was a mixture of laughter and curses from the mounted men who stood in silhouette across the hillside, but Bera threw the old man to the ground and kicked him in the chest with a grunt of rage.

"They've not seen a fucking fleet," he shouted for the benefit of those who had not heard. "Put the fire out. Elnoth! Tie this old bastard to a tree. I'll whip him until he'll never feel the cold again.

The warrior called Elnoth dragged the old man to his feet and without quite knowing how I had got there, I was suddenly stood between him and Bera.

"Leave him be. You've scared him to the edge of death, he doesn't need a whipping too." I heard the words as if someone else was saying them. Bera glared at me. He had taken his helmet off and his thick hair now stuck up from the top of his head.

"You stand aside unless you want a whipping too," he spat.

"He's old enough to be your grandfather. Whip him and he'll probably die." The old man wriggled weakly, his scrawny arms and legs twisting in Elnoth's grip.

"If the bastard dies, then he won't light the fucking beacon for no reason again will he? You go back to your fyrdmen and find your armour. At least then you might look like half a man." I glanced around and I felt the same fear I had felt outside Ragnald's cottage, realising there was nobody to support me.

"Leave it boy. The bastard deserves a whipping," said a voice from somewhere close to the fire. I wanted to leave it. I wanted to walk away, to throw my pride to the ground and avoid a beating, but I could not. I felt myself moving towards Elnoth, reaching out to wrench one of his hands from the wretched old man's neck. Then I felt myself falling and rolling on the ground, punched down by one of Bera's mailed fists.

"Do you want to die, boy?" said Bera's voice, and I sprang up on to the balls of my feet, ready to launch myself at him, but suddenly there were hands gripping my shoulders and arms around my chest pulling me back.

"Wulfred you fool!" said my father's voice. I twisted around to see my father on one side and   Oswold on the other.

173

"He's an old man! They'll whip him to death!" I protested. My father looked at me without comprehension.

"He lit the beacon, Wulfred. He misled the king's army. All along the coast now, fires are burning and warriors are riding towards this hill, all for nothing. This fool deserves punishment."

I heard Bera laughing as they dragged me away. I felt the cool grass as they threw me down and stood over me. I felt a dull ache gathering on the side of my face where Bera had hit me. And as the fire dwindled and the horsemen began to ride away down the other side of the hill, I heard the slap of an alder rod against skin and the whimpering of a man who was too old and too foolish for war being whipped because he had wanted to keep warm in the dead of the night.

Two days later, on a breezy evening near the headland where I had stopped and wondered whether to turn my horse and ride away from battle, Ragnald came back to our little camp. He had gone to find a cottage he knew of where the housewife sometimes had ale to sell. But he came back empty-handed and grim-faced. While the others grumbled and shared out some gritty bread and a little sour ale from two days earlier, Ragnald led me up the coast path to the top of the headland where a makeshift gibbet had been erected. The old man's body hung by a rope under his armpits. His eyes had been taken by gulls and his naked back was a bloody mess of dark congealed blood and flayed skin, the bones of his ribs showing white in some places. Ragnald was no stranger to death, but he looked sick. I took out my knife and cut the body down.

"A warrior called Bera did this," I said to Ragnald. "The same man who did this." I pointed to my right eye, which was now bruised and swollen. "He had the body brought here so that I might see what he did to the man I tried to save." The wind gusted along the headland and I looked at Ragnald, searching for my thoughts. Ragnald looked steadily back at me. "Not long ago," I said, "my father told me that I would learn soon enough why men fight. I think I have learned that now."

9. LUNDEN

There are many beautiful cities in the world. I have heard men speak of the City of Constantine, the great light in the east, a place of shining glass and marble towers under a sky as blue as Heaven, scented with spices and ringing with the songs of every land. And of Rome, far to the south over seas and mountains, where the columns of palaces from which the world once was ruled still reach towards the golden sun, reminding men of what was once achieved and what they might rise to again one day.

Lunden stank. Crammed in between the brown broth of the River Thames and the old Roman walls were the homes of some eight thousand people. And between their houses, with walls of plank and plastered mud, roofs of thatch and turf, rose the crumbling bones of the buildings Rome had once planted in this land. The grand facades of palaces from which law had once been spoken and armies of bronze and steel sent forth were now the gathering places of crows, sprouting with weeds and falling stone by stone in the winter storms.

There was no city in all of England as big as Lunden. Alongside those who dwelt there, there could be half as many traders and labourers passing through at any time from all across this land and many others. And all the filth of so many people - all the stale food, the shit of men and beasts, the unused carcass scraps, rotten skins and bones - was scraped from the streets and dumped outside the walls, along the bank of the river. We knew we were near Lunden when we heard the squabbling of crows, saw kites circling over the midden heap and smelt the stench of things decaying.

"It is like the week after a summer battle," said my father, spitting out the foul air. "When the dead have rotted on the field."

The year was passing. We could taste the ghosts of winter in nights that would soon be longer than the days. I rode in a column of warriors summoned from the windswept coast to the royal hall at Westmynster. The fields had faded by then from the glorious green of early summer into brittle brown, and as our column wound its way northward along the old iron trading roads of Sussex, men who had so recently swapped their hoes for knives and axes to march with the fyrd now swung sickles and loaded carts with ripe corn. The apples were growing heavy in the orchards of Wessex, the fyrdmen were back in their fields and a gentle breeze from the north and east had kept the Norman fleet in its harbour all summer long. It would have been easy to believe that the shadow of war had passed over and everything was as it should be.

But then had come the news that was least expected. The king sent out riders summoning all the warriors of Wessex. For a Viking army had sailed up the River Humber and made landfall in the great earldom of Northumbria. And at its head was Harald Sigurdsson, ruler of the Norse and the greatest warrior king in the northlands.

I rode with Oswold and my father and all the followers of Magnus and Leofwin, fretting that war knew me by the sword I carried and that its talons reached through the changing seasons and across the length of the land to draw me back.

The village of Suthwerc huddled on the south bank of the Thames; a cluster of inns, stables and taverns for folk who had business in Lunden but whose purses were not heavy enough for them to sleep in the city itself. On either side were marshes and rough fields scattered with sedge grass and overhung by the stench of the city's middens.

And on the far side of Suthwerc was the great bridge that strode across the river and into Lunden itself. At either end, squat Roman towers stood guard, and beneath the massive oak beams, great stone pilings stood proud above the rushing water many centuries after the men who built them had passed beyond memory. I rode across the bridge amid the creaking of planks and cartwheels, the clattering of hooves and I felt a deep chill to see the sucking tides of that wild river clawing at the stonework beneath.

But there were more chilling things to ponder that day. The north seemed far, far away and invading armies of Vikings seemed like a bloody horror from fireside tales, something that should have passed from the world in the times of my grandfathers' fathers.

"Northumberland has never been anything but a thorn in the side of Wessex." I said as we crossed the bridge. "Will the king fight for it while we're still threatened by Normandy?"

"Northumberland is more trouble when Wessex does not control it." My father's voice was grim, but there was a gleam in his eyes. "And a king must fight," he said. "What king could stand with pride before his people and say he's given away half the land won by the swords of his forefathers?"

Pride, I wondered to myself. How could a king's pride be enough reason for men to be butchered?

"That's why we're summoned here," said Oswold. He was smiling broadly. "A king must seek the counsel of his people before making war."

My father's brow creased into a frown. "He might seek the counsel of noblemen and churchmen. But we are his warriors. Our king summons us because he has already chosen to fight."

Away to the east the Thames wallowed on towards the long sea roads. The north bank was shored up with stakes and planks, making a deep channel and a quay for cargo ships. Soon the trade routes would be closed for all but the bravest and most desperate, but now the harvest was in and England was rich, so the docks of Lunden were busy with ships, their sails furled and thick ropes lashing them to the quayside. Some were being loaded with cargoes of cloth by men who sweated in the heat and sang as they hefted the

178

clumsy bales. Other ships were being emptied and their sailors spoke in strange tongues. A dark-skinned man on the dockside pulled out a curved knife and held it high in some kind of warrior's salute to us, grinning as he called out words that none of us understood. A couple of Magnus' men raised their fists in reply, shouting the battlecries of Wessex. We watched goods being carried from the ships and into the great warehouses along the quay. There were stored casks of wine, bundles of furs, purses of amber, dried fruits, jars of oil, rare dyes and spices and goods from all across the known world.

Behind the dockyards was a market square in the crumbling courtyard of what had once been a cavernous Roman building - the hall of lords and governors long before the Saxon kings. Here were sold the goods unloaded at the riverside as well as meat, fruit, cloth and leather from the surrounding villages, pottery, glass and metal ware from the city's workshops and bread baked in oven-houses near the walls. Most of the stalls were closed now, and the traders counting their takings under the canvas roof of a tavern in the far corner of the square.

The mounted column turned westwards into the narrow alleys of the city and the traders glanced and muttered, no doubt discussing whether war would be good or bad for business. A priest sidled up alongside my horse and quietly chanted a blessing in Latin. Then he raised his head and looked at me, two steely eyes staring in expectation from above a sharp, hooked nose. It was usual for priests and monks to give their blessings to warriors on their way to battle. And it was usual for warriors to give them a penny for their trouble. But I had seen enough of the work of priests and I did not reach for my purse. A priest who has the scent of silver in his nostrils, however, is not an easy thing to be rid of.

"May the Lord strengthen your sword arm and grant you courage to endure the wounds of battle," he said, in a manner that suggested I was more likely to be wounded were I not to give him anything. "And may your foes lie slain upon the ground as thickly as the blades of grass."

Remembering words I had heard Father Cuthred speak, I shot the priest a questioning look. "You pray for the deaths of the Norse, but didn't Christ tell his followers to love their enemies?"

The priest shook his head and laughed as if I was a fool. "Love thine own enemy, yes. But love not the enemies of the Lord. Christ's kingdom will not come to be until the heathens of the north are cleansed from the earth." He smiled at me, like a man explaining something to a child. I saw Grimstan's scowling face flicker behind this priest's smile and I spat on the ground and rode on. On one side of me was Grimstan's world of holy books and spiteful whims and on the other was my father's world of blood and battle, and I wanted no place in either.

But I rode with the army of Wessex because it was the only thing I knew how to do.

In the narrow alleys beyond the market, the air was heavy with the smells of baking bread, stew and roasting meat mingled with the stench of dung and filth. Innkeepers paid boys to call out that they had strong ales kept cool in cellars and wines from across the sea. Girls stood in the doorways, their hair falling across their shoulders in the manner our priests so despised. Most of them wore clothes that were too flimsy or too tight and showed off the curves of their breasts and hips. They smiled and called out as we passed by. One of the men stopped to talk with a girl who wore what looked like a boy's tunic, short above her knees and with her breasts trying to push their way out, but Magnus rode up angrily.

"Ride on Ulf! You're summoned by the king of Wessex, not by the whims of your groin. There'll be time to whore and to drink later."

"Wait for me tonight my love," laughed Ulf, winking at the girl in the doorway. She flashed a wicked smile as our column rode on.

"A full set of teeth," my father grunted. "They say the best thing about Lunden is its whores."

"That one'll cost Ulf more than he'd take from a whole warband slaughtered in the Welsh hills," said Magnus.

"Then lucky for us we fight the Norse," answered a voice further up the column. "And let's hope it's a long winter - their silver will keep us in ale and whores all through it." Magnus gave a cold laugh and spurred his horse forward.

"The lord Magnus disapproves," Ulf smiled. "He likes them old and toothless - afraid of having his little cock bitten off." The men around me laughed and I laughed with them and I swallowed a bitter gob of loathing for a man who laughs along with those who he despises, just because he does not know what else to do.

Further west through the city, the alleys broadened into wide lanes lined by workshops and houses. These low thatched buildings were like those of any English village. Some had little gardens, green with herbs. Beneath the blue autumn sky a great orchard hung heavy with plums and apples. There were churches here as well, marked by wooden crosses above the doorways, and close to the river stood the monastery of the monks of St. Paul, built on Rome's old foundation stones.

And out beyond the city's edges, we reached a broad field of stubble that lay between the royal hall, King Edward's great church of St. Peter and the monastery's low stone wall. There were hundreds of sailcloth tents pitched around the field, and warriors in helmets and mail rehearsed the battles to come. The still air carried the clashing of blades and shields and the cries of sparring men. Close to the hall were carts laden with ale barrels and behind them were pits of wood and charcoal for cooking. One or two girls from the city loitered, looking for business and there were cries of approval from the men. A smile stole across my father's face like that of a man coming back to his warm home after a long winter journey.

"England has not seen such an army gather, not since the days of Aethelred," he said, his voice almost a whisper. Then he grinned savagely and his fist clenched around his sword-hilt. "At last, my sons, we'll fight shoulder to shoulder against the northmen, like the warriors of Aelfred, in battles that will be spoken of forever."

"Wessex!" he cried, drawing his sword and raising it high in salute to the men we rode past. The cry went up, and all along the mounted column, and the name of Godwinsson was raised aloud in honour of the king. Axes were beaten on shields and horns were blown to welcome sword-men and spearmen to King Harold's side. To welcome men to the mustering of arms that might bring death to every one of them.

While my father and Oswold greeted other warriors, I led our horses to a field behind the hall where there were posts to tether them, and troughs and barrels filled with water. As the horses drank I scooped up a bucketful of the murky river water to wash the dust of the road off my face and hands. The afternoon shadows were lengthening, but still the sun was hot and the cool water felt good. Hundreds of horses quietly cropped the grass, the sound of squabbling geese came from the direction of the river and a bell rang in the monastery.

"Hey, slave! These barrels are the king's property. Mind how you handle them!" I looked around to see a dark-haired boy rolling an empty barrel onto a cart. But the voice was one I had heard before.

Standing ten paces away, his arms heavy with the silver, was Bera, the warrior who had ordered an old man whipped to death on the clifftops just weeks before. He held a horn cup in his left hand, his weight shifted from foot to foot and slops of ale ran down his beard. Two more warriors, younger and just as drunk, stood behind him clutching their own cups and laughing. The slave, a thin boy of twelve or thirteen years, looked at him. He lowered his eyes, but there was a brave indifference in the way he shrugged his shoulders, turned his back and got on with his task. Drunk he may have been, but Bera felt that little spark of defiance like a fist in his belly and he strode across to the cart, his face set and his hand twitching on his sword hilt.

"Bow. Bow to me, slave. I'm a warrior of Wessex and you're a fucking Welsh bastard." The boy turned again, briefly lifted his eyes then wordlessly bowed. They stood there looking at each other. Bera still did not seem satisfied.

"I've fought your lot," he bellowed, drawing his sword and spilling ale. "I've fought with King Harold and with Magnus. This blade's tasted the guts of a dozen bastards like you. You come out of the hills to steal English cattle and rape English women, but you run like dogs from the swords of English men."

"I have never fought the English," said the boy quietly. "I was taken from my village by spearmen when I was a child." Bera's two friends lurched against the water barrels and watched with eager eyes. A dozen or so others had gathered beside them. I found myself moving closer to this small crowd.

"You lying shit!" Bera shouted. He slapped the boy's face with the flat side of his sword. The boy gasped, stepped back and touched his hand to the reddening mark left by the blade.

"You bastards raided and burned our villages and now you eat good English bread, drink English ale and sleep on a bed of English straw. We should have put every Welsh pig we caught to the fucking sword. We should be there now, driving every one of you into the sea." The boy, who had a lot more courage than sense, raised his eyes to his tormentor again.

"I was never a warrior," he pleaded. "I was taken from my village. Now I serve King Harold."

183

"Don't talk back to me you fucking pig." Bera raised his sword again, higher this time, aiming for a blow that, even with the flat of the blade, could have broken the boy's skull. But the blow never landed. Before he could bring the sword down, I grabbed his wrist.

"He's just a boy," I said. "Look at him. He's not old enough to have fought." A brief flicker of confusion crossed Bera's face, then his cold anger blazed anew.

"Who the hell are you?" He pushed me hard so that I staggered back and let go of his wrist.

"Leave the boy alone. He's a slave, doing his work. He hasn't harmed you." I did not remind him of my name. He did not seem worthy to know my name.

"You're that bastard we caught running away when the beacons were lit." Little droplets of spittle clung to his beard as he spoke.

"Leave the boy alone. Go back to your ale."

"Want his arse, do you?" he hissed. There was a sudden burst of laughter and I looked around to see dozens of eager-faced men now clustered about us.

"Fight!" shouted someone. "A half pound of silver says Bera breaks his neck."

"Smash his face in Bera!" yelled another voice. Bera was clearly more popular than he deserved to be. He glanced around the ring of men that had gathered, smiled a dark, dark smile then sheathed his blade and unbuckled his swordbelt. I saw men making wagers with each other, little piles of coin and silver lying between their feet on the trodden grass, ready for the winners to divide the spoils. If I didn't fight this warrior, then I would face the anger of many others.

"Wulfred, what have you done?" My father was there in the crowd, his face furrowed with incomprehension. But I did not have time to answer him. Someone grabbed my shoulder and pushed me into the middle of the ring. I dropped my swordbelt and faced my opponent.

Stripped to the waist, he fixed me with a hard stare and clenched his fists.

"It's good to see you again," he grimaced. "When I met you on the coast, I wanted to beat you 'til you puked blood. This time you won't get away." I did not answer. I shrugged as if his words meant nothing to me. I was looking for weaknesses. He was a bulky man, but his bulk was more muscle than fat. It was hard to tell where his beard ended and where the matted hair of his chest began. I knew how to fight with my fists and my feet – all warriors are taught these things because such brawling is what even the greatest of battles descend into. But I did not have the hard years of fighting that the gleaming silver on this man's arms spoke of. He spat on the ground and walked slowly towards me. The crowd yelled and stamped and I prepared myself to take a beating.

It is strange how fear can reach its height then flee from you. As my opponent closed in, I simply thought about how to get out of that ring with as little injury as possible. I knew that if I attacked him, my inexperience would show. Wait for him to strike. Dodge or block him, then try to hurt him while he was off balance. He was heavy and he was drunk. I was quick and my mind was suddenly as clear as the blue sky.

He feinted first with his left fist and I ducked to avoid it, just as another blow came from his right. If he had been sober, he would have knocked me out with that first punch, but he was fuddled and slow. I heard him roar and I just had time to move my head aside. Then I suddenly heard nothing as the blow landed in the corner of my left eye. I staggered and was caught and thrust back by the hands of the crowd. My opponent staggered too, unbalanced by ale and by the force of his own punch. I felt my skull throbbing from the blow and suddenly the hostile voices of the gathered warriors resurged as they cheered their champion on.

As Bera swayed around to face me again, his fists raised and ready, I dropped into a crouch and hit him in the belly with all the strength I had gained from years of pulling the bowcord. He barely seemed to notice. It was like hitting a tree. I saw him grin as he aimed another blow down at my face, but I was already springing aside and he reeled again as his fist found only the empty air. Blood ran into my eye from where one of his silver arm rings had torn into my forehead, but I hit him again - a left and a right into his flank as he struggled for balance. My fists slapped hard against his sweat-slick flesh but again he barely noticed and I skipped backwards into the open centre of the ring where I could move freely.

He followed me, his face now a livid mask. His steps were the uneven, over-careful steps of a drunk and I saw a cloud of frustration blur his face as he almost stumbled. But he closed in on me and he punched and I dodged the blow. He lashed out again and I ducked to the ground and kicked him in the knee as I rolled behind him. But his leg remained as firm as a post driven deep into the ground and I heard the laughter of the crowd. He turned and tried to smash his fist into my face again and I dropped to my knees and drove my right fist into his groin with all my strength. He doubled up with a gasp of pain and, springing back onto my feet, I raised a knee hard into his face, slamming both my fists down on the back of his head at the same time. There was a popping sound as the bones of his nose shattered. I saw his blood all over my knee as he fell, I heard him choking for breath then I stamped and stamped again on his face, the nails of my boots ripping his cheek open and smashing the teeth out of his gums.

And then I felt arms grabbing me around my waist and chest and pulling me away because the fight was over. And I had won, and my opponent lay in the trampled grass coughing and spluttering through the bloody mess of his face. And a mass of eyes stared at me, cold and silent. Oswold and my father hauled me away as they had done beside the beacon fire on the night when I first quarrelled with Bera. But this time the joy of my victory streaked through me like bolts of lightning and I felt I could take on that whole ring of gathered warriors and never be beaten to the ground. I stared back at them, growling, daring them all to step forward and take me on.

"Idiot!" said my father's voice as he bundled me away across the field. "You pick fights with the king's best warriors when our enemies run loose across the kingdom." I pushed his hand off my shoulder.

"Bera's a piece of shit. I wish I'd killed him!"

"And there would be one less warrior to defend our land. Did you not think of that while you were punching him in the balls like some peasant brawling in a tavern?"

"He deserved worse than that," I snarled back, and I was surprised by the way the words burst from my throat as sharp and as certain as blades. "He killed that old man on the coast and he would have killed that slave boy. When the spears of our enemies take him the world will be better for it." My father saw my anger and there had been a time, not so long ago, when he would have called me a fool and wondered aloud how he had sired such a wrong-thinking son; when he would have just shouted me down, beating his staff on ground to the grinding rhythm of his voice. But instead, he took a step away, fixed his eyes on mine and spoke quietly.

"Save your anger for your king's enemies, Wulfred," he said. "You won't care how a man treats slaves when he stands at your shoulder in the shield wall, only that he knows how to fight."

And I looked back at him, and I realised that the expression on my face was the same as his. And I felt that we had looked that way at one another for as long as I could remember, and perhaps we would always do so.

In the evening, as the western sky turned red and the smell of fires and roasting meat began to drift across those fields of tents and horses, we were summoned into the royal hall, where King Harold would address his war host. The great doors were thrown open, with

187

the banners of Harold and his brothers planted on either side. Highest of them all stood the Dragon of Wessex – a ferocious beast's head, open mouthed with jagged teeth. It was made from plates of polished steel, edged in gold and silver, with chunks of gleaming jet for eyes and a great tail of red silk that would thrash above the battlefield. Harold's hearthtroop – a thousand of his finest warriors who were oath sworn to bring victory or to die at his side – called themselves the Dragons after this war banner.

The king himself greeted his followers as they entered the hall. It had been nearly three years since I had seen Harold Godwinsson, since the winter when he had invited my father to send me to the Welsh border with Earl Leofwin. I had nervously taken an oath to serve the sons of Godwin then, and we had all drunk mead to celebrate and seal the bond.

He had been the Earl of Wessex in those days, but even then his warriors had spoken of the day when their lord would be a king. Now he sat at the head of a great hall, at a finely carved table on a raised platform with the other highest-ranking men of the kingdom. The hall was vast and its walls decorated with religious tapestries and carvings of saints and of Christ on the cross. These were the symbols with which King Edward had impressed his Christian virtue upon his lords and they seemed out of place now, peering down at a mass of rough warriors with lust for battle burning in every scarred face.

"Saxmund, my friend and sword-companion!" he called out as we entered. His voice was powerful, well used to carrying far across a field of battle. He bounded down from the platform and as my father began to kneel before his king, Harold grabbed him by the shoulders and hauled him into a rough bear hug. It was not the way kings were expected to behave. Kings carried the royal blood of many generations in their veins, they were anointed by archbishops and were therefore close to God and distant from men. They did not shout and bawl and hug people. But Harold had not been born to be a king - he had been raised among warriors for whose loyalty he had had to fight. Our king was a little older than my father and although his face was lined by the years, he did not frown so easily. His hair was straw coloured like Leofwin's, with flecks of grey and he wore no beard, only long plaited moustaches that hung below his chin. He greeted Oswold and I warmly, saying that Earl Leofwin had spoken well of us after the battle at Riaburh. Oswold stuttered nervously and bit his lip. Then the king glanced at the bruise and the raw cut above my eye.

"And I hear you've seen battle here already Wulfred."

"I apologise for my son's behaviour, Lord King," my father began, but the king quickly hushed him.

"Don't apologise for him!" he barked. "I want men who like a fight, not milk sucking cowards who keep their fists in their breeches. Bera's a ferocious bastard and your son bested him. You should be a proud man, Saxmund." My father bowed his head obediently. The king turned to me, smiling.

"Hit him in the balls did you?" he whispered. Then he gave a burst of laughter and slapped one of his broad hands on my shoulder. "As my son Magnus always tells us, when a man fights, he fights for victory, not for honour. Just don't spare the bollocks of the Norse and the Normans." I grinned back at the king then at my father, who threw me a shadowy look.

Then Harold gestured us towards a bench where a few grim looking men shuffled along to make room. "Sit down, my friends. Take the weight of your belly off your leg Saxmund." Some of the men on the bench laughed aloud as their king walked back to his seat with the confident stride of a survivor of many battles. He wore a fine tunic of red silk, but he wore it untidily as if unaccustomed to such finery, like the rings and the gold torcs that he wore on his arms, but fiddled with as if they irritated him.

And the thane moot he had summoned was probably also an irritation to King Harold. A warlord on the field of battle makes decisions in the space of a heartbeat - decisions that lead to victory or destruction and in which the only certainty is that delay will bring defeat. But before a king could take a great decision, he had to make it look like he sought advice from half the realm.

"Men of Wessex," Harold began, his voice echoing among the high roofbeams as he rose to his feet. "I have summoned the strong, the brave and the loyal, and it gladdens my heart that so many have come. Through the summer we've guarded our shores against the war host of Normandy, but now we face a different foe. Harald Sigurdsson, King of the Norse, is at large in Northumbria"

"Let him keep Northumria," I whispered to Oswold. "We've enough to worry about with the Normans." At least, I thought I whispered. I heard the sound of someone rising to his feet behind me and felt the heel of a hand strike the back of my head.

"Let him keep nothing! This boy speaks like a pig's arse." I turned around to see a red-bearded man, one who had stood in the ring of warriors as I had fought Bera, now addressing Harold. "Lord King, heed not the words of cowards. Generations have fought and died so that Wessex might rule the north."

Another man stood, on the other side of the hall. "Edwin and Morcar - the sons of Aelfgar who call themselves the earls of the north - are treacherous men," he boomed. "They seek to throw off the rule of Wessex. Have they sent men to guard their king's lands against the host of Normandy?" The red-bearded man sneered at me as he sat down. Gyrth Godwinsson, the Earl of East Anglia, a big bald-headed man who sat at his brother's side, stood and brought his fist down on the table.

"Then we march north, crush the Norse King and take back the land the sons of Aelfgar undeservingly hold." There were cheers from many warriors, including my father. Oswold joined in a cry of "To York!" For a moment the matter seemed decided, but then another warrior stood.

"We can't waste time and men fighting in the north. The wind may turn any day. The fate of Wessex will be decided here, with the Bastard Duke in the south."

"It's too late in the year for the Norman fleet to sail," said Gyrth with a dismissive wave of his hand. The hall was suddenly filled with arguing voices. I saw Harold mutter a warning to his brother. Leofwin also sat at the great table, but said nothing. He stared at the roofbeams most of the time and seemed close to falling asleep. Beside him sat Stigand, the Archbishop of Cantaburh, a fat-faced, sly-looking man who wore his silver cross and ecclesiastical robes as uncomfortably as King Harold wore his gold. And beyond Stigand, there were two more bishops, with monks and priests in attendance.

"Is it too late?" Now it was Magnus' voice rising above the babble of the hall. "The Norse have come this late. Why not the Normans too? There are ships full of Frankish wine tethered at the Lunden quayside. If traders can come from Normandy, then so can warriors. Let the north look after itself."

The uproar of argument surged back in the wake of Magnus' voice.

"The king can't leave the coast of Wessex undefended," I said to my father, shouting above the din of voices.

"A king must fight for what he holds," he replied, "or be swept aside by foes and forgotten by his kinsmen."

"And if the Norman Duke comes when the army is in the north?"

"Then the greater our names will be when we turn from one field of victory and make another." My father snarled the words and brought his fist down hard on the bench.

It was as if the battle had already begun. For that was what these men had gathered for. There may have been decisions still to make, but in those moments of din and bluster I realised that the fate of the kingdom could only be settled by the edge of the sword and the point of the spear.

I thought of Hildelyth, and how she had tried to make me steer the course of my life elsewhere, and of Aelfwyn's words about men worshipping war and feeding only the ravens. The light of torches blazed, the cries for the coming battles raged and the wisdom of women seemed like a fading candle as the shadows of evening slunk through the hall.

The voices fell silent as Harold strode forward and addressed his son.

"And what does the Norman duke do, Magnus, when he arrives in England to find us already threatened by an enemy in the north?" He paused and the silence held. "Perhaps he makes a pact with the Norse King to join forces and divide England between them. Harald Sigurdsson. William the Bastard. Edwin and Morcar coming south with the carrion birds. The Welsh creeping out of their hills. And Wessex caught between them all. That is not a trap I wish to fight my way out of." The king looked around the hall as if inviting a response.

One of the bishops stood, an ancient man leaning on his crooked staff, and took advantage of the sudden silence. His voice was wheezy, but there was steel in his expression.

"The eye of God is fixed upon Northumberland. While Englishmen have followed the way of Christ since the days of the blessed Augustine, the men of Norway have only done so for a generation or two. There are many among them who still offend the blessed Christ with the worship of heathen idols. The city of York is a bastion of the true faith and if we let it fall, there will be abominations and foul sacrifices in churches across Mercia and Northumberland. Monasteries will decay, men's souls will be damned and God will turn his back on those who allowed it to happen. To fight the heathen foe is to defend the glory of God." Breathing heavily, the bishop sat down.

192

My father stood up, his fist clenched around his sword-hilt.

"Then we must take this army to York and put an end to the king of the Norse as our forefathers slaughtered the Danes at Ethandun." There was cheering at the mention of King Aelfred's great victory over the Vikings two centuries before, but it was cut short as Magnus rose to speak again.

"This army is needed to defend Wessex. We can win a victory in the north, but it will cost us dearly. Edwin and Morcar will side with the Norse and make their host even greater."

"No." King Harold's voice filled the great space of the hall again. "The sons of Aelfgar will fight with us. For the men of Norway bring with them one who will never deal with those who drove him across the sea. My once brother Tostig is at the Norse King's side."

A deep hush followed those words. The king's face looked suddenly older, the cheer with which he had greeted his followers fled into the empty spaces between the roof beams. This was news that nobody expected. The former Earl of Northumberland, driven from the land a year ago, his army broken on the banks of the Humber a few months before, still sought revenge on the brothers who had betrayed him. There was a darkness in the king's voice. If Harold did not easily act or dress like a ruler of men, he certainly spoke like one.

"The north is still a foreign land to many of us, still ruled by Viking laws and the sons of Viking lords. But I was chosen and crowned as king of all the English lands and I recall the names of kings who have ruled before me. I think of Aelfred, Aethelstan, Eadred, Eadwig. Men of Wessex. Warrior lords who pushed back the Danes, the Norse, the Irish and the Welsh, until words spoken in the halls of Wessex were law throughout England. Mercia and Northumberland are not lands that kings of Wessex are born to rule. But they are ours by right of blood and conquest and we'll fight for them and we'll rule them. Our fathers for two hundred years have

193

spilled their blood to bring England under the rule of Wessex, and we shall not dishonour their memory.

"Tostig will make no bargain with Morcar and Edwin. The men of the north will have to fight. The sons of Aelfgar have not the strength or the skill to win alone, but they will weaken the Norse army, and when Sigurdsson thinks victory is his, we will strike him like thunder from the autumn sky.

"Three thousand men will ride north with me. But my son Magnus is wise to remain wary of the Norman fleet. I will leave warriors to defend against it and if it is his wish, Magnus will pick his force and have full command all along the coast. He will hold the fate of the kingdom in his hands while I deal with the north." The king paused again, stern in the silence he commanded. I saw that the words my father had spoken on the bridge had been true. The king had made his decision to fight long before this moot of warriors had gathered.

"Magnus," he finally said "Will you do this?" Magnus stood and every face in the torchlit hall turned towards him. He scowled back at them. It was an offer, not an order and I am sure many expected him to refuse it. A fighting lord like Magnus would want to earn war-fame at the forefront of the battle line, not waiting somewhere far away for a fleet that might never come. But there was no hesitation in Magnus' reply.

"The Bastard Duke will come. And the men of Wessex will be ready for him. I accept this command Lord King." The king nodded, then he drew his sword and held it aloft for all to see.

"This is a war not for Wessex but for all of England. And it has come at last." Sword still in hand, he took his seat again. Even Leofwin looked like he had been listening. I counted my heart beat ten times before the stamping and cheering of men eager for battle began.

"Wulfred," a hand grasped my shoulder as the moot began to break up and men's thoughts turned towards food and ale. I looked around, fearing to see one of Bera's friends. But it was Magnus. His gritted teeth and deep-set eyes were hardly a more welcome sight.

"As I said to my father, the real battle will be here in the south," he said, leading me aside and handing me a cup of ale. "The wind has fallen. Soon it will turn and the king turns with it. The Bastard Duke will not keep a fleet in harbour and feed an army all winter. At the smallest chance he'll raise his sails. He may already have made a deal with the Norse King so that we're attacked in the north and the south at the same time." I nodded. Men had spoken of the Norman Duke and his plans all summer and by that time I could think of little more say about it.

Magnus' eyes were as cold as death and talking to him was unsettling. I sometimes think that maybe he liked me, but I doubt it. I doubt that Magnus was able to like anyone. When he looked at a man, he saw a shield in a wall of shields and a sword to kill his foes. When he looked at a woman he saw a womb to breed men for that shield wall. And now he looked at me in the echoing hall, shadows blackening the shaved stubble on his head and the bleak precision of his eyes.

"Most of our greatest warriors march on York, so I need men of cunning. And I need bowmen and spear throwers to harry the enemy. I need men who know this corner of Wessex. Think of the war-fame that will be ours if we turn back the Norman Duke while my father chases Vikings across Northumberland. Will you join me again, Wulfred?"

It should have been an easy choice for me – the certainty of battle in the north or the chance of a few more quiet weeks guarding the coast before winter drove us all back to our hearths. But the continued company of Magnus' men did not appeal to me much more than facing a horde of bloodthirsty Vikings.

The king's son sensed my reluctance. He scratched his chin with his thumb and said quietly, "I heard about how you brought down my father's man Bera this afternoon. It was well fought, but there are those among the Dragons of Wessex whom you would be wise to avoid in the coming days."

So I looked at Magnus, and I looked at the cup of ale in my hand and I agreed to join him again.

"Good man," he said, raising his own cup in salute. "Our swords will not go hungry."

10. PEFENSEA

"While kings may hold our world in balance today, it is the sons of kings, and the men who follow them, who will forge the future," said my father, before joining the long column to ride north. "And it makes me proud that my son will stand at Lord Magnus' side. But while we break our foes against the walls of York, I will look to the day when we stand together in the shield wall."

"And may the north wind ever blow for you," Oswold smiled, when he was sure our father could not hear him. I smiled back at him, but I felt I was letting him down. We had trained for battle together all our lives and when the moment came to face the enemy we should have stood side by side. I should have been there to protect his sword side with my shield and to beat down the spear that leapt out of the enemy line to cut his throat. But the prospect of battle that was a joy to Oswold was still a grim spectre of terror and pain to me Oswold's joy at the prospect of a great battle against a Viking horde was still a mystery to me. The face of the man I had killed at Riaburh and the spear-slain of the hall at Llyn Rhydderch haunted me more closely than ever. Yet I felt that twinge of shame and I turned my eyes to the ground as the great column of warriors rode out of Lunden, the king's banners flying at its head, heavy carts of shields and armour grinding along at the rear and the leaves of autumn turning along the road that led them north.

Earl Leofwin also stayed with us. On the morning his brother marched on York, he was dragged from the bench where he had slumped into a drunken sleep and brought out into the cool early light of day. Harold, mounted and with the dragon banner raised at his side, looked at him briefly and cursed beneath his breath. He gestured to a man close by who picked up a bucket of water and emptied it over Leofwin's head. The earl tried feebly to shake the water out of his hair, groaned and vomited. The two men holding him up muttered darkly as water and vomit splattered over their boots.

"Leave him here," grumbled Gyrth, his fat bald head reflecting the morning sun. "He'll only slow us down – drinking all night and sleeping half the day." Harold turned to him irritably.

"He commands seven hundred warriors. We can't face the Norse without them."

"My King," said an old warrior with a face ragged from the scars of many battles. He bowed his head and Harold looked a little embarrassed. "Our oaths are to my lord Earl Leofwin, but if he cannot lead us into battle, we will follow one who can." There was a brief silence while Harold gritted his teeth in thought. It was against all the customs of war for one lord to take command of another lord's warriors. Harold stepped up to his brother and pulled back his hair to lift his head.

"Leofwin, my brother, your oath-man asks that I lead your men to the walls of York. Do I have your consent?" Leofwin groaned and dribbled. "Leofwin! May I lead your warriors north? Speak now or I'll assume your agreement." Leofwin tried to open his eyes a little, then his head fell sideways and he said nothing. The king stepped away and turned to face the mass of warriors.

"To York!" he called out as he mounted his horse. "It will be a fine and victorious day, my brother," he said, looking down at Leofwin again "when next I see you." Then he grimaced and spat on the ground. "As it will be a good day when next I meet my once brother Tostig."

I rode south again with Magnus and three hundred warriors – his own followers and others he had chosen to join him in what he was sure would be the decisive battle for England. Nearly as many men again had been left to guard on the coast while the war host had gathered at Westmynster, and Leofwin rode south a few days later with about a hundred of his most loyal followers – those who would not leave his side even at the behest of a king.

And I roamed the shore in the company of warriors. Seabirds wheeled high overhead, their cries mourning the passing season, and the great swarms of shrill-voiced swifts and swallows disappeared into the grey meeting of sea and sky, seeking lands where the winter was kinder. Yellow leaves blew across the cropped fields and still I watched the sea as if I had not peace in my heart or a home to return to.

I was thinking of home very early one morning as I rode along the coastal pathway. The followers of Magnus and Leofwin clustered in camps among the woods and the villages north of the shore. Magnus himself, and the warriors who called themselves the Bloodhelms, were camped on Fierel Hill, whose wooded flanks rose up above the sea to the south and the fields and forest to the north. And there were rough huts on high points of the cliffs where the keenest eyed of the local men were stationed to keep watch. Magnus always sent a few men out of his camp at night to ensure that the lookouts stayed awake and watchful. I missed the people of Ellasham and if I could not be with them, then I wanted no company at all, so I was happy to have a task that took me away from fighting men who bellowed over their ale and smirked cruelly as they sharpened their blades.

The sea shimmered very faintly under a half moon and my horse padded along the stony path towards the next lookout point. The voices of corncrakes rose from a field away to the north and fading leaves rustled in the breeze, like the whisperings of those whose bones lay in the hills. Far in the east, the sky foretold the coming day with the very darkest shade of blue

I had not been in Ellasham for three months. Soon the first of the summer's barley would be turned into ale. I wondered if Eohric had passed on the secret of the winter mead to any of his sons, if something of the old brewer would live on in the celebrations of generations not yet born.

I wondered if my father and brother would return from battle in the cold wastelands of Northumberland and how they would greet me if they did. And I wondered if I would ever return home or if everything we knew had gone forever. Like Eohric, like the summer, like the joy I had once felt to see Hildelyth smiling as sunlight fell through the bright leaves of Andredsweald. I stopped my horse and took a deep breath as I gazed out across the dark and whispering water. Way out on the horizon, out in the fading of the world, the first glimmers of the coming day danced on the waves. I loosened my cloak, for although the summer was gone, the night was a warm one.

But as I watched those tiny beads of light, a coldness sank through me. The wind had turned. The ships of Normandy could finally sail for England. I remembered those words Ragnald had spoken in the dunes months before. Words about ships sailing at night carrying lanterns to guide the rest of the fleet. Lanterns which, at a great distance, might look like the first glimmers of dawn dancing on the waves.

I sat there and stared at the sea for a long time, my horse tearing at the stunted grass of the path's edge. That cold fist of fear turned in my belly again, the way it had when Ragnald had woken me that night in the dunes. I tried to tell myself I was worrying about nothing, that those far pulses of light were truly just the first glimpse of dawn. But they were in the south. The faint lightening of the sky was away to the east and there was blackness between it and these lights on the waves. I looked along the coast, straining my eyes to see into the furthest distance, looking for the red glow of a beacon fire, but there was nothing. If this was the coming of a great fleet, then I was the only one who knew of it.

The hour of dawn grew closer and the lights brightened and spread further across the horizon. I wanted to ride away, far away from a duke whose claim to kingship was more important to him

200

than the lives of men; far away from Magnus whose greatest joy would be to lead his warriors into the jaws of death. But where would I go? If there was any man in Wessex who could find a way to hold an army at bay, to drive the coming war back into the sea, then that man was Magnus.

I gently kicked my horse's flank and, keeping an eye towards those blinking, still distant lights on the sea, I rode along the stone-strewn pathway until I came to a place where a smaller, earthen track turned away from it and led to the Bloodhelms' camp on Fierel Hill.

"Wake up!" I shouted. "There's a fleet at sea." By the time I reached the tented encampment, the trees and the grass were silvered with the brittle light of dawn and the hills beyond were turned to mist. And the deep grey distance of the sea far below crawled with dark shapes and the lights of ships.

The guard at the camp's edge woke with a start, sprang away from the tree he was leaning against and scrabbled about on the ground to pick up his spear. I pointed down the hill, across the trees to where the blaze of a beacon fire had erupted from a distant clifftop.

"Shit!" the guard muttered. Had he not been dozing at his post, he would have alerted the camp long before my arrival.

"Light the beacon," I said to him. He ran of across the smooth grass towards a mound of wood piled at the hill's summit, and I kicked my horse into a gallop and rode into the camp.

"Lord Magnus! Lord Magnus!" I shouted. "The lanterns of a fleet. The Bastard Duke has come!" Magnus was suddenly there, in the half light, his eyes red with sleep. He did not have to ask me to explain myself. I pointed to the south and he saw the lantern-lights and dark shapes on the brightening water.

"They've come at last," he said, his voice almost a purr. "Good man," he added and I did not know whether he addressed me or the distant Willelm of Normandy.

The smoke of burning tinder blew across the camp as the great beacon of Fierel was kindled and there were shouts and hastening footfalls, curses and the glimmer of blades in the dawn. War had burst upon the quiet coast of Wessex and I was already at its heart.

The darkness of night descended again as Magnus led the Bloodhelms down the woodland pathway that led to the coast. The weight of my shield beat against my back and the rough edges of a stuffed leather tunic chafed at my neck and wrists. There was no time that morning for the heavy carts that hauled loads of arms and armour behind an army on the move. I and the men around me rode straight to battle, mailed and helmeted, holding reins in one hand and a spear in the other.

And there was quiet in the woods. The high branches swayed, leaves fell and birds whistled in alarm and bolted at the approach of men and horses. But the trees loomed over and for a while I felt protected by their deep shadows.

Then we broke out of the woods and onto the coastal pathway. The morning was already bright and the sun sent low shafts of light glancing across the waves. Those ships I had first seen as points of lantern light in the darkness were close now. The men around me fell into excited chatter, pointing spears and shaking their fists at the Norman fleet. For a moment I stared across the rolling water, at and the shields lining the gunwhales of the ships, the tiny silhouette figures of the men aboard them and the crosses and carved beast-heads that rose at their prows. I tried to count the ships of our enemies, but there were so many of them. Some were big trading ships, large enough to carry horses and maybe fifty men, others were little open boats like those used by fishermen, but there were more than a hundred of them visible, and they disappeared around a headland which must have hidden many more.

"Their sails are turned to the east," Magnus shouted, above the wind and above the babble of his men. He drew the sword Ironclaw and held it aloft, the slanting rays of the sun shivering blue and grey along its edge. "So we ride east. Ride for Wessex!" he cried, and a volley of whoops and war cries went up as his men followed him at a gallop, a hundred men against a host of thousands borne by the sea. And I followed with them, feeling powerless to do anything but ride on into the approaching battle.

The land rose up onto high cliffs and the sea spread out below us and revealed more of the fleet. All summer long there had been rumours of five hundred, six hundred, even a thousand ships waiting to carry an army out of the ports of Normandy. I had dismissed those claims as stories told over and over and getting bigger with each telling. But now the fleet seemed to stretch as far as the sea itself. There were seven hundred warriors scattered along the coast to oppose this fleet and the fleet had as many ships as Wessex had men.

The cliffs plunged down to lower ground once more and the wind blew at my back, and all around the followers of Magnus roared and hollered and drove their horses on in a mad ecstasy of battle lust. But the wind drove the Norman fleet faster still. Groups of armed and mounted men rode out of the woods, drawn by the sight of beacon fires and smoke billowing along the coast. They greeted Magnus and bowed to him as the son of their king and we all reined in our horses for a few moments while words were exchanged. And all the while the fleet outpaced us.

Finally, we reached another headland and Magnus called us to a halt. Raising a hand to shield my eyes from the level rays of the morning sun, I looked down on a bay of shingle close to a cluster of houses and fishermen's huts called Pefensea. In that bay and on the jetties at the edge of the little town, a mass of Norman ships were already ashore.

"Shall we give them a taste of Wessex steel, my lord?" One warrior held his sword aloft and other men gathered at his side.

"Shut up!" Magnus snapped. "There are thousands of them. If we fight now, we die and they take the south before the king returns." Eager warriors looked at their lord doubtfully, but we all followed as he led us along a low gully out of sight of the bay and into an outcrop of woodland to the north.

"How many are we? Two hundred spears?" he said, turning at the wood's edge. "By nightfall we'll be six hundred strong. We'll summon the fyrd and they'll arrive in their hundreds tomorrow and the day after and every day. But we'll still not have the strength to turn back the host of Normandy. We must hold them on the shore and await my father's return." There were mutters of dissent– the king was in Northumberland facing the axes of Norway and his return was far from certain – but Magnus brushed them aside.

"There are hundreds of ships in that bay. Thousands of men and horses. And between us and our foes lies half a mile of marsh. If we attack them now, they kill us and they break loose in Wessex. If we stay behind the trees and the marsh where they can't charge their horses, if we hide our numbers, then we can pin them down here until the king arrives."

Magnus' plan made sense and his men reluctantly dismounted and spread themselves out along the edge of the wood.

"Wulfred!" he called to me before I had time to get off my horse. "Get out into the marsh." My bow was in a long leather sheath strapped to my saddle and Magnus pulled it out and thrust it into my hands. "Stop the enemy getting too near. I don't want them to see how few we are. Bowmen!" he shouted, turning away from me and riding along his thin-spread line of men. "Bowmen into the marsh. Keep those bastards at a distance."

I dismounted and, ignoring the warriors who were spreading out along the copse's edge, I looked across the marsh. Less than half a mile away, I could see the masts and sails of Norman ships rising above a beach hidden by sand dunes. Among the dunes, closer still, I saw spearheads reflecting the morning sun, and spears with coloured pennants flying from them moving swiftly as the Norman lords deployed their men. Between myself and those spears was a stretch of flat boggy land, thinly scattered with bushes and a few stunted birch and alder trees.

"Take this, it'll be better protection if they have their own bowmen." A bearded warrior leant down from his horse and handed me a long shield. Its end was tapered and when I touched it to the ground, the top still reached my chin. A few warriors favoured such shields for the extra protection they gave a man's legs in battle, but most found them heavy and hard to manoeuvre. I dropped my round shield, lifted the long shield and stepped out of the cover of the trees. Along the line of the wood and the marsh, other men were doing the same, some dressed in mail and helmets, others with leather caps and padded tunics. They all carried bows and they had bags of arrows hanging from their belts.

The rains of autumn had not yet come and the marsh was dry. Across the flat ground, among the spears and the pennants, I saw the iron-clad heads of a few men above the dunes. They pointed and they waved to others. I saw a man put his hand to his mouth to shout a command, but the wind stole his voice and I heard nothing. Glancing left and right, I saw the other bowmen hurrying forward and against all my instincts, I rushed towards the enemy to keep up with them.

Two bowmen to my left reached a thicket of brambles and birch that stood before a low expanse of reed-covered, waterlogged ground. There was another patch of undergrowth just ahead of me and, pausing to look over the lie of the land, I decided to take cover there.

"We will hold them here!" Magnus' voice carried across the level ground. "We and we alone hold the throne of Wessex for King Harold. We few are the heroes tales will speak of." The men among the trees behind me began to call out insults at the distant Normans, but their voices were puny in the silence of the marsh. They had placed spare shields all along the line of trees to make Magnus' force look bigger than it really was. I hefted up the long shield again and ran the last few paces towards the undergrowth.

And it was just as I reached the tangle of gorse and broom that the first arrow flew. But not from the bow of a Wessex man. I saw it streak across the reedbed from the sand dunes and it clattered through the birch branches above the two men on my left. They both glanced over at me as the arrow fell into the sedge-grass. I thrust the end of my shield into the soft ground so that it stood before me as protection. It was painted white and red and would be seen easily through the tangled branches, but it was better than crouching among thorns waiting to be shot.

An arrow whispered through the air above as I strung my bow. The two men among the birch trees on the left shot arrows high over the marsh to land in the sand dunes where Norman archers stood exposed as silhouettes against the sky. I scanned the dune-tops with an arrow nocked to my bowstring, picking out a target. But before I could even aim, something smacked hard into the top of the shield, splitting the wood and leaving the corner hanging on by its iron rim. Stuck half way through the broken planking was an arrow only the length of a forearm, but thick, black-fletched and with a wicked iron point. On top of one of the dunes stood what looked like a priest holding some kind of cross.

For a moment I watched him in confusion, then he lowered the object and I realised he held a crossbow. It was a weapon little known in Wessex, a thing from the east which shot its bolt further than an ordinary bow and at great speed, but which was slow to shoot again. The man on the dune pointed his bow to the ground and put his foot in a stirrup to hold it while he used both hands to draw back the thick string. He was foolish to stay in view and I drew back my own arrow and loosed it at him. It cut a swift arc through the air and struck. The man fell back, disappeared down the far side of the dune, and I could not tell whether I had hit him or the bow he was drawing. The two men on my left whooped and I raised my bow to them.

The arrows did not fly for long. Arrows are well-crafted things, straightened and fletched with care by skilled men, the tips cut and hammered by smiths, sharpened up and bound with great skill to the shafts. A man must have a good weight of coin to buy arrows and even dukes and kings are loath to see them wasted them on the empty air.

The coloured pennants of those who commanded the Norman host still flitted back and forth, but there were no more heads raised above the mounds of sand. From time to time I heard bursts of tuneless singing from the woods at my back as Magnus' men roared out battle songs to show their confidence and their numbers. The sounds of hoofbeats rolled across the quiet marsh as more warriors arrived from further along the coast. From the beach in front of me I heard bursts of shouting in what I guessed was the tongue of Normandy, though it was distant and indistinct. To the west, a makeshift banner was raised on the high ground above the sea and marsh. It looked like a man's tunic nailed to a spearshaft, but it showed that Magnus of Wessex controlled the high ground and the men of Normandy were confined to the beach. Sometimes, I caught the sound of digging coming from the edge of the beach, and it was a sound I was glad to hear for it told me that the Normans were making banks and ditches and preparing to defend the scrap of land they held rather than planning to break out of it.

The sun climbed higher into the cloudswept sky and the salt-tasting wind played among the sedge and rattled the drying reeds. In the shield wall, a man relies on the warriors to his left and right to protect him and he in turn protects them. The bowman, alone in the emptiness between two armies, has only his eyes and his ears and his quickness. Those were lonely hours, and I feared to even blink lest a Norman should emerge from the marsh grass and rush at me in my tiny moment of blindness. Late in the morning and oblivious to the men of Wessex and Normandy, a flock of curlews made its way across the flat ground, probing for worms and watching the flat landscape. Their presence was reassuring - I knew they would take flight and give me warning if any foe tried to creep unseen towards where I crouched.

It must have been just after noon when the Normans came to parley. First I heard the sound of monks singing dirges, blown in on a stiffening wind. I had been crouched behind my shield all morning, scanning the line of sand dunes with a dozen arrows stuck into the soft ground close to my right hand. A group of figures appeared over the dunes and I plucked an arrow from the soil. If this was an attack, I was in a bad place. I could shoot arrows and kill my attackers, but only so many of them. There were less than twenty bowmen in the marsh, and thousands of Normans waiting in the ships and on the beach. If they knew how few Magnus' men were, they would surely attack and I would be one of the first to die. I glanced back at the woods. If I retreated, would Magnus have me killed for running away from battle? Probably.

The figures stepped forward and the curlews took flight, their plaintive cries soaring above the droning of the monks. At their head was a tall man in war gear. His sword was sheathed and in his hand he held a staff topped with a polished gold cross. At his right stood an elderly priest in black robes embroidered with gold, carrying a heavy leatherbound Bible, and behind him came a group of twenty warriors with long spears and armour that flashed like fishes' scales when the sun glanced through the clouds. Monks walked on either side and they ceased their chanting as the whole group knelt to pray and to hear the old priest read from his great book.

This did not look like an attack. The nobleman at the front looked too important to lead a charge and the warriors seemed too few. But I kept my arrow nocked on the bowstring.

"It is Odo, the Bishop of Bayeaux!" I heard the voice of Earl Leofwin rise from the edge of the woods. "He has slave boys sent to his bedchamber to sing him to sleep, and they seldom walk for days afterwards." There was laughter among the trees and when I looked around I saw Leofwin and Magnus and a dozen warriors striding out across the marsh. The Normans ceased their prayers and picked their way forward until they stood at the far side of the reedbed, with Magnus and Leofwin at the near edge, only a few paces from where I crouched. I knew of Odo. Bishop of Bayeaux, half brother to the Bastard Duke and a feared warrior, spoken of as a man with a sword in one hand and the cross of Christ in the other. Today his sword was sheathed, but his cross was bright among the brown weeds of the marsh.

Magnus nodded to me and I nodded back and then the bishop bellowed something in a language I did not know.

"Leofwin, Earl of Middlesex, son of the outlaw Godwin - where is your brother, the usurper Harold, Earl of Wessex?" called the elderly priest. Although he spoke the English tongue well, he was toothless and his voice was thin compared to the roaring of the bishop. Magnus and Leofwin glanced at each other. It was the older man who spoke.

"My brother Harold was chosen as king by the Witan, in keeping with our laws. You have no business in his realm. You war host is like a cluster of flies perched on the snout of a mighty bear. I ask you to leave now before we swat you away."

The priest translated for Odo and the bishop's face flushed red. I could see him well for he stood little more than fifty paces away. Within an easy arrow-shot in fact, though I had taken my arrow from the bowstring now and stood to watch and to listen to this encounter of enemies. Odo was a big man – fat as well as tall – and his anger gave him the look of a drunk trying to remember what he was arguing about. Again he shouted across the reedbed, wasting his voice on men who understood little of his tongue.

"The crown of England was promised to my brother William, Duke of Normandy." The men stood behind Magnus and Leofwin roared with laughter and tried to imitate the priest's piping voice until the earl held up a hand for silence. "Harold of Wessex swore on sacred relics to support the Duke. He has broken a holy oath. Let him come forward."

"My brother the king is a busy man." Leofwin smiled and gave a dismissive wave of his hand. "He has churches to build, arguments to settle among farmers. He must collect rent and tribute from his people and listen to beautiful women sing him to sleep in the evening." Again, the warriors hooted with laughter and beat weapons against their shields. "He has no time to speak with you. Sail for home before you face the spears of the Dragons of Wessex." The priest must have been tactful in his translation, because Odo looked at him and at Leofwin doubtfully before he spoke again.

"The Dragons of Wessex are not here Leofwin. I do not see their banner. You have only four or five hundred men? My lord Duke Willelm commands thousands, from the farthest ends of the Christian world. His host is blessed by the Holy Father himself. Withdraw your rabble before we break it."

The dozen warriors who stood with Leofwin and Magnus were not laughing now, I noticed. I did not know for sure how many more men had arrived at the copse over the course of the morning, but four or five hundred was not a bad guess. Our position was not nearly strong enough to hold and the enemy knew it. I tried to swallow my fear, and looked at the arrows lined up in the soft ground, wondering what I would do if the Normans tried to cross the marsh in force. Leofwin must have feared attack too, but his reply showed no such fear.

"Five hundred, my lord bishop? I command the warriors of Glowcestre, of Crogendene, Basingastoc and Swinedune. There are men here – spearmen and axemen - from Berlesdun, Tantun, Bristelmestun, Breguntford and all over Wessex. Men who could behead one of your plough-horses with a single axe blow. One man of Wessex is worth a dozen of the perfumed bedchamber boys you bring." The earl stood on his toes and peered at the horizon, at the clusters of masts just beyond the dunes. "If you tried to break us here Lord Bishop, how many would you have left to face the might of King Harold? Sail for home now and perhaps the king's fleet will let you leave in peace."

There was a brief discussion between the priest and the bishop, probably about whether the towns Leofwin had mentioned were real or not. They had clearly never heard of them. Magnus looked across at me, staring hard and grinding his front teeth together. I felt that he was willing me to take up an arrow and shoot down the Bishop of Bayeaux.

"You are a fool and the servant of an oath breaker," Odo finally decided. "Your gang of nothing-men will break like rotten wood before the spears of Normandy…"

"Where is your master?" This time it was Magnus who shouted out, interrupting the priest's translation. "Where is the Duke of Normandy? Where is the Bastard of Falaise?" The priest looked blank for a moment then translated the question. Odo began muttering a reply, but Magnus cut in again.

"Perhaps he would not have the hearthside tales of generations yet unborn recount that he set his foot on English soil only to have it driven off again. Perhaps he thinks it better to remain on his ship." Magnus' men jeered the bishop while the priest translated again. Then, with a roar of rage Odo hurled garbled words across the sand and stamped back through the weeds and the long grass. Struggling to clutch his Bible as he stumbled backwards, the priest squeaked the reply at us.

"Death will find you all pierced by Norman spears! And you Magnus, bastard-born son of Harold the Abomination, will go to Hell with the sword of Christ in your neck!" In the priest's voice, it sounded like a feeble whine and the men of Wessex bleated like sheep at their retreating backs.

Leofwin grimaced at me and at the other bowmen as he set off back towards the trees. The earl had been confident and calm in the hope of convincing the bishop that his force was strong enough to hold its ground. But Magnus had lost his temper and I could only guess at how the Normans might react. At that moment, I expected them to attack. If they did, I would make my way back across the marsh, shooting arrows as I went, rather than run for my life towards the woods and risk ending up on the wrong end of a Bloodhelm's spear. But I glanced back towards those woods and thought of the country that lay beyond them. Rough, scrubby wasteland that ran northwards for at least five miles before it reached the thick cover of Andredsweald. Country upon which the Normans could use their horsemen to scatter, chase and slaughter an army. If the enemy could cross the marsh in force my chances of escaping into the forest were non-existent.

But the attack I awaited did not come. I watched the pennants of the Norman lords pass back and forth against the sky and the grey sea. I heard the snorting and whinnying of horses and the sounds of digging, but nobody sent spears and swords or even arrows against us. And at the edge of the trees behind me, the hawk banner of Earl Leofwin fluttered on the wind. Although the day was still warm, the dampness of the marsh crept through the leather of my boots and through the cloth of my breeches. The smoke of cooking fires wafted across from the beach and my stomach growled with hunger as my throat chafed with thirst.

When the shadows of evening began to lengthen, another group of bowmen, mostly fyrd from the looks of them, scrambled across the marsh and I was sent back to rest in safety.

Back among the trees, I unstrung my bow and put the cord into a leather pouch at my waist to keep the damp of night off it. There was a cheer from some of the warriors in the wood as a wagon loaded with barrels of ale arrived. I sat on a log eating a bowl of barley stew strengthened with strong herbs and pigs' blood, and I thought about the arrow that had whistled above my head in the marsh, and about how dismal a thing it would be to die in battle alongside such men as followed Lord Magnus.

212

The sun faded far to the west and for a while the whole of the distant sea glowed as it clung to the last of the light. And thus passed the first day of the war against the Norman Duke.

I did not sleep well that night. Wrapped in a fur-lined cloak I huddled close to a smouldering fire on the damp ground and listened to the noises in the woods. Sword-men and spearmen travelled through the night, guided by the trail of beacons that still burned along the coast, and by the rumours of ships and war hosts that snaked from one village to another.

At every hour of the night, groups of warriors arrived, their horses rumbling through the shadows and their voices loud in greeting. Magnus and Leofwin were just as noisy in welcome, hoping their voices carried across to the Norman watchmen clustered among the sand dunes. I do not think either man slept for any of the time that we lurked among the trees at Pefensea.

In the morning, I peered through the early mist at what at any other time, would have been a large gathering of warriors. The smoke of many fires mingled with the mist, some warming pots of broth and stew, others just sending out smoke and flame for the Normans to see. Men bustled about, chopping wood, building shelters and benches from branches and fallen trees, shouting orders and greetings. Some sat at the fires drinking ale and singing songs of war. There was enough noise for an army three times as great as we were. And perhaps the Normans believed our deception, for still they made no move to cross the marsh.

With the coming of daylight, the first of the fyrd began to arrive too. They drifted in from the villages of Sussex, some scared and some snarling as they picked their way through the trees. And as I scooped a bowl of mutton and barley from one of the cooking pots, Ragnald and Godric appeared through the smoke of campfires.

"Welcome my friends, it is good to see you again." I hugged them both and grinned like a fool. It was indeed good to see them.

213

So good to see men for whom life was something other than spears and battle. They had left the shore at harvest time two months earlier, gone home with the disbanding of the fyrd. Ragnald greeted me like a lost friend, then a more sombre expression stole over his face as he stared out across the marsh. Just visible through the rising mist were the banners that the Normans had planted along the sand dunes. They flapped and rolled in the breeze, a show of strength by an enemy that would not yet show itself.

"So it has come to war at last," Ragnald said. Then he raised his eyes to the yellowing branches of the wood's edge. "The leaves turn and the war begins." Behind his eyes, he had suddenly gone somewhere distant, into the places he had looked when my father, Cuthred and I had blundered into his cottage on that snow-bright morning at the dawning of the year. Godric strutted and looked excited.

"So we drive these bastards back into the sea and go home, eh?" he muttered. He carried a long pole with a wicked-bladed knife bound at one end and he jabbed it clumsily in the direction of the beach. It was not the knife that Earl Leofwin had given him, of course. That remained in its sheath at his belt. And for some reason I thought of Godric then as an old man, fifty winters from now, with the sons of Godwin and the dukes and bishops Normandy all long dead and himself sat at the door of his house, proudly showing his grandchildren the knife once given to him by an earl as a reward for courage and skill.

"We drive these bastards into the sea when my father returns," growled Magnus, who had been listening close by. "When we've got three thousand spear-trained warriors here and at least as many fyrd."

"A war lies between us and our winter hearths," said Ragnald, turning from his contemplation of the trees.

"It does." Magnus noticed the knife-sheaf at Godric's belt. "Your friend is wise, you are brave and your lord here is a cunning

214

warrior. You will be well rewarded when our foes are beaten."
Wise, brave and cunning. He might have been right about Ragnald.

More fyrd arrived through the morning and the warriors ordered
them about, got them cooking up big pots of barley and onions,
digging latrine ditches and pointing their makeshift spears up
through the berry-laden elder trees so that the most keen-sighted of
the Normans saw a tangle of wicked iron points. There were already
many shields hung among the low branches, to look like a line of
men awaiting the enemy's charge.

Although the mist cleared, a steady rain began as the day set in
and warriors sat around the cooking fires and huddled into their
cloaks against the misery of it. A few fyrdmen, more used to
spending their days out in the fields with the rain on their backs,
were climbing trees to try to get a glimpse of the Norman host and I
joined them. I pulled myself up through the low sweeping branches
of an old elm tree, then higher into the middle branches until they
swayed under my weight.

Across the marsh and the sand dunes I could see Norman ships
hauled up on the beach, anchored in the bay and tied to the little
jetties of Pefensea. There were a few big ships, like the wide, flat-
bellied vessels used by traders, with carved beast-heads and crosses
on their prows, and there were many little ships, many more than I
could count, the kind used by fishermen, but newly built and
brightly painted with images of sea-beasts and saints and charms to
protect them from the whims of the waves. And I could see the
Norman warhorses being exercised along the beach, their hooves
throwing up sand and pebbles, their riders steady with spear and
shield as if the battle for the kingdom had already begun. I
wondered what it would feel like to stand against a charge of such
men and horses. My father had always dismissed such tactics,
saying that mounted men are no more capable of breaking a shield
wall than men on foot - that they only look and sound more

215

ferocious. But I found it hard to imagine that any man would stand his ground when such a charge came thundering on.

As I watched, a huge flock of plovers winged across the bay, turning and twisting through the sky as one, their black backs and their pale underbellies alternating as they went. They did not stay to face the cold dark coming of winter. They turned their backs and followed the path of the sun to warmer, kinder lands. I thought of Aelfwyn as the birds disappeared into the grey meetings of the sky and the sea. But Aelfwyn was as distant as the moon over the midsummer trees. On the rain-washed edge of battle there were only blood hungry men with furrowed brows and cold fingers curled around their spearshafts.

"The birds are not fools like us," I said to Godric and Ragnald while we ate stew and hard bread that evening. "They know death is coming and they fly away. They don't wave a sword in its face."

"Maybe men have forgotten more than they have learned," nodded Ragnald, that faraway look still in his eyes. Godric looked at us as if we were both mad.

"Well when you learn to fly, teach the rest of us and we'll follow the birds," he said.

And it was there in the fading light, as warriors sat down to their food and their ale and as sodden men crept in from the marsh to report that the enemy had made no movement all day, came the news that nobody in that wood had dared to hope for so soon.

"Victory! A great victory in the north! The Norse King is slain, and with him the traitor Tostig, and their army destroyed on the field of battle. King Harold rides south to join us!" The messenger galloped along the edge of the marsh, his horse kicking up mud and his voice ringing into the grey sky. Ragnald looked up from his bowl, an uncharacteristic grin splitting his face, Godric brought his fist down on his knee with a whoop of triumph and I felt a surge of hope. The battle that my brother and father had ridden away to fight had ended in victory. There was a good chance they were alive and the great army of Wessex was heading south to where we clung to this strip of coast. The Norman Duke had not yet fought his way through a few hundred warriors. When the full might of Wessex swept down from the north, his army would run for its ships. Before the falling of the leaves the war would be over and I would be back in Ellasham, and I thought of its bright hearths and quiet, darkening fields and the people whom I loved.

And I thought of Hildelyth. And everything was suddenly simple. There may be princesses of Wessex in the world whose beauty eclipsed the dawn and whose words wove spells beneath the moon, but Hildelyth, waiting among the dark hills to the north, was as much a part of me as my heart and my blood and that without her smile and her gentle mockery and her warmth there could be no dawn or midsummer moon to compare princesses of Wessex to.

Magnus ran across the woodland pathway to intercept the horseman, his iron-shod boots thundering on the ground and we rose to our feet with the cheering spread along the wood's edge. It was as if victory was ours already and, overwhelmed by that sudden moment of celebration, I clapped a hand on Godric's shoulder.

"When this war is won I'll marry Hildelyth," I said to him. "And we'll live long and in peace and with full bellies and one day we'll tell our grandchildren of these times." On any other day it would have been a foolish thing to say to Godric. On any other day he would have sneered and made some joke about there being enough madness in his family without me marrying into it. But on that rainy evening as the news of victory surged through the trees like fire through a field of stubble, he smiled and clapped a hand on my shoulder and said nothing. Ragnald was still grinning. A loud chant of 'Godwinsson' went up into the darkening sky.

The celebrations went on into the darkest hours. The rain dwindled into mist and war drums, great oak barrels with hardened pigskin stretched over one end, hammered out their brutal rhythms and the braying of horns rolled across the marsh. Songs of victories past were sung with a great roaring and stamping, every scrap of wood the fyrdmen had gathered was thrown onto the fires. One fire reached up into the branches of a tall ash tree so that its flying sparks were visible for many, many miles around. And the Normans on the beach and in their ships must have believed that it was King Harold's army itself that had brought the news of victory from the north.

And late in the night, as men finally drifted into sleep, the wind fell away and a dense fog rolled in from the south and the west. I awoke before dawn in a chill that felt heavy with the souls of the battle-slain. The fog was so thick that a man or even a horse might have passed just a couple of paces from where I lay in my cloak and I would have noticed nothing. The only sound was the quiet rustling of the branches. I propped myself up on an elbow and listened out for the noises of mailed men advancing across the marsh to attack us in the blind darkness. But there was nothing. On a night like that a man could look around him and not know if he was alive or dead. But I knew I was alive and I knew that hope was alive in my heart again. I buried my head deep in the hood of my cloak and went back to sleep.

Dawn crept like a whisper across the silence of the sea and the marsh. And it was hours after the dawn before the fog lifted. And when it did, three parts of the duke's fleet were gone.

11. BLOOD ON THE FIELDS

"Loose!" At my command the first flight of arrows streaked across the grey afternoon sky. Mine missed the leading horseman by a hand's breadth, but another black-feathered shaft spitted a man through the neck and brought him crashing down, hammered into the ground by the weight of his mail. Another warrior fell with an arrow in his chest and a wounded horse threw its rider and fled across the field. The half dozen men at my side picked up new arrows and drew their bowcords again.

The leading Norman raised his shield and shouted orders. His men closed in around the two wagons, raised their own shields and spurred their mounts into a trot, while the draymen whipped the lumbering carthorses into whatever speed they could muster. I sent three more arrows hard into that cluster of men and horses before they reached the far edge of the stubble field. One of the dray horses took two arrows in its flank and kicked and stumbled until the wagon ground to a halt. The two men who had driven it leapt away and scrambled away towards the safety of the woods that lay beyond the field's edge. One of the Normans, hit in the thigh by and arrow and thrown from his horse, called for help as he dragged himself through the stubble behind his companions.

"That's enough," I called out, raising an arm and signalling my men to stop. The Normans were close to Magnus' position and I did not want to face his wrath if our shafts fell among his men. "Good shooting," I added. The man on my left grunted reluctantly as he lowered his bow.

"That's the last village those bastards will burn," he muttered. It was Ulric, the poacher who had once saved me from a Northumbrian spear beside the walls of Riaburh. He had been brave and desperate that day, a condemned man given the thinnest of chances to redeem himself. Now he was calm and cold, a man forged into a warrior by Magnus.

The first spear flew from a thicket of ivy-tangled elder and glanced off a Norman's shoulder. I saw his shield arm drop and he slumped forward in the saddle. The second hit their leader low in the belly. His horse bolted, leaving him flailing in the damp stubble, his yellow-plumed helmet rolling beside him. And when he fell, the enemy broke. Spears and axes flew in both directions. Horses reared and screamed. One of the riders called out and held a sword aloft, trying to rally the others until he fell with a spear jammed under his helmet. Another was brought down as Magnus led his Bloodhelms charging in amongst them – fifty spearmen in tight ranks driving their long blades through thirty panicking riders. A few horsemen tried to meet the charge, while others hung back to defend the wagons. But the Bloodhelms moved in a tight wedge with their spears held high, stabbing at the faces of horses and men, and the Norman riders wheeled in confusion. I knew nothing of their tongue, but I could tell that three or four of them were all shouting different orders to the others. Then another horseman fell into the blood-slick stubble and the survivors fled, galloping back over the crest of the hill, leaving the wagons of meat and grain where they stood. The sound of their hoofbeats faded into the grey afternoon. I picked up my arrows and led my bowmen across the field.

There were calls of greeting and congratulation from Magnus' men, but Magnus himself was knelt on the ground beside the spear-pierced leader of the Norman raiders, shouting questions in some clumsy version of the Norman tongue. The man on the ground had his hair shaved off at the back and sides in the Norman fashion. He muttered weakly, his teeth clenched in pain and his hands fumbling at the spear still stuck in his belly. Magnus roared with rage and twisted the shaft. The man screamed and spat blood into the stubble. Rising to his feet, Magnus kicked the Norman and cursed his dying soul. The fallen man tried to roll away, but screamed out again as the blade dug deeper into his guts.

"Kill the wounded," Magnus called to his men. "Except this bastard here. Let the crows finish him." He cursed again in the

Norman tongue as he ripped the bloody spear free and tossed it to one of his men.

A man in a brown cloak darted from behind one of the carts and plunged towards the trees at the field's edge. He was one of the draymen – probably from the plundered village, forced at spearpoint to drive the cart for the enemy. I would have let him go, but Ulric whipped out an arrow and loosed it across the field. It caught the fleeing man behind the knee. There was a shriek of pain and he tumbled into the weeds at the edge of the wood. Two warriors dragged him back. The other drayman was already captured and he whimpered with fear, staring down in horror at the knife held to his throat.

"Tie their hands and feet," Magnus growled. "And drag them through the villages behind your horses. The rags of their flesh and the trailing bones will teach the people what happens to those who aid the king's enemies."

"My lord, we had no choice…" One of the draymen fell at Magnus' feet to beg for mercy. Magnus brought his knee up hard into the man's chin.

"Shut up. Your life is finished." The other man lay pale and groaning, blood running freely from his leg as two warriors tied him. If he was lucky he would bleed to death before the stony roads ripped the flesh from his back. I wanted to speak out for these men, but Magnus' rage was rushing like a torrent and there was no way to stop it. I glanced at Ragnald and saw a look of pain and horror such as I had never seen on his face before.

"What about the food?" I asked instead. The two carts were laden with sacks of grain and pigs' carcasses taken from a nearby village.

"We keep it," Magnus snapped. "If folk let the enemy take their supplies, they don't deserve to have them back".

It would have been pointless taking food back anyway. A short distance to the north, a grey smear of smoke loomed into the sky and I knew there would be nothing left of the village but ash and corpses.

From the top of a bramble bush, a butcher bird eyed the dead men on the ground and the dying Norman lord who clawed the ground and gasped for breath. The draymen screamed and pleaded as the horses began to drag them away.

"If my father lives," I said while Ulric and the other bowmen cut their precious arrows from the flesh of the dead and stuffed their leather pouches with whatever plunder they could grab. "At least I can tell him I fought for the people of Wessex while he was in Northumberland." Ragnald slipped the linen cord from his bow and looped it around his belt.

"In Northumberland the people would gladly have a ruler from across the sea to cut them loose from the chains of Wessex," he said. "But these bastards have nothing to offer here but theft and murder."

War had found us, and in war things change terribly. I saw my enemies dying and that was no longer a dark and haunting thing. It was only better that they should die than continue their bloody work.

No fewer than twenty villages had been destroyed since the enemy fleet left Pefensea. At first the foggy morning had been a time of panic and argument. A messenger brought news that the Normans had moved through dark and fog and by both land and sea to take the port of Haestingas at first light. Magnus had lost control of the war and it was Leofwin who finally said that we should abandon Pefensea and find a position from which we could harass the enemy when they tried to move deeper into Wessex.

Heading east and inland, Magnus and Leofwin's column passed dark stains of smoke and ash where villages had once stood. Among the ruin of houses, I saw fire-shrivelled bodies, grown men and women shrunk to the size of children with the ash around them turned black by the fat from their bodies. In the harvested fields, corpses, some with their insides spilled around them, buzzed with flies. People who had escaped into the woods told us Norman warriors had taken the meat, the grain and the women, slaughtered men, children and the old and burned every house. Again I remembered that night in the spring, that night that already seemed so long ago, when a strange new star shone like a warning fire in the dusk and my father had told me I would soon learn why warriors fight. Amid the blood and fire that now raged through the land, every turn of the road threw up a new reason to fight.

While the Norman host had dug in behind the earthworks of Haestingas, Magnus and Leofwin split their forces into smaller warbands camped in the forests north of the town. We ambushed Norman raiding parties, protected local villages as best we could and struggled to keep the Duke in his stronghold. The fyrd joined us from all across Sussex and Kent and beyond, but they did not have the horses to ride quickly from one place to another or the skill to fight horsemen. And many more people came to the woodland camps to seek refuge from the enemy.

As the column of warriors rode away from the bloody field of our little victory, three bedraggled women and a small boy came stumbling out of the woods.

"My lords!" called one of them. "Spare us some bread. Our houses are burned and our winter grain is gone." Her face was stained by smoke and streaked by tears, but I saw her blue eyes and the golden hair falling from her ragged grey shawl, and I had to close my eyes and take a deep breath when I realised she reminded me of my mother.

"And our husbands murdered!" wailed another woman, who just sat helplessly beside the path and sobbed. One by one Magnus' men rode past them in silence.

"Pray for God's help!" shouted one man, turning to them with a scowl. "If you still live, then you have His favour."

I nudged my horse aside and untied a leather bag from the saddle. There was a loaf of bread and some smoked meat in it and I passed it to the golden-haired woman.

"God bless you Lord," she stammered, clutching the bag to her breast. The small boy clung to her skirts and looked bewildered.

"Lord Magnus is camped in the woods three miles north of here," I said. "You might find shelter there."

One of the men frowned as I rejoined the column.

"Leave them to look after themselves," he grunted. "We are at war. We can't afford to feed those who don't fight."

"Women can always look after themselves," said the man who rode in front of me and a ripple of bitter laughter passed along the column as those desperate survivors scuttled away into the trees.

"They could just take the food they need." Godric spat into the campfire and stared angrily at the rising smoke when I told him of our ambush. "The bastards don't need to kill everyone."

"They need more than food." Magnus paused by our fire and lowered himself onto a tree stump, his grim face lit redly by the flames. "They need a battle. If we can stop their raiding and cut off their supplies by sea, they'll starve in Haestigas. They'll be eating their horses before Christmas. So the Bastard Duke slaughters the people of Wessex and burns their homes to force my father to face him in battle for his land and his people. Wessex was my father's land long before England was."

"Why doesn't he break out now?" I said. "He has thousands of warriors penned up in the town."

Magnus smiled with his teeth. "We couldn't stop him if he did. But we'd hurt him badly. We'd fight him in the woods, the fields and the villages. And he'd beat us. But he'd lose hundreds of men and horses and he'd still have my father to face. When the Bastard Duke fights, he needs to fight the king and all the men the king commands, with the crown of England as the prize. The tale of that battle would be told and told again until the ending of the world." A few sparks flew among the falling leaves. Magnus cast a hard look around the faces gathered at the fire. "But if my father is wise," he added. "He won't give the Duke that fight and it will be a tale never told."

12. OSWOLD'S TALE

Every day messengers came and went from at the woodland camp, so the sound of hoofbeats was not enough to make me look up.

"Lord Magnus! News from your father the king. My lord King Harold has returned from victory in Northumbria. He is at the royal hall of Westmynster and will join you in seven days to drive back the host of Normandy."

I looked up when I heard the voice, and not only because of the message of hope he brought us. For it was the voice of my brother.

Men cheered, Magnus summoned his swiftest riders to carry his own news back to his father, and I rose to greet Oswold.

"It's a fine thing to welcome you back, Oswold." We clasped each other by the hand and the shoulder.

"Thank you brother. It's good to be back. And to know that soon we'll face the Normans together." They could have been my father's words. Oswold was different – half brother, half stranger. He had been gone for only three weeks but his wispy beard seemed thicker, his hair longer and his whole body leaner and more powerful. His eyes shone as if the windy moors of the north had left a little of their wilderness running through his blood.

My brother told his tale that night as we sat around a fire on logs and rough benches – Oswold and I, a couple of Magnus' warriors, some of Ellasham's fyrdmen and a few children, brought to the supposed safety of the camp from villages stalked by spears and fire. There was a rumour of frost in the fallen leaves around our fire.

"It was a hard ride we had to York. We rode at first light each morning and didn't rest until the sun was setting. On the fourth night we stopped beside a great river a few miles outside the city. We'd ridden through forests, swamps and barren heaths, but the valleys around York were as green as anywhere in Wessex.

"The next day we broke camp before dawn and entered the city while the sun was still low. The gates were open and the streets were silent. There were no spears raised against us, but neither was there any cry of greeting to hail our arrival. Many had spoken of fighting a battle at York, but there was not an enemy to be found.

"Or a friend. The houses were closed to us. Those people must have suffered great loss already. The army of the north had been cut down outside the city's gate and we passed that field on our way in. The dead lay thickly across a marsh, half eaten by wolves and crows. Even the hardest warriors among us rode in silence. Those Northumbrians who'd survived the battle were scattered and few came out of the woods and villages to join us.

"What about the earls of the north?" I asked my brother. "What of Edwin and Morcar? Did they survive? Did they come to the king's side?"

Oswold shook his head. "It was said that they left the field alive, but King Harold heard no word from them until after his own battle was fought." He spat into the fire in disapproval, one seasoned warrior cursing the cowardice of another.

"We rested in York for less than an hour. A few bowmen came out of a tavern and told us that the Norse King had led a large part of his army east to collect grain and cattle from the villages, so King Harold ordered that we take the eastern road that leads towards Bretlinton. My father was hungry for battle, riding in his mail and helmet, but it was a hot day and I wore just my breeches.

"'You should get used to the weight of your armour," he told me. "Put your mail on when battle begins and it feels ten times heavier.'"

"At noon, we reached a village called Stannaford, by a bridge on a river called Deruent, and there we found the host of Norway at rest. Although we saw them first in the far distance, like sparrows scattered on a harvested field, we could tell that no more than a half the enemy was there. And as we drew closer we saw that, with the day being so hot, few of the Norsemen had shields, helmets or mail. They knew nothing of our presence in the north."

Oswold smiled as he recalled this, but it was not the boyish smile he had worn for so many years. It was the smile of a man relishing the doom of his foes and I felt he had become as different from me as was my father.

"So we raced our horses down from the hills, hoping to take them by surprise. But the enemy rallied fast. They retreated across the bridge and into to a great flat meadow. Their king left less than a hundred men to defend the bridge, and those few men held us up for a long time.

"They fought like devils, like boars cornered in a forest lair. They were so few, and with only one shield for every three of them, but it would have struck fear into God himself to see how they wielded their great axes. My father went forward in the first rush - him and a Kentish man, both screaming like madmen. I saw him knock a Norseman aside and for a moment I thought he would break their line, but the Kentish man fell to an axe stroke and my father stumbled - tripped by a low spear thrust - and the charge faltered behind him. Then those few Norsemen were coming forward, trapping our warriors against the ranks behind and cutting them down."

I looked across the fire at Oswold and he nodded back reassuringly, acknowledging a question that did not need asking. "I helped to pull our father safely away from the enemy axes," he told me. "But many of our finest thanes watered the ground with the day's first blood.

"The Norsemen fell back before their line became overstretched. They'd shown their strength and well they knew it. They formed a stronger wall using the shields of men they'd killed. At their backs was the bridge and on their flanks the river." Oswold drew out battle lines on the ground with a chicken bone. "They held a strong position and they jeered at us, insulting our courage, our land, our mothers, our king. Some even insulted our Christian God. Many among their ranks dressed in the skins of bears and wolves and called upon the powers of Balder, Thor and Odin and a hundred other old names. I'd heard about men such as these. They knew death was coming, so they prayed to their gods for a great slaughter, a heroic last battle and a swift passage to the hall of fallen warriors. But I saw that others wore crosses and knelt in Christian prayer. And they stared at us over their shields and over the dead men lying between us, with neither hope nor fear on their faces.

"We charged the bridge five times. And every time that scrap of Sigurdsson's army held its ground, until their axes and their wolfskins were black with drying blood. With every attack, a few more were cut down, but each of them took two or three of our spearmen with them. The pagans believe that men they slay in such a battle will be their servants in the next world. If so, then those Norsemen will feast well in the hall of the dead."

A man sitting to my left coughed disapprovingly and touched the cross that hung around his neck. Irritated by the interruption, I gestured to Oswold to continue, because although it was a grim tale of bloodshed, my brother told it well and I was eager to hear more. Oswold gathered his thoughts and continued.

"At last, the final twenty or so warriors turned and walked away to join their king. They were not defeated and they did not run like defeated men. They had fought bravely and the lives of their companions had bought Harald Sigurdsson enough time to prepare his army for battle. Many of our warriors raised their swords and cried out salutes to the retreating men.

229

"But they left a single axeman on the bridge." Across the flickering light of the fire, Oswold grinned at two young boys from a nearby village. They looked back at him, their eyes wide and their mouths agape. "An ogre of a man he was, with eyes burning like red embers and two great horns on either side of his head. The skins of serpents hung in his beard, he roared like a bull, blew steam from his mouth and the blade of his axe was as broad as the wings of a buzzard." The boys shrank back fearfully.

"A demon," one of them whispered.

"Perhaps he was," grinned Oswold. "And one by one, the best of the king's hearthtroop stepped on to the bridge to fight this beast. And one by one, they felt the killing edge of his axe. They stabbed at him with spears and swords, but he was quick and cunning and the bloody boards of the bridge were soon covered with the bodies of those the river had not claimed. And all the time, he laughed at us, a spitting, rasping, evil laugh. Sometimes he cursed us in his own tongue, and sometimes he spoke in a strange northern kind of English. He called us the offspring of worms and toads. He threatened to castrate us, to hang us by our own innards and carve the blood eagle in our backs as an offering to the gods of the north.

"I believe there was fear among even the best of the king's warriors by then. The sun had already passed its height and the bodies of the slain lay thickly around the bridge and along the banks of the river. There were mutterings that this axemen was indeed a creature of Hell and that no man could kill him. On hearing this, King Harold himself stepped forward in full mail and a gold-crested helmet, his sword in his hand.

"'He is a man and he will die like any man. If those whom I thought the greatest warriors in the land will not fight him, I shall fight him myself.'" At this, the hearthtroop of Wessex rushed forward to defend their king. At the back, we pushed the whole mass of men forward and the Norseman screamed and swung his axe, spinning and prancing away from the spears so that the whole bridge shook with the slamming footfalls of his iron shod boots. I saw blood flying and bodies falling into the river and then the Norseman stepped back and for a moment he stared hard and silent at the king's men and they stared back at him. The men of Wessex were halfway across the bridge and they would not take a single step back. The Norseman breathed hard, but a murderous light still gleamed in his eyes and I wondered if he might even be able to hold that bridge until nightfall.

"But just as I was wondering, a spear flashed up from the other side of the bridge and spitted him below the armpit. There was a ragged cheer from the king's men and one of them ran forward as swift as a deer in the fields, raising his sword. The Norseman grunted in surprise, clutched at the spear that pierced him and glanced down at the river to see where it had come from. Then running man's sword cut deep into his neck and at last he fell, stumbling over the low rail of the bridge and splashing heavily into the bloodied water below, just as a warrior stripped down to his breeches and riding on a barrel floated out from under the bridge.

"And that's how we took the Deruent bridge. Its last defender joined his fallen foes in the river. It may not have been an honourable way to slay such a champion, but what man of Wessex could tell with any pride that all the mightiest thanes of Christian England were held at bay by a single heathen warrior?"

Oswold picked up a jug of ale and drank deeply. He wiped his mouth on the back of his hand and stared up through the dark trees with a distant look in his eyes. It was the look our father had always worn when he spoke of the battles of his youth and in that moment I felt I had lost the brother I knew to the gods of war as surely as if he had fallen to the spears of his enemies.

"So what about the Norse King?" Godric asked, and Oswold continued his tale.

"We crossed the river and formed up for battle on the opposite bank. Sigurdsson's army faced us in a great ring of warriors – four or five thousand men, their spears bright in the afternoon sun like

231

sickles ready for the harvest. They placed what shields they had at the front of their circle, but there were scarcely enough to call it a shield wall. It was only the war banner raised at the centre of their army struck fear into the hearts of the men of Wessex.

"Landwaster, it was called. A great square of blood-red cloth embroidered with a black raven. Its edges were ragged, as if a thousand swords had fought beneath and torn at its folds. There was a skull nailed on its pole. An old yellow skull with teeth filed to points and its mouth and eyes plugged with black wax, like the head of a ghost. Landwaster looked fearsome enough, but it was more than just a banner to the Norse. Since an unremembered time it had flown above the armies of a thousand pagan kings and carried the dark magic of those days into our own age. And it was said that no army to fight beneath the dusk-dressed raven had ever been defeated. Those who bore it into battle claimed it had the power to summon fire and lightning from the skies and open up the very earth to swallow whole armies. There are songs that tell of Landwaster's voice calling the old gods into this world.

"For it had a voice too. The skull must have been filled with gravel, which made a hissing, rattling sound as the warrior below shook the pole from side to side and flung out the banner's folds. The rulers of the northlands may say they follow the way of Christ nowadays, but in war it is to the old ways that these men turn."

Again the eyes of the two small boys widened with fear. And when my brother paused to draw a long breath and let the fierce tapestry of his story weave itself in his listeners' minds, the only sound was the slow hissing of new-cut logs on the fire.

"I was called to the front of the battle line. My father had been placed near the centre and he wished me to stand at his side. I wanted my spear to taste blood that day, but the Norse warriors sang slow death songs to the rhythm of Landwaster's laughter and with every heartbeat my fear grew stronger, until it felt like a cold hand gripping at my throat.

"The kings of England and Norway met to parley in the green flatland between us. Sigurdsson rode out from his war-ring, a great tall man in a sky blue cloak, and Tostig, clean-shaven and carrying a black shield. King Harold and Earl Gyrth went to meet him, and each king had twenty warriors at his back. I was told later that Sigurdsson mocked our king for the cowardly way in which his champion was killed on the bridge. The finest skalds of Norway, he said, would soon be composing verses to immortalise the mighty Ostman of Berghavn, but no such songs would ever be sung of Harold Godwinsson.

"It was also said that our king offered his brother Tostig earldom over Mercia and Northumbria in order to split the Viking host, but that he would give Sigurdsson only enough English earth to serve as his grave. And Tostig replied that his honour forbade him from accepting such terms. The king and his men rode back, hard-faced and ready to fight. A cry went up into the afternoon sky. Horns were blowing. And our battle line went forward with the westering sun high at our backs.

"I have been told that fear is the greatest foe a warrior will ever face, and I fought it hard as we approached Sigurdsson's army. When Wulfred and I fought at Riaburh, there were only two hundred or so warriors on either side. But on that great meadow in the north I marched forward as one man among thousands. It would have been an easy thing to die unnoticed in that host.

"We walked slowly. I thought our advantage in armour might frighten the enemy - that they might break and run. But their songs and shouts only became fiercer and we could see the iron determination in their faces. Harald Sigurdsson himself roared from the battle line that by nightfall our bodies would feed the crows, our halls would be the feasting places of Norsemen and the bellies of our women would be plump with Viking children. If there was fear in the shield-ring of Norway then it was fear well hidden.

"But the greatest warriors of England were around me and, like our enemies, they buried their fear and I fought to bury mine also.

233

Many times I felt the shield of the man behind me push me on. Our few bowmen ran ahead, loosing arrows before the armies met. I heard the men around me beating weapons on their shields and a chant went up of "Out Out! Out!" Out of our blessed land, filth of the north!

"The Vikings jeered back, promising us death and singing of the massacre they had made of the Northumbrians and Mercians outside York. Then, when we drew within fifty or so paces of them, a cry went up from King Harold's hearthtroop and we ran as one towards the enemy's spears.

"I expected a hard and bloody fight. And in the very first moment, as blades sang and I smelled the sweat, the ale, the stale leather armour of men who would find joy in my death, I thought I would vomit in terror. I wondered if I was really fighting a battle, or lost in some evil dream. But it was only for a moment. I thrust out with my spear, caught a sword blow on my shield and suddenly I knew the enemy's weakness. Those without shields and armour, but with others pressing them from behind - they fell quickly. Where a blade should have hit a helmet or been checked by mail, it tasted blood and bone instead. The songs of the Norsemen turned to pain and panic. My father and I advanced shoulder to shoulder, cutting through their front rank. My spear found the bellies of four Norsemen in the first few moments of battle. My father swung his sword with the strength of a man half his age and with blood splattering his shield and face, he laughed. He roared a great bellowing laugh amidst the slaughter.

"I do not know how much time had passed, but it only seemed like moments before the shield ring broke and I stumbled over the dead and into the centre. The Norse tried to hold their ground. But they died as they did so and we saw the banner Landwaster undefended in front of us. That's when the Norse King himself charged at the head of his finest warriors. Howling like the winter wind they came. Harald Sigurdsson was a giant of a man, an armoured terror from forgotten times. His cloak flew behind him

234

like the storm-wracked seas of the far north, his sword cried out in the air and his blue eyes were sharper than any blade carried by men that day.

"And I looked straight into those cold eyes as his shield battered against mine. With an angry bark, he swung his sword and my shield was smashed to splinters. I fell into the flattened grass, saw the blue sky above me, saw my father's spear jam into Sigurdsson's shield. But the king brought down his blade again and broke off the spearshaft. I groped through the grass to find my fallen sword, but Sigurdsson's sword was already raised above my head, his eyes fixed upon me. I can only remember seeing his blade and his eyes and the great raven on his shield calling out for my death.

"But the sword-blow never fell. An arrow from one of the York bowmen skewered Harald of Norway through the neck. He sank to his knees and slumped against his shield, choking and spewing blood. The defiance fell from the voices of his followers for now they knew everything was lost. The Wessex men who had been pressing in from behind rushed forward and trampled me. As I raised my head among the boots, I saw a dozen spears being driven into the Norse King's falling body. My father let out a yell that could have rent the hills apart and lunged wildly with his sword. The blade cleaved Sigurdsson's skull, but the king was dead before his body reached the ground. The greatest warrior king of the northlands fell less than a spear's length away from me, just a heartbeat before his blade would have cut me down. Even if I live a hundred years, it is a sight I shall never forget."

Awed, Oswold looked into the licking flames at the edge of the fire and slaked his thirst again. Warriors tell wild tales and Oswold was truly a warrior now. I threw him a questioning look across the fire, wondering how much of his story he had dreamed up on the long ride south, but there was not a flicker of a smile to disturb that faraway look on my brother's face. Nor was there a word, nor a murmur around the fire.

"The Norsemen carried the body of their king to the foot of his banner," Oswold went on, his voice quieter now. "And I took my place in the shield wall again. The great meadow lay scattered with the dead and dying. Landwaster still rolled in the breeze but the fear it had struck into us had gone. If the greatest king of the northlands could die beneath its folds, then all its magic was surely spent in the pagan past.

"King Harold offered mercy to the survivors and pardon to his brother, but they just raised their shields and glared back at him. Tostig took off his helmet and strode forward. He looked a lot like his brother the king and carried a fine sword, held bloody in his hand and with gold at the hilt. Behind him, a big Norseman began to swing Landwaster to and fro to draw out the skull's laughter again.

"'It shall not be said,' Tostig called out, 'that Tostig, son of Godwin, brought Harald of Norway to this bloody field only to see him slain and then betrayed! Come forward Harold my brother! Come forward men of Wessex! You'll have no victory while any man of us still breathes English air!' The enemy roared out their defiance. The voice of Landwaster rattled above their cries. My father passed me a whetting stone.

"'Keep your blade sharp,' he said. 'More blood will flow today.' A bearded, bald-headed Norseman with a black boar painted on his shield stepped out of the enemy's new battle line.

"'I still serve Harald son of Sigurd, King of Norway, overlord of Orkney and the isles of the far west, ruler by right of Denmark and of England. I follow my lord to victory, not to shame!' The enemy cheered, hurled stones at us and rattled their weapons.

And after that, we killed them all, though the fighting was harder. Many of the Norse had picked up shields and mail from the dead and they fought with the desperation of men already beaten.

Tostig fell, pierced by swords as the sun lowered towards the west. And the remnant of the Norse army finally broke, three parts

236

of them caught between the spears of Wessex and the sucking waters of the River Deruent and the other half fleeing into the woods to the south.

"When they fled, my father ripped his sword from a new-made corpse and raised it towards the evening sky, a bloody blade against the blood-red clouds, and gave a great shout of victory. And the whole field took up the cry, swords and axes raised in salute to the gates of Heaven. Two priests hauled down Landwaster. King Harold himself smashed the yellow old skull, and there beneath the darkening skies, the dead lay as thickly upon the ground as the very blades of grass."

Oswold paused to drink again. The dry leaves above us rustled quietly. Someone threw a couple of logs on the fire and sparks scattered into the damp darkness. My brother's story echoed with the glory of battle and the joy of victory. It was the first great tale he had ever had to tell and he told it well. Our father would have been proud to hear him. I wondered if a time would ever come when I would speak of battle with such a voice.

"But we did not linger on the red field of our victory. The woods to the south were full of our foes, some fleeing, some riding north from the Norse fleet, coming too late to aid their king. In the shadows of the forest we tore them apart. Those who had their wits about them turned their mounts and galloped back towards the ships that might still bear them home. Those with the courage of fools or without horses were slaughtered as we swept across them like a tide.

"I threw down my shield and some men even stripped off their mail to speed the pursuit. We ran across stubble-fields and through woods in the gathering gloom and we spared nobody. In the black hours of night, I came to the river where the ships of Norway lay beached. Our king had sent horsemen who had reached the ships long before us, slaughtered the few warriors left to guard them and set the whole fleet alight. In the midnight blackness there was another field of dead men beside a burning river and I knew the kingdom was saved. The warcries and the battering of blades were suddenly gone and the only sounds were the splitting of burning wood and the hiss of the river as it fought the flames. Then I just fell into the dewy grass, and like a dead man lying among the dead I slept in the cool night and dreamt of nothing. The Viking fleet burned, the last few bands of Norsemen came to King Harold with their surrender, fugitives slipped away through the woods and I slept so deeply that I am surprised I ever woke."

Oswold looked up, watching a thin trail of smoke climbing into the dark treetops. Owls were calling in the woods. A freshening wind murmured through the branches with the cold autumn voice that calls wolves down from the hills.

That was the tale that my brother told that night, in a camp of warriors, fyrdmen and frightened villagers beneath the yellowing trees. It was a long time ago – nearly a lifetime ago - and I may have changed his words a little. But if I meet him again, in this world or another, I am sure he will forgive me for it.

Our father remained with the king at Westmynster, resting after the long marches and the battle. But many of the men who had fought in the north joined us in the woods around Haestingas. The Norman army was trapped inside a ring of iron and although a winter of war lay ahead, it was a war in which the King of England and the men of Wessex controlled the battleground.

So the days that followed were quiet. Our forces in the woods of Sussex were too strong now for the Normans to risk more raids on villages. But a group of monks, protected by Norman warriors rode out form Haestingas early one morning. They bore messages for the king in Lunden, so we let them pass under escort and we let them return, stony-faced and indignant, two days later.

"Remember the feast last Christmas?" said Godric as we watched them ride away towards the port their duke still clung to. "Hildelyth said we'd both go and hide in the forest if war came to England." He chuckled grimly.

"Well, let's drink to the Christmas to come," I said, passing him a jug of the weak ale that Magnus provided to keep his men sober. "May we all be back in the hall with meat and songs and strong mead."

"I hope so," Godric muttered, "I'd rather starve in Haestingas with the Norman bastards than be still stuck here drinking this piss."

My father arrived at the camp in the afternoon of that day. He came with Leofwin and a hundred or so other warriors and he flung himself down from his horse and strode towards Oswold and I with barely a hint of a limp. He greeted us with rough embraces and a wild-eyed smile.

"I hear that the men who rode south with Magnus are now the heroes of Wessex," he said to me, and that was generous praise from a man who had fought in the battle which had broken the undefeated king of Norway. We spoke of the days that had passed. But Earl Leofwin had greater news to tell.

"I bring word from the king, my brothers of the shield wall," he called out, reining in his horse next to the rough shelter of logs and sailcloth where Magnus and a few of his men rose from their fireside seats to greet him. "We will face the invader with the sword's edge, beneath the dragon banner of Wessex. King Harold commands all who would hold true to their oaths to gather at Sandlac Hill." The Earl tried to sound enthusiastic, but his voice was stilted.

Magnus faced his uncle with a look of disbelief. "Sandlac Hill is ten miles away. The Bastard Duke is here in Haestingas."

"This is the command of your father the king. We face the men of Normandy on Sandlac Hill."

Magnus spat on the ground. "Then you can tell my father I am busy here. He may have scourged the north, but the Bastard Duke has yet to take his fleet home. If my father wants to keep his throne then I would bid him come here and join us."

The two men held each other's gaze for a few moments. If the king had sent this command with any lesser man than his brother, Magnus would have dismissed it and sent the messenger back, probably with a bloody nose. Leofwin sighed, dismounted and spoke more quietly.

"Magnus, your father has decided to fight. To end this war before the winter sets in."

"Then my father has lost his mind! We have them pinned down here. Nailed to the coast. Winter will bring them only cold and hunger. Winter is our ally. Would he have us open the trap and let our foes swarm across England?"

"Our villages have been burned, our people slaughtered. It is the duty of a king and a king's warriors to defend their people with their strength and skill on the field of battle."

"It is the duty of a king to win battles, and with my father's hearthtroop at the gates of Haestingas and his ships in the Narrow Sea, we cannot lose."

"You father has spoken. Will you come to his side or will you betray him."

Magnus fixed his uncle with an angry glare, but Leofwin did not flinch. I wanted to speak up, to take Magnus' side for the first time. The attacks on the villages had stopped. The Normans had lost every advantage they ever had. And as a hungry winter set in, I thought there was every chance that the Duke's army might return to its ships and slink back across the Narrow Sea without a fight. But this was an argument between two noblemen and nobody else was invited to share their opinion. So I turned to my father instead.

"What of the earls of the north?" I muttered, but Magnus overheard me.

"Yes, what of the north?" He nodded to me in acknowledgement then turned back to Leofwin. "Have Morcar and Edwin brought an army to the king's side?"

"The tide of war is with Wessex," said the Earl. "The king will fight. He will not wait for Mercia and Northumbria."

"He will not wait because he knows they're not coming. He knows they've betrayed him. Shit!" Magnus kicked out at an empty cooking pot that lay beside the fire. "My father's been made mad by victory. The men of Normandy won't just flee as soon as they see us standing on a hill pointing spears at them." He looked at the faces of Leofwin's men and they looked coldly back at him. To publicly doubt the wisdom of a king was not a wise move. Leofwin clapped a hand on his nephew's shoulder.

"The Bastard Duke is desperate for a battle, Magnus. So desperate that he'll face us on whatever ground we choose. Sandlac is a fine position to fight from and with God's help we'll drive them back into the sea."

"With God's help?" muttered Magnus. "We have no need for God's help. We could beat them here on our own and God could go and piss into the wind." He turned to face his men, many more of whom had gathered at the sound of raised voices. "We leave before nightfall. Gather the sentries and call in the patrols. We fight with my father the king at Sandlac Hill." There was a little dutiful cheering, though the faces gathered around him shared Magnus' doubt. "With God's help, hopefully," he mumbled.

13. THE DAY OF BLOOD

There are those who say that Willelm of Normandy was aided by the Devil in his bloody work on Sandlac Hill. That among his army rode witches chanting curses, that the warriors who battered against our shields that day were not men, but the Host of Hell.

They also say that were he not thus cursed, King Harold could have thrown aside fifty men at a time with each sweep of his sword, and hurled their bodies into the sea as a warning to all of England's enemies. Harold Godwinsson strangled warhorses with his two bare hands, they say, Harold could speak with the saints of Heaven, Harold could turn back the tides of the sea. I have heard the story that Harold was struck through the eye by a Norman arrow and that he simply wrenched it out and fought on, as if such a wound would not simply leave a man whimpering on the blood-sodden ground, reaching out to be carried to safety by his comrades. There are even those who say King Harold yet lives, wandering as a one eyed hermit through the wastes of the north.

These people are fools. The young men who speak such things were not even born when we fought on Sandlac Hill. But for many who have come into this world since those days, Harold is the greatest of our heroes.

If they had walked the path of my life they would not believe such things.

Men died because of Harold. He saved nobody. Warriors fell on the battlefields, women and children were slaughtered in their homes and now wolves stalk the deer fawns in weed-ridden fields once tilled by our people. The Norman Duke ordered their deaths, but they died because Harold had been king. When people splutter drunkenly of the terror that came to England and the great king who fought against it, I see how easily the truth is lost.

I am sure Harold could have been a good ruler. He was popular, he thought well of his people, he had humility and in some ways he was wise. But he was not a great man. He could not heal the sick, he could not drain fields and bring forth corn from flooded land, he could not raise strong children or weave cloth or make shoes or build houses or sing songs of love and youth with the old and the lame and the blind.

He was only a king.

It was close to nightfall. Low in the western sky, the sun lingered like a blood red shield, throwing long shadows across the grassy hillside. The golden leaves of Andredsweald were still and the smoke of a hundred campfires gathered like a mist, woven through with the fireside songs and the muttered voices of an army. The sounds rose and fell like specks of dust in a boundless silence. I have heard skalds and poets tell of the gathering of the souls of long dead warriors before great battles, and under the early stars in the evening of that day I could well believe such a thing. The silence of the great darkening sky was like something living, deadening the sounds of men. But this was the place where Harold Godwinsson had chosen to face his enemy and fight for his kingdom. I tried to imagine the quiet hill swarming with iron clad men and spears and horses, the stillness shattered by death and steel, the grass slick with blood. But there was only a silence stronger than any sound, and the setting of the sun.

Forest covered the northern side of Sandlac Hill. The southern slope was bare and steep, a grazing place for sheep and cattle, slipping down into a dry valley before rising again. My father, Oswold and I and the fyrdmen of Ellasham made our own fire near the hilltop where the trees of Andredsweald petered out. At the summit were the tents and banners of the king and his brothers. The dragon of Wessex stood silhouetted against the evening sky. There was no sign that the earls of the north had come to their king's side, but my father was already convinced that victory was certain.

"We beat the Norse with ease because they lacked their armour," he said. "Here it will be us who are defending, as the Norse were. But we have mail and helmets and shields on the high ground. All we must do is hold our position and the Normans will break against us."

There were thousands of men – warriors and fyrd - on the hill that night, but they all seemed distant in the eerie quiet. Some men drank and sang long into the dark hours, and their voices were like tiny points of light in a vast landscape. Again and again I slumbered and woke to see only the stars creeping across the great bowl of the sky. I dreamed of home, of childhood, of the king accepting the Duke's sword in a bloodless surrender, of the wraiths of ancient warrior lords at my side in the shield wall and of fleeing through the woods with the enemy's spears at my back. I did not dream of death because death does not come in dreams.

Death comes only in the iron light of the waking day.

We were awoken by horn-blasts at dawn.

"The enemy has broken camp!" Men walked among us beating drums, hammering on shields and calling out the news that would rouse an army. "Willelm the Bastard is marching. Today we feed his army to the ravens!" I peered into the chill grey morning to see shadows stirring all across the hill.

I rubbed my eyes and stretched my hands to the last of our fire's warmth. Birds sang in the damp forest while men cursed and muttered.

"This will be a magnificent day," boomed my father. He was admiring the blade of his sword as the sun crept above the far horizon. "A glorious day for battle." He would have said the same thing in freezing rain and if we had awoken to find that cattle had dunged on us in the night. Oswold sat on his cloak, studying the rolling land to the south where a curtain of mist was still settled. Above it the wooded hills floated like islands in a ghostly sea. Woodsmoke purged dampness from the air as men stirred up embers to cook a last meal before battle and the gathering light revealed briar patches, grey stubble fields, and a herd of cattle moving across a distant hill.

As the sun rose, a light breeze from the west fingered the trailing banners planted along the hilltop. For the first time I saw King Harold's new standard, the Fighting Man - a blood-red cloth with a man wielding sword and shield embroidered in threads of gold and silver.

"Back to the swinefields of Rouen, you cockless bastard!" Leofwin laughed, swinging his sword vaguely in my father's direction. The earl looked like a man who had taken his breakfast at the ale barrel. My father gave a fierce roar and the two warriors' swords clashed.

Oswold silently picked up his shield and checked that the iron boss was well riveted. Then he ran his hand along the hide edging. His expression was dark now, the misty dawn sucking from him the fire of victory in the north.

"I dreamed of charging horses," he muttered.

"Fight bravely Oswold," Leofwin said, clutching him by the shoulder. "Man and horse the Normans will run from your spear as did the warriors of Anlaf and Sigurdsson."

"They will, Lord." Oswold's reply seemed lifeless in the gathering light.

Still laughing, Leofwin loped off across the hill, playfully swiping at shields and greeting friends as if they had come to feast rather than fight.

My father handed me a rough sack.

"Food for the fyrdmen," he explained "Give it to them. Tell them victory is certain. Then join us to hear the king speak." For a moment he gave me a hard, frowning look, then he and Oswold turned and walked towards the top of the hill.

There was bread in the bag, and cheese, boiled eggs, smoked meat and even some honey. The village men sat in a circle around the rekindled fire and said little. There were twenty-three of them – I counted their heads and wondered if there would be as many by the day's ending. Men who had been my friends since childhood. Men who had drunk ale with me a thousand times. Men who stood at my side when I defied my father and led them against the priest Grimstan. For the first time I felt that they were my people more than my father's. There was a silence after they finished eating. They fiddled with knives and buckles and the hems of their cloaks.

"Victory will be ours," I said, still obedient to my father, though I had no idea of how the battle would go. Godric looked up doubtfully as he cut a piece of ham. "The king will place at least four ranks of warriors at the front – you'll have to push us forward and chase the enemy when they're beaten. Then you just kill them and take their silver."

"So easily?" Ragnald asked. He was afraid. He hid it well, but there was an unfamiliar shadow in his eyes and he clasped his hands together in his lap as if to stop them from shaking.

"Yes." I tried to sound certain. "We're in a strong position. We have woods at our back and gullies on the flanks. All we have to do is hold this hilltop and not let them break our shield wall."

"What if they do?" Fear did not stop Godric from eating more than his fair share, but his voice was unsteady. Suddenly, from distant memory, an image of the villagers of Llyn Rhydderch slithered through my mind – those brave but hopeless men who had tried to defend their lord's hall so long ago.

"Then run," I told them.

"What of the oath of the fyrd to serve our lords until death?" Now it was Brichteva's father who spoke.

"Fuck the fyrdmen's oath. If the battle goes badly, run for the forest."

King Harold looked tired that morning, but there was a shaft of steel in his voice. He sat on his horse beneath the blue open sky and spoke of victory. He no longer wore the gold trinkets of a king on his arms and at his neck, just the padded leather coat and the grey mail of a fighting man as his warriors gathered in a great circle around him.

"One more battle," the king roared, standing tall on a rough hummock of the ground, one knee bent as if ready to charge the enemy and a fist clenched on his sword-hilt. "I have already asked much of you. You gave your strength and your courage in the north and I am proud to call you the greatest warriors in the world. And now we must stand together one more time in this autumn of war. Another day of blood and another day of victory. Through our strength and our blades Harald Sigurdsson is gone from this this world. And Tostig the Nothing is gone from this world. Willelm the Bastard will soon join them in the cold, dark grave. And when the sun rises tomorrow, it will be the first dawn of a thankful winter of feasts."

He named many of the warriors who had fought at York and spoke of their deeds in battle. He promised fame and wealth to all who stood at his side that day and immortality in songs and stories to the man who slew Willelm the Bastard. Men cheered him, beat their sword-hilts on their shields and their spearshafts on the dew-wet earth. Others shouted out to carry his words across the long crest of the hill and along the length of the army.

I think he had planned to speak for longer, but there was a cry of warning and we all looked to the south. And we saw glimmers of light among the distant trees   beyond the next hill.

247

"Spears!" my father shouted. "It's the sun reflected by a thousand spears. The Bastard is here." He grabbed Oswold and I by the shoulders, shook us joyously and laughed aloud. Other men stamped on the ground and cheered.

"To battle then, my friends," the king roared when the voices had subsided. "Shield wall across this hilltop. Remember the great lords of Wessex. Remember Cerdic who sired five centuries of kings; Ecgbryht who brought the Welsh to heel; the great Aelfred – slayer of the heathen Danes, and Aethelstan whose sword ruled all of Britain. Their ghosts will stand at our sides today!"

The warriors of Wessex raised their swords and cheered. War drums hurled a sound like thunder across the hills, and long battle horns bellowed into the still sky.

Below us, in a saddle of land between the hills, the first banners of the Norman host appeared from among the trees.

A shirt of iron mail is heavy to lift, but when its weight is balanced on the shoulders it is easy enough to wear. My mailshirt hung to my knees and its sleeves fell below my elbows. Beneath it I wore two layers of thick leather stuffed with horsehair. The leather was old and hardened by years of sweat. I also had padded boots, which almost reached my knees. My shield hung from a long strap across my shoulders so I could have both hands free to hold spears – I carried three of them at the start of battle - but it also had arm loops for more control when I drew my sword. Sword, axe and knife hung at my belt and the weight of my helmet put me off balance so that the act of simply glancing left or right could turn into an ungainly lurch. I had tied my hair and stuffed it up under the helmet to stop it getting tangled in the rings of mail.

Somewhere behind me the war drums crashed and a bagpipe wailed its defiance as thousands filled the cloudless morning with the songs of the heroes of Wessex.

248

"Hold this ground," shouted Magnus, walking in front of the shield wall and brandishing Ironclaw at the blue sky. "Do not break the line. And any man who turns his back gets a spear in it - from the Bastard's men or from me."

I stood with Oswold and my father on the right flank of the army – the forest at our backs beyond the mass of the fyrd, the sandy stream gully from which the hill took its name to the right and a steep part of the slope in front of us. Magnus commanded here and his followers formed the front rank. They seemed like good men to have between myself and the enemy's spears, and good man to have on the flank of an army. In a battle like this, the flanks were the keys to victory or defeat. If one side of the army collapsed, the enemy would surge through and destroy the centre from behind.

My father and brother stood at my right. As veterans of the battle in the north they might have expected to be at the very front of the shield wall, but Magnus had filled the first rank with his own men.

"There will be time enough to stand face to face with our foes before the day is out," my father said, nodding grimly at the broad back of the man in front of him.

Somewhere among the duke's army, his own war drums pounded, driving the mail-clad ranks forwards. Slowly the green space between the armies shrank away. At their centre, marching towards the dragon banner of Wessex were shining rows of men in bright armour, their mailshirts polished like silver, their helmets throwing back the light of the morning sun. Their shields were newly painted with crosses and swirling patterns and the beasts revered by their ancestors. Above them, coloured banners filled the bright sky, many of them carefully sewn with the images of saints in silk and golden thread. I had seen the men who marched beneath these banners at Pefensea and I had fought bands of them in the woods and fields around Haestingas, but not until now had I realised just how great the enemy were. There must have been five

249

or six thousand relentlessly striding towards us, and at least another thousand mounted men still snaking out of the trees in long columns. Six thousand, seven thousand warriors – true warriors, trained warriors. There were no peasant soldiers in Duke Willelm's army. Each man wore armour and carried a sword and spear. Each man had years of training to guide his sword arm. Of such warriors we had only half that number. King Harold's victory over the Norse must have cost him a thousand of his best men, while others still lingered on the roads of the far west, distant to reach their king's side in time to fight.

But we had the high ground, the strong position, I told myself, and that made victory ours to take. As I had heard again and again, all we had to do was to hold our line, stand our ground, wield the sword and thrust the spear until the enemy broke against the strength of Wessex.

The Bastard Duke had recruited his army from all over the lands he ruled, and the men on his left flank, the men who marched up the hill to meet Magnus' followers, looked very different to the Normans in the centre. Wild looking men, they were, with helmets of horn, leather and iron. Most wore mail, though some had tunics of thick hide and fur, and they sang gloomy songs to the rhythm of the war drums and the wailing of flutes and pipes. Their gold and silver shone more brightly than their armour - arm rings and neck torcs - rewards for courage and for killing foemen. Their hair and beards were long and dark beneath their helmets. And their shields and banners bore the staring eyes of beasts, birds and serpents – the emblems of heroic ancestors who fought such monsters when the world was young. And the bear. So many of them carried the image of the bear. And it was from that sign that we knew them, for the bear was the old, old banner of Arthur, the doomed Welsh ruler whose deeds are still so well remembered across the River Sefern.

There was muttering among Magnus' men, and the muttering grew as the enemy drew near until someone yelled aloud "Welsh! The Bastard Duke sends Welshmen to die on our spears!" and suddenly there was laughter and mocking from all around. Men bleated at them like sheep and called out "Brunnanburh!" - that great battle in which the men of Wessex slaughtered the Welsh and their allies.

These were not the Welshmen we knew, of course. They came from the Breton lands, along the wild coast west of Normandy. Not many years earlier, the Breton lords had fought against the Bastard Duke, and Harold Godwinsson himself had ridden into battle with the men of Normandy to blood his warriors and to forge alliances. But now the duke had chained the Breton lords with oaths and they went into battle at his side. Perhaps they also came to fulfil ancestral oaths, for the Bretons shared much with the Welsh. Their language was similar and their songs and stories told of the same heroes. Far back in almost forgotten times, when the English first conquered this land, it is said that many of the Welsh fled south across the sea to seek refuge. Maybe these were their grandsons by many generations coming to reclaim the lost land.

But Magnus' men laughed and jeered at them. If they looked and sang like Welshmen, they must fight like Welshmen, and fighting the Welsh was something they knew how to do.

"One charge, that's all they have in them," said my father, lowering his shield to smile reassuringly. The man in front of me also turned and spoke.

"They drink mead and ale for courage and they'll run at us like a herd of randy bullocks. Once a few of them die on our spears the rest will shit themselves and run."

But the men who came towards us did not blunder like randy bullocks, neither did they stagger like drunks. As the warriors of Magnus laughed and called them cattle fuckers and sons of whores, they stared darkly ahead, the icy damp of the grave woven into their slow battle songs and our slaughter like a dark promise in their eyes.

The noise of impending battle swelled and I began to beat my spearshaft against my shield. It stopped my hands from shaking with fear. I tried to join in with the jeering and the battlecries, but my throat was dry and suddenly I did not want the enemy to notice I was there. This was not like Riaburh where I had faced only a small warband across an empty slope and along the shaft of an arrow. I had my bow slung across my back, but in the press of the shield wall there was not the space to draw back the cord. And, if I were to slay four or five of the enemy with arrows, would I be marked for death by them even more surely than I already was?

Closer still, and I could see courage and hatred in their shadowed eyes. Their faces were like the bloody dead of Llyn Rhydderch coming back for me across the grey borders of death and I could almost feel their long spears on my flesh.

With about twenty paces to go, the Bretons cried aloud and broke into a run. The shouting and the beating of shields stopped. Magnus' men in the front rank braced themselves to meet the charge and I could suddenly measure my life by the length of the Breton spears.

The men in front of me stepped forward. We in the second rank took a half step forward and someone's back was thrown against my shield and the back of his helmet was in my face.

"Spear!" the man in front of me shouted. I thought of nothing in that moment when the battle for the kingdom began. I only know that the terror which had twisted my stomach was gone. Years of training had taught me that fear brings death and action brings victory. While the first clash of spears and shields still rolled along the battle line, I thrust my first spear over the shoulders of the front rank, aiming at the nearest of the enemy. Like so many others, he carried the mark of the bear on his shield and he went down rasping and gurgling with my spear in his mouth. The warrior in front of me stepped onto his flailing body and put his sword through the man's throat. And I thought nothing of his death as the shaft of my second spear hit the helmet of the man standing behind me then bounced off a shield boss.

"Steady!" my father shouted. The third spear was ready in my hands. I paused to pick out a target. The sudden chaos of clashing armies had passed. We stared at each other over the rims of shields and down the lengths of spears, across a stride-length of grass that kept the two armies apart. The horn blasts and the frantic war drums seemed distant now. From the corner of my eye I noticed the breeze plucking at Leofwin's eagle banner. I had expected the enemy charge to be followed by a wild thrashing of blades and the breaking of shields, not this sudden calm. Closer to the centre of the hill I heard shouting, the battering of iron and wood where the enemy were trying to push through the shields of the king's best men. A few wounded men groaned as their shield-brothers dragged them to safety. The stench of the day's first blood was rising from the torn throat of the man I had speared, mingling with the odour of men sweating in their padded war gear. A black bearded warrior faced me across his shield. He wore so much silver on his right arm that it was hard to see where his arm ended and his sword began. I tried to aim my spear, but he raised his shield and fixed his gaze on me.

"Out! Out! Out!" The battlecry that had been raised against the Norse roared along the shield wall. I saw fear creeping along the enemy line. They glanced from side to side, watching our faces and our weapons. I had been taught that if a shield wall is going to break, it will break in the first moments of battle, when the charge hits home. But the shields of Wessex held like the gates of an iron city. Our foes could only jab and lash out, afraid of coming too close. I saw spears flying into the enemy, thrown by our rearward ranks, but none of them killed. The Breton bear shields were held high. My father stood grim-faced beside me, a spear at his shoulder and a steel-bright glare in his eyes as he stared down the men opposite. Beyond him a man in the front rank swung a long axe over the rim of a shield. Beating off a spear with his own shield, he tugged the axe back. Oswold pushed his spear into the gap made by

253

the opened shield, the men around him shouting their support. The warrior flailed backwards away from the blade. My brother pushed down and twisted the spearshaft, but the blade only cut through his mail and into the leather he wore beneath, and the man next to him pushed it aside. Then the noise of the Breton drums thundered once again.

"Hold your ground," my father snarled, his eyes never leaving the enemy. "These cowards will not fight us, so the Duke is driving others up the hill to push them on. The ones that face us now - they are doomed. You come to your death!" He screamed across the shield wall and by the faces of the enemy, I would have guessed that they thought so too. The jeering and howling from our line swelled into a wild chorus. Some men called out the names of their lands and villages, others cried Godwinsson in honour of the king. I drew the axe from my belt and hammered it against the rim of my shield as, all along the shield wall, men tried to drown out the sound of the enemy's drums. From the centre, a great roar of "Dragons!" went up from the king's own hearthtroop.

But the drums drew nearer and the enemy came forward again. There were shouts behind them, sounds of pushing and shoving. I could see the thick press of men tightening. At first some of them shuffled, trying to hold themselves back, out of reach of our spears, but finally, with great cries of courage and terror, they threw themselves against our shield wall.

And many of them died. The growling, black-bearded Breton fell to a sword blow just as my father pushed the man next to him to the ground with a spear at his chest.

"You should have stayed in your hovels and died in your beds!" he yelled, punching down another man by ramming the spearhead under his helmet and pulling it back with a vicious twist and a spurt of blood. Oswold made his first kill of the day, sending a Breton screaming to his knees with blood gushing from a vein in his groin. The axeman in front of him landed a blow that split an enemy's helmet in two. It seemed like there was no air left to breathe, only the odour of blood and sweat.

Then the man in front of me fell. He stumbled into me, his shoulder a mess of blood and bone and broken rings of mail. His shield fell and his body arced as two spears smashed through his ribs. The Breton warriors rushed forward, their eyes wide, their teeth bared.

"Push him!" my father shouted. He flung his spear into the enemy and grabbed the body with his free hand. I shoved with my shield and together we thrust the dying man into our charging foes. They stumbled under his weight and suddenly I was in the front rank of the battle, my shield overlapping with those of Magnus' men on either side of me.

"Sword!" shouted one of them, but I knew what to do. I had already hurled my spear into the faces of the enemy and was drawing my sword.

There is nothing good about battle, but the battle fought when two shield walls grind together must be a horror unimaginable to anyone lucky enough not to have been there. The only way to survive is to kill and to kill fast. I kept my sword moving. To yield the small space of empty air in front would have been to invite the soul-stealing blades of the enemy. Again and again I jabbed forward, splitting the edges of shields, shearing flesh from men's faces, breaking their teeth. I swung the blade high, beating down spears and other swords, hammering the mail-clad shoulders and iron helmets of the enemy. The heavy shield dragged at my arm, but I kept it up and pushed it against those of the men facing me, trying to steal their balance. Attack, I had always been told. Do not watch and wait for the swift blade to come - attack the enemy with all your strength before he has a chance to attack you. From a place in my soul where I had not walked before, something murderous arose and I howled my defiance until my throat bled. *Break their line! Break their bones! Break their spirit!* Hearing the words I had heard again and again since childhood, I battered my shield into the shields of

255

the enemy and lunged my sword at anything in front of me. I did not see the sword that swung in high from my shield side and crashed into my helmet's nose guard. My whole head jerked sideways, the swordpoint lodged for a sliver of a heartbeat just a finger's breadth from my eye. Then another blood-blackened sword hissed up from the other side and opened my attacker's arm from elbow to wrist. He screamed and fell back, his sword hitting the ground at my feet and his blood splattering across my face.

The man to my right, the warrior who had just saved my life, crumpled and a Breton leapt forward trying to force a gap through our wall. He hunched low to keep his face behind his shield, but I swung at him with all my strength. My blade did not even pierce the thick mail that hung from the back of his helmet, but still he fell, the bones of his neck shattered. My father stepped in beside me, the dead man's shield propped against his legs. With a howl of rage he swung his axe over a bear-painted shield and tugged so viciously that the enemy warrior lost his grip. Before he could even raise his sword, Oswold's spear was in his neck and his blood was soaking the men behind him.

A bright spearhead flashed from behind the line of bear shields. I raised my own shield, rocked back from the impact and saw the point sticking through the planks, level with my face. Taking half a step forward, I punched the shield at the man in front, hoping to shake the spear free. At the same time my father's axe chopped at the shaft of a spear that had been aimed at my exposed side. A big chunk splintered away from the top of my shield, the ragged wood leaving my left shoulder open to the enemy. I lifted the broken shield as high as I dared. The muscles of my sword arm were numb, my right hand wracked with cramp, but still I stabbed and hacked to keep those deadly spears at bay.

Another spear smashed into my shield and split it in half. Desperately I punched the iron boss into a man's face before he could lunge at me. But by then we had done enough. There was a great cheer suddenly rising from the packed ranks of warriors and fyrdmen behind me. And, like a golden sunrise after a howling night of winter, the open sky rose into view again. Keeping their battle line intact, the enemy shuffled down the hill. The crashing of blades and the screams of the wounded gave way to roars of victory. I felt the men behind me pressing forward to chase and rout the battered foes, but there were voices above the din ordering us to hold our ground. There was blood on my sword and on what was left of my shield and a tide-line of broken bodies ran along the foot of the shield wall. But the shield wall stood. The strength of Wessex was unbroken. The dragon banner trailed lazily against the blue sky.

Shouting and stumbling, the enemy fell back and struggled to rebuild a shield wall. The wounded moaned beneath the autumn sun. A fresh smell of damp earth and falling leaves misted out of the forest to mingle with the blood-reek of battle. I lowered my sword, stretched my arms and legs and felt the life flow back into them. But all around me, the men of Wessex cleaned their blades and took up new shields. For the Duke had only begun to unleash his army.

All that summer there had been talk of how the Normans fought on horseback. And now the grey-mailed mass of men on foot drew back and we watched the Norman warhorses snorting and stamping on the slope below us.

"Fear. That's their weapon," said Oswold, wiping the sweat from his forehead. He tried to sound confident, but I could see from his wide-eyed look that, despite his triumph in the north, the fight against the Bretons had shaken him.

"Only fear," our father replied. "Stand your ground and all they can do is turn around and trot back down the hill. We made easy work of their Welshmen and we'll make easy work of their horses."

"Won't they force the horses into the shield wall?" I asked him.

"Horses aren't stupid enough," he frowned. "Would you run onto a man's spear?"

I shook the shaft of a spear to check its strength. And I threw down my broken shield and picked up a Breton bear shield. The man who had carried it lay dead on the ground, his whole left side soaked with the blood that had pumped from a deep sword-cut though his neck and shoulder. I glanced at his face, saw his dead eyes staring sightlessly back, and felt the cold shudder of the hall at Llyn Rhydderch and the day when I first watched men die. I stepped back and turned away from the corpse, but there was no escape from the sword-harvest of battle. Fyrdmen carried our wounded to the rear, to have their wounds bound or to die in the shade of trees. The enemy wounded, if they could not crawl away down the hill, were killed where they lay. While Magnus' Bloodhelms cheered their victory over the Bretons, pleading men dragged themselves along the ground away from the blade that came to cut their throats. Their mailshirts and weapons were given to the fyrd and some village men started stripping the dead of rings, cloakpins and other valuables, until Earl Gyrth rode along the length of the shield wall ordering men back to their places.

"I won't have my brother's army descend into a plundering rabble!" he blustered, red-faced in the saddle. Harold himself stepped carelessly through the mangled dead.

"There will be time for plunder when victory is ours." He stopped close to our part of the line and kicked a broken spearshaft down the hill. "The horsemen of Normandy are coming. Stand firm on the soil of Wessex. Trust your shield brothers. They will break as the Welsh did." Again there was cheering and the beating of shields as the king worked his way along the line.

Magnus brought more of his men forward to fill the front rank again and my father and I returned to our places in the second. We both had spears wrenched from the hands of the dead. Leofwin promised that we would all be drinking Frankish wine in Haestingas by sunset.

The Norman horse-warriors - close to a thousand of them - began a slow trot up the hill. They wore bright mail and helmets like the men on foot and they carried long spears and the tapered shields that protect a rider's leg. Their armour shimmered in the sun as they spread out across the hillside. There was a moment of silence. The Bloodhelm who had taken my place in the front rank adjusted his helmet strap and I felt thankful that another man stood once more between me and death.

Then a high-pitched horn blast rose above the field and was immediately drowned by the thudding of hooves as the horses came lumbering over the grass towards us. I saw the men in front of me flex their knees and crouch behind their shields. The thunder of those hooves seemed to fill the whole world. I saw the horses' eyes, crazed and yellow, and the grim faces of the men who rode them. In the shield wall, many took up their chants of battle again, and some called upon the aid of Christ, of God, of the Holy Virgin and of Thor, but their voices were feeble beneath the hammering of hooves. I just fixed my eyes on the riders, clutched my spear and shield and tried to swallow my fear. And then the charge hit us.

The man in front of me stumbled as the flank of a horse drove against his shield. He staggered to his feet, holding his shield high and the beast reared up, battering shields and men with its hooves. Just to my left, a horse screamed and part of a shield was smashed off, spinning over the heads of the warriors behind. The man in front of Oswold fell as a spear struck down into his face. I heard bones splintering and he collapsed into the grass, the blood spraying with a shrill rasping noise from a ragged hole where his nose and mouth had been.

Again, the man in front of me stumbled under the flailing hooves, but this time, as the horse sank back to the ground I rammed my spear hard into the soft flesh between its leg and breast. A bone cracked, the beast shrieked and went down, ripping the spear from my grasp and I saw my father's spear flit in front of me to tear out the rider's throat. He wrenched the bloody blade free and turned to me, grinning madly.

259

"Wulfred!" he called out in a voice that rang out above the roar of battle. And for a few moments, the men who had seen me fell the beast raised my name as a warcry, and those who had survived the first charge stepped forward to fill the places of the fallen, a couple of them slapping me on the back and offering hasty congratulations. I stood bewildered before the wreckage of man and horse, wondering at how I had become, for one brief moment of battle, the hero of the shield wall. Further along the line, another horse screamed more horribly than a man or woman ever could. Men lunged forward to spear the stricken rider and the spears of the second rank stabbed high to defend the first. Somewhere behind me a horseman had smashed his way through the shield wall and was spinning in a tight circle, hacking wildly with his sword as fyrdmen jabbed at him with pole-knives and axes.

"Go for the legs!" I called out, my spirit borne aloft by my moment of victory. "Break the horse's legs!" The man on my left carried a heavy long-shafted Dane axe. He slung his shield across his back and stepped out of the line. Roaring like the Devil, he swung his weapon at the nearest horse as if cutting down a tree. The animal went down white-eyed with terror as one of its front legs was sheared through, left hanging by a sinew shred. The rider fell, trapped beneath the bellowing beast. In one swift move, the axeman hefted his weapon up over his head, then brought it down on the Norman's neck. A couple of other horsemen spurred their beasts forward, but our advancing spearmen jabbed their blades at the horses' eyes. One horse rasped and spat blood as a spear cut its throat. The axeman picked up the Norman's severed head and held it up, dripping blood and dangling shreds of flesh. Careless of the spears clashing all around him, he first turned to us and let out a roar of triumph. It was echoed along the shield wall. Then he turned to face the enemy.

"Go home while you've still got your fucking heads!" There was more cheering as he hurled the bloody head back at them.

260

And that cry of victory rose to a crescendo as the horsemen rode away down the hill. A final flight of their spears winged over our heads and then our drums hammered out their blood-mad dances, the blasts of horns and pipes soared across the sky and I joined with the men all around me, roaring the songs of Aelfred and Beowulf and Woden and all the blood-drenched heroes of our forefathers. A tide of noise tumbled down the hill at the enemy's back. Men shouted for the horse warriors to come again and waste their strength against the shields of Wessex.

I felt as I had done at the moment when I first faced the Northumbrian at Riaburh, when I beat Bera to the ground at Westmynster. I felt like I could never be defeated.

And the dead lay still, the dying cursed and prayed and bled, and ragged wheels of ravens darkened the autumn sky.

That final flight of thrown spears before the horsemen fled had fallen into our rearward ranks where the less fyrdmen were packed together with few shields and little armour. I found the men of Ellasham gathered around where Godric had fallen. He lay doubled up on the ground, his hands slick with the blood that pumped from a deep spear wound in his belly. He looked up at me, his skin like melting snow and his eyes already blurred by the shadow of death. The faces around him stared up at me as if I could do something. These were men who had lived alongside death and disease and hunger and the killing frosts of winter and these things they bore because they were born to them. But they had never seen friends and brothers slaughtered on the battlefield.

Those days when Godric and I had been children in the fields and the forests seemed so far away. I wondered if he could see me from the edge of death. Then he choked as pain cut through his body and he wept like a child and begged to be taken home.

"I'll be safe there. We'll all be safe," he gasped. But Godric could never be safe again in this world. If he did not die before the sun set, he might cling to life for two or three days, the flesh of his torn belly rotting and stinking. All his questions would be left unanswered, gathering dust in the shadows. I cradled Godric's head in my hands and could find no words. Ragnald crouched next to me and muttered to him about old Eohric's ale and catching salmon in the river. Slowly, Godric prised blood-slick fingers away from his stomach and clutched one of my hands.

"Hildelyth. Keep her safe," he whispered and his eyes were drifting wildly into an unknown place. And before I could reply, Magnus hauled me to my feet.

"He's a dead man. Cut his throat and make it quick," he said to Ragnald. Then he turned to me "And you can get back to the shield wall. The Welsh come to be slaughtered again."

He pushed me away and, feeling sick and only briefly looking back, I took my place in the battle line again. So Godric was lost. Even now, I sometimes find it hard to believe that he died there on that field of blood so long ago. Warriors died in their hundreds, of course, but that is what warriors do. What did Godric know of spears and the black rage of battle? He should be sat across the hearth from me right now, bald-headed and white-bearded, among his sons and his grandchildren, laughing, singing, remembering times long gone.

Again, the Bretons linked their shields and faced us across the hillside, the Norman horse-warriors held back for a moment when they might turn the battle.

It was a harder fight those Bretons gave us then. I could not measure the time that passed as I fought off sword and spear in that God-cursed line of slaughter. I have been told that Duke's army fought us without pause until the morning was long gone. But it seemed as if whole ages were passing. The autumn sun was hot, the air filled with the reek of death and the screams of the dying, and the blood of both foes and companions mingled with the sweat that

262

ran down my face. Again the man who stood in front of me was killed. A sword's edge took his throat, but the press of men was too great for his body to fall. So blood from the gaping wound sprayed across my face and the breath of his life choked and rattled and ceased as me and my enemies pushed his limp body back and forth with our shields and swung our swords over his lolling head.

But all around me I felt the strength of Wessex growing. Again and again I stepped forward over the bodies of the newly-slain and the bear shields of the Bretons were pushed back down the slope of the hill. The warcries, the cheering and the taunting grew louder. Axemen stepped through our shield line, their great blades whirling to cut through spearshafts and break shields. The pushing of fyrdmen gathered behind us as they sensed victory and plunder.

And eventually, the hard pressed Breton bearshields broke once again. And when they broke, the tide of battle turned.

Amid a riot of horn-blasts and shouted commands, the Bretons stepped back a spear's length and as they did so a volley of spears and axes rushed over our heads. The fyrdmen at the rear cheered as their missiles drove down into the second, third and fourth ranks of the Bretons. Many of them fell and the men of the front rank glanced around at empty spaces where warriors had once stood. That was when I heard Leofwin's voice above the din of battle.

"Wessex!" he cried, charging out of the shield wall with his sword held high and the eagle banner raised at his back. And the whole battle line went forward with him.

There was no longer any grass beneath my feet, just the bodies of fallen Bretons and Normans. As the enemy line stumbled back, I stepped up onto a shield that covered a corpse and brought my sword down on the bearded Breton in front of me with enough weight to smash iron and bone. I saw the terror flashing in his eyes, but I only heard the words my father had shouted as he trained me to the sword, and I drove the blade down into his neck, and as he fell I saw the sky and the grass behind him. The sky and the grass

263

and the chain of low hills that led southwards towards the sea. The Duke's army was in chaos. The men behind were turning and fleeing faster even than the sword-battered front rank.

I sprang through the gap I had made and bounded down the hill, seeing the men of Wessex rushing forward all around me and tasting cool, bloodless air. Earl Leofwin ran on ahead whooping and yelling, his sword cutting circles against the sky. The enemy packed together in their retreat, trampled over one another, and we flew down the grassy slope of Sandlac hill, warriors and fyrd together in pursuit.

Our fyrdmen were ferocious in that fight. Face to face with a Norman shield wall they would have been slaughtered in their hundreds, but they were like a pack of wolves among the breaking army. I saw a Breton warrior trip on a fallen shield and before he had a chance to rise, two fyrdmen had planted their feet in his back and were clubbing him to death. Others came charging out with knives and axes and with fallen weapons picked up from the field. And as soon as they had killed, they began to plunder. The hillside was strewn with the dead and for each fallen foeman there were two or three peasants stripping off armour, searching for the trinkets and talismans, crosses of gold and silver, prising rings from the arms and fingers of the dead. Some fallen warriors had helmets decorated with gold. And swords. Any sword would fetch as much silver in the markets of Lunden and Wincestre as a village man was likely to see in his whole life. But a sword from the field of Sandlac, from the broken army of Willelm the Bastard - from the battle that saved England from the thralldom of Normandy - such a sword would be the most precious thing in all the land.

I never reached the bottom of the hill. Some of the fleeing Bretons rallied and turned and formed a ragged shield wall and by that time most of the fyrd had lost interest in killing as they stripped corpses on the hillside.

"Rally to the eagle!" Leofwin's voice rang across the hill. I saw the black eagle of his banner flying and his sword lifted to the sky

264

as men gathered to his side, ready to break the Bretons again. And I would have joined them, but before I could move, I heard the braying of war horns from the hilltop. The king was summoning us back.

A hand grasped me by the shoulder and I spun round ready to duck and to strike low with my sword. But it was Ragnald.

"The horses are coming!" he shouted, his face a fleeting moment of panic as he ran on across the hillside to warn the clusters of fyrdmen. I looked around and realised for the first time that the enemy had not truly broken. The Breton flank was in disarray, but the great mass of their army remained at the top of the hill, their shields locked and their spears level. Behind me, the warriors of Wessex were waving madly and shouting at us to return. My father and brother were still there and so were Magnus and his men. Some of the men now scattered across the hill were rallying to Leofwin, but many others began running back to the shield wall. After just a moment's hesitation, I joined them.

Because the Norman Duke thought fast in battle, and from behind the mass of warriors who had held their ground, he sent his horsemen out again.

Leofwin's men were doomed. A few broke away in a desperate race to rejoin their king. Others glanced from the foemen in front of them to the horsemen pounding towards their flank. The fyrdmen who had rallied to the Earl's side were already running. I saw Ragnald leading a group of them away into the stream gully and the hawthorn thickets beyond which lay the forest where horse riders could not chase them. Some of them might live to sell their plunder and to tell wild tales of the day when they stood alongside King Harold in the Great Battle for Wessex.

But I was a warrior, and I was a fool that day, and although I knew it was the only wise course to take, I could not run from battle. Instead I fixed my eyes on the hilltop banners and sprinted hard against the slope. Other men were running alongside me.

Under the warm sun, the tall grass clung to my feet and the weight of my mail and shield dragged me down. Screaming with war-rage, the foremost of the mounted warriors plunged on four or five horse-lengths ahead of his followers, his sword raised and ready. I prayed silently and my prayers were answered as he led the bulk of his men down the hill towards Leofwin's pack of warriors. But a few split away to skirt the shield wall. I heard a scream and saw the mailed man on my right brought down by a Norman spear. He tumbled into the grass, his legs thrashing and the long shaft in his back pointing at the sky. But I was lucky. The rider was past me before he had time to draw his sword. A few more paces up the hill and the sweat was stinging my eyes and the shield across my back pulled me down towards the slaughter at the foot of the hill. I remember bending double under its weight and grabbing handfuls of grass to haul myself along.

I heard voices calling from the shield wall, shouting out at us to run. The horseman who had missed me turned, singling me out from the straggle of running men. Another rider caught a man on my left, smashing a mace into his helmet with the careful aim of a smith beating out an iron bar. Up ahead, a spearhead flashed in the sun and flew from the shield wall. It arced high in the air and hammered into the shield of the first horseman as he rode at me, his sword already raised for the kill. He swayed in the saddle, cursed in his Norman tongue and knocked the spear to the ground. It just gave me enough time to lurch towards the row of painted, war-splintered shields. I saw more spears raised above me to protect me from the horseman. I heard him curse again then I felt hands grab the mail at my shoulders and pull me through the shield wall to safety.

"It's good to see you so eager for battle," grunted my father as he passed me a horn cup filled with watered ale. "But we'll chase them when the command comes." Heaving for breath and sitting on the grass among the feet of the men who had saved me, I guzzled it down, trickles running out of my mouth and washing the sweat from my neck.

"Slow down," said Oswold. "We're not celebrating yet."

"Did you not hear the king's command? Hold this ground, he said," muttered one of Magnus' men. He had cropped red hair and a fat, angry face. "We could have wheeled left and trapped them, made them fight on two flanks uphill." He pointed down the hill with his sword. "See what happens to that idiot Leofwin now."

The horsemen were riding along the edge of the stream gully. Those who had lost their long spears in their first attack drew swords and the whole pack of riders turned in a circle that would bring them back down upon the Earl's force. From the other side of the hill, another band of fifty or sixty horsemen rode in to join the killing. Faced with a resurging tide of Normans and Bretons, Leofwin and about three hundred followers had fought their onto a hump of rising ground. Perhaps he hoped to break out through the tangled bushes of the dry gully. But many of his men were already bleeding on the ground. They were almost out of earshot at the foot of the hill, but we knew their cries were for us to help them. And they must have known just as well that if we left the shield wall it could only bring us death and do nothing to save them. Magnus had stepped forward to watch his uncle make a final stand, but the expression on his face said nothing.

Leofwin died, and all his most loyal warriors beside him. They formed a defensive ring but horsemen and footmen came at them from every side and they were scythed down like corn in the harvest fields. They fought and they roared their battle cries beneath the eagle banner. They called out to us for help as the tide of foes swirled around them. And then they were finally silent. The Normans cheered when the eagle banner fell, the bodies of three hundred men bloody on the grass around it, and on the hill we could only watch.

The band of horsemen broke apart, fists and weapons raised in triumph. Some of them galloped up the hill brandishing Saxon spears and axes. From amid the pack one man rode to within a spear's throw of our line carrying that banner of black eagle

267

embroidered on a field of blue and gold. Bloodstained and ragged, it flapped stiffly as he reined in his horse. Then he spoke. His English was broken, but his voice carried clear across the flattened grass and the bodies of the dead.

"The eagle falls! Brother of Harold Oath-Breaker is dead! Men of England, you yield or you die!" He drew back the shaft of the banner and hurled it high. The blue and gold cloth swept over our heads and landed somewhere to the rear, more a piece of discarded rubbish than a trophy of battle.

It was past noon and the sun was high, but it took the enemy a long time to find the courage to meet us again. A new battle line formed in front of us, now more Norman than Breton and sweating in the mild warmth of the day. They passed skins of ale and pots of water along their line as we did. Rank on rank of mail-clad men, ready to deal out death once more.

There were some grey-bearded men in the lines opposite us. Old warriors tempted from halls and villages deep among quiet fields by the call of so great a battle as this. But most were young men, bright eyed and beardless, hiding their fear behind scowls and clenched jaws. Some had summoned courage with screams of joy and hate as our shields had crashed together. Others had pissed themselves at the sight of blood and bone.

"Don't look too long at their faces," said a voice beside me. And it spoke so softly that at first I did not know it as my father's. "They're not devils. They are men just like us. And if we look too long, we see our fathers, our brothers and our sons. See only the iron of their blades and think of the druid kings and foul beasts of ancient times." A buzzard circled above the corpse-strewn hillside, making the thin mewing call that would summon others to the feast. I could think of nothing to say to my father. It was as if another man was speaking. A man who, until this day, had lived only as a pale shadow.

268

"You fight well," he went on and there was pride in his smile. "If you still know fear, then you show none. The drums of war beat in your heart, Wulfred."

He rested his spear against his shield and reached across to clasp a scarred hand on my shoulder. We said no more, for there was a sudden cry of command and a hundred stones whirled through the air over our heads.

"Slingers!" Oswold shouted, and his cheer was echoed along the line. On the hill below us, the enemy huddled beneath their shields. The force of a smooth stone launched from a fyrdman's sling was enough to break a shoulder or even kill if it struck an unprotected head. The Norman warriors staggered back from the hail of stones. Their leaders rode among them shouting orders and beating men back into line. A horse reared as a stone hammered into its flank. Then the arrows began to fall.

I felt something hit my shield and looked down to see a white-fletched shaft sticking through the torn leather covering.

"Cowards!" my father yelled, but he quickly ducked behind his shield as a volley thudded home. Some arrows whipped into the grass and the dead men in front of us. Others smacked into shields and glanced off helmets and shield bosses. The tip of the arrow had come about a thumb's length through my shield and I used my knife to cut off the murderous iron point. A third volley rose from behind the Norman ranks, flying higher to land behind our shield wall. There were screams in the still afternoon as the fyrdmen began to die. I no longer had my bow – it was lost somewhere on the slope below, so I just lifted my shield like the other warriors and cursed. And listened to the screams of the wounded and the dying fyrdmen at our backs.

After five volleys of arrows the drums and the horns sounded and the enemy came forward again – another line of shields and iron helmets and a hedge of spears, chanting songs of blood. And this time they ran, the shields wavering as they stumbled through

269

the corpses. I jabbed out with my shield to turn an enemy spear coming from the left, then stumbled as an axemen blundered forward on the other side, his weapon smashing through a Norman shield. I had just enough space to push my spear over the broken shield and into the Norman's throat. His scream rasped a blood-mist into our faces and I turned my head briefly to the axeman. I nodded to him, but the expression he shot back at me was unreadable. Half his face was covered in a thick black beard and the other half was a horror of pus and half healed scabs, a few broken teeth showing clearly through a ripped-open cheek.

Bera, the fyrd-killer and slave-beater I had quarrelled with on the coast and kicked senseless outside the hall at Westmynster. My father had told me at the time that I would not care what kind of man stands at my side in the shield wall, as long as he could fight and kill. But for the first time since the battle began, I felt a tremor in my knees and a clutching of fear at my throat as Bera's wolf eyes glared back at me. He made a dribbling grunt of a sound, the words lost in the wreckage of his mouth, then spat and growled at the enemy, his axe sweeping fast and deadly just above their shields. I followed the axe with my spear again, this time feeling the jarring of metal as the blade struck a Norman helmet. The axe swung again, broke another shield and Bera leant back to bring the weapon over his head again. But this time I did not see the axehead smashing down into the enemy. This time I felt a hand pushing me hard between the shoulder blades and I heard a mangled snarl as I tripped forward into a place of whirling blades and broken shields. A weight like an iron fist smashed into the side of my head. I remember a greybeard Norman fixing his eyes on mine. I fought to stay upright in the shield wall, but my legs staggered beneath me and the strength washed out of my body. My shield dropped and a spear cut through the air over my head. There was blood in the old Norman's beard, the sky darkened, the enemy warriors loomed and my father's elbow was in my face, his mail scratching the skin from my nose and lips as he pushed me back. Someone was dragging me by the arms. A thin-faced old man mumbled something in Welsh as he cut the leather chinstrap from my helmet and prised it from my head. I remember the tearing pain of metal in my flesh. Stains of red and black spread across the sky and thunder rolled in from distant hills.

I remember a great darkness gathering.

14. THE BREAKING OF ARMIES

Not many years after we fought on Sandlac Hill, I saw a great cloth in Cantaburh being embroidered with scenes of Duke Willelm's campaign against the English. Its making was ordered by Odo, the Norman Bishop whom Leofwin and Magnus taunted across the marsh at Pefensea. And its purpose was to immortalise forever the Duke of Normandy in his moment of triumph.

I do not know where that cloth now hangs. In some great church across the sea probably, where people will look upon the images of English warriors and make the sign of the cross because they see evil in them.

Or maybe it hangs in the royal hall of Westmynster, where Harold once mustered his warriors on a day of boasting and brash hope so many years ago.

The Norman Duke is dead now, killed when his horse threw him to the ground in the burning ruins of another town he had conquered, and I cannot find it in my heart to wish his soul any peace. His son followed him, red-faced and raging, drunk on English ale and Frankish wine and wringing from England all the corn and the silver it could give until he too was struck down, pierced by an arrow whilst hunting on a royal estate where men and women were once free to stalk deer, gather wood and graze their pigs and cattle. Now another son of the Bastard Duke sits throned in the hall of Westmynster and I wonder if the faces of Harold Godwinsson's warriors of Sandlac Hill gaze down from the walls, immortalised in thread and cloth, fixed in the throes of battle and mourning the fate of their people.

The darkness passed and the sky was blue again, but with the sun much lower in the west. The screaming and roaring of men, the battering of hooves and shields and the crashing of weapons went on. My shield lay across my chest and there were arrows sticking out of its edge. There were many more arrows in the flattened grass and in the bodies of men that lay all around. There was a sticky crust of drying vomit on the rings of my mailshirt. A wounded man groaned feebly nearby. The corpse on my right, close enough to touch, had two arrows in his chest and one in his groin. Flies crawled around his open throat, cut across to release him from pain.

The sounds of fighting and hoofbeats subsided with a few hoarse cheers. I rose up on my elbows and fell back as pain roared in my skull. Much more carefully, I raised my head again, blinking against the light and swallowing the sour taste in my mouth. The men of the shield wall seemed few. Of the fyrd, more lay arrow-pierced on the ground than remained to push the warriors forward. Corpses, broken shields and men who still half lived lay before and behind the battle-line. Some of the survivors sharpened their blades, some drank from skins of ale and water, others just leaned on their spears and shields, gulping at the air. A few arrows fell and tired warriors raised their shields. Was this real, or was I dreaming that the great strength of Wessex had ebbed away into the dimming sky.

As the pain in my head began to fade, I found my sword, crusted with blood and battle-dented, still at my side. I looked around for water, but instead I found Magnus. He did not greet me. He just looked down with his hard blue eyes.

"Curig!" he bayed across the corpse-field, and the thin-faced old Welshman came scurrying over. To my relief he handed me a hare's skin filled with water. "Curig, did you tend this man's wound?"

"Yes my lord."

"Will he live?"

"He will, lord. If not, I would not have bandaged him." The old man drew a finger across his throat and they both looked grimly at the throat-cut corpse that lay beside me. "His helmet was split apart and the metal cut into his flesh, but the bone of his skull is still whole." The old man held up my helmet, the side of which had been gashed by a sword or axe-blow, with blood and hair still stuck to the splintered metal.

Then Magnus grasped my elbow and hauled me to my feet. Blinded by pain, I had to clutch at his shoulder to keep my balance.

"The battle's not over." He wrenched the helmet from an arrow-slain corpse and threw it at my feet.

My father grinned blackly through his bloody beard. He had lost another tooth and had an open cut along his right cheekbone, but among warriors on the field of battle he looked tireless.

"How's your head, Wulfed?" he asked.

"Still on my shoulders, no thanks to that bastard Bera." The order to lock shields together rolled along the line of the army. But before he lifted his shield, my father pointed to his sword to a corpse, one corpse of many, that lay face down just a pace or two in front of us. The thick mat of hair that covered its neck was drenched with blood and I glanced back at my father, to ask how my enemy had died. But my father was poised for battle again and staring over the raised rim of his shield. Norman warriors, silent and grim, were advancing back up the hill. Oswold tried to smile at me before he turned to face them, but he was pale and wide-eyed, the corner of his mouth twitching.

So once more I stood in the press of warriors and fought the men of Normandy. Still dazed, with my head throbbing inside a dead man's helmet, I stood in the second rank, but had not thought to pick up a spear from the fallen weapons on the ground. All I could do was to wave my sword over the shoulders of the men in front of me. I heard a man shouting "Spear! Spear!" and I saw him pull open a Norman shield with the barbs of his own weapon. But the Norman was beyond my reach and he quickly pulled back his battered shield and fought on.

From far away to my left, in the centre of the field, the sounds of blades and shields smashing together thundered out across the hillside and the air was filled with the wild screams of warriors in victory and in death.

"Wessex will stand forever!" my father shouted at the line of hard faces in front of us.

"Your Duke will be a corpse on a dungheap tonight," cried another man.

But when the Normans finally fell back, their shield wall still unable to break ours, the news was very different.

"What's happening up there?" Magnus called out when a red-faced warrior from the king's hearthtroop came rushing down the line. He moved close to Magnus and spoke in a hushed voice, but I was close enough to hear.

"Gyrth's men broke. The Normans breached the shield wall of East Anglia on the right. The king himself led us into heart of the battle. We drove them back, but we must have lost a hundred men."

"Shit!" Magnus spat on the ground. "And my father's orders?"

"Stand firm." The king's warrior shrugged. "The light's fading. Once darkness falls, our victory is certain."

I looked at my father. He had overheard the king's man and he frowned a warning at me not to spread rumours of defeat along the shield wall. For there were other stories now passing from man to man. Someone told me that Gyrth Godwinsson himself had fallen, thrown from his horse and hacked to death by Normans as he tried to rally his men. Another said that men who had fought hard all day had turned and fled towards the forest when the Norman Duke drove his horse-warriors into the shield wall again.

I put down my shield and ran a stone along the edges of my sword, trying to drive out the fear of defeat. How many men must die, I wondered, before we could lay down our blades and submit to the Duke of Normandy? Leave our weapons on the field and go back to our homes. But, of course, I could say no such thing.

275

The red-faced man continued along the line, urging men to stand their ground until darkness or victory ended the fight. He was answered by tired cheering and the groans of the wounded. The desperate calls of those staring into the eyes of death and the voices of the carrion birds that wheeled above the field almost drowned out the pounding of war drums. The older wounded men lay still, their lips moving in silent prayer, welcoming death as a friend they had served all their lives. But younger warriors, lying broken on the ground, screamed as if their voices could vanquish pain, and pleaded with God for just one more moment of life.

A man who lay bleeding to death gibbered that he could see the very shadow of Christ himself rising above the Norman army.

"If Christ stands with our foes, then he shall also taste my sword this evening!" my father shouted across the field. His voice was tired, but the men around us roared their approval and the wounded man died on the hillside, his eyes fixed on the wheeling birds in the darkening sky.

For evening was coming at last. Away to the west, the red sun faded into the weald. Darkness would leave the duke's army battered, bleeding and lost in an unfamiliar land, while the army of Wessex swelled with warriors and fyrd arriving from the far west and perhaps with the armies of Morcar and Edwin riding down from the north. Darkness was the greatest ally we had.

I prised a spear from the grip of a corpse. Its blade was jagged from the fighting, but it would kill as well as any other. Arrows thudded into our shields again.

Then the order to fall back went out along the line of battle. King Harold no longer had enough men to hold a strong position across the whole hilltop. We were to retreat fifty paces and make a half-ring four ranks deep around the king's banners. In doing so, we yielded much of the hill's flat summit. The enemy would no longer be attacking uphill, but at least we could make a solid shield wall. We stepped among the bodies of the dead, skewered with arrows, sprawled and hunched on the bloody grass. Those masses of fyrdmen who had stood behind us in the morning waiting to tear the heart out of a defeated enemy were reduced to almost nothing. Many were killed by the arrows that had rained on the hilltop while I had lain unconscious among the dead. Others were cut down with Earl Leofwin on the hillside below. But I looked at the dead and I looked at the frightened and foolhardy few fyrdmen who now picked up shields to fight at the sides of their lords and I hoped that many more had fled the field, slipped back into the weald and begun their journeys back to the villages they should never have left. I remembered Godric dying on the flattened grass. I shivered and swallowed hard and prayed that the rest of Ellasham's men had run before death could catch them.

But the dragon banner of Wessex still flew on Sandlac Hill and there was no such escape for warriors. King Harold walked among his thanes and his hearthtroop. His brow was furrowed but there was still strength in his voice and in his stride as we approached the final hour. Some of the king's men rode the length of the shield wall and pushed the men on the flanks back until we formed a semicircle backing onto the weald that the Normans would not easily outmanoeuvre. The king carried a shield across his back, and his sword was drawn in the reddening light. He would fight to the death if necessary and he expected his warriors stand at his side against whatever fate held for them.

I thought of home then, of the women waiting anxiously for their menfolk, of the quiet evening in the shadows of the great trees in a place where such slaughter could surely never come. I am almost sure that I would have fled into the forest had the warriors of Glowcestre not been gathered around me. They were grim-faced, but spoke not a word of defeat.

"Rest while you can," Magnus ordered his men. "Sharpen your spears."

"Our enemies grow weary," the king told us as he once again walked the length of his battered war host. "And you, men of

Wessex, have fought like the heroes of old. The daylight fades and our foes are failing. Gather weapons from the field. There will be gold and land for every man upon this hill of victory."

I looked at the faces of the dead as we picked up their fallen arms. The Norman army waited within a stone's throw of our own. Their drums and horns fell silent and they glanced nervously at each other while mounted warriors at the rear shouted and threw wild gestures towards our line. The first chill of night was beginning to move among us.

"Now we come to the breaking of armies. No priests, no gods, no songs this eve. Just men and blades and blood." My father spoke calmly, his voice cut through with awe as light drained from the world. His mail was crusted with the blood of foes, his shield hewn by many blows and the war banner of Wessex high in the evening sky at his back. Oswold, wild eyed and unfamiliar, was beside him and I clasped them both by the shoulders. The three of us stood side by side and there was strange joy in that moment, joy and a surge of hope. Hope that if we three had withstood all of the fight so far, then the day could still be ours to tell of through long and quiet years to come.

The Norman drums sounded again. My father took his place between myself and Oswold and we overlapped our shields to face another attack in the half light.

Horsemen rode among the Norman host crying out orders and shouts of encouragement. But their men gave little answer. Doubt crawled upon their faces. They outnumbered us badly now, but the sight of a shield wall built anew filled them with fear.

"Come on you bastards!" my father yelled across the field. "The sky darkens! Why do you wait?" I heard Oswold make a strange whimpering sound and when I looked across at him all the brash courage he had brought back from the north seemed to have gone. His eyes stared, his hands shook and my father put down his spear for a moment to place a hand on Oswold's shoulder. I wished I could comfort my brother. I wished I could take him back to Ellasham, far from the swords of Normandy.

A volley of stones came from the men to my left. It caught the Normans unprepared and a section of their line stumbled back a few steps. Horns blew among the army of Wessex and I began to hope that maybe we had done enough and that the Norman host might not have the stomach to face our swords again.

"Run like sheep," laughed a voice from our line. "Fight like women and run like sheep! We have men here who'll fuck either. Go back to your ships!" We bleated like sheep at our foes and there was laughter in that darkening hour.

A Norman horseman in a bright blue cloak rode along the enemy line urging his men on. I saw the way they looked up at him and guessed he was a well-loved warrior lord in the land across the Narrow Sea. A bringer of victory, a giver of gold in his hall. Now he stood dark against the sky in the level rays of the fading sun. Warriors looked up in admiration and some of them raised their spears for him to touch with his own blade. Maybe he was a fighting priest or a bishop, giving blessing to his followers. He turned his back on us and as he did so, our line opened. Magnus stepped forward and hurled a spear at the horsemen. At that distance he could not have missed. The blade punched straight through his mail and into the middle of his back. His words of encouragement died in a grunt. His horse turned and circled as its rider fought for breath. Four Norman warriors broke from their shield wall to catch his body as he fell to the ground.

Then, from the rear of the army, a man galloped forward and threw his helmet to the ground so that all might recognise him.

"It's the Bastard himself!" my father cried. The horseman called out to his faltering warriors while we bleated and threw spears and stones. He did not look like a great leader of men – he was plump and red in the face – but at the sound of his voice, they lifted their shields, fixed their gaze upon us and we knew they would fight again.

The man on my left held out a small bronze figure.

"Odin," he said. "Spear lord of the warriors' hall. This is his day. May we have victory before we meet him." I touched the figure, but I did not pray to be worthy of the death halls of my ancestors. I silently prayed to still live in this world when the day was ended, and never to stand in the line of battle again. My father growled and raised his shield up to his chin. The songs of death and the songs of victory had passed. There was only the cool dusk, the tramp of the enemy's feet and the groans of the dying. I did not need my father to tell me that this was a fight that awed voices would recall at their hearths until our people faded from the memory of the world.

The Normans were slowed by the grisly mounds of the dead and dying where our shield wall had stood all day. We hurled the weapons gathered from the fallen. I threw a spear that struck a man full in the chest as he stumbled on a corpse. He fell back among his comrades and the men around me punched the air and gave a brief shout, their breath beginning to mist in the cool air. I had three small axes too, hung from my shield strap, but the axe is a clumsy weapon to throw and I saved them for when the Normans closed in.

Heedless of our missiles, the Duke forced his way through the packed ranks, yelling and screaming at them, striking out with the flat of his sword. His army stumbled over the piled bodies, shields up and spears forward. We threw the last of our axes, aiming low at the exposed shins and feet beneath their shields. A few men fell, but the others knew that to hesitate now meant death and the wounded were trampled as the shield-line rushed on.

And with another roar of battlecries the two lines met again. As one, the shields of Wessex rose to meet a great line of spears. Some men lunged out with axes to break the long shafts. Keeping my shield lapped tightly against those on either side, I rammed my spear hard into the neck of the Norman facing my father. His blood misted the air, his breath rasped from the wound and I pushed his body back into the ranks behind him. Abandoning the spear, I drew my sword, screamed out and stabbed at the faces in front of me. They leaned back, fearful of the blade, but not far enough. Like a flash of light in the dying day, my father's spear twitched across, sliced off half a man's face, then flew quickly back and buried itself in the belly of a warrior caught by the press of men behind him. The man in front of me fell and curled up on the ground, gibbering and clutching at his butchered face while my father's laughter bellowed across the field.

The enemy were cautious. Glancing up, I saw the noblemen of Normandy riding among the mass of grey-mailed men, roaring at them to push forward. When they did, they met our swords and spears and began to make a new tide line of slaughter. From over my shoulder, one of Magnus' warriors hefted a Dane axe to split helmets and skulls.

The sun had fallen into the western trees. The Day of Blood had withered and evening was as grey as unpolished armour. But still the strength of Wessex seemed unbreakable.

And in that desperate moment, as King Harold shouted words of victory above the din of battle and the Normans must have wondered why they fought on, the Duke made his final gamble.

It began with cries of confusion from the Norman warriors in front of us. There was pushing and shoving in the ranks behind. Beyond the reluctant warriors who faced us, a mass of Normans broke away and, with horsemen at the front and rear, I saw them streaking across the hilltop to hit the far right of our shield wall.

"Glowcestre! To the flank!" It was the voice of Magnus. He saw the danger straight away - that a final desperate charge on the right flank could still break the shield wall and give the Duke his victory. Holding Ironclaw aloft, he gathered men to face the new threat. The Bloodhelms slipped from the shield wall and other men took their place, leaving no part of our line more than two men deep. The Norman facing me made a poorly judged stab and I caught his sword high on my shield. The axeman at my back swung his weapon over my shoulder and smashed the Norman's elbow. He fell into the grass, his blood running blackly in the half-light. A tall warrior with a patch covering one eye took his place. The cold grip of fear came with him as I recalled a Viking tale of one-eyed Odin appearing in the battle line before men about to die.

Then a wall of noise erupted from the right as Magnus' men crashed against the flank attack on the weald's edge. A dying horse screamed above the fighting. My father's sword hissed through the air and glanced off a Norman helmet. And yet again the enemy stumbled over the bodies of the slain to try to break through one last time. The one eyed man slipped and I rammed my sword hard into his stomach, splitting mail and pulling out his guts as I twisted it free. Death had missed me again. Then suddenly, where that fallen warrior had stood there were hooves.

The horse reared up and battered down the shield of the man on my right. For a heartbeat, the whole shield wall quivered. The Norman Duke must have led his horsemen straight through the packed ranks of his struggling warriors. The screaming of horses and the cries of their riders suddenly broke out from both sides. My father looked at me, anxiety shadowing his face for the first time. The man on my right was down, so I took a half step back, to allow a man behind me to come forward and to avoid the horse's flailing hooves. But a spear from above hammered hard into my shield and I fell. There were hooves and running feet all around. Covering my face with my shield I thrust my sword up at a black mass above me. It sank into a horse's belly and blood and filth gushed onto the ground. The horse shrieked and hurled itself backwards. The rider fell a few steps away from me. He rolled over and lumbered to his feet, but I did not stop to fight him. I was up, my shield slung across my back, running into the gathering dark. A man running in front of me was cut down by a rider's spear. I ran past the horseman, hacking at his leg. Then I felt a blow from behind and heard the dull clang of a spear glancing off my shield boss. I was on the grass again, but I managed to parry the long spear as it came for me a second time. I saw the hard jawline and the eyes of an iron clad man looming above me. He stabbed again and this time I grabbed the shaft of his spear, used it to pull myself to my feet, and lunged at the horse below the saddle. The animal bellowed and reared and I turned to run again.

The edge of Andredsweald was only a hundred paces away, but the shield wall that had held all day was shattered and the foes who had smashed through our flank now stood between the fleeing warriors and the possible safety of the forest. On both sides I saw men cut down by the high spears of horsemen and the swords of those on foot. The trees were closer now, a dark line separating death from life. The sword was ready in my hand, sticky with the blood of horses and men. But four warriors loomed out of the darkness in front of me. Bretons, they were, with bears painted on their battle-torn shields and their dark hair mingling with the night and the far trees. Three of them had swords and one carried a long boar-spear that could gut a man through mail and leather. They advanced on me, their faces savage, their mutterings deadly in their unfamiliar tongue. These were men who had been humiliated in battle that morning and now they came for vengeance. There was nowhere to run. All I could do was to rush the enemy, take them by surprise, lash out at the nearest one and try to outrun the others. I took a few steps back, trying to show them fear, to make an attack the last thing they would expect. Close to the hilltop a horse reared and kicked a man down. Together the Bretons advanced on me, swords ready, that great boar spear snaking forwards as its bearer cursed me. A roar of battle arose somewhere to my right as Norman riders battered into the Dragons of Wessex.

Then one of the Bretons stepped forward. I raised my sword. This was death - the enemy coming at me before I had a chance to make a move. The fire of the shield wall had fled from me. Somehow I managed to walk forward, to face this black shape carrying my doom out of the darkness while three of his

283

companions waited behind to ensure I would never get away. My foot touched one of the hundreds of arrow-slain bodies that littered the hill. The Breton warrior dropped his shield a little.

"Wulfred!" he said quietly. "Knock me down you fool and run for the trees!" I saw the eyes glimmer beneath the iron helmet, the ragged hair and the unexpected face of a friend. For a moment Idwal smiled as he stepped forward, then he raised his sword and howled a warrior's cry. I rushed forward at him, pushed him with my shield and he fell, pretending to stumble on the corpse at our feet, and I was past the three Bretons before they knew what had happened. As I ran, I heard one of them laugh at Idwal and another cursing him for a fool. There were men running to my left and right, turning and weaving to avoid the horsemen who hacked at anyone they could reach. I saw a man throw down his shield to run faster, but a spear took him in the back before he had made more than a few strides.

I do not know how many Normans tried to kill me in the chaos of that shattered army. I only know that none of them did. I ran like a wild pig with the hounds at its tail. I plunged through a bramble thicket and over rough tussocks of grass - anything that might slow down a pursuer, until I finally scrambled over a fallen tree at the edge of the woods, missed my footing and rolled into the long grass and nettles.

Before I could even get to my feet, there were hands gripping my arms, pulling me up. I fought to shake them off, reached to pull the knife from my belt.

"Hey steady friend. We're not the Bastard's men." Confused, panting for breath and trying to free my arm from a tangled shield strap, I looked up into the face of Magnus. "Wulfred of Ellasham," he said. "You live. And I'm not surprised Wulfred Fleetfoot. You run from battle just as your father always feared!" His voice was as toneless as ever, but there was a grim smile on his face. "This time you were wise to do so." Then he turned and shouted orders at a small band of spearmen.

284

Looking back into the dimming light of the battlefield, I could see only Norman warriors riding triumphant across the field. But there were dark shadows of men among the darker undergrowth of the treeline. Magnus threw me a spear. I caught it and he smiled that wintry smile again.

"It's still not over Wulfred. We have much to avenge this evening."

"Have you seen my father? Or Oswold?" Magnus shrugged his shoulders and looked out across the dark battlefield.

"They stood beside you. I had my own men to deal with. It was your part of the line where they hit hardest. My men met the charge and fell back in good order. The king and his hearthtroop still fight in the centre. But the men between us and the king? Most of them are dead on the field. Not all as swift-footed as you."

My father could fight like a bear, but he was no runner. And would he have even thought about fleeing from his king's foes? Perhaps I should have looked for him when the shield wall broke. But what could I have done except to die by his side? And what of Oswold? I slumped to my knees, gripped the spearshaft and closed my eyes and I felt suddenly alone in the chill grey evening. I thought of Oswold as a boy, plump-faced and sure-footed, smiling with pride as he lifted a sword made for a man three times his size, still innocent of all that the blade was forged for. I remembered him laughing as he wrestled me down into the mud of the south field while half the village watched. A warm rush of tears crept into my closed eyes. What little chance was there that my brother still lived? Could Ellasham ever be home again without my father's rage and my brother's smile? How could I go back there and tell my mother that I had left them both for the wolf and the raven?

But there was no time to dwell on such things. As Magnus had said, the fight was not over. A couple of men stood on the fallen trunk that I had stumbled over and their calls to any survivors still fleeing dragged me back to the battle.

"Rally to Magnus!" they cried. "To the trees!" But very few managed to stumble off the hill, and the calls alerted the enemy.

They gathered as silhouettes in the failing light. The great constellations were already shimmering above the battlefield. The wind gathered strength as the day died, rattling the branches and blowing dead leaves across the weald's edge. We heard the beating of hooves and shouted commands in the Norman tongue. About fifty of their horse-warriors were gathered along the skyline. Magnus stood near me. We both held spears poised over the great tree trunk. Spears already so dark with blood that they blended with the hungry ground.

"Now they'll see the men of Wessex do not die easily," Magnus called out.

"The men of Wessex do not die!" added another defiant voice from the darkness. I had seen about thirty men spread among the bushes, but I could hear the voices of others in the shadows beyond them. I rested my spear on the fallen tree. It was an old, old tree. A witness to the storms and the battles of centuries.

The horses turned to face us and their hoofbeats rose into thunder. I heard Magnus chanting some old song of battle. I gripped hard on my spear again and raised it at a patch of sky between the branches. And suddenly the terrible hooves of the warhorses flailed at us again. The rider turned his mount too late and it reared against the tree trunk. I thrust up with my spear and heard it strike dully against his helmet. The blow was enough to knock him to the ground. A couple of spears stabbed out just short of him as he struggled to his feet and fled from the dark shadows where death was lurking. Another horseman, night-black against the sky, lunged down at the man to my right. I slammed the spear hard into his shield and wrenched it upwards. The shield came away and another spear found the gap. The man's breath spluttered in his throat and he slumped from the saddle to land gasping among the nettles and stones. Protected by our shields and the shadows of the wood, we held the enemy at bay. And on the flanks, our men hurled spears out of the darkness. The horsemen fell back to the hill and there were a few ragged cheers from the forest's edge.

Then, out of the war-ravaged evening, others came on foot. Rounded up from the looting of the dead, the riders gathered a band of warriors and drove them towards the forest. I saw Magnus look for a moment towards the hilltop, where there was enough light to see the dragon banner still flying above a mass of struggling men. But then he looked at the grim silhouettes marching towards us.

"Fall back!" he called out. "Into the trees." His order was passed along the line and, following the men on either side, I stepped away from the protection of the tree trunk, into the darkness.

Immediately, the bushes along the forest edge came alive with the black shapes of men and the air was rent by the whoops and cheers of an army drunk on victory. A roaring warrior charged at me with a Dane axe taken from the battlefield, but he did not know how to wield such a weapon. I beat it aside with my shield and pushed my spear into his face. It went high and sparks flashed through the darkness as it scraped against the iron of his helmet. Another spear came in low from the left and hit him in the knee. I heard a crack of bone and the axeman fell. As quickly as it had begun, the whooping and cheering ceased as the Normans realised they were blundering in the dark towards enemies still able to fight.

They fell back and kept their distance. Their voices were replaced by the sounds of horses among the dark woods on either side. I cursed the ill luck that had led me straight into Magnus' position. I could have run on into the weald and been far away from death, one man amongst a million trees and a world of shadows. But instead I had found Magnus, and Magnus would surely fight to the death in a battle already lost, and take every man he could muster into the shadow world with him.

"They're surrounding us," I whispered.

"They don't know this place," said a voice from my left. "They're walking to their deaths."

287

It was a part of the forest I did not know either, but it did not seem to me that death awaited the enemy. They were on both flanks and many of the horsemen carried lit torches. I tried to count the eerie lights flickering among the trees, but there were too many, picking their way through the black forest to get behind us.

It felt like a long, long retreat through the trees. The men around me spoke little. They watched the flickering torches, listened for the shouts of warriors and tried to tread light and quiet through the leaves of the forest floor.

We reached the edge of a clearing. Suddenly the stars spread out across the open sky like the blazing dust of the sun and the rest of Magnus' men leafed from the darkness as clusters of black shadows from blacker shadows. There were more than I had first thought. Sixty or seventy. I felt the pace pick up and the tension of the men around me rise. We were on open ground now. In spite of the darkness, the horsemen might still charge and turn us into carrion for the grey wolves. All along the edges of the clearing, in front of us and on our flanks, the shadows of armoured men slid out of the night.

"Run!" yelled Magnus. His voiced rang from one wall of trees to the other. "Run for the ditch!"

As one, we turned and lumbered across the black and scrubby clearing. I should have been exhausted from the day's battle, but with the riders of Normandy behind me I hardly noticed the weight of my armour. Magnus led us to one side of the clearing and along a narrow path. Down to the left was a wide, shallow ditch filled with weeds. To the right was a great pit of rock, crumbling earth and the faint glimmer of stars reflected on water. It was one of the quarries that pitted Andredsweald, the places where Britons, Romans and Saxons had dug for the stones that make iron. The path turned left, leading behind the ditch and away from the pit.

"Spread out!" cried Magnus. "No shield wall! Stand alone. Let them come against us."

It was madness. It was madness to fight on in a battle we had already lost. But to spread ourselves thinly behind a ditch hardly deep enough to slow a charging horse? In the grip of that madness, some of Magnus' warriors now let loose their cries of battle again and beat weapons on their shields, inviting the enemy to battle. The forest behind me was thick and tangled with thorn bushes. A man fleeing would be caught in those thorns and slaughtered. It was a stupid place to die after all that we had lived through.

"Why here? What are we doing?" I asked the man nearest to me. He was a big, thickly muscled warrior with a dark beard and he grinned at me, showing broken teeth and setting fresh blood flowing from a gash on his cheek.

"That ditch is a place of death, cursed by the old gods." His voice was slow and something menacing growled in it, but in the ditch there was only grass and straggling brambles. So, at the end of the long day's battle Magnus had nothing left but to trust in the malice of ancient gods.

I closed my eyes and prayed to those gods, prayed to Christ, prayed to any god that might listen, for the madness to be over, for a chance to see the sun rise at the end of this dreadful night. And when I opened my eyes, the enemy were crossing the clearing under the light of the stars. They did not attack quickly. They sent men out to the flanks, who must have returned to report that the woods were thick - that there was no safe way through to surround us. The dark-bearded warrior handed me a leather bottle half-filled with sour ale and as I drank I finally felt the weariness of the day throbbing in my arms and legs. The Normans gathered on the clearing. Those on foot stood back and the horsemen came to face us, bearing many torches to show off their numbers. I counted sixty mounted men during the long wait for death. The stars roved silently above. The battle on Sandlac Hill was already passing into history as we waited to play out its final throes. Eventually, two horsemen rode forward, dragging a roped captive between them.

"The Earl of Wessex, he is dead," one of them shouted. His accent was harsh and strange. He hit the prisoner across the back with the flat of his sword. "Speak." The man staggered to his feet. He gasped for breath and struggled to shout across the ditch.

"King Harold fell in battle. The dragon banner was cut down. The Norman duke holds the field." The man slumped to the ground again and the riders threw down the ropes that bound his wrists. One of them urged his horse a few steps forward.

"So who will call himself lord of England now?" There was silence for a few moments. Then another cry chased his voice across the darkness.

"We're the fucking lords of England you bastard!"

The rider waited for its echoes to fade. "Then submit to Willelm, Duke of Normandy and King of England, or you die with Harold the Oathbreaker." There were a few more shouts of defiance and some of Magnus' men threw stones across the ditch. And then the silence of night fell again. The two foremost horsemen looked at each other and drew their swords.

"Your heads be our final trophies of this day!" one of them called. The whole mass of horsemen rode up behind them and I prepared to face battle yet again.

In a tight shield wall, a man can barely move for the closeness of those around him. The shields overlap and the wall is almost unbreakable. That is how it had been on the hill all through the long day. But now there were two or three paces between each man. The dark-bearded warrior began to laugh as the riders came closer. It was an evil sound, rumbling in time with the deadly approach of hoofbeats, with the chill of the night, with the cold glint of starlight on steel, with the tomb-black woods all around us.

The riders swept down the shallow slope, their silhouettes half hidden against the trees behind them. And just as I braced myself and flexed my bone-weary spear arm, the men around me cried out as one and ran forward to meet the enemy. Somehow the Normans were floundering in the ditch. Those who were carrying torches dropped them as their horses reared and fell. And in the flamelight I could suddenly see that the brambles, the hawthorn and the ivy grew thick and tall, and in the darkness they made the ditch look shallower than it really was. Mud and water splashed around their thrashing hooves and I knew that we had a chance - not of turning the day's defeat into victory, but of surviving - a chance of living to tell tales, to drink ale and taste bread and sleep again. I plunged forward with the rest of Magnus' men.

And in the thrashing shadows of that bloody night I felt the cold, I felt tired and I felt hunger and thirst, but I knew that death was as far away from me as if I was sat at the fireside. For a moment, death was something for my enemies to taste and battle was no longer a distant horror, but a fragment of ice in my soul. The dying faces of Llyn Rhydderch were no more a nightmare, just something old, and lost between dream and memory. I rammed the spear hard into the shape of a Norman struggling to control his horse, drew my sword as he fell and plunged in among my foes. In a knot of flying steel and flailing limbs I heard again the scraping of blades tearing into iron mail, the cracking of bones, the spluttering of blood from pierced lungs, the screams of fallen men and dying horses. And they were sounds as ordinary as wind blowing across the thatch and logs crackling in the hearth. The Normans tried to turn their horses, but the ground was pitted with rocks and water-filled holes. I learned later that it had been the site of the kilns where folk had once turned rock into iron. And now defeat was turned to vengeance and Normandy's finest warriors into an army of souls, sent screaming into the next world.

On the sodden ground in front of me, a man lay struggling to free his legs from beneath the bleeding body of his horse. He looked up at me and babbled in his foreign tongue. He held out his hands in some kind of plea and by the light of fallen torches I saw my sword at his neck and terror blazing whitely in his eyes.

And I saw him scramble off through the mud and the bramble bushes as I stepped away. From the top of the ditch, I saw the Norman warriors on foot, still waiting on the other side, hesitating to go into the slaughter to the aid of their mounted lords. The dark-bearded man I had stood beside hurled a severed head into their ranks and they began to shuffle away. And when a few more heads were thrown, they broke and ran from the horror that had found them when they ventured too deep into the forest.

There was a tiny gap in the bushes behind the ditch, and while the men of Wessex and Normandy struggled in the brambles and the mud, I found it and slipped through. Behind me, the fight was dying and the cold quiet of night slid back across the forest. Men searched the dead for anything of value. I heard their voices remarking upon the ease of the killing or upon a gold ring found on a dead finger. Pinpricks of sound in the great silence.

The fight at the ditch was a victory, but it was only enough victory to let us live for another day. On Sandlac Hill, across the haunted wilderness of Andredsweald, the banners of Normandy proclaimed victory for Duke Willelm.

The great strength of Wessex had failed.

And I was going home at last.

15. THE FIELD OF CROWS

I heard the braying of geese from across the slow river and there were cattle grazing the stubble fields. A mist rose above Walland Fen, carrying the gentle smoke of hearthfires stirred up against the chill morning. For a moment I thought nothing in the world had changed.

All night the weald had raged with ghosts. Alone in the darkness, I heard voices in the hungry blackness of the trees, but never the voices of things that lived. Not an owl shrieked, not a fox barked, not a breath of wind touched the dry leaves. I heard the crashing of weapons and the shouts of warriors in the shield wall. I saw the faces of men whose lives I had taken and of men who had fallen beside me. They flooded from the shadows as shapes of light in a great darkness and in an instant they were gone into something darker still. I saw blood and I saw splintered bone showing white through the wounds of dying men. I heard screams and choking sounds and the weeping of those who went unready to their deaths.

And my arms felt like thick bars of iron, my legs like old wood that will break before it bends and my head was like a bell of lead. Somewhere among the still trees and the wraiths, I sank into the cold ground and slept.

And early in the morning, as weary as a man who has seen a hundred winters, I stood, turned my face to the brightening east and walked on. The misty light was as strange and unwelcome as our defeat in battle. So many had died, and I wondered if I was one of them. My father was surely among the dead. He would not have run from the swords of his king's foemen. And how could Oswold have survived when the warhorses of Normandy smashed through the shield wall? Would he have run as I had? And the king? The prisoner the Normans brought before us at the ditch said the king had fallen. But I did not care about the king.

I tried to think of home and whatever remained of my people. But the dead walked with me like a fever, cold and clinging even as the sun drove its bright shafts through the tangled trees. There was a great pain in my head and I had to close one eye against it, stumbling half blind through the forest. I pressed my hand against the wound above my ear, the place where some sword or axe had battered against me in the shield wall. But I felt only the cold iron helmet I had worn as warriors fell all around. I cut through the leather strap and hurled it into a thicket, then staggered and fell at the foot of a tree as my head suddenly span like chaff blown before the west wind.

But I stood, and I walked again, heading towards the morning sun while the ghosts of that long day's fight still screamed and struggled.

And finally I reached the River Leman at a place where it slowed and pooled and the autumn trees were reflected like fire in still water. I took the pathway leading north and sometime in the afternoon I came to that swift blaze of light, when I stepped out of the weald and looked upon a world unchanged.

I crossed the south field and tried to remember Oswold and Richard fighting with blunt swords back in the spring. But I could not see their faces, just the whirling of their limbs amongst a hundred others. I saw blood in the stubble at my feet and death in the eyes of cattle that bellowed like warhorns.

And then, cutting through the battle-sounds that still raked the air, there were voices. Real voices, the voices of people who had rushed out of the village towards me. The voices of the living. And then there were faces – living faces. I mumbled the names of those I recognised. Someone took off my belt with the heavy sword. I felt hands pushing me down into the stubble and lifting my arms to hoist the mailshirt over my head. I remember the ripping sound of the dried blood that glued the iron mail to the leather tunic beneath.

The days that followed were broken and uncounted. There was rain and the river swelled and voices spoke of the ditches filling up. They spoke of the slaughter of pigs, which would begin as soon as the acorns and beech mast were gone from the forest floor. There was talk of a wedding in a village a little way upriver. And while the wind from the west brought in the year's turning, great gangs of rooks and ravens soared the other way. From the cold wastes of Walland Marsh they came, singing songs of carrion and flying to the feast on Sandlac Hill.

Ragnald lived. Brichteva's father came back, though two of his sons had fallen. Ecgbert, Godric's friend who had lost an ear fighting the Essex fyrd, still lived. A boy called Bulig who was younger than Oswold proudly showed off his finger, the tip of which had been torn off by an arrow. His mother had wept way back in the summer, when he had left with the fyrd. Now she boasted as if her son had been the only man to stand between King Harold and the host of Normandy. Most of our fyrdmen lived. If they had ever had much stomach for a fight, they had lost it when they saw Godric die, and quietly found ways of slipping away into the weald.

Hildelyth sat at my side as I slept until the nightmares faded into the hell they had sprung from. I had last seen her at the height of summer when something empty and hopeless had stretched between us. Now she was close again, but it was a closeness without joy. I told her that Godric had fallen in battle and I held her as she wept for him, and her warmth flowed back into me like the stirring of spring. Ragnald had brought back the knife with the hare-engraved sheath that Earl Leofwin had once given Godric on a day of sun and laughter, and Hildelyth wore it at her belt even though it was stained with her brother's blood.

295

A baby was born in the village and was named Harold, after the king who had probably died in the battle. Traders from Walland brought bundles of newly cut reeds to exchange for corn. The ground shook as Ragnald and a few others felled trees at the weald's edge to provide us with fuel as winter stole slowly in.

The birth of one child seemed such a little thing after so many had died.

It was not only myself and the fyrd who had fled to Ellasham from the sword-feast of Sandlac. There were other warriors in the village. Wounded men who had limped bleeding from the field and travelled through the weald for a night and a day until they found the shelter of our hall. Some had saved their horses from the chaos of defeat and now the beasts strutted around the village cropping the short grass that should have sustained our livestock into the winter.

The wounded warriors were like the shadows that fighting men leave at the hearthside – quieted men whose restless eyes tried to shun the ghosts of battle, men who flinched away from spear thrusts where there was only empty air. Most were not badly wounded. They would not have made it to Ellasham if they were. One man was carried in on a makeshift litter dragged by a horse, his blood-caked breeches tied as a rough bandage around his belly, but he had died somewhere in the weald and his friends rested briefly then wandered off with vague talk of joining other survivors and fighting on, leaving us with a corpse. The dead man was buried close to the church. His friends had not even mentioned his name.

Rumours still ruled our lives as if the battle had changed nothing. The survivors in the hall spoke of Norman warbands in the weald hunting down the remnants of King Harold's army. And they muttered fearfully about bowmen and horsemen and of how close we had been to victory. None of them had seen the king fall, but nor had any seen him leave the field alive. Some said that the earls of the north had arrived in Lunden on the day of the battle and that their swords would now decide the future of England. Others questioned me about the whereabouts of Magnus, proclaiming that, as the son of Harold, the kingdom should be his.

I do not recall the names of all those men – there were maybe a dozen of them and they only stayed with us for a week or so in a time of darkness. But I do remember Wigod, a man who needed his mouth sewn shut more than his wounds.

"I was wounded in the arm," he babbled, as if I had asked. "That's why I had to leave the field. It was my sword arm – I could not fight on. Where were you at the day's ending?"

"I was in the weald with Magnus. We cut down sixty horsemen at a ditch deep in the forest." He seemed disappointed to hear this.

"And I would have been there at your side, my friend, if I had not been wounded." He touched his right arm and winced as if it hurt.

"And where were the fyrd?" he went on. "They fled like cowards rather than falling at their king's side. You see the man sat by the fire?" He dropped his voice to a whisper and he pointed across the hall. "His name is Coenraed. Not a man to have at your side in the shield wall. He was carried from the field with an arrow in his leg. A leg wound! Since when was a man with a leg wound unable to swing a sword for his king?"

The other warriors looked up to Wigod, as he claimed to be the ealdorman of a place called Gipeswic. I would not have been surprised if he was a half-witted monk from the kitchens of some monastery who had put on a mailshirt by mistake and hurt his arm walking into a tree. Once or twice, Ragnald mixed Wigod's ale with a draught of mugwort to make him sleep all day.

"I must go to Sandlac Hill and find your father's body." My mother looked at me across the hearth. My father's body. We had disagreed on so many things, but without him I felt the balance of

297

the world fall away and our lives were like an empty ship thrown on the whims of a storm.

My father's body. She did not mention Oswold. Ever since she was married, I think my mother had been quietly ready for the moment when her husband would give himself to something he loved more than life. But she did not mention Oswold. Her face was pale and solemn in the light from the doorway, but her eyes were dry while I felt my own fill with tears. She did not speak, but her quiet strength was there and I tried to grasp it.

"I'll go with you." I did not mention Oswold either. Going with her was the last thing I wanted to do. I knew that field of blood and bone would stay with me forever and I hated the thought of seeing it again. But I could not let her go alone into the heart of the victorious enemy.

"You can't come with me. They are hunting the full length of Andredsweald, killing any Englishman they find carrying so much as a sickle."

I glanced across at the swordbelt that now lay on the table, where someone had cleaned the blade and oiled the leather. "Then I'll go without weapons."

"You don't have to go back there, Wulfred."

"I fought at his side. If he fell, I'll know where to find him."

When I first stood on Sandlac Hill, I looked like some terrible figure from an ancient battle song. Clad in heavy mail, with my helmet polished bright under the autumn sun, I carried spears and a great shield edged with iron and covered with bright-painted leather. There was a sword at my belt and I stood with a king, with earls and lords and thousands of men - spearmen and fyrd - all armed for war.

When I returned I was dressed as a priest. Cuthred gave me an old monk's habit, which smelt of mice. The top of my head was shaved in a priestly tonsure and I shivered at the weird sensation of the cold wind blowing across my scalp. Cuthred assured me that the Duke's men would not harm a priest assisting the souls of the dead on their journey to Heaven, but I cannot have looked a very convincing priest. To this day I have never seen a priest with a shaved tonsure and hair reaching half way down his back, but we had to leave it long and tie it to hide the obvious battle-wound above my ear. So, although the rough cloth chafed my scalp, I kept my monkish hood up. Cuthred also tried to teach me a few words of Latin to mutter over corpses on the battlefield, but they felt clumsy on my tongue and I quickly forgot them.

A murderous band of night-black birds patrolled the treetops ahead of us, growling their carrion calls as our cart crested the hill and the trees thinned out. Beyond the trees lay the death-field of Sandlac.

I do not know how many died in that battle. Six thousand, a priest once told me and he may have been right, for such are the ghoulish accounts kept by the Church. Six thousand corpses, their eyes torn out by crows and their bellies opened in the night by flesh-feasting wolves and foxes. Along the top of the hill it was impossible to take a step without stepping on the dead. The crows were ten to a corpse. Bloated and greasy with blood, they screamed at each other, mobbed the kites and buzzards that circled low over the field and fought their own battles among the refuse of ours. And flies were buzzing, frantic among the filth and the dead. The sky was grey that day, but just a little of summer's heat still lingered and the flies feasted while they could and laid their eggs in empty mouths and in ragged purple eyeholes that stared up in mute appeal to the saints of Heaven. The dead had not yet begun to rot, but the hilltop stank of blood and shit and vomit. It stank of war.

I had expected to find Norman warriors still guarding the crow field as lords of the slain, but they were gone. There were only women and priests searching among the wreckage of husbands, brothers, sons and fathers. Weeping and prayer were the only sounds to interrupt the black choirs of crows.

We found my father's corpse lying where we had fought when the enemy broke the shield wall. There was a spearhead deep in his chest and his beard was matted with dried blood. That wound would have taken hours to kill a man. He must have laid there under the black sky as men slowly died around him, choking to breathe through the blood pooling in his lungs. There were already maggots squirming in the wound. Three fingers of his right hand had been hacked off by the battlefield scavenger who had taken his sword. He was no longer my father. No longer the man with whom I had forever quarrelled had struggled to understand, whose voice in joy and rage had rolled like thunder through the world. Just a piece of carrion, broken on the cold ground.

My mother knelt beside him, held his left hand for a while then clasped her hands together in silent prayer. And for the first time she began to weep. I knelt too and put an arm about her shoulders and said nothing as a small breeze blew the stench of stale blood across our faces. I remembered Bera's body lying on the hill, stabbed through the back of the neck and I wondered if that killing had been done for me – my father's last murderous act of love.

We found Godric on the west side of the hill, his belly ripped open and his throat cut across. Wolves had stripped the flesh from his ribs and his face had been torn apart by crows. I do not know how Hildelyth even recognised him. Were it not for his wounds and the place on the field where he lay, I would never have known that carcass of bone and offal as the remains of a lifelong friend.

I have seen so many dead, but never as many corpses as lay mangled on that dreadful field. I wish I had never seen it, I hope one day it will be washed from my memory and I pray to any god that will listen that men and women will never have to look again upon such sights. But I am sure by now that the gods do not listen. And when gods are deaf and blind, men take up the sword and believe, like unforgivable fools, that they can make gods of themselves.

I spoke to a priest before we left the hill. He was standing apart from two women who wept over a corpse among the carnage where once had stood the Dragons of Wessex. He was a younger man that Cuthred - the ring of hair around his tonsure was dark - but he had the same kind of thin, scholarly face. Dressed as a priest myself, I did not know how to address him.

"The love of almighty God be with you, brother in Christ," I said quietly. He looked at me as if I had said something strange.

"And with you, friend." He made the sign of the cross and I wondered if I should have done so as well. He shook his head sadly. "The Lord is just, but his wrath is a thing of dread to those who sin against him." Priests say some very stupid things.

"It is not for men to understand His ways." It sounded like the right thing to say, but the priest looked at me again as if I was a madman.

"It brings to mind the words of St. Oswald," he pondered. "For did the blessed Oswald not say that called unto God are those most beloved of him?"

"Do you know where the Norman host has gone?" I got to the point. It had been a difficult enough conversation before he brought St. Oswald into it.

"They marched east two days ago. Their duke had awaited the lords of England to acknowledge his victory and submit to him, but none came. Now he has sent news to his countrymen across the sea and called for more foreign warriors to join him. This I heard from a monk who came with his fleet. The Duke intends to capture the ports of Kent and the holy city of Cantaburh. May the Lord in His mercy spare the poor folk of those places."

"Are there warriors who will fight him there?"

301

"There are warriors in the weald and some have fled to Lunden. But I know of none in Kent. Even Bishop Stigand has abandoned his priory, and Cantaburh is preparing to submit. The servants of Christ will not see the city's sacred cloisters stained with blood."

I noticed that he omitted to call Stigand the Blessed Archbishop, as was usual, and wondered if it was a sign of the Church preparing to side with the victorious.

"So now the villages of Kent will burn like those of Sussex."

It must have sounded unpriestly, because he looked at me strangely again. "If God wills it, so it will be." His voice was stern and he made the sign of the cross again. "But the foreign lord has promised to spare any town or village that will welcome him as conqueror and king. I pray that he keeps his word."

"And what news of King Harold?"

"A body was taken from this field and buried on the shore close to Haestingas. The Norman Duke said that Harold could guard the coast in death as he had done in life."

"Was it really the king? Did anyone see the body?"

The priest gave me another disapproving look and shook his head. "Those who did said it was terribly mutilated and disembowelled. They say an arrow struck him in the eye and the vengeful warriors of Normandy cut his body apart until it was barely recognisable as a man let alone a king, may the Lord God grant him sweet rest. If he still lived, we would know of it."

The priest was right. If Harold lived, the call would have gone out across Wessex and into the north for what warriors remained to rally to his side. The King of England was surely dead.

We did not find Oswold. And we spoke of him for the first time.

"He was here," I told my mother, looking down at the ground where my father had lain before Ragnald and I hefted his body onto the ox cart. "He fought beside us all day. This is where he was when the shield wall broke." We both looked away towards the forest, where black carrion birds perched high among the thinning leaves. There were many bodies between the hilltop and the trees, but we had not found my brother's.

"Could he have got away?" Hope gleamed in my mother's eyes and her hope was more painful to me than her sorrow.

"I did. It was almost full dark. The horsemen couldn't chase us through the trees."

"He would have come home."

"He may have been with other warriors. He could be deep in the weald. Or in Lunden." Over her shoulder I saw a raven tearing out the entrails from beneath the mailshirt of a corpse. "He was frightened. Pale. It was if he was seeing men die for the first time." My mother nodded. I did not truly believe that Oswold could have survived, but she could believe nothing else. She turned and walked back towards the cart. The raven scrambled up onto the corpse's head, opened its bloody beak and rasped into the grey sky. We wrapped Godric's ghastly remains in a cloak and laid them beside my father's and three more of our fallen fyrdmen. The chorus of the crows rattled on, spilling across the hill and the weald and across all of Sussex and Kent.

Lord Saxmund was buried in the damp ground beside the church in Ellasham. I had wanted to lay his body in the old sleeping ground of Oxeneye, so that his bones might rest alongside those of the blood-drenched ancestors he revered. But my mother insisted on a proper Christian burial and I did not argue with her. All his life, my father had respected the law, the authority of the king and the power of the Church so it was only right that he be buried as a Christian warrior of Wessex.

303

I remembered the day far back in springtime when we had laid Eohric in his grave. There was singing and flowers and the sun of a new day breaking over budding trees. At my father's burial there was only the weeping of women, the useless Latin of Cuthred's holy books and the grey drizzle falling from a grey sky onto a grey autumn land. The whole village gathered at my father's graveside and the people were as drab as the landscape. Only fear lived in their faces.

A thin mist shrouded the mound of Oxeneye that day. I do not think my father would have truly cared that his grave was not there among the pagan lords. He died at his king's side and that was all that mattered to him. Nothing that he loved lay beyond it. His spirit had fled from the world when the shield wall of Wessex crumbled.

The days passed and the rumours festered like unwashed wounds sewn shut. There were few traders and travellers walking the roads of Wessex in those times. Ordinary folk stayed huddled in their villages, clinging to the things they knew, waiting for fate to find them.

We heard no more news until two weeks after the battle, when a group of monks passed through Ellasham.

"We are the Poor Monks of Cynehelstou, sent by Earl Edwin of Mercia, a pious and holy man," said an abbot called Lyfing. He was a broad-faced man, and plumper than one whose life was devoted to poverty and prayer ought to be, and he seemed to be in charge. Before he spoke of his mission, he questioned every one of the warriors who gathered around him in the firelight of the hall, their wounds healing and their ears eager for news.

"Pious and holy perhaps, but not a man who rallied to his king's side!" Wigod began, but I held up a hand for silence, Wigod grunted and the abbot continued.

"He bids me journey to the camp of Duke Willelm, to pray with the duke while my brothers in Christ assess the strength of his army and learn of his plans."

"Are the sons of Aelfgar in Lunden?" I asked.

"My lords the Earls Edwin and Morcar arrived in Lunden as news of the battle arrived from the south. Edgar the Atheling is with them and the Witan has declared him King of England." There were a few mutters of surprise from around the fireside.

"Harold is still our king!" one man said, spitting on the floor in disgust. The abbot made the sign of the cross.

"It is believed that King Harold has joined the host of Heaven."

"Then what of Magnus? He was alive and still fighting after the battle. The king's son should be our king."

"Magnus is in Lunden," said Lyfing patiently. "And warriors have rallied to his side – those who fought and lived and those who had been in the far west mustering the fyrd. But the Witan has chosen Edgar as king and Magnus has sworn an oath to him."

It made sense. The northern earls would want a weak ruler like Edgar whom they could control, rather than a strong Wessex king. And perhaps it suited Magnus to keep Edwin and Morcar happy until he was in a position to challenge them.

But the news that Magnus was in Lunden sent a buzz of excitement from man to man. If there was one warrior in all of the land who could gather what remained of England's strength and lead it victory against the Norman Duke, then Magnus, son of Harold, was that man.

Much discussion followed. The monks ate and drank and prayed and heard the confessions of the warriors who could give them a penny or two and avoided the villagers who had nothing to offer. Abbot Lyfing, it seemed, was a greatly esteemed man of the Church who had once translated the Life of St. Cynehelm into the English tongue. It was commonly believed that God would look kindly upon a man who had confessed his sins to Abbot Lyfing

Wigod gathered the men around him. Nobody trusted the lords of the north, but they held Magnus in the greatest esteem. And the Bastard Duke was still the worst of their enemies, and their place was at the side of whoever opposed him. After a lot of shouting and bluster, it was decided that they would ride for Lunden on the following morning to join Magnus and swear allegiance to King Edgar.

That was the first time I heard the title of King Edgar used. It was a name that would be another curse upon England in the years that followed.

"I'm staying here with my people," I told Wigod in the morning when he instructed me to gather my sword and armour for the journey. It was a grey dawn with a mist that clung to the faded willows along the riverside and settled like a frost at our feet. There was a smell of smoke lying heavily on the air. It may have been the smoke of autumn waste being burned, or the smoke of burning houses, but the faces of the villagers showed that they feared the worst.

Wigod gave me a harsh look. While the wounded men who had come to Ellasham had had their clothes washed and mended, polished their buckles and cloakpins, oiled the leather of their belts and boots and taken great pains to preserve their appearance as lords and warriors, I had done no such thing. I wore a plain grey tunic and a pair of patched breeches that I had eaten and slept in. The hair that had been shaved from my head was growing back in spiky clumps and my beard grew wild. I must have looked more like a peasant of the fields than a man who carried a sword and served a king.

"In times like these," Wigod went on "your place is at the side of your king. The Witan has chosen Edgar, and this is his hour of need."

"My place is where it always was – with my people," I repeated.

"How can you fight our enemies as one warrior alone amongst a village of peasants? In times like these, no free man of Wessex must bow before a foreign lord. Would you have it said in the tales of winters yet to come that you shirked the sword while the Lord Magnus and King Edgar laid low the Norman host and won the greatest victory in all the stories of our people?"

I thought about that for a moment, and wondered if it was really possible for two scheming earls, a puppet ruler and the murderous son of a fallen king to hold an alliance together for long enough to even raise an army, let alone face the might of Normandy.

"The tellers of tales will do as they always have," I finally said. "They'll tell whatever tales the great lords want from them."

"So be it." Wigod stepped away and looked across the village. "I thank you for your hospitality, Wulfred of Ellasham. But it will be remembered that you refused your duty to your king." I shrugged my shoulders, eager to see him go. I had sworn no oath to serve this Edgar and I certainly had no love of Magnus.

"You! Bring my horse," he bellowed at Ragnald. Ragnald glanced back at him with eyes like winter. Wigod turned to me instead.

"What's wrong with the surly bastard? Doesn't he know the voice of a lord when it commands him?"

"He's no slave."

"He should be a slave. He's a fucking coward of a fyrdman who ran from the battlefield rather than fall at his king's side." Wigod picked up my father's staff which I had stood at the doorway of the hall in memory of him. Ragnald held his ground, still glaring as the

307

warrior approached. But before he could strike, I kicked Wigod's left leg out from under him. With one arm still bandaged and the other raising the staff, he could not reach out to break the fall, so he sprawled in the mud and I stood over him.

"On the day you sweat and break your back in the fields beside the men of the fyrd, maybe they'll be ready to die at your side."

"And fetch your own fucking horse," Ragnald murmured, smiling the first smile I had seen in many days.

Warriors rode away, monks walked south along the river and in the damp chill of the day's evening, my people gathered in the empty hall. I was their lord now and they needed to know what the future might hold.

"Are the foreign warriors coming?" a woman asked me. Her name was Elfitu. She was young – Oswold's age perhaps. She was married to Wada who was known for his strength steering the plough and who had fled the spears of Sandlac to return to his family. Their first child, less than a year old, was asleep in her arms. The child was a girl and I think she was named Ealswith.

Every day, I think of my people and I try to picture them and recall their names. It grows harder as the years pass, but still I try to remember. When those too young to have known such times speak of the thousands who fell at Sandlac or the uncounted folk killed and scattered in the years that followed, it can mean little to them. But my people had names and faces. Although the bones may lie in woods and ditches and unmarked places, their mothers and their fathers gave them names and for a while their lives shone as brightly in this world as new-kindled flames or sunlight glancing off flowing water. Their memory is a burden to me, but it is a burden I will bear and a burden I will pass on.

"We cannot be sure of what they will do," I said. I looked around from face to face across the glowing hearth. It was less than a year since the Christmas feast when Godric had worried about the health of King Edward and Idwal had sung and tried my father's patience. Now Godric and my father were dead and Idwal fought for our enemies and I only lived because of luck and a friendship remembered.

"I spoke to a priest on Sandlac Hill and he said the Duke was taking his army east, to Cantaburh and the Kentish coast."

"And when they reach the coast," said Ragnald, "they can only turn around and come back this way."

"What about the earls of the north? Edwin and Morcar? Those monks said they were in Lunden. Will they not fight the Bastard's men?" One of Eohric's sons, who sat at the bench where Leofwin had sung the song of Aelfred while the summer moon wrapped the hills in silver, was answered by a tiny murmur of enthusiasm.

"They didn't come to fight on Sandlac," someone growled.

"They might fight for their own land. But not for Wessex," said Ragnald, his eyes fixed on the fire embers. I felt a coldness deeper than the chill of autumn as I remembered those words he spoke in the dead of winter – a village of ghosts and a church in flames.

"The northern earls are treacherous," I said. "They've come to Lunden to grab what they can from the defeat of King Harold. The Duke is summoning more warriors from Normandy. Edwin and Morcar don't have the strength or the spirit to stand against him."

"So what will happen to us?" I cannot recall whose mouth those words came from, but it was the question on every face.

"Maybe the Normans will not come here until the war is over and the kingdom is settled again. If they come sooner, we must be prepared to welcome them. The priest told me that the Duke has promised life and peace to any town or village that submits to his rule." There was a flutter of relief at this news. But not from everyone. A woman with grey eyes and a voice that could split firewood stood up to speak.

"I've heard about this Bastard Duke. He eats the flesh of Saxon children roasted on a fire of their mothers' bones," she squawked. I had not heard this rumour and I was fairly sure it was untrue. It probably came from Earl Edwin's monks.

"The Duke is not a monster, he is a lord like any other," said Cuthred. He rose from his bench. Gaunt and grey, he looked older than ever in the dim light. His back was stooped as if the years of his life were hung from a yoke upon his shoulders. "He fears God, but his greater fear is defeat and to show weakness. I have heard of villages burned since the battle, villages which surely could not have tried to fight his war host."

"Which villages have been burned?" I asked him. I did not want to trust the Normans either, but I saw no other choice. Cuthred sat down again with a weary sigh.

"A monk who travelled with the blessed Abbot Lyfing spoke of people fleeing to Lunden after their homes were burned. There has been smoke on the wind. I have prayed to the Lord Almighty for guidance, but still I would not place my trust in this foreign lord." For a moment those walls that had heard music and song heard only the silence of fear.

Then it was my mother who stood and spoke.

"I shall go to Cantaburh. The town will to surrender to the Norman lord. I do not believe the Duke will commit murder amongst our most sacred places. Those who fear him may travel with me as pilgrims to the holy shrines of the city. We will be protected by the laws of God and men." Her voice was quiet and gentle, but sadder now, as if her summer had passed.

My mother's words gave more comfort to the people of Ellasham than mine had. Some immediately chose to go with her, mostly women who wanted to save their children from the wrath of the Bastard Duke. The old and the sick would have to stay of course. Cantaburh was at least two days walk away across a land heavy with the mud of approaching winter and with frost reaching hungrily into the long nights. But in hard times the old and the sick are released from the sufferings of this world. Such is the way it has ever been.

Others did not wish to leave their homes and I found that harder to understand. Coming home to burnt homes and plundered byres is a terrible thing, but houses and cattle can be replaced. Only death is the end of all we know.

But many changed their minds that evening. About a dozen people – men, women and children – came to Ellasham from a village across the weald called Halasley. Norman warriors had come to their hall for meat and corn to feed the Duke's army. The villagers had submitted and given everything they demanded, until one warrior grabbed a young girl as if to take her away with them. The girl's father had raised his voice in objection and the village had been destroyed. A grey old man told me about it, his hands shaking and his eyes wet with tears.

"'You cannot take my daughter,' that is all he said to them. And they set their swords and spears amongst us. They killed men and women and cattle and pigs. They tore the thatch from roofs and set every house aflame. Nothing now stands where Halasley once was. These are not men but beasts sent by the Devil."

They would not stay in Ellasham, even for one night, such was their fear of being somewhere the Normans might come. They walked on into the darkness, going north towards Lunden where English lords still held sway. We gave them blankets and food for the journey. Better that they should have our meat and grain than it be taken by the men of Normandy.

There had been a tavern in Halasley where the ale was sweet, flavoured with honey and the blossoms of the elder tree. The first wolves of the winter howled deep in Andredsweald as that band of survivors vanished into the gathering night.

And in the morning, it was Ellasham's people who left their homes.

The house where Eohric had lived was empty now, its roof fallen in for the last time, its little herb garden swept aside by weeds and its walls were now a haunted place of spiders and cold shadows. Beside it, the ford ran deep after the rain of autumn and the children of the village had to be carried across. Beyond the river, they would take the old stony pathway heading east towards Cantaburh.

They took as much food as they could carry and little else. Food and one another was all that was precious to them. Everything else stood abandoned in the cluster of houses below the hall, where hearthfires that had smouldered for the lifetimes of generations dwindled and died.

Cuthred went with them. He knew that the whole village could not be persuaded to leave together, so he had prayed all night and finally decided to go where his guidance would benefit the greatest number of our people. And I suspect that in such troubled times he wished to be close to God in Cantaburh. Cuthred had offered to disguise me as a priest again so that I might travel safely among them, but I refused. We had fought and lost, and now was the time for me to lay down my sword and face the new rulers of Wessex. To run and to hide would only lengthen the days of uncertainty.

"May God bless you and protect you," murmured the old man as I knelt obediently before him outside the shell of Eohric's house. "And may His wisdom guide you through these troubled times."

"Look after our people," I said to him as the trail of frightened villagers began to struggle through the ford. "And make sure the Lady Estra is safe." It felt like an odd thing to ask. Cuthred was frail and bent-backed and did not look like a man who could walk to Cantaburh through mud and frost, let alone look after anyone. But Cuthred had an iron will to live and to serve his heavenly lord. While God still needed him, Father Cuthred could not die.

312

"We shall return," my mother said. "Even before the ground is frozen, our people will come back to their hearths and kindle their fires again."

"Go safely," I said to her, and smiled weakly. I did not want to prolong the moment of saying goodbye, to make it seem like we would never meet again. "At Christmas we shall feast together again."

"When peace returns. And when your hair has grown back. You look like a shaved hedgehog." The spark that lived in her eyes flickered briefly and she almost laughed, but then something else caught her mind.

"And before then, you must find Oswold." I still could not believe that Oswold was alive, but my mother could not believe otherwise.

"I will find him. Before the year ends, Oswold will be back among us." I held her close to me, felt the strength that lived so resiliently in her slim body, and then she walked away. I saw her pick up one of the village children and carry him across the ford on her back. As the desperate procession slipped away into the trees along the northern edge of Walland Fen, I heard the voices of the women, frightened but unbroken, raised in a song of love and home.

Most of Ellasham's people left that morning. Alongside the old and the lame, Ragnald and some of the fyrdmen I had led along the coastal paths and into the sword-feast of Sandlac chose to remain at my side. Brichteva stayed with Ragnald. She had scratched Grimstan's name into the blade of a knife she wore at her belt. She also muttered about vengeance for her brothers who fell under Norman arrows at Sandlac and I wished she had gone to Cantaburh with the others. Wada, the big ploughlad, foolishly insisted that he would not lead his wife and baby daughter out onto the cold roads.

If his lord stayed, he told me, he would stay. But those who remained were only a quarter of the people who had once dwelled between the river and the weald. Already the ghosts of those who had gone seemed to linger. And far worse than seeing a ghost is to see an empty bench at a cold hearth in an empty home.

Hildelyth took my hand, turned me away from the chill riverside and pointed towards the church. The cross Ragnald and I had raised in the winter still stood outside it, and above the wood-tiled roof there was also a weather vane, a thin wedge-shaped piece of leather which blew with the wind and which the villagers consulted in the spring before they muttered and mumbled about when to sow the barley.

"Eohric used to talk about the weather vane when we were children," she said. "He said that the south wind brings joy and the north wind brings sorrow."

"It's the other way around this year."

"But he said the wind always changes. 'Sorrow fades into joy and pain melts into laughter,' that's what he used to say. Do you remember the snow of last winter?"

"Of course," I said.

The cold wind lifted her hair, she swept it back off her face and her brown eyes held me rooted to the empty riverside. As much as I wished she were safe from whatever fate held for us, I was glad that she stayed at my side. "It came in the night. And it changed the world. For a while everything was white and frozen. But in time it melted and the winter passed, and summer came back to us."

Hildelyth looked at me and smiled. Against the bleak landscape and in that time of darkness, she smiled and for a moment I forgot the battle and the deaths of so many and the fear of what was to come.

Hand in hand, we wandered back into the quiet village.

314

16. THE MERCHANT'S DAY

"Horsemen are coming! Mailed men with spears! And the merchant leads them!" It was the boy Bulig, his finger still bandaged from the work of that arrow on Sandlac Hill, who came running up the village path to bring us the news. His father ushered him indoors, still pointing and shouting about spears.

"Sigered?" said Hildelyth. Her golden hair hung lank in the cold drizzle and fear moved like a shadow across her face.

"I suppose so. He is a man who would side with the victorious. And he knows the Norman tongue. Perhaps they come to talk with us." I stepped out into the cold rain to face Wessex's new masters.

So many were gone. My father and Godric dead. Oswold vanished in the fury of battle. My mother fled with most of the village three days earlier. Ragnald keeping watch somewhere in the woods. So many whose presence and wisdom might have made the day a little easier. Hildelyth remained at my side, but I could not let her stay.

"Go indoors. It would be better if they thought all the women were gone." She understood. She squeezed my hand and kissed me and hurried back into the village.

"Remember the broken fence," I called to her. "Be ready to flee." We had loosened planks in my father's rebuilt palisade fence at a point close to Ragnald's cottage and at another behind the hall, so we could escape into the forest. I prayed we would not need to.

Not everybody went to their homes. A dozen or so villagers stood by the pathway, watching as a band of horsemen came into view. They were mostly men, foolishly eager to show that they feared no enemy. I stood close to what I still thought of as my father's house. It would be a mistake, I thought, to stand at the edge of the village as if to bar their way.

Sigered was dressed in his finest as he rode into Ellasham. He wore a tunic of closely woven red linen trimmed with black and yellow silk. His cloak was deep blue, darkened to purple by the rain. Behind him there were twenty or thirty horsemen, all mailed, carrying spears and shields and with swords sheathed at their waists. Their leader, riding at Sigered's side, wore a helmet crested with a golden boar.

But it was not just Norman horsemen that Sigered led into our village. At his side, Grimstan walked barefoot in a black cassock and holding a staff mounted with a cross of twisted iron, like the one Cuthred paraded around at Easter. His sandals were tied to his belt and I wondered if he had only just taken them off in some pretence of piety before he entered the village. He scowled at a second man who walked painfully beside him, a man bruised and bloodied from a heavy beating. A man whose wrists were tied by a rope that one of the horsemen held. It was Ragnald. I nodded to him as they approached. He raised his head to nod back, but Grimstan slapped it down viciously.

"Eyes to the ground heathen!" the priest shouted. "How dare you set your face towards Heaven!" Sigered gave Ragnald a stern look then cast the same eye over me. They reined in their horses and the merchant dismounted.

"Greetings Sigered," I began. I tried to make my voice sound bold and confident, but it was not easy. Ragnald's capture complicated things. Grimstan wanted him dead. What could I offer Grimstan in return for Ragnald's life? "So you have sided with the host of Normandy?"

"These men are no longer our enemies Wulfred. They are the lords of England now. Duke Willelm will soon be crowned our king." I looked at him silently, challenging him to explain himself further.

317

"It is the way of things. Every man must serve his master. On Earth or in Heaven." He glanced at Grimstan who leered approvingly. I ignored the priest and looked at Ragnald, but he kept silent and his expression told me nothing. I unbuckled my swordbelt and dropped it onto the wet ground.

"It is indeed the way of things." I raised my voice to address the Normans. "I am Wulfred, son of Saxmund. Since my father's death I have been lord of this estate. Now I submit to the rule of Duke Willelm, that my people might be spared." There was some muttered translating among the Normans. But it was Sigered who spoke up.

"In the name of Willelm, Duke of Normandy and Conqueror of England, I accept your submission."

"You accept it Sigered? By what authority do you accept the submission of a lord of Wessex?" My tone was accusing and the horsemen glanced at each other and shifted their grips on their spears.

Sigered looked embarrassed, but Grimstan answered for him. "My lord Sigered rules here in the name of King Willelm. This is his estate now." I turned back to face the merchant.

"Ellasham will be yours? What did you do for them?" Sigered still looked awkward, but this time managed to answer, albeit feebly.

"For years I have traded across the Narrow Sea. I have many friends in Normandy as well as in England." He wanted to say no more, but Grimstan, in his triumph, could not hold himself back.

"He gave them ships, you fool. The Lord Sigered helped my Lord King Willelm to build the fleet that brought the holy host of Normandy here and rid us of the heathen usurper Godwinsson. Five ships, three hundred spearheads, silver to buy the swords of lordless men in Flanders. The spears that did God's work on Sandlac Hill were made at my lord's command as a gift to King Willelm."

So Sigered had been betraying us all along. Even as myself and Ragnald had saved his son's life, he had been aiding those who sought to destroy us.

But it no longer mattered. Perhaps it was a good ending to a dark time. Sigered may have been a traitor, but he was a reasonable man and he would not want to let the spears of Normandy loose among the people of his new estate – the people who would grow his crops. It was only Ragnald that I was concerned about.

"And what of Ragnald the woodsman?" I asked. "Why does he stand tied like a thief?"

"He was caught on the weald's edge with weapons. These men apprehended him as a rebel." Sigered indicated the watchful band of mounted men at his back.

"I sent armed men out to patrol and keep watch. We did not know what to expect. Now I have submitted, Ragnald will submit also." We all looked at Ragnald. His hands were tied and he had no weapon to drop, so he merely bowed his head in mute surrender. Sigered remained silent, but Grimstan looked at him expectantly. In the end it was once more the priest who had to speak.

"You have defended this abomination too long! Well you know that this demon you call a friend is more than a rebel. He is a heathen, a witch, a maker of spells and a tool of the Devil. He must face the judgement of Almighty God. Only when his kind and those who give them succour are scoured from the earth shall the blessed Christ return."

"Sigered, please order the priest to shut his filthy mouth and free Ragnald." I spat on the ground at Grimstan's feet and there were angry stirrings among the Normans. Grimstan was more popular, I guessed, among those who did not understand what he was saying. Sigered glanced worriedly over his shoulder.

"The law of God is above friendship, Wulfred. It is men such as Ragnald that bring God's anger upon the world. War, plague and

319

famine are unleashed because we suffer the heathen to dwell amongst us." I looked hard into the merchant's eyes. I had always seen him as a man of good sense. Had Grimstan twisted his mind completely?

"Ragnald saved your son's life, Sigered. His healing was all that stood between Richard and death."

"Ragnald brought witchcraft into my house. We have been at prayer ever since to beg the Lord's forgiveness."

I could see no way out. Sigered had won the game and Grimstan was intent on using his master's triumph to settle an old score. There was nothing I could do, but how could I do nothing? "And what will Grimstan do now that he has Ragnald at last? Baptise him?" Sigered gritted his teeth as if our conversation had gone on for too long.

"Grimstan will do what God requires of him."

"He will burn!" Grimstan roared, prancing about and slapping Ragnald's face with his skinny hand. "I will burn the demon out of him in this world and his soul will burn for all eternity in the flames of Hell. Had you not let this devil escape us in the spring, then God's punishment need never have come to our land. His evil has awoken the swords of divine will." I looked to Sigered again, but he nodded to the priest.

"God is just," he said. We eyed each other in silence as the thin autumn drizzle fell. I could not let them pass and let my friend die. Yet I could not stop them. The faces of my enemies were hard and cold. Fat crows mocked me from the treetops of Andredsweald.

Then, in a moment, everything changed.

"Let me speak with him!" Brichteva burst from the doorway of her father's house and ran towards Ragnald. One of the Normans moved to draw his sword, but their leader held out a hand and barked a hasty order. The rest of them were distracted by Grimstan's shrieking.

"Witch!" he howled. "She is no woman, but a beast that ruts with the Devil! The evil in this kingdom was not spear-slain in battle, it walks amongst us still!" Sigered glanced from Brichteva to Grimstan, but before he could decide what to do, Brichteva was stood before Ragnald. With her left hand she grabbed the front of his bloodstained shirt and pulled him towards her as if to kiss him, but with her right she drew a knife from inside her cloak. In a single movement she slashed the blade up through the rope that bound Ragnald's hands and tethered him to one of the horseman. For a fragment of a heartbeat I saw Ragnald look all around him and weigh up the situation before Sigered or the Normans could react.

A horse screamed and reared. Brichteva had drawn back the knife and, with a curse worthy of any seasoned warrior, thrust it into the chest of one of the warhorses as its rider tried to level his spear at her. The armoured warrior crashed to the ground and horse's blood sprayed across the muddy path as the beast twisted and staggered. The leading Norman shouted an order, but Ragnald was ready for what must come next.

"Run!" he shouted, and that nervous little group of onlookers turned on their heels and began a desperate race across the village.

"Make for the broken fence!" I yelled out, grabbing my sword belt from the ground. Some ran for the fence and others were rushing out of their houses. Sigered shouted something in the Norman tongue, but his voice was lost among the beating of hooves.

Two horsemen came straight for me and I ran between the houses, vaulting over hurdle fences in the hope that they would slow the riders. There were splintered voices coming from either side, but whether they were the cries of people fleeing or people dying I could not tell.

I ducked around the side of house just as one of my pursuers appeared from the other side. He aimed his spear at my chest and I threw myself across the path of his horse, lashing out at its eyes

321

with my sword. The horse reared up and as the rider fought for control, I rolled to my feet, but tripped again on a bundle of reeds. The second horseman came from behind me, his sword raised to strike down, but a spear glanced off the top rim of his shield and knocked him off balance. Hildelyth threw down the spear, pulled me to my feet and we ran again.

The wet grass slid away beneath our feet, the fat grey clouds of autumn twisted overhead and we ran hand in hand, with the chaos of war smashing through the village at our backs. For a brief and perfect moment we were children again, running from our parents, charging headlong towards the shadows of the weald where the leaves would whisper their secrets, memory would endure forever and we would be safe from all the spite of the world. The thunder of hooves was loud behind us, but there was not far to go. We would kick the loose plank away, slip through the fence and keep running until we were as free as children in the forest.

Hildelyth stumbled as we approached the fence. She gave a small cry and her hand slipped from mine. I turned to help her, but the horseman was too close. His beast stepped over her as she rolled aside and he came for me instead. I saw her scramble to her feet and flee from the circling hooves that gathered about the gap in the palisade. She ran back into the village. Back to where the Norman warriors were searching the houses, dragging out those who had tried to hide. Back to where our people screamed as death came for them. Smoke was belching from the doorway of one of the houses, and three or four bodies already lay on the rain-soaked ground.

Someone grabbed a handful of my hair and hauled me roughly back towards the fence.

"Get out!" Ragnald shouted. I remember seeing his gritted teeth out of the corner of my eye. My forehead scraped against one of the wooden posts as he pushed me through the gap in the fence. I heard a spear hammer into one of the planks as Ragnald dived through after me. Then he was behind me, pushing me down into the ditch and hauling me up the other   side.

"Hildelyth!" I panted, staring back towards the fence.

"She's gone. It's all gone." Ragnald pushed me towards the trees. I saw Brichteva, standing beside the gap in the fence, stab her knife into the face of a Norman who leapt from his horse and tried to follow us. Then she sprang into the ditch, scrambled out and ran for the trees. The sound of hoofbeats came from the south – some of the horsemen had ridden out of the village gate and were coming around the outside of the ditch. There were other villagers still running, disappearing into the trees with Brichteva. And Ragnald and I looked at each other and I have no idea now what terrible thoughts raked through our minds, but there was only one thing we could do.

We ran hard into the weald, heading for the thickest trees and the steepest slopes where riders and armoured men would not follow.

Where the leaves were falling and home became no more than a memory.

17. BLOTMONATH

In troubled times, the shadows that cover the land reach deep into the souls of men. The month which the Church calls November is the month for slaughtering livestock and the country folk still call it Blotmonath – the Blood Month.

A lifetime ago, these things happened. But still it is hard to speak of them.

"They've nailed back the plank we came through, but the one behind the hall's still loose. I tried it just before dawn. Covered myself in shit so their dogs couldn't smell me." Wada scowled and used the back of his knife to scrape at some of the cattle dung he had smeared over his clothes.

Wada, the ploughman, tall and broad-shouldered but barely old enough to grow a beard sat opposite me with a face as wintry as the grey-wreathed sky. His wife and daughter were lost in the chaos when Sigered and Grimstan came to Ellasham. It had been as painful as anything I have ever lost to see this strong, work-hardened man huddled weeping in a corner of Ragnald's hut on Blood Hill for two days and nights. But now there were no tears left, only dark, bright eyes, glowering from a face that might never smile again.

We squatted round in a tight circle on the lee of the hill. It was grey in the early morning with ragged ribbons of cloud scudding across the forested hills. Wada and Ecgbert had been out all night scouting the weald's edge. I looked around the circle at those few who had escaped from Ellasham. Their hair and shabby cloaks were tugged by the wind and thoughts of vengeance throbbed like open sores just as hunger twisted in their bellies. Ragnald could feed himself from the forest and the river but not the twenty of us who huddled there. And we dared not hunt and forage too far back towards the village for fear of the Normans who ranged the weald with their hunting dogs, searching for any who still held out against the new rulers.

"The houses are empty," said Ecgbert, scratching the red scar that marked the missing chunk of his ear. "I looked for smoke and firelight, but I saw nothing. There are strangers – strangers wearing fine clothes and silver – at the hall, and the warriors are still there. Their horses are tethered close to the river and they have dogs to guard the place. The merchant and his wife went into your father's house just before darkness fell." He looked up at me as if to declare that he had finished and it was my turn to speak. Like Wada, his eyes were cold and filled with hatred.

"And none of our people remain?" someone asked when I failed to say anything.

"Our people are dead or enslaved," Brichteva spat, still looking at me with narrowed eyes. "Death or slavery. That's all they'll offer to any who fled from home or stood and fought. Those who went to Cantaburh have nothing to come back to."

"The wind comes from the east," said Ragnald. "It will be in our faces and carry our scent away from the dogs. Tonight?" He too looked at me. His expression was clawed by a doubt uncommon to him. Brichteva crouched beside him and her face asked the same question. We were hungry. There was corn and meat in the hall at Ellasham.

It was because of Brichteva that death had come to our village and I never truly forgave her. But would I have stood aside and allowed Ragnald to die so that others might be spared? Perhaps I have not deserved to, but I have lived many years since that day, and still I do not know.

325

"Tonight," I eventually said. The wind hissed through the trees below the bare crown of Blood Hill. We stood. And the circle broke.

When we came to the weald's edge there was just enough light to see by. The palisade fence of Ellasham rose blackly before us and above it the dark sky was strangled with cords of cloud.

We waited there. The sky blackened and the bare trees roared in the wind. There was a short stretch of open ground between the treeline and the ditch, but nothing moved in the darkness. I shut my eyes and listened for sounds blown on the wind. Ragnald nudged my arm and pointed at a white owl, the ghostly death bird of children's tales, still feared by many. Silently it swept out of the rattling canopy and vanished into the sky over the village. Grim-faced, Ragnald turned away.

"You lead them into the hall," I said to him. He nodded once but he did not look at me. "I'll take two men to the gate."

When darkness was full and the dank stench of frost-killed reedbeds blew in from Walland Fen we waited longer still. We waited for a time deep in the bowels of night when men slept so deeply that they struggled to wake even with a knife at their throat. The high branches of the weald lashed out and sang eerie songs to the hidden places of the night. Dark clouds raced across a darker sky, the eyes of stars winked for a moment and were gone. Some men prayed, but to what gods I did not know. Had there ever been gods to rule over nights like that one? Eventually, well after midnight, we slid silently into the ditch and clambered up the other side. Ragnald and I worked the plank loose and laid it carefully on the ground. Through the gap we could see the great dark shape of the hall merging with the black ground.

I went through first and crouched low, scanning the dark village for movement, listening out for any sound beneath the rushing of the wind. Wada followed me, then Ragnald and Brichteva, her pale face like a phantom in the blackness. I nodded to Ragnald as the rest of my people, armed with clubs, knives and axes slunk back like wary beasts to a lair they had been driven from. Then I led Wada and Ecgbert silently towards the clustered buildings. Our nightly scouts had reported that two guards were posted at the gate. They would be the only people in the village ready to oppose us and as the only trained warrior, I gave myself the task of dealing with them.

At our backs, Ragnald and the others were breaking into the hall, catching in sleep the Norman warriors and whoever else Sigered had brought to our village. The wind gusted strong and we heard nothing as they hauled the great doors open, but at the sound of barking dogs, we crouched beside an empty house and drew our weapons. The sword I had tried to surrender slid soundlessly from the lambswool of the scabbard and blended with the night. Wada carried an axe he had taken from the field of Sandlac – a one handed war axe with a blunt hammer opposite the blade. And Ecbgert clutched a wickedly sharpened seax, its cutting edge more than a foot long.

Alerted by the dogs, the two guards lumbered up the pathway, black shadows among blacker shadows with the wind twisting their cloaks into monstrous shapes and their footsteps heavy on the damp ground. The first one was lifting a horn to his lips to blow out an alarm call, but he went down as my sword ripped up beneath the skirt of his mail and into his groin. I heard the thud of steel as Wada's axe smashed into the second man's helmet and a rasping gurgle as his throat was cut. They both cried out, but by that time the noise of fighting in the hall was already surging into the night. A dog leapt at me from the darkness, all teeth, black eyes and flying slobber. A hunting dog is a fearsome foe to a man fleeing alone in the woods, but it is nothing against a group of armed men. I pushed my sword into its gaping mouth as it jumped for my throat and Wada hammered it to the ground. For a moment it twitched and whimpered, then there was a blade across its neck and blood steaming on the ground.

A few silhouette figures ran from the hall, but I pointed in the opposite direction across the village.

"Sigered," I whispered, and set off at a run into the dark. The others followed.

My father's house stood like a squat, black tower on its hump of rising ground, sharp edged against the night and raised above the unquiet riverside trees.

Sigered had replaced the old leather curtain with a door of wooden planks, but with an axe blow and a kick it was quickly open.

And we were inside. Wrapped again in the warm fireglow of the old house. There were furs on the benches now, and embroidered cloths on the walls. Pictures of saints and Christ and holy men, all illuminated with bright dyes and golden thread. Behind the hearth stood a polished table where rich men might drink wine and argue over the price of goods and the best places to buy and sell them. A few candles burned low around the walls and strangers were stirring in the beds. But it was still home and my footsteps faltered on the familiar old planks.

To my companions, though, it was nothing but a hive of foes. Ecgbert rushed at the box bed in the far corner where Oswold used to sleep and I almost cried out in warning as he raised a long knife over it, unable to imagine anyone but my brother lying there. But the blade fell, there was a half-waking shriek, a spurt of blood and the spell was broken. Something dressed in white linen rushed out of the shadows and I caught it by the throat. I drew back my sword and found myself looking into the boyish face of Odda. He looked terrified, like he had when Oswold fought his brother in the South Field, like he had when Ragnald had cut off Richard's arm and saved his life. I hesitated, but there was a knife in Odda's hand. Clumsily he fumbled it at my belly, and before he could strike, an axe hammered into the side of his head. He fell to the ground and with a roar of animal rage, Wada took three blows to hack the head from his shoulders.

Ecgbert cried out and stumbled back from the ladder to the loft where my mother and father had once slept. Sigered knelt at the top of the ladder, with his hair awry, his eyes bleak with horror and a stout cudgel in his hand. He called out something in the Norman tongue, trying to summon warriors from the hall.

"They're dead Sigered," I shouted back at him. "Ragnald has led the men of Ellasham into the hall." I plucked a smouldering log from the fire and hurled it up into the sleeping loft. It crashed against a roofbeam in a shower of sparks, and flames soon flared from blankets and the straw mattresses.

They both leapt down from the loft, Sigered and his wife together. Ecgbert, half blinded by the blood running down the side of his face, cursed and stabbed and the woman fell. Sigered ran for the door, straight into Wada, who grabbed him by the neck and threw him down. Across the room, I saw another body croaking and twitching as blood ran from its throat. Sigered rolled over, but before he could scramble to his feet I took the axe from Wada and hammered at the bottom of his spine until I heard the crack of breaking bone. He lay there spluttering, his arms flailing wildly, his legs still and dead.

"Sigered, the ghosts of your grandfathers weep with shame. You betrayed all of Wessex and sold my people to their foes." Light flared through the house as a chunk of burning thatch fell into the sleeping loft and sparks tumbled around us. The faces of my companions, red and sweaty in the rising heat, stared down at the crippled man.

"S-spare me!" Sigered spluttered. He tried to push himself up and howled with pain as the bones of his shattered spine crunched together. Wada kicked him in the belly and he screamed again. Through the open doorway came the sounds of fighting and other screams borne on the wind.

329

"You sold us all like so many ragged furs in the marketplace," I shouted. Or tried to shout. Sigered had betrayed us, Brichteva had smashed whatever deal he had made and let death loose amongst us and now I had brought fire and sword to destroy my home forever. A great weight crushed me and I could do little more than sob at the dying man. His wife's body lay beneath the sleeping loft and the flames caught her hair with a bright flash and a pall of stinking smoke.

"I tried to save you!" he howled. "Spare me. Get me out of here. I'll give you everything I have!"

Wada kicked him in the side of the head. "We've crippled you and slaughtered your family. If you were half a man, you'd beg for death, not life." He crouched and held a knife at his throat, looking up at me questioningly. Behind me I heard the rattling of silver as Ecgbert scooped out the contents of a chest. The heat of the flames prickled on my face and knew that we must get out before the whole house blazed up and fell in on us.

"You have nothing to give us, Sigered. You are nothing. A man with a sack of gold and no honour." I heard myself say that, but it seemed more like the ghost of my father still echoing around the roofbeams of his house. One of those beams cracked, more burning thatch crashed down and Sigered screamed and pissed himself as it scorched his arm. "Get up," I said to Wada. "Let him burn."

Outside the air was mercifully cool, though fountains of sparks rose up where other buildings were in flames

"Help me! Help me! I'll give you anything!" Sigered's howls from within the burning house were terrible enough to tear the sky to ribbons. And those were his last words spoken to this world.

That was the night when the church burned. Ragnald's winter prophecy came to pass as another winter fell. The painted faces of God and Christ and Satan melted from the walls and vanished into the black sky. The hall burned too, and the blazing thatch that flew on the wind caught most of the houses and reduced them to ash.

Like an old story told to tired ears from a fading memory, Ellasham was lost that night. There were corpses scattered across the ground. To this day I do not know who they were – those folk who died while the village burned. The Norman warriors who had been sleeping in the hall. Sigered's friends, the wealthy merchants of the Norman ports, come to celebrate their lord's victory, to feed while they could on the carcass of Wessex before the Duke hammered some kind of order upon the land again. The women who came to serve them at their feasting benches. Perhaps some of the men who had once worked on Sigered's land down the river. All I know is that they died. I saw their bodies, hunched and bloody in the mud while the killers I had brought there raged through the dark and everything we had known was eaten up in a night of fire and blood.

The river was swollen with the rains of autumn. That river had many moods and voices but it was black with menace that night. I felt it waiting in the darkness for my back to turn so that it might leap up and drag me down to a cold, choking death. While the flames of Ellasham roared in the wind, the willows on the riverbank flailed their limbs and groaned with songs of mourning and the hungry chill of winter.

I do not know where the others went after we left Sigered to die. I turned my back on the screaming and the fires and when I reached the river I was alone.

I remembered sitting in the long grass of the village, looking down towards the river with Aelfwyn on that warm midsummer night that seemed as distant as Heaven. She had spoken of the folly of men and their petty wars, but I had drifted into places darker than we could have dreamed of. And now she was only a dream, vanished into the wild lands beyond the Irish Sea. And Hildelyth was gone too. Was she dead? Or raped and enslaved by the men of Normandy? I had hoped against hope to find her in the village, but neither she nor any others we left behind were there. With his last breaths, Godric had begged me to look after her, and in the rout of the Blood Month, I had failed him.

I walked south, following the river down to the pathway that led out of Ellasham. There were sparks and smoke still flying on the wind, but the screams of the dying and the vengeful had passed. Only the dead remained. Close to the gate a bloody corpse lay spear-pinned to the ground. And as was as I left the village I felt a pain throbbing up my left arm. I must have burned my hand as I plucked the log from Sigered's fire, though at the time I had felt nothing. To this day, the flesh is shrivelled along one side of my palm, and the pain always returns as winter draws near. It feels like a knife slowly slicing open my hand from wrist to fingers and sometimes I think it grows worse with every year. But I welcome the pain because it means I cannot forget that which must not be forgotten. I feel the chill of the grave as I think about it. And it is right that I should, for the time will come when I will have to account for that night, before the god of Christ or the older gods or the ghosts of my forefathers or whoever else it is who rules the world of men. Perhaps I will be forgiven, for justice and mercy are luxuries only the victorious may wield.

Or perhaps I am damned.

In the weald, the damp taste of fallen leaves purged the smoke from my lungs. I scanned the black treetops and listened to the wind whipping rain through the naked trees. Rain to quench the fires we had started and cleanse the earth for something new to take root. But the horror of that night was not over.

I thought at first I was hearing the sounds of battle madness rage through my head again, or the screams of newly slain ghosts seeking a way to leave this tortured world. But the screams did not surround me like the nightmare of a battle entangled in memory. They came from somewhere in the weald. And for some reason – the madness of murder and remorse perhaps – I followed the howling voice. It was like the sound of a wildcat caught in the net of fire. There was a weak grey light in the eastern sky, but day could not ever break while such suffering still sounded in the world.

I stumbled through brambles and the dead undergrowth of summer. Shapes seemed to rush by like the shadows of a people put to flight.

At the edge of a small clearing, there was a great yew tree reaching up into the sky. The light was still feeble, but it was sufficient to make me wish for utter blackness. Something was dying there. Its arms were stretched out behind it and its wrists and feet nailed to the tree trunk. It was red and running with blood – a half skeleton, with flayed skin hanging in ribbons. And from its opened belly, the coils of its guts stretched up to tangle in the low branches. Its screams were weakening. It retched and spluttered, trying to speak, but no words forged in the world of men could escape that thing of blood and pain. Those eyes, burning white in the darkness, staring with horror into a ragged corner of Hell. When the night storms of winter howl across the hills, those eyes still pierce my dreams.

Ragnald sat cross-legged in the middle of the clearing, staring bleakly into the silhouette trees. Brichteva pranced around the yew tree, screaming curses, her voice hoarse and her face smeared with blood. She whipped the raw flesh with a willow rod, and her victim gagged and spluttered in resurging pain. And when Ragnald looked up and saw me, the horror on his face was barely less than on that of the corpse Brichteva was making. There was a moment of near silence as the sound of the wind in the trees seeped back into the world. Brichteva grabbed the bloody, drool-slobbered chin of that hellish face and stared into its dying eyes.

"The sun will rise," she said, her voice carrying across the treetops. "And today you will die. The carrion birds will wake with the dawn. The rook and the raven will tear out your heart and your liver and break open the cave of your skull. In the end they will take your eyes. But they will leave them long enough for you to see everything else torn apart. Today, Grimstan, you will die."

18. WINTER

Winter had come. The leaves had fallen and redwings had stripped the brambles that edged the forest and fields. The fat spiders of autumn were gone, leaving old webs traced with frost. The cold air stung our throats and dry grass cracked underfoot. The high branches around Blood Hill rattled like spearshafts above a shield wall.

It is the end of winter when death usually comes, when the warmth of spring is close, but the months of cold and hunger finally take their toll. Those who have already seen generations rise and fall slip away into the great darkness. Babies and children live through one winter and lose the will to see another. But it is in the first dawning of winter that I remember the dead most keenly. Sometimes I speak to them in the cold silence of a still night. And when they finally answer me I do not think I will fear them.

One night a vast flock of geese swept low over Blood Hill on their way to grazing grounds north of the weald. The beating of their wings and their rasping voices were as fearsome as the sounds of battle. Good Christian folk are taught to fear the great goose-gatherings of winter. For some reason priests imagine the honking and squawking and flapping to be the noise of Odin's wild hunt thundering through the winter skies. Grimstan had once demanded that I hand him my bow so that he might shoot the evil birds out of the air.

"Can you use a bow?" I had asked as he stumbled around and tried feebly to draw the string.

"It does not matter. Almighty God will guide the bolt I shoot." The arrow span off to the side and brought down the rotten thatch of one of the huts of Godric's family. It had led to a row as Godric's grandmother, whose shouting and squawking was worse than that of the geese, demanded that the priest provide them with reeds to

334

repair the roof. Grimstan refused of course, saying that he was doing God's work and that if the arrow had flown towards their house then perhaps there was something in there that God wanted slain.

"That'll be you," I had heard Ragnald whisper, nudging Godric in the ribs.

But by the dawning of that winter, Godric's mangled body lay in the cold ground beside the ashes of the church and Grimstan's was flayed and nailed and ripped apart by crows in the weald. There are very few who deserve to die, but perhaps Grimstan was one of those few.

Sigered was not. He did not live in our world. He thought he could shape the future with gold and silver. He believed a man's life was worth no more and no less than the wealth he possessed. He was a greedy, and he was twisted by Grimstan's spite until he betrayed us all. But looking back over the many years that have passed, I can see he was not an evil man. Murder is a thing far worse than greed, and I murdered Sigered. And perhaps one day my ghost will kneel before his and beg for forgiveness.

In the night we heard the wolves of Andredsweald, louder and more menacing than ever as they slipped out of the weald's darkest places to feast upon the slain of Wessex. There were villages where the dead lay unburied beneath the frigid wintering sky. There were rivers into which bodies were thrown, only to be washed up in a tide of blank eyes and bloated bellies. There are places where, since that time, only the dead have ever walked.

And in the daytime, we heard the distant sounds of Norman hunting dogs and sometimes even the hoofbeats of horsemen still scouring the weald for those who had fled from the enemy and those who had made outlaws of themselves.

"We cannot stay here." Ragnald spoke the words that I was already thinking. Brichteva gave him an angry look but said nothing. Ragnald's hut kept the wind off us, but the chill of winter still crept in. He had made it from logs laid across a frame and covered with turf. One end was open to let out the smoke from a small fire. Outside on the hill, some of the others who had fled Ellasham with us had built their own rough shelters, but the people were gone now and the wind was tearing down the flimsy frames of ferns and branches, old blankets and cloaks were blowing threadbare in the wind.

"So where do we go?" I said. "Cantaburh?" It was the first place that came into my mind. My mother was in Cantaburh, and many of our people. If I lived and if my mother lived, then the day would come when I would have to face her and tell her what had become of Ellasham and what my part in it had been. But at that moment, on that cold hillside in a winter of smoke and hunting dogs, I longed for the familiarity of my people and what remained of my family.

Ragnald shook his head. "If Cantaburh has submitted to the Normans, we are outlawed there. We are the rebels who destroyed a village, killed the Lord Sigered, the priest Grimstan and twenty Norman warriors. There may be none who live to bear witness, but the enemy will know well enough to hang us as a warning to the townsfolk."

"I'm a lord of men. I led the attack on Ellasham. You and Brichteva are nothing in the eyes of the Normans. There must be a hundred or more villages destroyed by the Normans and you could be fleeing from any of them. Maybe I cannot go to Cantaburh, but for you it might be safe."

Those whom I had led back into Ellasham had already fled; some to Riaburh, some to Cantaburh, all to a fate none of us knew for certain. They were protected only by their wits and a share of the silver we took from Sigered and from the hall – enough to keep them fed and sheltered through the winter or enough to get them hanged as thieves. At least it was better than shivering in the winter

336

forest waiting to be run down with spears or torn apart by dogs. Not all of them had even come back from Ellasham. Brichteva had seen her father die in the hall, cut down alongside two more of our men by a Norman warrior who managed to reach his sword before his throat was cut. Wada had gone home. He took corn and meat plundered in the sacking of the hall and walked back to the village again, insisting that he would bury the dead, repair his house, sow a patch of land and bring life back to a dead place. A quiet madness had crept into Wada and we let it take him. Perhaps we should have knocked him senseless and tied him to a beam in Ragnald's shelter. Only the darkest of gods could know what the Normans would have done to him if they found him in the burned village among their own dead.

"Would you go to Lunden?" Ragnald asked me.

I shrugged. "At least Saxon lords still rule there."

"Will they fight again?"

"Magnus will fight somehow, though he won't have the strength to face the Duke in open battle. And if my brother lives, he will be with Magnus." I had promised my mother I would find Oswold. Could I face her without news of him? Ragnald lowered his eyes to the flickering embers. He knew as well as I how small were the chances of Oswold being alive.

"There is a power in this place," Brichteva whispered. She sat close to the hut's open doorway and although the wind blew her hair across her face, I could see that her eyes still burned with the vengeance that had slaughtered Grimstan. "The spirits of those who once fought here will protect us."

Ragnald bit his lip and stared into the smouldering fire, but I looked at Brichteva, wondering if she was actually serious. "An army of ghosts? Against Norman spears?"

Brichteva fixed her eyes upon me and it was not the cold of the winter day that made me shiver.

"The hounds they follow know this place is sacred. The men know nothing, but they will fear this place if they find it." She jabbed a stick into the fire and sent a bright whirl of sparks into the gloom of the little shelter. Ragnald looked up and spoke at last.

"They fear nothing, especially not old legends they don't even know. Gods there may be, but none that have power in this world. Only men can shape the fate of men." Brichteva looked at us again, but finding no support, she turned away and stared angrily across the windblown hill.

I had not been in the hall to witness the slaughter of sleeping men and the women who followed their camp. But I heard chilling reports from those who were there and wished they had not been. They spoke of how Brichteva rushed in through the doors wielding a jagged edged knife and hacked and stabbed at anything; man, woman or beast, shrieking like a demon from a dark otherworld. I heard that she tore a struggling man's nose off with her teeth and that when the Norman warrior who had killed her father was cornered and brought down, she placed a foot upon his throat and slowly crushed the life out of him. Grimstan had forged a streak of murder in her soul and it was awakened that night. Ragnald loved her, and that seemed to me like a foolish thing in one so wise.

Night fell, and despite the smouldering fire embers, we shivered beneath our thick cloaks. The wind blew the clouds away over Walland Marsh then dropped to a whisper. Dawn stole in through the bare tree branches, bearing with it the first hard frost of winter.

And in that dawn we followed the clear stream of Blood Hill down through the silent trees. It brought us to the River Leman, running deep and cold far to the west of Ellasham, and beyond it an empty field, the stubble of autumn all frosted and bristling in the early sun like a land cast in silver. The field was part of the estate of Piasfield, a village much further up the Leman. But Piasfield had been burned as well and there was a whisper of smoke on the wind.

In those days on the cusp of winter there was always smoke on the wind.

We learned later that the Duke and his army burned and killed their way from Cantaburh to the Thames. They left a trail of ash and butchered families in an attempt to terrify Lunden into submission. Along the line of Duke Willelm's march not a house still stood and not a man, a woman or a beast still lived.

Would our people ever return, I wondered as we hauled Brichteva, spluttering and shivering, up the bank of the freezing river. If not, then many generations would pass before these fields yielded corn again. The weeds would take hold, the marsh would haul itself upwards from the river and the forest would creep down to meet it. Away down the valley, what remained of our houses would become haunted ruins in a dark, forgotten wood. After a dozen winters, foxes would raise their cubs among the ghosts of my people.

Fieldfares squabbled among the barley stalks, their shrill voices carried on the west wind towards the frosted graves of Oxeney. We rubbed our feet to coax back a little warmth, then wrapped them in fleece and pulled our boots back on. The horses waited patiently, their faces to the frozen ground and their breath billowing like plumes of smoke. They were beasts taken from the enemy in the sacking of Ellasham. Norman warhorses, now loaded with food for our journey, blankets, spears and shields. I still wore my sword like a curse I feared would follow me all my life. Earlier, in the half-light of dawn, I had thrust it into the ground on Blood Hill and walked away. Ragnald called me a fool, picked up the blade and pushed its hilt back into my hand.

"A sword never did good for any man," I told him.

"And what will you do when the Normans try to ride us down?" Brichteva spat. "Sing a fucking song?" They were right of course. Perhaps there were men who had the power to end this war, but I was not one of them. Reluctantly, I shoved the blade back into its sheath.

And we had not even crossed the field when we saw the horsemen. They were already across the river. Perhaps the shrill gangs of birds, rising at our approach, had alerted them.

"Shit!" muttered Ragnald, glancing around to see how far we were from cover.

"Only three of them," Brichteva snarled. She was already pulling a spear out of the leather loops that hung from one of the horses' packs. I looked at Ragnald and he looked back grimly. If we ran back towards the forest, they would catch us at the river. In every other direction the field just stretched out wide and flat, a killing ground made perfect for Norman horsemen.

"Shit!" said Ragnald again. He took one of our two shields and handed it to Brichteva, swapping his long bladed seax for her spear.

"Move apart," I called to them. "If we stand together, we make a bigger target." The horsemen were coming at a canter, only about fifty paces away. I thought that if we stood apart then I might get a chance to throw my spear at the flank of whichever horseman attacked Ragnald and Brichteva. I could see that they were both struggling not to show their fear and they reminded me of hunted deer at the end of a chase. The riders came in closer still. Their cloaks were blue, a shade darker than the winter sky. These were sights and sounds too familiar to me now. The iron grey of mail and shields daubed with bright crosses. The hammering of hooves across the cold ground. Two of them lowered their spears, their horses showing teeth and the men's eyes hidden beneath their helmets. And the other, the one who seemed to lead them, had a plume of red ribbons flying from the crest of his helmet and he spun his sword through the empty air. Three mounted warriors, bred to the sword and the saddle against the three of us. Ragnald had wit and nerve enough to wield a spear, but lacked the skill and training

340

for a desperate fight such as this. And Brichteva, ferocious though she was, could kill only the defenceless. I thought not of how we might win, but of how any of us might escape alive. A hot shaft of pain shot up my arm from the hand I had burned when we unleashed fire on Sigered and his family, but I raised my shield high, steadied my spear and tried to meet the eyes of my enemies. Death and blades of iron. Death had been like a wolf on my trail since I had cheated it in the Great Battle.

But suddenly, Death faltered. The leading horseman tried to lift his shield, but it slipped to one side and fell across one of his horse's ears. With a grunt, the horse dug its hooves into the earth and turned. And the other warriors swayed in the saddle as they fell into graceless confusion behind him.

"He can't ride!" I called out to the others. What kind of Norman warrior could not handle his shield and weapons and charge his mount into battle? Something was wrong and we had just a small chance to strike before they could recover.

"Charge them!" I ran forward across the stubble field, howling at the enemy, my fear and the pain of my burned hand thrown aside like a cloak in the summer. One of them twitched at his reins and hurled a spear at me. But his horse moved and I glimpsed the spear out of the corner of my eye as it flew somewhere far over my shoulder. I heard Brichteva screaming with a voice she must have taken from Grimstan as she cut him to pieces. I rammed my spear hard at the nearest rider. He raised his shield just in time and the top of it splintered as he turned his mount under the weight of the blow. I jerked the blade free and jabbed it at the horseman's back. The blade glanced harmlessly off his thick mail, but the rider squawked with fear, kicked out and galloped away beside the man in the crested helmet who was still trying to take control of his horse. And to the left I saw the other rider crash down among the frosted barley stalks, felled by Ragnald's spear punching through the mail at his shoulder. Brichteva threw down her shield and leapt with a wildcat pounce, her hair flying like fire in the cold light. She pinned him

341

down with her knees, raised the antler-hilted seax high and drove it down hard, through mail and leather and flesh, through his stomach and into the ground beneath. He roared with pain and clawed at the frozen barley stalks. Brichteva spat in his face. Silently, Ragnald bent down to draw a knife across the dying man's throat.

But I did not see the warrior die. I stood staring at the third man – the rider with the plumed helmet who had led the attack and whose blundering had caused it to fail. It was not horse-skill that he lacked – it was his right arm. At his shoulder was just a hand-span of stump to which his shield had been strapped. The shield now flapped uselessly as he sheathed his sword and fumbled for the reins. I sensed Ragnald and Brichteva scrambling to my side and stopping as I had done.

"Move!" he shouted, jerking at the reins with his one hand. "You're nothing better than a tanner's hide!"

The hoarse calls of a crowgang rolled across the winter sky and the rider's familiar accent turned the shiver of recognition into aching truth.

"Your time has passed Wulfred." he said. I stood almost speechless on the frozen field. All I could say was his name.

"Richard," I whispered, and the sound of my voice slipped seamlessly into the frosty dawn. Richard, who had mocked my brother and I in the spring and had paid dearly for it. Richard son of Sigered, the last survivor of a family whose slaughter I had caused.

"You had your chance to make peace with England's new lords. My father gave you life and peace. You spat it back and paid him with death."

"Your father was a nothing without shame or honour. He was the betrayer of my people."

"Murder, Wulfred. That is your crime. Murder of my father, an honourable lord and loyal servant of King Willelm. Of my defenceless mother and brothers. Of the guests of Lord Sigered.

342

And of the most holy priest Grimstan. You came among peaceable folk with fire and sword. For that you'll choke at the gallows and I will bring you to that justice." I feared the truth of his words. If the Bastard Duke was to be our king, then I could have no place in his kingdom, but I tried to hide my fear with defiance.

"With a horse you can't ride and a sword you can't wield?"

"The full might of Normandy hunts you Wulfred. This year is dying, but you will die before it."

Then he turned his beast, mustered his horse-skills and drove it into a clumsy gallop away across the field. The other horseman – the one who had survived my spear – waited for him and they rode together towards the morning sun. My hands were numb and my spear just a weightless lump clutched in them. Brichteva took up the other spear and hurled it at Richard's back, but she had no spear-skill and the ghost-warriors of Blood Hill did not aid its flight. The two fleeing men were a blur in the distance before I could turn and face my companions again.

We stopped for the night somewhere to the west. Somewhere way beyond the village of Piasfield, which had become a grey smear of ash on a grey winter landscape. We had lingered briefly among the pitiful remains of houses and listened and stared across the fields and into cold dark woods, trying to catch a glimpse or a voice of any survivors who might be hiding nearby. There was nothing. Only ash and the charred bones of men and beasts.

The night came down early, the red sun slipping into a horizon caged by bare trees. We built a shelter from branches and dead ferns, still crisp with the frost of the night before. And when the darkness came down and the silent frost of a new night started to bite at our fingers, we made a little fire and huddled around it, wrapped in cloaks and blankets. We had not dared light a fire before nightfall for fear of the smoke giving us away.

Our horses were gone. We had taken a few weapons and as much food as we could carry, then driven them northwards across the slopes of Oxeneye and away into the fields and woods, using stripped branches as whips. Those who hunted us, we hoped, would follow their trail through the frost while we slipped away to the west.

The tiny light of our fire trembled in the great darkness of winter. The land was empty, silent. A hollow wilderness haunted by walking shadows and wolves. There was danger in the night – danger of ambush by thieves and foemen, of malevolent ghosts that steal a person's soul, of sinking suddenly into unseen swamps. No warriors would ride through those long black and freezing hours. But still I feared the eyes of the enemy and we piled stones, earth and fallen wood around our fire to hide its feeble light.

A branch shook somewhere behind us and we all started. Brichteva was on her feet, staring blindly into the darkness, her eyes too dazzled by the firelight to see anything. Ragnald's hand was on the hilt of his seax. The silence swept back in a great wave across the forest. Brichteva sat down and shrugged.

"An owl hunting." she muttered.

"Or a murdered ghost," I whispered. So many had been severed from their lives that we knew the woods and hills were shivering with panicked, weeping ghosts still searching for home, searching for those they loved.

Ragnald slid his blade back into its leather sheath. "We need not fear ghosts. Only the swords of men."

"And you need not travel with me," I said. "They hunt me and if they catch me I will die and you with me. There must be hundreds driven from their homes and seeking shelter. It would be an easy thing for you to vanish among them." The silence of the forest crept back across our little camp. Brichteva bit her lip and Ragnald stared away into the black treetops.

"Once we were villagers," he eventually said. "We had fields and woods to work and your father was our lord. Now we have no homes or fields. But today we fought at your side and you brought us victory. We will stand beside you." He held my eye with that steady look of his. Brichteva looked at me too, and for once her eyes burned with something a little warmer than Hell and defiance.

"You fought for me in the summer," she muttered. "When the priest would have taken my life. And now I fight for you." A small gust of wind rattled the trees, as if the old gods had witnessed an oath. Ragnald shoved a thick branch a little further into the fire.

"It must be nearly Yule," he murmured. "I'd give half the gold in Wessex for a cup of Eohric's mead."

"And to hear music and to dance," said Brichteva. She gave a bitter laugh as if the world she remembered was gone forever.

"My mother said they would all return to Ellasham before the frost came. Now I hope they never will."

Ragnald looked at me sharply. "They can return and they might. What was destroyed was only houses. Wood, turf and thatch. They are passing things. They can be replaced. In one lifetime men and women can build more than any war can destroy." He put his arm around Brichteva's shoulders and she huddled in close to him. I thought again of Hildelyth and wondered if she still lived somewhere out in the black winter night, and what kind of life she might live at the hands of her Norman masters. In the firelight, Ragnald breathed a long plume into the freezing air and the silence beyond our little circle was so great that whole world seemed to listen. "There will come a day when all the things we remember will return to us."

In the morning the sun rose in red and gold as if the hills were on fire and the very sky was bleeding. The ground was hard and frost-bright again. Somewhere in the land, armies marched and the lords of men tried to take control. Broken and scattered, people huddled in frozen forests, silent towns and burned villages and they waited in fear for the next move in the bloody play of kings and those who would be kings.

And with everything we knew turned to ashes and shadows at our backs, we walked on into the iron heart of winter.

CPSIA information can be obtained
at www.ICGtesting.com
Printed in the USA
LVHW011530181021
700760LV00028B/1861

9 781326 723996